Streaming Stars

Transcender Trilogy Book 2

Vicky Savage

ISBN-10: 0985901926
ISBN-13: 978-0-9859019-2-9

To my family, Michael, Jessica, Colter, Katie, and Bella.

Much love.

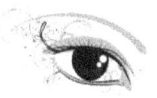

ONE

*L*ove makes people do stupid things. Climbing into Agent Ralston's sleek, black limo, I can't shake the feeling that this may be one of them.

Agent Constantine Ralston of the Inter-Universal Guidance Agency (IUGA for short) showed up unannounced at my door this morning and made me an offer he knew I couldn't refuse. For the last twelve months I've been searching for someone. A man I've never met—in *this* world, at least—yet I'd know him instantly by sight. His memory is indelibly burned on the hard drive of my mind, inerasable, inescapable. Each look, each word, each moment we shared—collected, compiled, and captured on a looping screen-saver of dreams.

Mostly I see him that first day at the lake, before we'd ever kissed. Standing near the edge of the water, silver light glints off his ebony hair. Dark brows and thick lashes frame sky-blue eyes. Full lips curve appealingly as my gaze follows the beads of water trailing down the honey-copper skin of his bare chest and abdomen. I'm swept away by his beauty, nearly sick with desire, knees weak as a newborn fawn. It's all there, the warmth of our intermingled breath, the salty-sweet taste of his mouth, the pure rightness of his embrace. Fresh and intense as it was that day.

What would I do to be with him again? *Almost anything.* And Ralston knows it. That's why he came calling this morning. That's

1

why I'm climbing into this obnoxious car and leaving my home behind—maybe forever. Because he's taking me back. Back to Ryder Blackthorn. Back to my mother. Back to the life I thought I'd never know again.

"You're looking well, Jaden," Ralston says, clambering in behind me and settling into the seat opposite mine. "Fit as always."

"Thanks. You look good, too." *Maybe a little stressed.* "Nice suit. Very Armani-ish."

The corners of his mouth respond faintly to the compliment. "It's Zegna, actually. I do favor the Italian designers," he says, brushing his fingertips across the fabric. "May I offer you some refreshment?" He pops open a wooden panel concealing a small refrigerator.

"Sure. What've you got?" My eyes are still adjusting to the dark interior of the car. It has the tang of a rich man's study in here, like fine leather and wealth. I nestle deeper into the buttery-soft seat.

He peers into the compartment. "It seems there is only water. Still or sparkling?"

"Actually, I'm not really thirsty, Rals. Let's just cut to the chase, okay? I have about a million questions I need answered before I go through with this."

"Yes, I know. All in good time, my dear. Why don't you make yourself comfortable?" He places plump, green bottles of Perrier in our cup holders. "We have a bit of a ride."

"Why? Where're we going?" I squint out the tinted window.

"To a safe house of sorts. It belongs to an IUGA agent who is assigned to this sector." He smoothes a hand across his thinning, sandy-brown hair, and checks his watch.

"You have agents in Connecticut?"

He looks at me over the top of his glasses. "We have agents everywhere."

I'm still not totally clear on what his agency, IUGA, does, but their motto is *Destiny is our Duty*. From what he's told me and what I've gathered, it means their job is to make sure events in the universe go down exactly the way they're supposed to.

Ralston and I met last year when a freak electrical storm catapulted me into a parallel world—a post-comet-collision version of earth, where most of the surviving population resides inside three gigantic domes. He rescued me from a sticky situation and helped me assume the identity of my *mirror* in that new existence, while his agency worked on a way to get me home. The way Ralston described it, in parallel worlds everyone has a "mirror"—someone who looks exactly like them, has the same temperament and the same name, but a completely different life. In Domerica, my *mirror* just happened to be a princess.

The problem was, Ralston didn't exactly tell me the truth about how I landed in Domerica in the first place, and about the fact that I didn't have to leave if I didn't want to. When the *powers that be* discovered I'd been bounced back to Connecticut against my will, the entire agency got a giant slap on the hand, and I got the chance for a do-over.

Ralston leans forward in his seat, clasping his hands in front of him. "Jaden, on a personal note, I wish to thank you for accompanying me today. It was quite a blow to be demoted after my years of loyal service. But, in hindsight, I agree that our handling of your situation was not entirely appropriate.

The fact that you're a Transcender should never have been concealed from you, and the Transcenders should have been allowed greater access to you. What I regret most is separating you and young Blackthorn. I knew better. The perpetual contract between the two of you should have taken precedence. Even though the legal department and my director advised me otherwise. For that, I sincerely apologize."

Ralston lied to me about the fact that I'm a *Transcender*. Translated: *freak of nature*. Something unique in my genetic makeup allows me to shift in and out of parallel worlds. I'm told there aren't many of us in existence. I've met only one other. I was completely unaware of my ability until last year, and don't ask me how it works because I don't really know... yet.

When Ralston appeared at my door this morning, the deal he offered was pretty simple. He takes me back to Domerica. I have thirty days to decide whether I want to stay there, return home, or join the other Transcenders, which, by the way, I never seriously considered. I don't know much about them, but they sound like a cult, and I'm not into cults. In the meantime, my life in Connecticut just sort of freezes in place. If I do this, Ralston gets a shot at winning back his old position as Senior Agent.

I guess I kind of owe him something. Ralston comes across as a stodgy old, buttoned-up British-type, but I know another side of him. While I was in his care, he taught me to fence, ride horses, and comport myself as a member of the royal family. He was my mentor, protector, and friend ... until he kicked my ass out of Domerica.

"Don't worry about it," I say. "You probably already know I'm not doing this just for you. Mostly it's for me. I have to see Ryder again. And my mom. Even if it's only for a short time. You knew I'd say *yes.*"

My Connecticut mom died in a fiery car crash two years ago. It's impossible to describe how devastating it was. It changed *everything*. I struggled just to make it through each day. So when I found my mother alive and well in Domerica, it was a gift of unimaginable joy. Our reunion will always be one of the most cherished events of my life.

Also, Domerica is a fairyland under glass. Sure it's backward as far as technology and science are concerned, but its beauty is beyond compare. Lush verdant hills dip softly into warm green valleys; countless orchards of flowering trees give way to pastoral meadows strewn with lively wildflowers. Idyllic farms and quaint towns emanate the steady hum of contentment and prosperity. And an ethereal light created by the silvery dome shell suffuses everything with a radiant glow. So after falling in love with Ryder and the strange and beautiful dome world, I decided I wanted to adopt that life as my own—permanently. IUGA had other plans.

Ralston leans closer, a conspiratorial glint in his eye. "I have something for you. A peace offering if you will." He lifts a small brown pouch from his jacket pocket and hands it to me.

I upend it, spilling the contents into my hand. Tears leap into my eyes. It's a silver wolf-head pendant on a woven chain. "My necklace. How did you get this?"

"I took it from your personal effects before we sent you home. Strictly against the rules, you know, but I hoped we might meet again someday. If not, I would have found a way to return it to you."

I slide over to the seat next to him and throw my arms around his neck. "Thank you so much. I thought I'd never see this again." Ryder gave me this necklace. I promised him I'd wear it always, but when I got booted back to Connecticut, I was sure it was lost forever."

Ralston pats my back paternally. "It's all right, my dear. Consider it a small step toward making amends. Now we must talk. There is much ground to cover before your return to Domerica." He quickly checks his watch again.

I scoot back over to my own seat and slip the necklace over my head. "How come you keep looking at your watch, Rals? Are we on some kind of time schedule?"

"You may remember, old girl, these inter-dimensional shifts must be precisely orchestrated, with down-to-the-second timing. You'll be using your Transcender skills to return, but I must ensure that I am in place at exactly the right moment, or I'll lose my slot."

"Whoa, hold the phone. I don't know how to use my Transcender skills. I thought we agreed on that point. I'll never make it back by myself. I could wind up in some primeval forest as a breakfast burrito for a triceratops."

"Triceratops are herbivores, Jade," he says dryly. "But I assure you nothing like that will happen. You shall have competent assistance. All will go swimmingly."

"Yeah well, I'll reserve judgment on that issue. But how's this supposed to work anyway? I mean, I can't just show up in Domerica after a year of being gone. Like '*Yo, waddup? Long time no see.*'"

Ralston rolls his eyes. "Honestly Jaden, can you possibly imagine I would have undertaken such an important assignment without a solid plan?"

I shrug. "I guess not. Sorry Rals. I trust you." *Well, sort of.* "So what's the plan?"

Carefully removing his charcoal coat, he folds it neatly and places it on the seat next to him. "I called in a favor from Melor Thaddeus. You remember the elder of the Cleadian colony? He and his wife agreed to assist us with our small ruse. Since they're aware you're a Transcender, it wasn't difficult to explain your disappearance and reappearance to them."

White-robed, white-haired, and very reclusive, the Cleadians live in their own protective structure outside of Domerica. I met some of them once while shopping in my father's village. They rely on the Domericans for some goods and services, but generally don't mingle with outsiders. To the world at large, they're descendants of survivors from Nova Scotia who migrated to the area long ago. In reality, they're aliens from the planet Cleadies, whose ancestors were trapped on the planet back when the comet hit. They possess some remarkable powers, like reading a person's essence with just the touch of a hand. Melor discovered I'm a Transcender, and a princess-pretender, by simply shaking my hand.

"Jaden, you must listen carefully." Ralston eyes lock onto mine. "I'm about to relate our agreed-upon story. We must be in complete accord on the details."

I tilt forward, focusing intently. "Okay, shoot."

"Because you disappeared during the disastrous fire last year, everyone assumed you perished in the flames. But that was not the case. The following day you were found wandering in the woods by a group of scavenging Outlanders. Your clothing and hair were singed, and you had an obvious head injury."

My fingertips absently trace the scar on my forehead where I was actually reinjured during the fire.

"You were in shock, and mostly incoherent. The Outlanders took you back to their outpost. Eventually you regained your physical health, but had no recollection of your name, your family, or the location of your home." He twists the top off his water and takes a few quick swallows.

I know a bit about the Outlanders—scattered groups of mostly misfits and some outlaws who live in homemade structures outside the domes. "I'm with you so far," I say. "But where do the Cleadians come in?"

"Be patient, I'm getting to that." He screws the cap back on and wedges the bottle into its holder. "This next part is true, by the way. A number of weeks ago, an Outlander settlement suffered a severe outbreak of influenza. Most victims recovered on their own without medical attention, but a few remained gravely ill. Aware of the remarkable healing powers of the Cleadians, a group of Outlander women brought three young people to Melor, pleading for his assistance. Melor graciously agreed to help, and soon the lot of them were back on their feet, feeling fine."

I nod. "And …?"

"Well that's where you come in. You see, *you* were one of those young people."

"Oh!"

"Melor's account will be that upon first seeing you, he believed you bore a striking resemblance to Princess Jaden, whom he had met once briefly. When he heard the tale of how you came to be with the Outlanders, and of your nearly total loss of memory, he strongly suspected that you were, in fact, the missing Princess. He did not express his suspicions to the Outlanders for fear they would attempt to ransom you or take advantage of the situation in some other way. Rather, he convinced them to allow you to stay on at the compound so he could assist you in discovering your true identity."

I'm swept up in the story now. "All right, I get it. So Melor succeeded in restoring my memory and …"

"… confirmed that you are indeed Princess Jaden, whom everyone presumed to be dead these many months." Ralston finishes my sentence. "He immediately contacted me for verification, as he knew I was once your professor. And I, in turn, contacted your father. The two of us have arranged to travel together to collect you from the Cleadians later tonight. Afterward, we'll go directly to the Enclave, and then deliver you to your mother at Warrington Palace the following day."

My parents are separated in that existence. So, while my mother's Queen of Domerica and lives in the palace, my father is the Governor of the Enclave, a small walled city within the dome, but not subject to its laws or authority. That was a stipulation of their separation agreement.

Reviewing Ralston's apocryphal tale in my head, I search for holes or inconsistencies. Nothing glaring jumps out at me. "You know, that's pretty good, Rals," I say. "It's simple, part of it really happened, and the rest is impossible to disprove. It just might work."

"It is a fairly air-tight chronicle, if I do say so myself." He sits back and visibly relaxes. "The Cleadians are masters at keeping secrets, I trust them completely. And, as you've pointed out, it is utterly impractical for anyone to determine the veracity of the Outlander portion of the story, since they're notoriously nomadic and avoid dome-dwellers like the plague."

"The amnesia part's a little hokey," I say. "Something right out of a soap opera. But hey, if we told the truth, they'd never believe us."

He chuckles. "I'm afraid that is so. Truth is undoubtedly stranger than fiction at times. Sir Arthur Conan Doyle relied heavily upon that adage when bringing Sherlock Holmes back to life. The public was so delighted with Holmes's resurrection, they didn't delve too deeply into the details. Let us hope the same holds true for the princess."

"Yeah, let's hope. There aren't any loose ends I should know about, are there? The princess's body was never found, right?"

"It was not. There were a number of casualties in the fire. Some of the bodies were burned beyond recognition. It was assumed her remains were among the unidentified."

"That works. But, out of curiosity, after I disappeared, what did IUGA do with Princess Jaden's bod…" I wave my hand and shake my head. "You know what, never mind. I don't think I want to know. What about Gabriel?"

"Your horse was found two days after the fire, riderless and suffering from burns."

"Is he okay? He didn't have to be put down did he?" I hold my breath.

"He is fine. A section of his mane may never grow back, but otherwise he's healthy."

Whew! "Okay, this is good," I say. "I'm down with the story. Now fill me in on the rest. I'm dying to know what happened after I left." I tick-off questions on my fingers. "You said back at the house that my mom's not well. What's wrong with her? Is Ryder okay? Was the Xtron ever recovered? How bad was the fire? And have the Unicoi moved to Domerica yet?" The not-knowing has been hell.

TWO

*R*alston rotates his head from side to side as if to relax the kinks in his neck. "We've not enough time to go into specifics on any of this, but I'll touch upon the major facts with which you should be familiar. You may have to wing it a bit, but people will expect you to be vague on current events since you've been absent for a year."

He begins with a rundown on the enormous fire raging inside the dome at the time I was sent home. According to Ralston, the fire was contained without widespread damage; a dozen people lost their lives, but it could have been much worse. The fire could quickly have sucked all the oxygen from the dome, thereby extinguishing itself, but not before wiping out every living thing inside.

"No time for details at the moment, but the Dome Operations Center was eventually recaptured, and the fire was doused by a carefully-orchestrated deluge."

"That's great news, Rals."

"You'll also be pleased to know that the entire Unicoi nation was successfully relocated from their contaminated cities to Domerica several months ago. That is something of which you should be very proud, Jaden, since you were largely responsible for saving the population from certain death."

"Thanks," I say, thrilled to hear that the project we started was seen through to completion. "You had a lot to do with that too, Rals.

It must have been amazing to witness the exodus of so many people and animals. I'm sorry I missed it."

"Yes, they say it was quite a feat, but I understand construction of Unicoi Village is woefully behind schedule, and I've heard rumblings that the transition is not going as smoothly as we had initially hoped," he says.

"What do you mean *you've heard*? You don't live in Domerica anymore?"

He adjusts the knot of his burgundy tie and clears his throat. "When I was demoted, I was reassigned to a job at IUGA headquarters. I haven't been out in the field for months. I get updates from the senior agent who replaced me, Marshall Chelmsford. Good man."

"Geeze Rals, I'm sorry."

"What's done is done, my dear. We'd best get back to business." He taps the face of his wristwatch to remind me of the time constraints.

"Regarding the Xtron energy cell, it was recovered intact."

The Xtron, an item of enormous power, had been stolen by Damien, a rogue prince from the country of Dome Noir. He and a group of his henchmen were bent on destroying Domerica. Damien was captured before I left, but Ralston says many of his men got away, taking most of the explosives they stole with them. It's assumed they returned to Dome Noir.

"After his capture, Damien disclosed the location of the Xtron in exchange for Queen Eleanor's agreement to release him into the custody of his father in Dome Noir," Ralston says. "An unfortunate incident occurred, however, when Damien was being transferred to the Dome Noir representatives."

"What kind of *incident*?"

"He was assassinated. Gunned down with a long-range rifle."

"Good God! He's dead?"

"Quite so. King Philippe was enraged at the news of his son's violent death, even though Damien was an admitted thief and murderer himself, and despite the fact that Damien had at one point threatened to overthrow his own father. In any event, relations between Dome Noir and Domerica are terribly strained at this time. Philippe has suspended all trade until Damien's assassin is found and brought to justice."

"Do they even know who did it?" I ask.

"Not really. The type of firearm used, coupled with the fact that Damien had murdered a Unicoi warrior, cast suspicion directly upon the Unicoi people. After a brief and, I am told, less than thorough investigation, a warrant was issued for the arrest of a young man. You remember Ryder's close friend, Alexander?"

"Oh my god. Not Alexander. I know he hated Damien, but he couldn't be responsible. Could he?"

"Agent Chelmsford says he's not, but the identity of the real culprit is being well-protected. For now, Alexander remains a fugitive, while others work to clear his name."

"What about Alexander's wife? Don't they have a child now?"

"Mother and child are being well cared for by Ryder's sister, Catherine."

I snort. "That's uncharacteristically kind of Catherine."

"Actually, Jade, she's become quite a paragon for the Unicoi people. Chief Blackthorn finally succumbed to his advanced lung cancer several weeks ago, and Catherine has taken on a major role in easing the transition of her countrymen to their new home. Of course, Ryder was named chief and has assumed responsibility for governing the tribe."

I shake my head in amazement. "Chief Blackthorn dead. Alexander on the run. What a mess. All of that on top of my disappearance. How's Ryder holding up under this stress?"

"Truthfully, I haven't seen him in quite some time. But he is a strong individual and dedicated to the welfare of his people. I'm certain he's doing the best he can. Your reappearance will certainly be a source of great joy and comfort to him. However I'm afraid you'll find many things changed in Domerica, Jaden."

"Well, give me the rest of the bad news. What about my mother?"

Ralston gazes out the window and frowns. He punches a button on the console of his armrest. "Driver, can we hurry it up a bit? We're running late."

I hear a click and an amplified, "Yes sir." The car immediately picks up speed.

Focusing on me again, Ralston's expression becomes grave. "Jaden, I am terribly sorry to have to tell you that your mother is terminally ill."

"What! She was fine when I left. What happened? What illness?"

"It's a type of leukemia." His pale eyes turn soft and sympathetic.

"No." I cover my face with my hands. "This can't be happening. I already lost her once. I don't know how I can take losing her again." I draw in a shaky breath. "Can't leukemia be treated?"

Ralston explains that while some forms of the disease are treatable, Mother has an acute form, resistant to medication. He says Domerica isn't very advanced when it comes to treatment of cancers, and that the medication she's receiving will prolong her life for only a month or so.

My mouth goes dry, and my mind grasps for a loophole to make it not so. "Can't we bring her medicine from here?"

"You know we cannot. There are strict rules against inter-dimensional transfer of medications."

Ralston pulls the cap off my Perrier bottle and hands it to me. I take several large gulps. The bubbles sting my throat and help me swallow my tears.

"Fortunately, you've been given the opportunity to see her once again. I hope you will find some comfort in that," he says.

I nod slowly. That's more than I got when my Connecticut mom died. I guess I should be grateful, but I'm hollow and angry inside.

Staring out the window at the neighborhoods fleeting past my vision, it hits me that I've been so absorbed in searching for Ryder's *mirror* I hadn't noticed spring has arrived in Connecticut. Tender leafy shoots make gray, naked trees look lovely and young again. Cheery-headed daffodils bedeck bare flower beds, and nature's renewal project has repainted all the lawns, transforming the dull yellows and browns to bright baby green. The cycle of life. Death and rebirth. It happens whether or not you're paying attention.

After a respectful moment or two, Ralston pushes ahead. "Jaden, as a result of your mother's illness, your uncle, Prince Harold, and your cousin Princess Osrielle, have moved into the palace."

"Why? What can they do?" I mutter into the window glass.

"They are there because your cousin, Osrielle, will become queen once your mother passes."

I snap my head around. "That's ridiculous. Oz is only twelve years old. I mean, she's smart, but she can't rule a country."

"True. She is still quite immature, but your mother has appointed Prince Harold as Lord High Steward of Domerica until Osrielle reaches the age of majority, which means that, for all intents and purposes, your uncle will be running the country."

I grimace. "Uncle Harold?"

"You sound as if you don't care for him."

"I don't really know him. Here he's a big shot on Wall Street. Owns his own investment firm. The families aren't really close, though. He and my dad don't get along."

"Why is that?"

"Uncle Harold kind of looks down on Dad for being a nurse. Like, you know, he could have done better things with his life. And Dad calls Uncle Harold *Preacher Harold* behind his back, because according to Dad, he'll quote scripture to you while picking your pocket."

Ralston raises his eyebrows. "I see. Well, nevertheless, you may find him to be quite different in Domerica, having been raised as a prince."

"I guess it's possible. He did write a nice letter for me when I applied to Yale. But didn't you tell me that people are basically the same on the inside from one existence to another?"

"In most cases, that is true," he says.

I hold my hand out palm up. "Well there you go. So how come Mother doesn't just change the laws or whatever so Drew can succeed her?"

"We've been over this, Jade. Only female heirs of the queen may ascend to the throne. Your brother is not eligible. It's the one law in Domerica that is sacrosanct. Constitutionally, it may never be altered. Therefore, Osrielle, as your mother's niece, is next in the line of succession."

"Okay, but when I get back, I'll be the next in line, right?"

"Correct. Should you decide to stay."

"And I'm already eighteen, so I don't need a Lord High Whatever to run the country for me."

He nods.

I may be a bit of a pampered princess in Domerica, but I'm not one of those fragile, shrinking violet types. I'm five foot ten in my bare feet. I weigh a hundred and … well, none of your business. I hold a third degree black-belt in Tae Kwon Do, and I'll cut the Netherfields off of anyone who threatens me or my family.

"I'm not really fond of Uncle Harold," I say, "and I definitely don't want him up in my face for this gig."

"Perhaps he would be a source of significant support as you adjust to your new responsibilities," Ralston says. "But you needn't keep him at court if you feel capable of handling things on your own."

I stare at him. "Seriously? Of course I'm *not* capable of handling things on my own. I mean, I won't even graduate from high school for another three weeks."

He shrugs. "The decision is entirely yours, my dear. You'd have other assistance, of course. Your mother has a competent Council of Advisors. And there is your father and Prince Andrew."

"Will you be there? Will you be assigned to me?"

"If you wish," he says.

Geeze, Jaden, what have you gotten yourself into? I prop my elbows on my knees and drop my face into my hands, trying to wrap my head around Mother's illness, grappling with the momentous implications. I knew if I stayed in Domerica I'd someday take over the throne. I just thought I'd have thirty or forty years to grow into the job. This changes so many things. But a quick gut-check tells me I'm still going back.

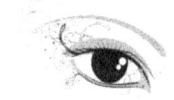

THREE

We ride along without speaking for a few miles while I stare out the window, mulling over the information Ralston shared with me. When the silence threatens to become awkward, Ralston tries a lighter topic of conversation.

"Are you still practicing your Tae Kwan Do, my dear?"

Grateful for the distraction from my thoughts, I turn to him. "I keep up with it," I say. "But you know how you suggested I look into fencing lessons? Well, I took up Kendo this year."

He raises his eyebrows. "Ah, the art of samurai swordsmanship. Impressive. I hear it's a rather difficult sport, and quite noisy as well."

I crack a smile. "Yeah, there's some weird shouting and grunting involved, but I'm kind of loving it."

"I look forward to seeing a demonstration sometime."

Lifting his jacket from the seat, he slides it on and straightens the lapels. The car slows and makes a right turn before coming to a full stop.

"We're here, Jade. Are you ready?"

That question is fraught with implication. *Am I ready? I don't know. But here goes nothing.*

The driver opens our door, and I climb out into the driveway of a pretty yellow clapboard house in the middle of a normal-looking New England neighborhood. The lawn and shrubs are neatly trimmed, and honeysuckle blossoms spill fragrance from the pretty white trellis framing the front steps.

"This is the safe house?" I ask.

"Yes it is. What did you expect?"

"I don't know, Wayne Manor, or something a little more imposing."

"IUGA's approach is rather low-key. The idea is to appear to 'fit-in'."

"Ergo the limo and the designer suit?" I say with a smirk.

He shoots me a look over his shoulder as I trot up the steps behind him. Ralston rings the bell, and the door is quickly opened by a bearded young man in an oxford shirt and khakis. Hey, I know this guy.

"Mr. Nordgren?" I say.

He smiles. "Yes, Jaden. Come in, both of you. I believe everything is ready for you." We follow him down a short hallway to the back of the house.

I tug at Ralston's sleeve. "Did you know he's my physics teacher at Madison High?" I whisper.

"Of course. He's been keeping an eye on you in case of any further unexpected shifts."

Mr. Nordgren, correction: *Agent* Nordgren leads us to a lamp-lit study off the right of the hall. A messy desk is parked at one end of the room. Mismatched chairs are scattered around haphazardly. A large whiteboard, scrawled with arcane mathematical formulae, takes up most of one wall. The other walls are lined with oak bookshelves chaotically crammed with hundreds of well-worn volumes.

My stomach roils now that we're here, and the enormity of what

I'm about to do becomes more real. All at once, this whole thing seems like some crazy ass idea. I'm pretty sure I can't really pull it off—sail through different dimensions, potentially take over as queen of a small nation. *What am I, Superwoman or something?* I reach up and caress the wolf-head necklace at my throat, reminding myself that Ryder waits at the other end of this journey. My second-thoughts fade to a quiet roar for the moment, and I'm able to gather my resolve again.

"I apologize for the clutter," Mr. Nordgren says more out of courtesy than concern. "Please make yourselves comfortable. Your other guest should arrive at any moment." He softly closes the door as he leaves.

Turning to Ralston, I ask, "Who's our other guest?"

"I knew you would need assistance with your first controlled shift as a Transcender, so I invited a friend. Someone who has been instrumental in arranging your return."

I wrinkle my forehead, but before I can ask the question, the door opens and a tall, lanky hunk in jeans and a leather jacket saunters in. *Asher! I should have known.*

I grin, genuinely glad to see him. "Hey," I say.

"Hey, yourself." Asher has striking, light-green eyes and a delicious smile, like he's got this tantalizing secret he can't wait to share. He hugs me tightly. God he smells good, like sun and spice and maleness. I haven't been this close to a man who wasn't a relative in twelve months. A warm little thrill shimmers through me.

Asher's the only other Transcender I've ever met. He tried to explain what the Transcenders were all about during my last stint in Domerica, but I always had my hands full with other things and never took the time to hear him out. I've regretted that decision at least once a day every day since I was unceremoniously dumped back in Madison.

"You're going to help me do this thing?" I ask.

"Oh yeah, and you're going to love it. The first shift can be a little scary, but there's no bigger rush in the universe."

The door opens again and Mr. Nordgren pops his head in. "They're waiting for you, Agent Ralston," he says. "Time is of the essence."

"Tell them I'm coming," Ralston replies. He turns to me. "Before I take my leave, there are a few things I must go over with you. Your point of arrival will be inside the Cleadian compound. Melor and his wife, Bithia, are expecting you. Oh, and before I forget …" He fishes in his jacket pocket and extracts two Hershey's candy bars. "I've promised Melor chocolate. Please be sure he gets these. He's quite the chocophile."

I stash them in the pocket of my hoodie.

"Your father and I will come to fetch you, late this evening or early in the morning. Ryder is spending a few days at the Enclave to pick up supplies. He should be there when you arrive." An involuntary shiver shakes me at the mention of his name. "We'll spend the night there, and then take you on to Warrington to be with your mother."

"Got it," I say.

"Now, may I have your cell phone?" He stretches out an expectant hand.

"My phone? But no, Ralston, please. Can't I keep it? My life is on that thing. It has all my music and everything."

"That's precisely why it must stay here. You cannot possess such a device in Domerica."

"Please, Rals. I won't let anybody see it. I promise." He impatiently wiggles the fingers of his outstretched hand. "Ah hell. That's just brutal," I whine, reluctantly releasing it to his custody.

"I assure you it will be returned to you if and when you find yourself back on this earth. Meanwhile, mind your language, Princess." He smiles. "*Bon chance*, old girl." He gives me a two-fingered salute before slipping out the door.

"Am I really going to be able to do this?" I ask Asher.

He laughs. "Of course. I have a little something here that will ensure your safe arrival."

He hands me a shiny black box. "Open it."

I raise the lid to reveal a beautiful gold cuff bracelet with an interesting octagonal silver medallion in its center. The medallion has three small shooting stars running diagonally across the face. Each star is inlaid with a tiny diamond. "You brought me jewelry?" I ask.

"It's much more than that. It's a TPD, a trans-dimensional positioning device. Essential tool of the inter-dimensional traveler. Go ahead, put it on."

Carefully lifting the bracelet from the box, I examine it. An inscription inside says: *timeas non plures semitas vitae* and underneath, *Jaden Beckett*. "Hey, this has my name on it."

"It's yours. Every Transcender has one. This one's programmed especially for you."

I slip it on my wrist. It looks awesome. "Wow, thanks. What's the decoration on the top?"

"That's the Transcender symbol, a kind of a coat of arms, *Streaming Stars*. But it's what's underneath that's really important. Release the latch on the side and open it up."

I do as he says. The medallion opens like a locket, and instantly a three-dimensional hologram rises from the opening. "Whoa," I say, moving my arm, causing the hologram to skew sideways. "What's that?"

"It's a holographic map. They're called interstitial maps. They represent the different dimensions. Transcenders chart them. Hold your arm straight so you can see it."

I bring my arm up horizontally so the map is at eye-level. Familiar looking streets and buildings loom in front of me. "Is this Madison?" I ask, turning my wrist from side to side to get a better view.

"And surrounding areas, yes. See that green dot there? That's you. The purple dot next to it is me. It shows you where you are at all times, and the locations of the other Transcenders. Down here," he points to a virtual keypad at the bottom of the image, "you can program in the coordinates for any destination you like, and it will take you there in a flash. Just double-click the latch on the side of the medallion."

"For real? Like anywhere?"

"Yeah."

"Why does it say 'Earth 7Y12'?" I ask.

"That's the designation for this world. That's where you're from."

"Really? Show me some more. Where are you from?"

"Hold your wrist steady." He touches a few keys on the virtual pad. 'Earth 39G428' shows at the bottom of the image, and a new holographic map rises, replacing the map of Madison. It doesn't look like Madison did at all. Buildings are crammed close together and, besides a few main thoroughfares, the streets are narrow and crooked. No green or purple dots show up in this hologram, but I see a red dot moving slowly in the outer corner.

"What's the red dot?" I ask.

"That's the location of your *mirror* on that earth. It's important you avoid shifting in too close to your *mirror*. It can cause all kinds of complications, as you know from your last little journey to Domerica where you wound up in the princess's body."

I shudder at the memory. The princess was supposed to have died after a fall from a cliff, but I accidentally got shifted into her body, changing everything that had been predestined to happen as a result of her death.

Ralston explained the whole thing about parallel lives to me by using a meteorological example. He said, "It's like when a hurricane heads toward land and the weather centers generate spaghetti models of the potential paths of the hurricane by feeding the best information they have into their computers."

According to Ralston, it's similar when someone is born—all the potential paths of their life can be charted like a spaghetti model based on the trillions of possible decisions they might make. "Except," as he explained, "one must layer that spaghetti model on top of all the other models for all the other universes in the multiverse, which are legion, and that's the number of possible paths a person's life might take."

Just as with hurricanes, though, sometimes things go wrong and a person veers off on a path that was never predicted. That's what happened to me when I got shifted to Domerica during that storm. It was like I jumped the tracks and ended up in a completely different life.

"I'll teach you a lot more about the TPD when we have the time," Asher says, "but right now I think the Cleadians are expecting you. I'll program in the coordinates of Domerica." He presses a few things on the keypad and another hologram appears. I recognize the dome, and my heart beats faster.

He manipulates the map with his fingers moving to the west of the dome. "This is the Cleadian Compound." He points to an odd-looking structure just outside the dome and enlarges the area by spreading his thumb and forefinger on the image. "These rooms are Melor's residence. And this little room is where they want you." He uses his index finger to zero-in on a spot. "If you don't have exact coordinates, you can lock-in the desired location by pinpointing it with your fingertip. Then press 'enter,' right here." He demonstrates. "And you're set to go. All you need to do now is double-click the latch and you'll be on your way."

"Okay, that sounds simple enough. How come Ralston didn't use one of these?" I ask.

"They only work for Transcenders."

"Oh." I take a deep breath. "So that's it? Are you sure? Just click the latch?"

"Yes. I've done it a million times. It'll take you exactly where you want to go."

I squint at him. "I've never seen you use one of these things when you shift in and out."

He grins. "Experienced Transcenders don't need them very often. Only when we're going someplace we've never travelled to before. But I wear mine all the time, just in case. I used mine to get here today." He shoves up the sleeve of his jacket and shows me his TPD. It's a black leather cuff with a pewter medallion on top bearing the same three-star symbol.

"What's the meaning of the streaming stars?" I ask.

"You'll see," he says. "Now, are you ready?"

"Wait a minute. You're coming with me, right?"

"I can't. I'm in the middle of an exploration. I left my partner alone so I could be here for you, but I need to get back. I'll check on you in a day or two."

My heart bangs against my chest like a bird trying to escape a cage. "I don't think I can do this alone, Ash. What if I screw up? You're sure all I need to do is click the latch twice?"

He smiles his sexy little smile. "I'm sure." Stepping close to me, he zips my hoodie all the way up, and kisses me on the cheek. "You'll be fine, Beckett. Good luck and have fun!" He steps back. "Come on. You can do it!"

I take another calming breath and double-click the latch. For a nanosecond nothing happens. Then *Zzz!*

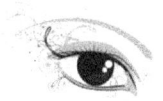

FOUR

Woohoo! I'm flying through silken space. The whoosh both stings and tickles my skin. My entire body is brilliantly incandescent, and is actually streaming stars. It's utterly surreal. I see only shades of light and shadow—a flash of color here and there. Then, after an eternity of seconds, a room becomes visible. But, disturbingly, I'm looking straight through the wall I'm hurtling toward … until, abruptly, everything comes to a halt, and I'm on solid ground again.

Part of my body still thinks it's flying, and I clutch the table beside me to steady myself. Melor rushes to my side.

"Oh wonderful, you're here. We've been waiting for you." He grasps my arm and holds out a small basin for me. "Take this. You may need it."

I do as he says, but when I release my hold on the table, I instantly sink to my knees and throw up all over the immaculate white floor. My nausea abates at once, but I'm totally embarrassed at my less-than-graceful entrance.

"I am *sooo* sorry." I hobble to my feet, still holding the basin. Only now do I realize why he gave it to me.

"No need to worry." He spreads a small towel over the mess. "I've heard the first time is always the worst," he says, leading me to a single bed covered with snowy white linens. "Why don't you lie down a moment and rest? I'll summon Bithia." He cocks his head toward the door as though he's going to call out to her, but says nothing. Then I remember, Cleadians communicate among themselves mostly through mental telepathy.

Sinking into the incredibly soft feather bed, I close my eyes and exhale. *Oh man, that was an amazing ride—thrilling and terrifying at the same time. My synapses need a minute to reboot. I just travelled across I don't know how many dimensions. Holy shit!*

Melor quietly tidies up the floor as I rest. After a few minutes, new footsteps enter the room. I open my eyes to find a female replica of Melor hovering over me. Her hair is long and white, her soft face generously lined, her eyes an eerie milky blue. Melor introduces me to his wife Bithia.

"I'm so happy you made it safely," she says. Her smile is crinkly and kind. "Are you feeling any better?"

"Yes, thank you. Sorry about the mess," I say.

"Don't give it a thought, young one." She extends her open palm to me. "May I?"

"Oh, sure." I place my hand in hers.

Her eyes grow wide, and she releases me with a little giggle. "Fascinating! You're my first Transcender."

"I'm still kind of new at it," I say. "Thank you both for allowing me to come here and for everything else … you know."

"We are honored to have you," Melor says. "We are most happy to be of assistance to the Transcenders and the Inter-Universal Guidance Agency. It's not often we have such excitement in our midst." Beaming and obviously pleased to be part of an inter-galactic intrigue, he rubs his hands together eagerly. "Now, do you have kisses for me?"

Huh? I cover my mouth. "Dude, I just threw up. Plus, I don't really know you that well."

Raising a gnarled knuckle to his lips, he stifles a laugh. "No child, you misunderstand. I mean *Hershey's*. Ralston promised me chocolate."

"Oh, right. Sorry. No offense." I sit up on the edge of the bed and take the candy bars from my pocket. They're in perfect condition, which is amazing considering the trip they just made. I give the bars to Melor. He holds them as if they're solid platinum.

"Bithia, look Hershey's bars," he says reverently, transferring one to her hand.

She smiles. "How wonderful."

Melor puts his nose close to the brown wrapper and inhales deeply. "Aah, just splendid. Have you ever been there?" he asks me.

"Been where?"

"To Hershey, Pennsylvania, on your earth?"

"Uh, no."

"You really must go if you have the opportunity. They say the air is so thick with chocolate you can almost taste it."

I nod. "All right."

"Let me put these in a safe place for later," he says, retrieving the other bar from his wife. "Bithia will get you a change of clothing, and we hope you will join us for dinner." He glides from the room.

Bithia opens a closet and takes out a beautiful white robe and sash similar to the one she is wearing. "I believe these will fit you, my dear. You'll find slippers on the shelf, and the bathroom is well-supplied. Leave your other clothes on the chair, please. Agent Ralston has asked Melor to destroy them, for security reasons. I hope you don't mind."

"No. That's all right." *Damn Ralston! These are my favorite jeans.*

"Why don't you take some time to refresh yourself? I will come for you at the dinner hour."

"Thanks," I say, fingering the lush fabric of the robe."

Peeking out from under my sleeve, the TPD bracelet sits securely on my wrist, seemingly intact. The star symbol makes total sense to me now.

I undress and slip into the long robe. It's luxurious against my skin. A small white bathroom is connected by a metal door, and I check out my reflection in the mirror. I'm nervous about seeing my Domerican father again, since I'm in my own body this time. My hair's shorter than the princess's, but it's the same honey-brown shade as hers. It falls to the middle of my back instead of well past my waist. Other than that, the princess and I are identical: same frame, our mothers' green eyes, same voice, although we have slightly different vocabularies. In Domerica, I need to drop the Americanisms from my speech. Slang is out. Words like "okay" and "dude" are unheard of.

After freshening up, I've nothing to do. The lighting in my small chamber is subdued. The room is spotless, with shiny metal walls and a compact white table and chairs. No books, trinkets, or decorations of any kind are visible. I open a couple of drawers. Nothing. My only option is to lie down again and wait until Bithia comes to collect me for dinner.

~~~~~

Next thing I'm aware of, Bithia is beside me, gently patting my shoulder. "Wake up, my dear," she says. It's dark, and my body feels heavy like I've slept for hours.

Slowly focusing on her sweet, grandmotherly face, I say, "I'm sorry. Did I sleep through dinner?"

"Yes you did. We thought it best not to wake you, but there is someone here to see you." She stands, and my father takes her place at my bedside. As his eyes connect with mine, his face becomes a shifting landscape of emotion. I can't tell if he's going to laugh or cry. Actually, he does both.

"Jaden!" he chokes. "I did not dare to hope it was true, but here

28

you are." He sits on the edge of my bed and hugs me fiercely. "I always felt you would come back to us. But this is nothing short of a miracle."

Over the moon to see him again, I cling to him for all I'm worth. Vibrant and handsome in his dashing Domerican clothes—billowy white shirt, leather vest, riding pants, and boots—he's so outrageously happy to see me, I can't help but get teary-eyed myself. Guilt tugs at my heart because I can't be entirely honest with him about where I've been this past year. But I silently vow to make it up to him.

"Father, thank you for coming to get me. I'm sorry my disappearance caused everyone so much pain."

"Shhh. It was all worth it to have you back again," he says, gently stroking my hair. "Ralston told me what you've been through. Are you truly all right?" His eyes search mine.

"Yes, I'm fine, thanks to Melor and Bithia. I'm just anxious to get home. I can't wait to see Mother and Ryder and Drew."

"They will be overjoyed at the sight of you, sweetheart. I've told them only that I have gone to investigate another rumor you'd been found. We've received many false reports of your survival since the fire, and were always disappointed in the past. I doubt that any of them is genuinely expecting to see you. This will come as quite a shock—but one of a most welcome nature." He smiles and holds both my hands in his. "Ralston has informed you of your mother's illness?"

"Yes. How is she doing?"

"She is frail, Jade, but I'm certain your reappearance will help rejuvenate her. She has missed you terribly. We all have."

"What about Ryder?" I ask. "Is he at the Enclave? Will I be able to see him?"

"Yes. He was there when I left. He promised to wait and hear what I had discovered before returning to Unicoi Village."

"And Drew? Is he all right?"

"He's well, Jade." A smile plays at his lips. "You may be surprised to learn that he is married."

"What! Drew?"

"Yes, last December. His wife, Adelais, is lovely. She and her family relocated to the Enclave from Dome Noir a little more than a year ago. Andrew met her at Summer Fest and was besotted at once."

"Wow. She must really be something to have captured Drew's restless heart. I can't wait to meet her."

"And you shall. Soon. But first, we must prepare for our journey home. I've brought some of your clothing. I hope you will find it suitable. I wasn't certain what you would require." He retrieves a satchel from the floor and puts it next to me on the bed. "Melor and Bithia have prepared a small meal for us." He glances at Bithia. "One of the many things for which we are grateful. And, then we must be on our way. There will be great joy and much celebrating upon your return." He rises from the bed. "I still cannot believe my eyes."

"We'll leave you now, dear," Bithia says. "When you have dressed, please join us in the dining room." She opens the door for my father. His eyes overflow with joy and affection, and he steps out with a backward glance my way.

With some trepidation, I unfasten the satchel to see what Father put together for me to wear. He'd thought of everything: beige riding pants, brown leather boots, a coral wool sweater—even clean socks and underwear. Nice job. I dress quickly, pulling my sleeve down over the TPD bracelet. After straightening the comforter, I place the Cleadian robe and slippers neatly on top of the bed. There's no trace of my other clothes. *I'm really going to miss those jeans.*

The door to my room leads out into a shiny metal hallway. The muted lighting emanates from small recessed tubes running along the floor and ceiling. I do a double-take when I see the walls which are adorned at intervals with plagues of tiny metal insect sculptures migrating across the expanse. It's seriously creepy. Cleadian art, I guess.

The location of the dining room is a mystery to me, but I didn't dare ask in front of my father, since supposedly I've been here a few weeks and should already know. I tread slowly down the hall, trying to minimize the clack of my boot heels against the metal floor. Father's voice carries through a door on the left. *Bingo.*

"Do we know how to reach these Outlanders?" he says. "I would like to thank them in some way for seeing to Jaden's welfare these past months. She was nothing to them. They could simply have allowed her to die."

"Unfortunately, I have no idea where they reside," Melor replies. "As you know, they're quite secretive regarding the location of their outposts. I don't believe they would welcome any intrusion, even if it was to receive your thanks. Should they ever return, however, I will convey your interest in making them a reward of some sort."

Father rubs a hand across his bearded chin. "I suppose you're right. Attempting to locate them would probably prove futile. We'll simply hope they will return someday to inquire about Jaden." He glimpses me standing in the doorway. "Here she is now." Smiling broadly, he comes to escort me to the dining table.

"You look surprisingly hale and hearty for your ordeal, sweetheart," he says. "You must tell me what it was like living in an Outlander post. It cannot have been easy for you, and yet you seem to have thrived."

I glance furtively at Ralston, sitting across the table. We didn't have time to discuss how I was going to handle these kinds of questions.

"Yes. I'm better now, thanks to the Cleadians. When I was with the Outlanders, I um, stayed inside mostly. They were nice to me. And, well it's all kind of a blur," I say.

"Of course it is." Melor chimes in. "You experienced several days of high fever with the influenza. And considering the extensive long-term memory work we've done lately, I imagine it all seems like a distant dream by now."

"Just like a dream," I agree, relieved. This guy's good. Maybe the best liar I've ever met.

Bithia arrives carrying a tray. "We have a small repast for you before you embark upon your journey," she says. The tray is filled with crusty bread, an assortment of cheeses, fresh fruit, and a small dish of sugared almonds. "The almonds are from Cupola de Vita," she croons. "They're divine. You must try them."

"It all looks wonderful," Father says, forgetting about my 'ordeal'… for the moment.

The conversation remains light for the remainder of the meal. Father enjoys recounting the details of Drew's wedding for me. Mother was feeling much better at that time and insisted on having a grand affair at the palace. I can't picture my big brother married. He's only thirteen months older than me.

My heart squeezes when I realize that, officially, I'm engaged to be married. Ryder and I entered into a marriage contract, but didn't have a chance to set a wedding date or make any plans before I was whisked back to Connecticut. My breath comes a little quicker when I think about that fact that I'll be planning my own wedding in the not so distant future.

FIVE

When we've finished our meal, we thank Melor and Bithia once again and prepare to depart the compound. "It's storming out there now, and travel will be more difficult once the sun has risen," Father says.

I'm not sure exactly what he means, but Ralston told me that when the Great Disaster occurred, and the remnants of Halley's Comet slammed into the Pacific Ocean, a permanent hole was ripped in the earth's atmosphere, and over eighty percent of the earth's surface was destroyed. Outlanders and others who travel outside the domes must wear protective gear at all times because the air is toxic, and the atmosphere provides little protection from the sun and the other elements.

Melor leads us through a maze of metal hallways to the main entrance of the compound. It's nearly 4:00 a.m. The halls are eerily quiet, except for the report of our footsteps, echoed and amplified by the metallic walls. Not another soul appears along the way. A large cabinet stands adjacent to the entrance door. A number of weird white suits hang from a rod inside. Melor removes three of them and passes one to each of us.

Father and Ralston immediately unzip the suits and begin stepping inside them, boots and all. Since I have no idea how these things fit, I just follow their lead. They look a little like hazmat gear, made of thick, rubbery material that sticks to my clothes. After we're all zipped-up, Melor hands each of us a helmet from the closet shelf. He helps me attach mine to my suit. It's heavy, and I instantly feel like I'm suffocating. Melor punches a button on the side of the helmet and, with a whoosh, oxygen begins circulating inside. In a few seconds, I'm doing much better. Father and Ralston attach their helmets, and we all pull on elbow-length gloves.

After our preparations are completed, Melor opens the gigantic metal door at the entrance. He gives a lantern to Father. "Godspeed, my friends," he says with a bow.

Father smiles reassuringly at me through his visor. I feel like Gumby trying to walk in this thing and, honestly, we all look ridiculous. I stifle the urge to laugh out loud. But maybe that's an effect of the pure oxygen I'm breathing. We step into a short metal hall with another door at the far end. Once we're inside, Melor closes the main door behind us with a heavy thud.

Ralston moves to the door opposite. It makes a loud scraping sound as he pushes it open.

We're immediately met with pitch-black coldness. The atmosphere outside is jarringly hostile. Tiny particles of crud bombard us relentlessly, chinking and pinging against our helmets. I'm nearly blown over by the howling wind, but Father steadies me, holding my arm securely. Heads bowed, we trek unsteadily across the gloppy earth. I hope we don't have to walk all the way to the dome, but conversation is impossible over the wailing wind, so I can't even ask how far we have to go.

Father leads the way with his lantern, a tiny beacon in the lurid darkness. After trudging along a rutted path for several yards, I glimpse a concrete slab ahead with two vehicles parked on top. The wind dies down for a moment, and we hustle to the nearest vehicle. It looks like a giant Snow Cat, with caterpillar-type tracks. Father opens the door of the large cab and pulls down a set of steps. I climb up and Ralston follows. Bringing up the rear, Father hoists up the steps behind him and clangs the door closed.

Aah. It's quiet and warm in here.

Father flips some switches in the cockpit, and the engine rumbles to life. Ralston and I settle into our seats. He heaves off his helmet and slips out of his gloves, motioning for me to do the same. We stuff our gear into netting hanging above our seats.

"Melor really needs to build an underground entrance for the compound," Father says, after removing his own helmet. "It would make travel much easier for the Cleadians, especially when these storms come up."

"I believe Melor fully intends to do so," Ralston says, "but things move a little slowly in the Cleadian colony."

I recall Ralston telling me once that the Cleadians have amazing respiratory systems, and this earth's atmosphere isn't toxic to them. Also, they're immune to ultraviolet rays, so the scorching sun doesn't harm them either. Guess that's why they're not in much of a hurry to build an underground entrance.

Our vehicle lumbers away from the compound on its continuous tracks. I can't tell if we're driving on a roadway or just making our own path. The headlamps beam bright shafts in front of us, and the giant windshield wipers sweep away the grit that unremittingly pelts the enormous square, tinted windows of our cab. But, straining my eyes ahead, I can't make out a thing. Father acts as if he knows where he's going, though, so I decide not to worry about it. The wind buffets our vehicle every now and then, but all in all, the ride is fairly smooth and comfortable.

Father concentrates intently on his driving, but does manage to fill me in on some of the news from Domerica. Mostly stuff Ralston's already told me, like the assassination of Prince Damien, Uncle Harold and Oz's relocation to the palace, Chief Blackthorn's death. But he does surprise me with one bit of news. Drew and his new wife are not living at the palace. In fact, they've taken up residence at Meadowood—a large estate belonging to Princess Jaden. Father wanted to prepare me for the fact that, once I was declared legally dead, Mother gave the property to Drew and Adelais as a wedding gift.

I'm kind of pissed about that at first. *How could Mother give away my estate?* But then I realize I'm being ridiculous, since she thought I was dead, and since it wasn't really mine to begin with. I tell Father I'm happy Drew and his bride have a great place to live.

We ride in silence for a stretch, and the sky begins to lighten and blush at the edge of the horizon. I'm able to get a better view of our surroundings—a staggeringly bleak display. The terrain is dull gray-black and formlessly murky, as if layers of volcanic ash cover every surface. Large, dark hills block our view on the left. On our right, random piles of sludgy, spiky debris lie scattered across an endless expanse of rocky terrain.

God-forsaken, life-forsaken, hope-forsaken. No color, vibrancy, or animation exists in this desolate landscape. *So this is earth outside the dome.* The reality surpasses even my darkest imaginings. A wave of profound sorrow shudders through me.

As if perceiving my somber vibes, Father turns and smiles. "Not much longer, sweetheart. We'll be there soon." He makes an arching left turn around the shadowy ridge of jagged hills, and I'm floored by the shining spectacle looming in front of us. The hulking hemisphere of Domerica dominates in the distance. Stunning in size and appearance, it's an otherworldly sight—as if the moon tumbled from the sky and lodged itself in the earth's crust. Gleaming in all its luminescent glory, it steals my breath away.

Buoyed by the magical facade of the dome, my thoughts turn to my upcoming reunions with Ryder and Mother. Nervous anticipation replaces my sober mood. The prospect of seeing Ryder again conjures a jumble of emotions. He's my passion, but he's also my weakness and I don't like feeling weak.

Ralston explained to me that Ryder and I have something called a *perpetual contract*—an agreement between two souls with a long shared history to be together in other lifetimes, but not necessarily *all* lifetimes. I admit I don't fully understand it, and I'm not sure Ralston does either. All I know is that last year IUGA decided, since their prediction models clearly indicated Ryder and Princess Jaden were not supposed to be together in this existence, I needed to leave the country fast or risk screwing up the future of the entire planet.

So I spent the last twelve months tracking down Ryder's *mirror* in my world, hoping if we met, we'd have the same attraction for each other. I was successful in discovering that he's with the Peace Corps in Zambia, and I was working on a way to get there when Ralston showed up to bring me back here. This way's better, *I think*. I guess we'll know soon enough.

SIX

*T*he sun inches above the horizon, but the sky roils with dark, fast-moving clouds. We catch only startling glimpses of blazing illumination through the cloud-breaks. On a clear day, the sun must be unbelievably brutal. Drawing near the dome, Father turns into a concrete passageway that looks like the entrance to an underground parking garage. We drive a short distance and park in a small area where a few vehicles similar to ours stand empty.

The helmets go back on, but we leave off our gloves. As I climb out of the cab, the howl of the frenzied crud storm makes me shiver. Father leads us to the dome entrance—a sturdy metal door with a thickly paned window. He presses a round disk on one side of the door. I hear the blare of a buzzer. In minutes, a face appears at the window. Father raises his hand in a salute, and the door is quickly opened by two members of the Royal Guard.

"Governor Beckett, may we help you inside?" a young sergeant asks.

We tromp into an anteroom; the second guard secures the door behind us. Relieved to be out of the elements, I pull off my helmet and shake out my hair. I'm sticky and sweaty in my rubber suit and antsy to get it off post-haste.

"Follow me," the sergeant says. We trudge behind the two guards to another thick metal door and repeat the same procedure. When this door is opened, four additional guards wait inside. They nod to us and escort us to yet a third door. Dome security is supposedly unbreachable. True or not, it sure as hell takes a long time before we're finally inside.

"I'll store your gear for you," the sergeant says, walking to yet another door.

"Thank you, Evers," Father says. "I believe you have some horses for me?"

"Yes. You may stow your things in here." Evers opens a large storage closet containing suits similar to ours. "May I have the names of your guests for our log, Governor?"

"Of course. This is Professor Constantine Ralston." Ralston nods at Evers. "And you know my daughter, Princess Jaden Beckett."

The sergeant looks at me for the first time, and the blood drains from his face. He bows low. "Please forgive me, Your Highness, I did not realize it was you." He focuses on my face again, regaining his composure. "I'm sorry, ma'am. I thought … Well I'd heard that you had perished in the fire last year. The story of your courageous attempt to recapture the Operations Center from the renegade Noirs is legend."

Embarrassed, I don't exactly know how to respond. Smiling awkwardly, I busy myself with peeling off my rubber suit. The fact is, I never made it to the Dome Operations Center. I struck my head on a low-lying tree branch and toppled from my horse. I woke up back in my bedroom in Madison.

"It's quite all right, Evers," Father says. "It was only recently discovered that the princess was alive and well. The story is rather remarkable, and I'm certain it will be widely reported in Domerica by tomorrow. But, we've been up all night and, at the moment we're most anxious to return to the Enclave for some rest."

"Of course," he says, bowing again. "I shall arrange for your horses at once."

The pinkish-silver light of the Domerican morning bathes the dome with a rosy glow as we begin the relatively short ride from the west entrance to the Enclave. The sun itself isn't visible from inside the dome, due to a protective layer of thick, silvery gasses within the dome's impenetrable double shell. The gasses are adjusted regularly to allow in enough sunlight to sustain the plants and animals, while screening out harmful UV rays. The freshly filtered morning air is exhilarating, though I believe I detect the slightest tinge of burnt wood. It's a pleasure to be on horseback again. I worried I might be a little rusty, but from the moment my seat hit the saddle, it was like I'd never been gone.

We reach the main gate to the walled city and are admitted by Nathan, the grizzled old gatekeeper. "Welcome home, Princess Jaden," he says in his booming baritone. "You've been greatly missed."

"Thanks Nathan. It's good to be back."

We steer our horses along the wide cobblestone main street. A few merchants sweep the sidewalks and arrange their wares in outdoor displays, but the little Victorian town is hushed and mostly deserted at this early-morning hour. No one pays much attention to us, just a fleeting look here and there. My heart lurches when we come to the tree-lined lane leading to Father's manor house. The blood sings in my veins, and every cell in my body is aware that Ryder Blackthorn is nearby. The little sorrel mare I'm riding seems to sense my growing excitement, and pulls anxiously at her rein. *Stay calm, Jaden. Stay calm.*

A stable boy meets us near the front steps, and collects our horses. Father wraps an arm around my shoulder, as if making sure I'm solid, and together we climb the stairs to the broad veranda. Ralston follows close behind. As we reach the top stair, the massive front door is opened by a middle-aged woman with an enormous smile and eyes brimming with tears.

She throws her arms around me and holds me close. Her embrace is pleasantly squishy, and she smells of cinnamon and hyacinth. "Saints preserve us! I can't believe my eyes. It's really you this time."

I'm momentarily thrown because I don't recognize this woman, but then Father says, "Mrs. Hornsby, you didn't have to get up so early to greet us."

Ah, Mrs. Hornsby, the housekeeper. I'd heard of her, but she was visiting relatives in another dome when I was here last. Her daughter, Erica, had temporarily assumed her duties.

"Thanks, Mrs. Hornsby," I say. "I'm glad to be home."

She dabs at her eyes with the corner of her apron. "You must be tired and famished. Come in. Let me make you some breakfast."

"I'm not really hungry," I say. "We ate before we left the Cleadians. Is Ryder here?"

An odd look passes across her face, and her hand flutters to her throat. "Yes, yes. He is here," she says tentatively, "but he's asleep. I believe he was up very late last night." She takes my hand. "Come and have some tea at least. I have fresh cinnamon muffins." She leads me toward the dining room.

"Baked in your honor, I'm certain," Father says, following us. "How about you, Professor?"

"Sounds lovely," Ralston says.

We sit in the dining room while Mrs. Hornsby bustles about serving us tea and muffins with homemade pommera jam. I sip at my steamy cup, and pick my muffin to crumbs. It's maddening to be this near Ryder and not be able to be with him.

At last Father says, "Go and wake him, Jade. He would want you to."

"Are you sure?" I ask, hopefully.

"Absolutely. And Ralston, you should get some rest. I need to check in at the hospital before we journey on to Warrington. I've a patient with a particularly frustrating case of pneumonia. It hasn't responded to any of the usual medications."

"Really?" Ralston says. "Do you mind if I accompany you? I saw a few such instances during my tenure in Cupola de Vita. Perhaps I can tell you about a poultice their physicians used for the most stubborn cases."

"A poultice? Yes, that would be wonderful. I welcome any suggestions you may have." He turns to me. "Jaden, will you be all right without us for an hour or two?"

Excitedly, I push away from the table. "Sure. I'll be fine. Take as long as you want. Ryder will keep me company."

Excusing myself, I make for the sweeping marble staircase, taking the steps two at a time. I pop into my room first, to check my hair and change my sweater. Everything is just the way I left it, as if Father had expected me to return.

Heart hammering wildly, I knock on Ryder's door. The seconds tick by. No answer.

Hand on the door knob, I lean in closer and call his name softly. "Ryder." Still no answer.

Slowly turning the knob, I crack the door slightly, and my breath catches in my throat. He's lying on his side, one long, bare leg draped across ivory bed linens. The David in repose. He's utterly splendid— luminous skin, elegant limbs, muscled back. Early morning light catches the sheen of his obsidian hair, carelessly splayed across the pillow.

Stealing to the edge of his bed, I kneel beside him. "Ryder," I whisper. His eyes remain closed, his breathing unchanged.

I tentatively reach out to stroke his hair. Quick as lightning, his hand darts out and grasps my wrist. A startled cry escapes my lips. He gapes at me for a split second before recognition dawns on him. Swinging his legs around, he gathers me into his lap.

"Is it you? Is it really you?" he says, azure eyes searching mine.

"It's me." Gazing at him in wonder, I brush my fingertips along his cheek, and the familiar electricity crackles between us.

He takes my hand gently pressing his lips to my palm. Then

crushing me to his chest, he hides his face in my hair and weeps. Warm tears topple onto my skin, as long shuddering sobs rack his body.

I'm broken to see him this way, understanding so richly the utter pain, the raw grief he has suffered. The relief of having him in my arms again is exquisite. I'm at once wounded and made whole.

"Shhh." I stroke his smooth back to comfort him. Silent tears spill from my cheeks, mingling with his, uniting joy and sorrow.

I hold him in a soggy embrace while he collects himself. Pulling away from me, he smiles and wipes tears from his cheeks with the back of his hand. "How?" he says, shaking his head. "Where have you been?"

Returning his smile, I relate an abridged version of the story Ralston and Melor concocted.

"It's remarkable," he says. "We searched for you for days. I was nearly mad with grief, and consumed with guilt because you'd gone missing while trying to help me. I should've known you would never stay behind as I asked." Wonder glints from his eyes. "But you've come back to me now, and that's all that matters."

He cradles my face in his hands and softly kisses each eyelid. Cocking his head, he says, "You've cut your hair."

"Yes." I nervously comb my fingers through the shorter, but still lengthy strands.

"I like it; you're more beautiful than ever."

I feel an odd shyness at the compliment.

He nuzzles my neck. "I'd almost forgotten your wonderful scent." Brushing his lips across my jaw toward my lips, the moment I've waited for, prayed for comes at last—Ryder's sweet mouth is on mine once again. All that's inside me flows up to meet his kiss, gentle and trembling at first. Then as emotion overcomes reason, he kisses me deeply, hungrily. His warm body shelters my own. Hot blood burns inside my veins, my pulse races wildly, swept up in the sheer rapture of our reunion.

After a moment, he pulls his mouth away, but I wrap my hand around his neck and draw him to me again. I require more of him, I want all of him. I've been with Ryder a million times in my dreams, but we've never actually shared more than a handful of passionate kisses. All that is about to change.

Tentative and restrained, he pulls away again. "Jade, I'm naked under this coverlet. Allow me to dress so we can talk."

"I don't want to talk." I grasp the hem of my sweater, pull it off over my head, and toss it onto the bedside chair. "There'll be plenty of time for that later. Right now I want to be naked and next to you."

"Jade, don't," he says, holding my arm to prevent me from removing any more clothing.

"Why? Are you worried about Father? He and Ralston are at the hospital. They'll be gone for hours."

He shakes his head. "It's not that."

"What then? You're not still concerned about appearances are you? We're engaged. Nobody will care. And if they do, to hell with them."

His face is tense, eyes unreadable.

"Ryder, what is it?" A small knot of fear gathers in my belly. "You still want to marry me, don't you?"

"More than anything," he says fiercely. "But we must talk. Please allow me to put on my pants at least."

"Fine. Put on your pants." I stand with my back to him arms folded, while he steps into his doeskin trousers. Grasping my shoulders, he turns me to him. My arms automatically wind around his waist.

"What is it, love?" I say. "If you still want to marry me, what's so wrong with us being intimate together?"

He bows his head and lowers his eyes. "You may no longer wish to marry me."

I laugh. "That's ridiculous. Of course I still want to marry you. Why—" But before the words cross my lips, the door flies open, banging loudly against the dresser. Framed in the entry is a flushed and breathless Erica Hornsby, ravishing in her anxious vulnerability.

She stares at me, wide-eyed. "So it's true," she says. Glancing at Ryder, her stunning face dissolves into an anguished portrait of pain, telling me all I need to know. She turns and flees, navy cape and long dark hair flying out behind her.

My heart, my breath, my entire world freezes in suspended animation. "Erica?" I whisper. "You and Erica?"

"Yes."

The air whooshes from the room. My heart and lungs wither in my chest. Clutching for the arm of the chair I sit down, hard.

"How long?" I ask, eyes straight ahead.

"Seven or eight weeks," he says softly.

"Do you love her?"

"No, of course not." He kneels beside my chair. I can't bring myself to look at him. "There is only one woman I have ever loved or will ever love. Erica knows that."

I hide my face in my hands. "But she obviously loves you."

"No!" he says. I lower my hands, piercing him with my eyes. "Perhaps," he admits.

"God, what an idiot. I never even considered that you'd found someone else."

"I haven't found someone else. Jaden, please let me explain." He gets off his knees and perches on the edge of the bed facing me. He reaches for my hand, but I jerk it away.

"Erica cared for my father in the hospital during his last days. She's training to be a nurse."

"I'm sorry about your father," I mumble, recalling with bitter irony that it was my brilliant idea for Erica to train at the hospital.

"Thank you. He was in much pain at the end, and Erica was very good to him. A few days after his death she brought food to our house. Catherine was not at home, so we shared the meal she had prepared. Our conversation was innocent. We spoke of her work, the unpredictability of life, the pain of loss. But near the end of the evening, she asked if it was true that when you were declared dead, I vowed never to marry. I confirmed what she had heard. She related that she had made a similar vow but for different reasons." He lowers his eyes.

"She suggested that the two of us could find companionship with each other without a permanent commitment. I said I would think about it and give her my answer later." His eyes find mine again. "I did not make the decision lightly, Jaden. I still felt a bond with you, even though I believed you to be dead."

"Yeah well, it didn't hurt that she's drop-dead gorgeous, did it?" I sneer.

"I cannot deny that she is physically attractive."

His words burn as if he scored me with a hot poker. Leaping to my feet, I snatch up the crushed sweater I've been sitting on, and pull it over my head. "Thanks a lot."

He scrambles to his feet. "What I meant is that for me it was only a physical relationship."

"That's a sweet little story, Ryder. But how could you? Seriously, how could you fall into bed with the first woman who bats her eyes at you?"

"It had been nearly a year, Jade. I thought you were dead."

"I don't care!" The shrillness of my voice startles me. "I could never have done that to you. I can't even *imagine* being with another man. I thought we felt the same. Now I know better."

"Jade, please." He rakes a hand through his hair.

I slowly shake my head. "I've heard enough. You'd better go and find Erica. She's probably as destroyed as I am."

"I want to stay here with you."

"No. I'm leaving in the morning to be with my mother." I futilely try to smooth my rumpled sweater. "Please go."

He pulls a shirt from the closet and slips it on, then tugs on his boots. Standing in the doorframe, his hair brushing up against the lintel, he asks, "What does this mean for us, Jaden? Do you wish to dissolve our engagement?"

I compose my face into a hard emotionless mask. "I don't know yet. I need some time to think."

He swallows audibly. "Please remember that in spite of my poor judgment, I love only you. Regardless of your decision, I shall always love only you."

"We'll speak in a few days, Ryder. I'll send for you when I'm ready." I turn away toward the window. The door clicks softly shut, and I fall back into the chair too stunned to even cry.

SEVEN

I want to wail like a banshee. I want to jump out of my skin, climb the wall, tear out my hair, something, anything, so I don't have to feel this way. Ryder and Erica. The image of the two of them together flashes in hi-def through my mind. She's so exotically beautiful. Smart too, and experienced when it comes to guys. Ryder claims he loves me, but can he ever forget how hot she is? Will he see her whenever he's with me? Dream of being with her? I mean, she's Angelina Jolie and I'm … *not.*

Grasping the hand mirror on Ryder's nightstand, I hold it up and stare at my decidedly un-glamorous reflection. What a pathetic, hopeless fool. I fling the mirror against the wall, and, like my dreams, it shatters into dozens of glittering shards and crashes to the floor.

Bolting out the door, I make for the staircase, not knowing where I'm going. I'll die of embarrassment if I run into Mrs. Hornsby. She probably knows everything. But I'll go insane if I don't get out of this house. Saddling-up and setting out to see my mother by myself is what I want to do, but I quickly rule it out. Highwaymen notoriously haunt the road to Warrington, and I've been attacked there before. I've just got to get away from *here.*

Stables. Horses. A quiet place to think. A meadow to gallop through, allowing the wind to blow away these dark destructive thoughts. That's what I need.

Peter, the head stableman, is intently mucking out a stall when I arrive. He raises his head and beams at me.

"I heard you were back, Princess. It's a true pleasure to see you again."

"Thanks Peter. May I borrow a horse until Father gets back from the hospital? That sorrel mare I rode in on this morning will be just fine."

"Of course. May I take you somewhere? I'll be happy to hitch-up the carriage and drive you."

"No. I just feel like a ride."

He narrows his eyes at me. "Are you all right, Jaden?"

I must look like a madwoman because that's how I feel inside. "I just need some fresh air and a silent companion," I say, doing my best to hold it together.

He smiles. "I'll have Lochlyn ready for you in two shakes."

The beauty of the day is a sharp contrast to my mood. Dome temperature is constantly controlled to be a perfect seventy-two degrees. The silvery filtered sunlight lends a radiant luminescence to the landscape. The Enclave is charming and unspoiled. Lush gardens of spring flowers in scarlet and lavender border the quaint city streets. Victorian houses, freshly painted in pastel hues, overlook well-tended yards, most of which are surrounded by white picket fences.

My sweet little mare is frisky and enjoying the exercise. Steering away from Main Street, which is now bustling with mid-morning trade, I search for a peaceful spot where I can sort through my thoughts and figure out how I'm supposed to feel about this. Skirting around the inside wall of the city, we eventually stumble into a quiet residential area. A large park unfolds at the end of small cul-de-sac. It appears deserted, so I steer Lochlyn onto the cobblestone road and make for the inviting refuge.

A small, ginger-haired girl romps with a spotted puppy on the lawn of a pretty cottage. She waves when she sees me. Smiling, I wave back. Her eyes and mouth instantly form themselves into perfect Os. "Princess Jaden!" she shouts.

I dip my head as if I haven't heard her and nudge my horse into a trot. The child spins on her heel and dashes into the house calling, "Mommy, mommy. Princess Jaden is back!"

Only a few more yards, and I can disappear into the park. Quickly checking over my shoulder, I glimpse the child's mother sprinting from the house, drying her hands on a kitchen towel. She rushes into the road and catches sight of me. Then, amazingly, she and the girl jog after me, the puppy nipping at their heels. "Princess Jaden, Princess Jaden," the woman calls, waving her towel.

In no time, the surrounding neighbors dribble out their front doors to see what the commotion is about. "It's Princess Jaden!" they cry out to each other. Near the park entrance, I steal another glance behind me. A small knot of villagers hurries toward me, waving and calling my name. *Crap! I'm done.* I don't have the heart to ignore them, and besides they're blocking my escape route.

I pull up on Lochlyn's reins, and turn her around. I don't know what to expect, but I suck in my breath, and urge her slowly in the direction of the burgeoning crowd. She snorts and shies as the throng presses in on us. I'm a little freaked myself, but they seem to want nothing more than to touch me or wish me well. "Long live Princess Jaden," they shout. Or "She's alive, she's alive!" Or "Welcome home!" Even a few "Blessed be the Chosen's"—the slogan of The Church of the Chosen—ring out.

I'm shocked by all the attention. The citizens of the Enclave aren't subject to my mother's rule, and have always been proud of their independence, but I guess someone just back from the dead is big news everywhere. *This was a monumentally stupid idea.*

Lochlyn and I carefully pick our way through the undulating mass of humanity. People offer up flowers, lace hankies, and even small cakes, as we pass. These gestures touch me, but I can't hold everything in my arms. Squishing it all together, I shove it inside the pouch attached to my saddle. Relief floods through me when we finally reach the end of the street. Steering Lochlyn toward Father's house, I turn and wave farewell to the crowd. To my chagrin, though, instead of dispersing, they continue to follow us, calling to passersby to join the procession.

By the time we reach the manor house lane, a veritable parade of townspeople tag along behind us. My father steps out onto the veranda, surveying the spectacle swarming up his drive. He stations himself at the top of the steps, hands on his hips. At first his expression is not discernible, but as we draw nearer, I glimpse amusement in his eyes and a twitch of a smile around his lips. When we reach the house, I bound off my horse and up the steps to Father.

"What's all this?" he asks grinning.

My face flames hot crimson. "I don't know. I just went for a ride and picked up a few friends. I'm so sorry."

The villagers gather at the foot of the stairs cheering and chanting my name. Father wraps an arm around my shoulder, and holds up a commanding hand. The noise dies down enough for him to speak. "Thank you all for this heart-warming 'welcome home' for Princess Jaden. We are thankful beyond words that she has returned safely to us. As some of you may already know, she has been through quite an ordeal this past year, and she is anxious to be reunited with her mother, Queen Eleanor. We hope you will excuse us for now, as we must make preparations for our journey in the morning. I promise you will be seeing much more of Princess Jaden in the coming months."

An appreciative cheer goes up from the gathering. Father waves one last time and steers me into the house. "Well, that was rather exciting," he says kissing my forehead. "Perhaps you should not go out unescorted for a time. Where's Ryder? Will he be dining with us tonight?"

At the mention of Ryder's name, a lead weight drops in my heart. "No. He has some things to take care of. He'll join us at Warrington in a few days."

Father's brow creases slightly. "Very well. Are you all right?" His eyes probe mine.

"Yes. That whole scene out there just threw me a little. I think I'll go up to my room and rest awhile."

"Of course, sweetheart. I need to make arrangements for tomorrow. We're taking some wagons with us to Warrington. Mrs. Hornsby has lunch prepared for you. I'll be home before dinner." He kisses my forehead again.

"Thanks Father."

There's no way I want to see Mrs. Hornsby right now. Once Father is gone, I make a bee-line for my room. Pulling off my boots, I sit on the edge of the bed and do the one thing I've needed to do since seeing Erica—drop my face into my hands and bawl.

Sorrow takes many forms. Loss. Regret. Despair. I've tasted them all. But this is a new kind of grief for me—jealousy, betrayal, and self-doubt, shaken together in one noxious cocktail of misery.

How could I have been so clueless? Of course women would throw themselves at Ryder. What reason would he have to turn them down? I was dead, right? I lie on my bed and stare at the ceiling, trying desperately not to think about anything, attempting to achieve a blissful catatonic state. *My mind is a blank slate. My mind is a blank slate. My mind is a blank slate.*

"Jade?" Ralston calls softly from outside my door.

I don't respond. *My mind is a blank slate.*

The door opens slightly, and he peers inside. "May I come in? I've brought you some lunch."

I continue to stare at the ceiling. *My mind is a blank slate.*

"I heard that Ryder departed hastily this morning. Obviously something is terribly wrong between the two of you. Since I'm responsible for bringing you here, I would very much like to speak with you about it."

So much for catatonia. I scoot off the bed and pull open the door for him. "Come on in Rals."

He sets the lunch tray on my coffee table, and we sit in the Queen Anne chairs facing the fake fireplace. I recount the ugly essentials for Ralston—the reunion with Ryder, Erica's unexpected appearance, my sending Ryder away. But I leave out the most embarrassing part about me standing there like some freakin' idiot with my sweater off.

He presses his lips together tightly. "Oh my. That was surely terrible for you, my dear. I must apologize. I assure you I had no idea they had begun a relationship. Agent Chelmsford did not inform me. Either he was unaware, which is inexcusable, or he felt it not worth mentioning, which suggests unforgivably poor judgment." His eyes are troubled behind his glasses. "Why, you might never have agreed to return had you known. I feel IUGA has brought you here under false pretenses. You have every right to return home immediately, if that is your desire."

I shake my head. "I can't leave right now. I need to see my mom first, and I have to sort through my feelings about this. It's still too fresh for me to know what I really want. Maybe after a few days it'll become clearer."

"Very well," he says. "Is there anything I can do for you right now?"

"Yes. Help me find a way to get my mind off of this."

His brow furrows momentarily. Then he raises his index finger. "Ah, I believe I have just the thing. Are you familiar with skittles?"

"You mean like the fruit candy?"

"No, I mean like the bowling game. I believe there is an alley near here. I could teach you."

This captures my interest, but then I remember. "I can't really go out in public. I almost got mobbed this morning. Word's out all over town that Princess Jaden is back from the dead."

He studies me, rubbing his chin. "I think we might be able to arrange a slight disguise. You could tuck your hair beneath one of my hats. I have a shirt and vest that should fit you. If we keep to ourselves, no one will be the wiser."

"Okay. It's worth a try."

The disguise works. Nobody gives us a second look as we enter the skittles alley, which doubles as a pub. Ralston pays for our games and a couple of mugs of ginger ale. He says the history of skittles dates back to medieval England. We spend a few minutes going over the rules. It's a lot like bowling except, instead of using a ball, you toss a big round heavy cheese, *real cheese*, at wooden pins. Kind of wacky, and a bit unsanitary, but it's a blast, and I'm disappointed when, after a few hours of lighthearted competition, Ralston says it's time to start back to the manor house.

"I'm not looking forward to dinner," I confess. "Erica's mother must know the whole sordid tale by now. She must hate me. She'll probably sprinkle cyanide on my green beans or something."

"I'm certain she doesn't hate you, Jaden. None of this is your fault."

"Maybe not, but her daughter's heart is broken tonight because of me. They both probably wish I'd never come back." I silently hope this doesn't signal a trend.

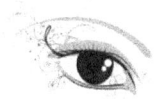

EIGHT

Dinner doesn't suck. Father's chef prepared a special menu for my homecoming. It's over-the-top delicious. Mrs. Hornsby is the epitome of graciousness and shows not the slightest hint that she knows her daughter and I are arch rivals for the affections of the desirable Ryder Blackthorn.

Sleep eludes me, though. My room at Father's house is large but cozy, and the bed is gloriously soft and comfortable. Each time I close my eyes visions of Ryder and Erica together play on an endless loop in my head. I push away the disturbing images by replaying old episodes of *30 Rock* in my mind. It works for a while, but I doze off and have a weird dream that Ryder and Tina Fey get married in a secret ceremony in the Caymans, and I find out about it from TMZ.

At daybreak I drag my weary bones out of bed and splash some water on my face. Catching my reflection in the mirror, I realize I look beyond wrecked. I don't care. It's a day for comfortable riding clothes and no make-up. These people are lucky I'm even brushing my teeth.

Downstairs, Father sips coffee in the dining room. "Good morning, Jade," he says as I stumble in.

Breakfast is laid out buffet-style on the sideboard, and I grab a glass of ruby-red pommera juice. I'd never heard of a pommera until I came to Domerica. It's a succulent, dark-pink fruit with juicy red insides, and I'm kind of addicted.

"I'm glad you're up," Father says. "We should get an early start if we wish to reach the palace by nightfall. I know your mother is anxious to see you. Would you care to ride in one of the wagons with Ralston, or do you prefer a horse?"

"A horse," I say. "That little mare, Lochlyn, would be great."

"Very well." He rises from his chair. "Have your breakfast, and meet me at the stables when you're ready. I'll ask Peter to prepare the mare for you."

I eat a muffin and finish my juice, stashing a few extra pommeras in my pocket for the road. Taking the long way around the house to the stables, I avoid seeing anyone else. Ralston's already seated in a wagon, but I'm surprised to see two additional wagons and several members of the Enclave army waiting to accompany us. I mount up and draw my horse next to Father's. "Are we expecting trouble?" I ask, cutting my eyes to the men.

"Not at all," he says. "I'm just being cautious. Instances of highway robbery have increased over the last several months, and we're carrying valuable cargo." He tips his head toward the wagons.

"What's in there?"

"Firearms."

"Guns? But they're outlawed in Domerica."

"They were, but Prince Harold has determined that there is a need for them now, so he's managed to have the law changed. When the Unicoi settled in Domerica, your mother had their firearms confiscated. I offered to store them in my armory for safekeeping. Prince Harold has ordered them transferred to the palace."

"I'm shocked Mother agreed to it. She's always been so dead-set against guns in Domerica."

"Frankly Jade, she may not even be aware of it. She has given your uncle enormous autonomy in his position as Lord High Steward, and he has made the most of it. Of course it is not *my* place to inform her of this development." He pins me with a significant look.

"All right. I get it," I say. "I'll make sure she knows about it."

Father and I ride to the mouth of the drive. He signals the men to follow, and we're off for Warrington Palace. My spirit feels a little lighter when we reach the open road, and I know that soon I'll see my mother again. It's unclear how much time she actually has left, but I vow to cherish every moment.

We haven't ridden far when evidence of last year's fire begins to appear. At first, it's only a small patch of burned ground here and there, but soon the landscape changes dramatically. Charred remains of trees and bushes litter the flattened forest. Some small shoots of grass and tender young saplings have managed to push through the rubble, but as we ride it's apparent that the fire took an enormous toll on this once-lavish countryside. Where flowering trees, lush vegetation, and plentiful wildlife once flourished, now lie acres of blackened earth, withered boxwoods, and piles of burned debris. An acrid stench of smoke lingers on the air. The term "scorched earth" comes to mind.

Father pulls his horse up next to mine. "I still can't get used to it," he says soberly. "Such a tragic waste."

Fire of any kind is strictly prohibited in Domerica because of the potential for quick and immediate destruction of everything living inside the dome. This fire was started when the band of Prince Damien's thugs sabotaged the Dome Operations Center and started a lightning storm inside the dome.

"How far does it go on like this?" I crane my neck in all directions.

"Around fifteen kilometers. Your mother was forced to cut back on the land granted for Unicoi Village. And, of course, there has been a shortage of lumber. Not all Unicoi have received homes yet. Many families have been forced to double-up, and many others are still in tents. The settlement is dreadfully overcrowded."

"Living in tents? For more than a year? That's got to be rough. Will we pass by the settlement on our way?"

"Yes. You'll be able to see some of it, but your Uncle Harold decreed that, for security reasons, the outer borders of Unicoi Village must be at least five kilometers away from the main highway."

"How does that make Unicoi Village more secure?" I ask.

"I don't believe it's the village he's concerned about."

"You mean he thinks the Unicoi are a threat to Domericans?"

"Honestly, Jade, I don't know what he's thinking. Perhaps you should query him on that issue yourself. He is rather orthodox COC."

What Father is referring to is that some members of the Church of the Chosen, or COC, think only people who originally populated the domes, and their progeny, are among the ones "chosen" by God to survive the Great Disaster. The Unicoi don't fit that definition. When the comet hit the earth in 1758, a community of people living on the edge of the Appalachian mountain range survived by moving into a series of caves. They were made up mostly of Cherokee along with British, Spanish, and Irish settlers.

Eventually they became a thriving society, building cities deep within the mountain, discovering an inexhaustible natural source of energy, and developing superior farming methods. They've even acquired some advanced forms of technology, like motorized vehicles and devices similar to cell phones. When I first met Ryder, the Unicoi population was slowly dying off from the effects of radiation and radon gas poisoning due to decaying uranium present in the mountain. Relocating them was the only way to save them, but not all Domericans were thrilled with that decision.

The remainder of our journey along the path of fire-destroyed terrain is long, tedious, and downright depressing. Thoughts of Ryder only make things worse. It's a relief when a swath of vibrant greenery and clusters of lively wildflowers come into view once again. Father, who has been riding abreast with me for the last several miles, mentions to me that we're nearing Unicoi Village. He points out an area on our left where numerous rectangle buildings rise from the earth. They appear to be much taller than any other buildings in

Domerica, but it's hard to make them out clearly from this distance.

"I'd like to visit the village soon," I say. "I'm interested to see how the transition is going. I hope the uranium-related illnesses have subsided now that the people are out of that mountain."

"We're still dealing with those who were stricken prior to the migration, but things are greatly improved from a medical perspective. I recommend you see the village soon, as many issues will require your attention in the near future. No doubt Ryder will give you a tour whenever you are ready."

Glancing at him obliquely, I say, "I was hoping you'd take me, Father."

He pulls his horse to an abrupt halt, causing the wagons and our guards to pull up short. "Let's take a brief rest," he calls to the group. Climbing from his horse, he motions for me to do the same.

The men dismount and shake out their legs. A few of them disappear into the bushes for a "pit stop." Father takes my elbow, steering me to a nearby tree heavily laden with yellow blossoms. The air is thick with their perfume. Once out of earshot of the others, he turns to me. "Jaden, please tell me what is amiss between you and Ryder."

"What do you mean?" I say, sounding stupid even to me.

"You know what I mean." His steady gaze holds mine. "I know him. He would not have let you leave his sight again once you were restored to him. What has happened?"

I can't even say the words. It hurts too much, and I don't want Father to worry about me. Staring at the carpet of saffron petals beneath my feet, I struggle to swallow the large boulder lodged in my throat. "Ryder and Erica have been … seeing each other," I croak.

This is not what he expected to hear. I know because he rocks back slightly on his heels. He pulls me into a gentle embrace, and I lean my forehead on his shoulder, crying quietly into his shirt.

"I'm so sorry sweetheart," he says softly. "I had no idea. You must be terribly upset. Does he intend to honor his engagement with you?"

"That's not the issue, Da… Father," I pull away from him, swiping at my nose with my hand. "He says he loves me and wants to marry me. The thing is, I don't know if I still want him."

"But Jaden, he thought you were dead. Surely you can't—"

I hold up a hand to stop him. "Don't even go there. I'm not ready to be reasonable yet. I feel betrayed and angry. It's not rational, I know, but it's how I feel. I need time to let my emotions settle before I speak with him again."

"I understand," he says. "Is there anything I can do?"

I shake my head. "Nothing. Just don't tell Mother, please. I don't want to upset her."

"As you wish. But she'll need to be told eventually. She will most certainly wish to begin planning a lavish wedding for you and Ryder now that you have returned."

"You think so? Already? But I'm not legally required to marry until I'm twenty."

"That is a correct statement of the law," he says. "But you know your mother. She will want to see you wed before she departs this life. Are you prepared to deny her that?'

Gulp. *Probably not.* "I'll figure it out soon. I promise, Father."

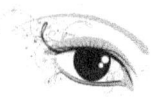

NINE

*A*fter several hours on the road, the stress of the last two days wears on me. I'm fatigued and glum, not to mention dust-caked and saddle-sore. But when Warrington Palace finally comes into view, my spirits soar. Not only because my mom's there, and because it's filled with wonderful memories, but also because it's one of the most beautiful places I've ever seen.

The massive structure itself is constructed of glittering white marble in the tradition of fine old English castles, with its share of turrets, crenellations, and one soaring round tower with a greened-copper roof and a graceful spire reaching heavenward. Ivy crawls endlessly along the northern walls, and scores of glistening windowpanes reflect the pearly-silver light of the dome, as if the palace emanates a celestial illumination. The castle is centered on the side of a fertile knoll and is surrounded by peaceful gardens, playful fountains, and blossoming trees. It feels like coming home, although it's more like the home of my dreams.

An enormous metal gate now stands at the foot of the promenade leading to the palace entrance. This is something new. It appears the entire palace grounds are now surrounded by a twelve-foot wrought-iron fence with guards posted every few yards. Father waves at the sentries guarding the gates, and they open them for us immediately. We're obviously expected.

Before we reach the hitching rail next to the front entrance, the massive palace doors swing open, and out step Uncle Harold and my cousin Osrielle. I have to smile when I see them both in all their Domerican finery.

Father and I dismount and make our way up the sweeping white stairway toward them. Ralston trails closely behind. Osrielle rushes to hug me. "Cousin! I'm very happy to see you. It was so sad when we thought you were dead."

I give her a big hug, and then hold her at arm's length to have a better look at her. She's the picture-perfect Princess in her blue satin dress and white sash. The toes of her prim satin slippers peek out from under the hem. Her corn-silk hair cascades down her back, held in place by a crown of silver twining vines. "Oz, you look beautiful," I say. "It's good to see you too." Back home, Oz, always the tomboy, dresses mainly in jeans and New York Yankees sweatshirts.

Uncle Harold holds out his arms for me. He wears a dove-gray cutaway coat and a yellow brocade vest, perfectly tailored to hug his rotund midsection. His plump face is more doughy-white in this existence than it is in Connecticut. His thin lips almost disappear in his smile.

"Dear Jaden. How fortunate we are to have you home," he says in his quiet, soothing voice. "This is truly a day for rejoicing. Blessed be the Chosen."

I give him a warm hug. "Thanks Uncle Harold. Nice to see you too. Is Mother inside? I'm anxious to see her."

"Come in, all of you," he says, shaking hands with Father and Ralston. The light glints off of an enormous diamond pinky ring on Harold's right hand. He's always loved his bling. Turning, he links his arm through mine and leads us all inside.

Applause startles me as we clear the threshold. Members of the household staff form lines on either side of the broad foyer, smiling and clapping. Each person bows or curtseys as we pass. I nod at Mother's longtime butler, Samuel, and stop to hug my maid and friend, Maria, truly happy to see her again.

Uncle Harold steers me toward the large drawing room. "Jaden, your mother has just had her afternoon dose of medication. She frequently becomes fatigued and nauseated immediately afterward, so she is lying down for a few moments. In the meantime, I have arranged for us to have tea so we can visit, and you can bring us up-to-date on your recent trials. We were horrified to hear that you were forced to live with savages for a time before being rescued by the white-robes. It must have been quite traumatic for you."

The drawing room has been laid out with all the makings of a formal high tea. Two maids hover near the sideboard, placing paper-thin china teacups on saucers. Silver trays arranged with pyramids of tiny tea sandwiches have been set out. Baskets overflowing with scones are flanked by cut-glass bowls brimming with butter, clotted cream, and assorted jams. A selection of sugar cakes and fruit tarts is arranged in a starburst pattern on a large round platter, and a golden dish piled high with chocolate truffles completes the mini-feast. The maids curtsey as we enter and shuffle to the side, whispering and staring curiously.

"Please, everyone, be seated," Uncle Harold says gesturing to the overstuffed sofas and chairs nearest the sideboard. "I should like to offer a small prayer of thanks, and then the ladies will be delighted to serve you."

"This looks great, Uncle Harold," I say. "Thank you so much for arranging it, but I really want to see my mother. It's been a long day, and I'm not very hungry. I'll just have tea in my room later."

A look of worry creases Uncle Harold's face. "I do not think it wise to excite your mother at this time, Jaden. Her condition is quite delicate, and she needs her rest. Come, sit for a while. It will be best for all."

"I appreciate your concern, Harold, but I think seeing me might be just what Mother needs. And I really need to see her, too." *Maybe I'm being selfish, but my boyfriend's just broken my heart and I a need a hug from my mom.* "I promise I'll be careful not to tire her out. Enjoy your tea." I kiss Father on the cheek. "Oh, Uncle Harold, is Drew coming for dinner?" I ask.

"Yes," he says softly.

"Great. I'll see you all then."

The family quarters of the palace are in the east wing on the second floor. I sprint up the stairs, hurrying to the end of the long hallway. The queen's suite is the grandest in the palace, with a mile-long balcony and a gorgeous view of the countryside. Mother's door stands slightly ajar. I wait outside, listening for a moment, in case the doctor is still with her. I hear no voices, so I slowly push the door open. Her curtains are tightly drawn, and the only light in the darkened room comes from a small bedside lamp. Mother lies asleep on top of the coverlet, but someone else is there also—in the chair on the opposite side. He's slumped across the bed, head resting on his arms

The scene feels a little awkward, so I step back outside the door and knock loudly. The man's head jerks up and, to my astonishment, I realize it's General LeGare. He springs to his feet and bows low.

"Princess Jaden." He's tall and young and tough-guy handsome, with line-backer shoulders and a shaved head. He's dressed in full uniform today, medals and all, his sword propped against the chair.

"General. What are you doing here?" I ask.

He carefully skirts around the bed and bows again. "Queen Eleanor sometimes has a difficult time with her medication. I sit with her in the afternoon to make certain ... Well, to comfort ..." He stammers and looks fleetingly at Mother. His usual badass arrogance seems to have vanished completely along with the giant ruby stud he always wore in his ear. His face holds only worry and something akin to sorrow.

"You sit with my mother? Every afternoon?"

"Yes."

I take a step toward him and put my hand on his arm. I always disliked LeGare because he seemed so self-important, and because he wore his affection for my mother on his sleeve. At the moment, I feel a sharp pang of sympathy for him, knowing the pain he must be

64

going through.

"Thank you, Charles." It's the first time I've used his given name. "Thank you for taking care of Mother. Not just now, but before too. I know you must love her. You've always put her welfare above your own."

He looks at me with watery eyes. "I am grateful that you've come home, Princess. I believe now that you are here, Eleanor will be more at peace. And now all of Domerica can rest easier knowing you will carry on her wise and capable governance."

His words are so unexpectedly kind, I have to swallow back my emotion.

Kissing my hand, he says, "I will leave you two. The queen was overjoyed to receive the news of your imminent homecoming. She has been eagerly awaiting your arrival."

LeGare softly closes the door behind himself as I move to Mother's bedside. Her face is pale and waxen, but still amazingly beautiful. A long graceful hand rests atop her slender waist. I lift it and gently touch it to my cheek. Mother's eyes flutter open, and a tender smile curves her lips.

"Jaden." Her voice is a wisp of its former self. "My lovely girl. My heart has wings to see you, darling. If only the rest of my body could soar as well." A tear slips from the corner of her eye.

I lean in and kiss her. "Mother, I love you so much. I'm sorry for all the pain and suffering I've caused you."

"Shhh. The things that bring us the greatest joy also bring the greatest sorrow, my dear. It is a simple fact of life. You'll know more about that when you have children of your own. I regret that I will not be here to know them."

"Mother, please don't talk like that. You still have plenty of time left," I say, knowing it's a lie.

"Well, perhaps enough time to see you married, at least. Is young Blackthorn with you?" She raises her head slightly to peer around me.

"He's not here right now. He had some pressing business, but he'll be here soon." Lie number two in about as many minutes. It's getting to be a habit with me … more like a way of life, actually. I don't particularly care for the way it makes me feel.

"Good." She closes her eyes and sighs. "Perhaps we can discuss your wedding date when he arrives," she mutters.

"I'm going to let you rest now," I say. "I want you to feel well by dinnertime."

"Yes. The medicine fatigues me so. The effects usually wear off within a few hours. Thank you for coming straight to me, darling. I was concerned that Harold might try to keep you from me. He's been so protective."

"Wild horses couldn't keep me from you, let alone Uncle Harold. I'm glad he's been taking good care of you, Mother," I say, kissing her again. "Rest well."

LeGare hovers patiently outside the door. "Is she all right?" he asks with careworn eyes.

You mean other than the fact that she's dying? "Yes," I say. "She's sleeping, but you can go back in. I'm sure she'd like that."

My next stop is the princess's room, my room now. The sight of Mother was like taking an express elevator from mildly depressed down to the depths of despair. I need a hot bath or a nap or a frontal lobotomy, some way to escape all this internal turmoil. Mother seems so weak. I don't want to think about what the coming weeks will bring, and worse, what I'll do when she's gone.

How the hell am I supposed to take over as Queen? Not only that, Father was right, she expects to plan a wedding for me. How do I deal with that? Even if I still want to marry Ryder, do I want to do it now? Is this really the life I'd choose?

Opening the princess's double doors, I'm relieved to find that the room looks exactly as it did when I left—warm, bright, and welcoming. Gaily-colored flowers spill from cut-glass vases. The fake fireplace has been turned on, and the crystal logs dance cheerily with red and gold light. I expected to find the place musty, cold, and vacant, but with a household staff of hundreds, that's not likely to happen.

I ease down into one of the brocade-upholstered chairs in front of the fireplace and tug off my boots. Someone knocks lightly. "Princess?"

Hurrying from my chair, I throw open the door for Maria. She's the closest thing to a girlfriend I have in Domerica, and I hug her warmly.

She beams at me. "I could not believe it when they said you were alive. Blessed Mother of God, it is a miracle."

"Come in and sit down," I say, pulling her by the hand. "How have you been? Is everything good with you?"

She takes the seat opposite my chair. "Oh yes. All is well with me. I am engaged now, too." She holds up her left hand, displaying a slim golden band set with a small round diamond.

My heart dips at the thought of my own teetering engagement. "It's beautiful," I say. "Congratulations. I'm so happy for you." I look away and swipe at an accidental tear.

"Are you all right, Princess?"

I sigh. "Yes. I'm tired, and I've just come from my mother."

"Oh. I am so sorry she is ill. But what can I do for you? Do you wish to bathe, or would you like to rest?"

"Both, I think. Bath first, then a nap before dinner."

"I will run the water and get your robe," she says kindly. "May I brush your hair out for you before you bathe?"

"No," I say, pulling my shorter braid over my shoulder. "I've cut it, so it's not nearly as hard to handle. I'll take care of it. But do you have any of that detangling tonic from Cupola de Vita."

"Of course. I'll set it out for you."

Freeing my tightly plaited tresses, I run my fingers down their length while Maria fills the pool-sized tub with steamy, hot water and aromatic bath beads.

"Would you like help undressing?" she asks.

"No thank you, but if there's any of Ralston's famous chamomile tea still in the kitchenette, I'll take a cup of that."

"I believe there is. Let me get it for you."

Shedding my dusty clothes, I step into the soothing bath. *Aah.* I'd forgotten how wonderful it is to have luxurious accommodations and servants attending to my every need. This part is nice, at least. And it could be the norm from now on... should I decide to stay.

TEN

I awaken from my nap to a gentle tapping on my door. "Who is it?" I call.

"It's Oz, and I've brought some friends."

I'm thrilled when I open up to find Oz holding a Skorpling in each arm. "Ethel! Fred! Come here. I've missed you so much."

Fred jumps from Oz's arms into mine. "Jay, Jay," he cries in his munchkin-like voice.

Ethel seems a little shy and disbelieving. She holds out a tiny, furry hand. "Jay?" she says softly. I lean down so she can better see my face. She strokes my cheek gently. "Jay." Crawling into my arms, she nestles her fuzzy head under my chin, making little mewling noises. I think she may be crying. My heart nearly cracks in two.

Skorplings are rare and remarkable creatures. They look like a cross between a monkey and a kola bear, gray, furry, and lovable. Besides being remarkably cute, they have a limited amount of speech, they smile, and they're tons of fun.

"Come on, Oz," I say, and we all pile on top of my bed. Fred jumps up and down on my pillows, but Ethel stays glued to my neck.

Fred wears a miniature green brocade coat, and Ethel's got on a matching doll-sized dress. "I like your new dress," I tell her.

"Jay home," she says in her tiny musical voice, keeping her face hidden in my hair.

Fred positions himself behind Oz, and begins playing with strands of her corn silk tresses. She laughs. "I love Fred and Ethel," she says. "Father allows me to play with them for an hour each day."

"That's all you get is an hour?" I say, petting Ethel's fuzzy head.

"Yes. I have my studies," she says wistfully. Her face quickly brightens. "Maybe now Father won't make me study so hard, since I'm no longer to be Queen."

"You sound happy about that."

"Oh yes. Very happy. I do not wish to be Queen. It seems to be a dreadful job. Father said he would do most of the work, but I would still have to live at the palace and be the *figurehead*, whatever that means."

"Don't you like living here?" I prop some pillows against the headboard and scoot back against them.

She sighs. "It's nice, but I miss my mother and my animals. I have a horse named Dido and two goats and dozens of cats."

Father told me that Aunt Judith had refused to move into the palace and was still back in Hempstead caring for the family farm.

Maria pokes her head around my door. "There you are, Princess Osrielle. It's time to dress for dinner. You are wanted in your room."

"Oh, I'm sorry," Oz says. "I'll just take the Skorplings back to the nursery first."

Maria looks at me. "It's time for you to dress also, Princess. May I help you?"

"Sure. Thanks Maria."

Oz gathers Fred in her arms, and I kiss his downy forehead. She reaches for Ethel.

"No, no, no!" Ethel squeals, locking her arms around my neck. "Ethel not go. Ethel stay here."

I pull Ethel's arms apart and hold her in front of me so I can see her face. "What's wrong? I'm home now. I have to go to dinner, but we'll play in the morning. I promise."

"No, Jay. Please. Ethel stay here." She makes the little mewling sounds again, and it tears me up inside. "All right, you two can stay the night with me," I say. "But you'd better be good. Don't break anything while I'm at dinner."

The corners of Ethel's diminutive mouth turn up. "Jay nice," she says and rewards me with a small kiss on the cheek.

"I'll stay with them while you are gone if you like," Maria says. "We had better get you dressed quickly, though. I believe Prince Andrew has already arrived."

"Drew's here?" I can't wait to see him and meet his new bride. Maria sits Ethel on a chair in front of the mirror, and gives her some strands of beads to play with. Fred is happily hiding under the covers of my bed. Maria works her magic on me—selecting a dress from the princess's impressive collection, styling my hair, and helping me choose my jewelry.

"There," she says, dabbing some gloss on my lips, "you look beautiful. Go and have a good time. I'll take care of things here."

When I reach the family dining room, Father and Ralston are deep in conversation with Drew and a pretty strawberry-blonde whom I assume is Adelais. Drew looks surprisingly princely in his black formal suit, despite the fact that his tawny curls are meticulously disheveled as always. He holds the hand of his new bride, eyes shining with pride and contentment each time he glances her way.

I run to Drew and embrace him heartily. He lifts me up and swings me around, even though I'm nearly an inch taller than he is. "There you are, Sister," Drew says with a laugh. "I knew we hadn't seen the last of you. You'd never go that quietly." Setting me down, he kisses my cheek. "Good to have you home."

He turns to his bride. "This is my *wife*, Adelais," he says, as if not quite believing it himself. Adelais curtseys daintily. Her skin is white as porcelain, and her periwinkle blue eyes sparkle as she slips her small hand inside Drew's. She appears far too prim to be married to my goofy brother, but they seem happy. Maybe he's cleaned up his act, or maybe she has a hidden spunky side.

I ask Adelais about her recent relocation from Dome Noir, and she tells me how happy she and her family were to be allowed to leave the troubled country. I'm about to query her for details when Uncle Harold enters the room with Mother on his arm. General LeGare and Osrielle follow behind them. Mother looks amazingly well. In fact, if I hadn't seen her in bed this afternoon, I wouldn't believe she was near death.

She wears a gold satin gown, a striking emerald necklace and a jeweled tiara. She says, "Good evening," to the assembled group, and Uncle Harold guides her to her chair at the head of the table.

Mother motions me to take my usual seat to her right. Uncle Harold graciously holds my chair for me. I have the vague impression that I'm displacing him at Mother's side. He probably sat here in my absence. But he takes a seat next to Osrielle at the opposite end of the table and appears to be in high spirits.

Sitting in close proximity to Mother, it is apparent that an expert makeup job is mostly responsible for her healthy appearance. Her eyes seem slightly sunken, her hands sallow and frail.

Waiters efficiently pour champagne into our crystal flutes, and Uncle Harold taps the side of his glass with his spoon for silence. Standing, he says, "Her Majesty wishes to propose a toast."

Mother remains seated, but lifts her glass. "We are blessed with a miracle this evening. Our Jaden is with us again." She looks lovingly at me. "All of Domerica rejoices at the safe return of the crown princess. There is much catching up to do," she says with a smile, "and another wedding to plan. Welcome home, dear."

A chorus of "Hear, hear," erupts from the table, as glasses are raised and clinked together.

"To Princess Jaden," Uncle Harold says enthusiastically.

Mother signals for dinner to begin, and giant shrimp cocktails are set before each guest. I wonder where the shrimp came from. Ralston told me all ocean life was destroyed when the comet hit. They must have found a way to farm them inland.

Drew, seated to my right, leans in and asks, "Where is your betrothed by the way? I expected to see him tonight."

Focusing intently on my plate, I cut off the tail of a shrimp. "He had some business to attend to. He'll be here in a day or two."

Drew places his hand on my arm. "Jade?" he says, arching his eyebrows in question. I never could fool him.

I shake my head slightly. "Not here," I whisper.

Tactfully, he changes the subject. "I suppose Mother told you Adelais and I are in residence at Meadowood. You should know that I'm looking to purchase an estate in the south near Somerset. We shall return Meadowood to you as soon as I can finalize the deal. You won't even know we'd ever been there."

"Drew, no. I'm glad you're there. I don't want you to leave. Meadowood is yours now. I don't need it."

He cuts his eyes to Mother for a moment and whispers, "Of course you wish to be with Mother for her final days, and you and Blackthorn will live in the palace afterward, but what will you do for a getaway? You'll need a place in the country to refresh when you feel as if you're about to have a breakdown. With Uncle Harold around, that may be a regular occurrence."

I laugh. "I'm not planning to have a breakdown anytime soon. But, if I feel like I need to get away, I assume you and Adelais will put me up for a while."

His eyes widen. "Well, you know what they say about

houseguests and fish?"

"Yeah, yeah, they both start to smell after three days." *Ha ha.*

Dinner is nine courses of culinary delights, and I sense Mother becoming more and more fatigued as the evening wears on. By the time dessert arrives, she appears exhausted. I place my hand over hers. "Mother, I'm very tired. Would you mind if I skipped dessert?" I ask.

"Of course not, dear. You may retire now if you wish."

"Would you like to leave now also?" I ask. "I'll walk you to your room. I'm sure no one will mind."

She seems hesitant and then relieved. "Actually, that would be wonderful. I'm ready to retire myself."

She rises from her seat. Everyone else at the table makes to stand also, but she stops them with a raised hand. "Please, keep your seats. Jaden and I will not be joining you for dessert and coffee. Thank you all for being here. Please enjoy the remainder of the evening."

I accompany Mother to her room. Several of her ladies-in-waiting escort her inside, and immediately begin taking down her hair and helping her undress. I know she'll be well looked-after, so I make my way to my own room, remembering with an internal groan that I consented to a sleepover with Fred and Ethel. It's okay, though. It'll be nice to have some furry little friends to cuddle with. It may help keep my mind off of Ryder and where he is tonight.

When I reach my room, the Skorplings are already fast asleep, curled up on my pillows. Maria says they were little angels. They had their dinner, and wore themselves out playing. I thank Maria for babysitting and wish her goodnight. It's wonderful to shed my evening dress and heels. I wish dinners at the palace weren't always so formal.

Slipping between the cool sheets, careful not to disturb my bedmates, I whisper a small prayer into the ether that I'll be able to sleep tonight instead of tossing and turning over my faithless boyfriend. Surprisingly I drift off easily.

Fred is the first one to wake. He scales the headboard and quietly twiddles with a strand of my hair. I open my eyes to find Ethel lying next to me on the pillow watching me intently. She reaches out a tiny hand to touch my cheek. "Morning Jay," she says in her melodious voice.

"Good morning, Ethel. Fred, stop that!" He's twisted a chunk of my hair around a spindle in the head board and is yanking it hard.

Somehow I manage to get my tresses unwound with most of the strands still intact. Fred scampers off to wreak havoc elsewhere. Rolling out of bed, I contemplate my schedule for the day. The first order of business is to get these rascals back to their own room.

I wash up and brush the tangles from my hair, anchoring it in place with a woven gold headband. Freshly-pressed riding clothes and spotlessly-polished boots are waiting for me in my closet *Ah, the life of a pampered princess.*

Taking a Skorpling in each arm, we set off for the nursery. As we approach the door, though, Fred becomes agitated, and Ethel locks her arms around my neck again. "No, Jay. No," she says.

"What's wrong with you two? Hold still, Fred." I open the door to their room, and my heart falls through the floor. Their beds and toys have been cleared out, and a giant, gold-plated cage sits in the middle of the room. *Unbelievable.*

Stepping into the hallway, I shout, "What is this?" Two maids and a butler scurry down the hall to me.

"Princess, what's wrong?" the young man asks alarmed.

"This is freakin' outrageous. What is this cage doing in the nursery?"

"Prince Harold had it made especially for the Skorplings," he says. "They're not allowed to be loose inside the palace."

"I want it out of there now," I roar, causing the three of them to shrink back. "Here, hold them for me." Each maid takes a Skorpling.

The nearest outside door leads to the tranquility garden. Flinging it open, I spot two groundskeepers in green uniforms weeding and raking the area. "You two," I shout. "Come with me." They drop their tools at once and follow me inside.

"Get this cage out of here. Destroy it. Chop it up, melt it down, toss it into the river. I don't care what you do as long as it's completely demolished. Not a trace remaining. Understand?"

"Yes, ma'am," they say in unison. They quickly drag the cage out the door and into the courtyard.

Retrieving Fred and Ethel from the arms of the maids, I hold them closely. "Have their beds and toys replaced immediately," I order. "Put it back just the way it was. Exactly the way it was before I left. The Skorplings will be in my room until that's done."

Stomping down the hallway, back to the family quarters, I can't remember ever being so pissed. What kind of jerk would imprison these thinking, feeling, loving little primates in a cage? It's despicable.

"I'm sorry guys," I tell my two buddies, kissing them both. "I promise I'll make this all better." Depositing Fred and Ethel on my bed, I tell them, "You two be good. Someone will bring you breakfast."

Fred jumps up and down. "Muffin. Muffin. Muffin."

"All right you can have muffins. Just don't get crumbs in my bed."

Hurrying to the kitchen, I put in an order for the Skorplings' breakfast. "Thanks, Cook," I tell the loveable old curmudgeon who runs the kitchen. "Have Maria take it up to them. I need to check on my horse." If Uncle Harold has caged up Fred and Ethel, there's no telling what he's done to my horse.

The palace stables are nearly as nice as the palace itself, with sweeping white arches, stone floors and polished mahogany walls. A stable-boy bows as I stride through the main door. "May I help you, ma'am?" he asks.

"Where's Gabriel, the black Arabian?" I crane my neck looking for him in one of the stalls.

"Down at the end." He nods to the right. "The young lady is already with him."

"Thanks." I make my way to the stall at the end, and I'm surprised to find Oz there placidly brushing Gabriel's sleek coat. A purring gray cat rubs against her ankles as she works.

"Hey, Oz. What's up?"

She smiles and comes to hug me. "Cousin. Good morning. I always come out here early, before my studies. I love being with the animals. Your horse is my favorite."

Gabriel swings his noble head around to gaze at me. My heart rejoices to see him again. Running my hand along his shiny coat, I breathe in the familiar smell of hay and horseflesh. Taking his chin in my hand, I kiss his velvety nose. He snorts his appreciation. *Ew*. It's a little wet, but I love it.

"You look good, boy," I tell him, combing my fingers through his mane, and examining the spot where the fire left a red and wrinkled patch of burned skin.

"It doesn't seem to bother him much anymore," Oz says. "Mr. Barksdale still puts ointment on it every day. He says the hair may grow back in another year or so."

Good old Barksdale, the crusty old head stableman. These horses are his kids.

Oz seems more like her usual self this morning in a pair of baggy old pants and a shirt that looks like it belongs to one of the stable hands. I cock my head to the side. "Hey, I'm thinking about going for a ride. I've missed my old friend here. You want to come with me?"

Her eyes grow bright with excitement, then dim just as quickly.

"That would be lovely," she says, "but Father would never allow it. I can't be late for lessons. Actually, I'd better go now and change. Perhaps we can ride some other time."

"Sure. Study hard," I say, smoothing my hand over her flyaway hair. "See you later."

She hangs the horse brush on a peg and dashes for the door.

"Guess it's just you and me, handsome," I say, taking Gabriel's bridle from the wall.

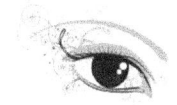

ELEVEN

It's a joy to be reunited with my horse. In looks and stature, he's noble and proud. He also possesses a huge heart and a talent for speed. I loosen the reins to give him his head, and he gallops with gusto. We reach the upper grounds in no time flat, and then slow to a relaxing trot. Everything looks pretty much the same as it did when I was here last, wide open meadows, thick piney forests, fields of grazing fargen—the super shaggy, super smelly beasts that provide most of the wool for Domerican fabrics. The peace and beauty of this place has wormed its way into my soul, and I have a weird sense of belonging here, even though it's only my adopted home.

I'm renewed and refreshed after my ride. Leaving Gabriel in the care of the stable boys, I head to the main dining room for lunch. A casual but bountiful buffet has been set out for the many palace residents and visitors. I wave to Father and Ralston, who are seated together at a small table near a window. As I make my selections from the many tempting dishes, Uncle Harold enters the room and walks purposefully in my direction. My cheeks grow hot as he approaches. I'd hoped I wouldn't run into him until my anger had subsided a little more. If he scolds me for destroying his gilded cage, I swear I'll take his head off right here in the dining room.

Harold bows deeply in front of me. "Princess Jaden, I wish to apologize to you. I understand you were distressed to find the Skorplings were being housed in a cage. I assure you that step was taken only for their protection. They are appealing, affectionate creatures, and it is tempting to treat them as something more than that. But ultimately they are feral animals. It's in their nature to attempt to escape back into the wild. Considering their enormous value, I felt it prudent to ensure that would not happen."

I barely control the urge to flip mashed potatoes in his face. "Listen Harold, I get it that you were trying to keep them safe, but Fred and Ethel have lived in the palace for eight years now. They're used to the freedom of their nursery, not a cage. You may not believe it, but they *do* have feelings. They were very upset. I don't like to see them hurt like that."

"Of course not," he says. "Again I apologize, but I hope to make it up to you this evening." He smiles brightly. "I've prepared a small entertainment for you. Something I believe will please you tremendously." He hands me a scroll of paper he's been carrying in his hand. "Enjoy your lunch." Bowing again, he exits the dining hall.

Father and Ralston both rise when I reach their table. Father sets my plate on the table, and Ralston holds the chair out for me. "Thanks," I say to both of them. Settling in my seat, I reach for the scroll Harold gave me and smooth it out on the table. It's an invitation of some sort.

The Honour of Your Presence is Respectfully Requested
at a Pageant in Celebration of the Glorious Return
of Crown Princess Jaden Victoria Hanover Beckett …

It goes on to give a time and place for the affair. I hold up the paper. "Have you two seen this?"

"Oh yes," Father says, smiling broadly. "I, for one, would not miss it for the world."

"I agree," Ralston says. "It promises to be quite an event."

I squint at them. "What's this all about?"

"Perhaps you should wait and see. We wouldn't want to spoil the surprise." Father winks at Ralston conspiratorially.

They're having fun with this little tease, but I'm not going to give them the satisfaction of begging for more information. "Fine," I say taking a mouthful of roast venison.

After lunch, I stop in to see Mother. Sitting at her desk poring over files, she looks rested and serene. Normally, she discourages interruptions while she's working, but today she invites me inside her office to visit awhile.

Unsurprisingly, the first thing she wants to know is what it was like living with Outlanders for nearly a year. I offer her an evasive sketch of what I imagine life in an Outlander outpost to be, and steer the conversation to the Cleadians, who I'm more familiar with. She's never met Melor or Bithia, so I suggest we invite them to the palace sometime. I don't tell Mother this, but I've wondered if the remarkable healing powers of the Cleadians extend to curing cancer. I'd feel strange asking them for so much, but if they were guests at the palace, maybe it would come up naturally.

"That's a wonderful idea," she says. "Perhaps we should invite them to your wedding. Speaking of which, when am I going to see my handsome future son-in-law?"

Another thorny topic of conversation. "A few things in Unicoi Village require his urgent attention," I say. "But I think he'll join us tomorrow or the day after at the latest."

"Goodness, what could be more important than your homecoming?" she says irritably. "I'm sorry he will miss the pageant tonight. Harold has worked so hard on it. I trust he is simply clearing his schedule in order to spend more time with you."

"Yes, Mother. I'm sure that's it."

Thankfully, Samuel shows up at Mother's door to remind her it's time for her medication, saving me from additional awkward questions. The doctor usually administers the meds in her room, and she naps afterward. I know Charles LeGare will be with her, so I don't offer to go.

"I shall see you at dinner, darling," she says kissing my forehead. "I'm happy to have you home. I missed you so."

~~~~~

The major topic of dinner conversation is the pageant scheduled for later in the evening. I gather from the chatter I pick up that it's some sort of play with actors. *Could be interesting.* With no movies or TV, Domerica is definitely lacking in the entertainment area.

As the dessert course is served, an announcement is made that the pageant will begin in thirty minutes in the palace theatre. *Geeze, I didn't even know we had one.* I glom onto Drew and Adelais and follow them and the rest of the crowd into what turns out to be a very cool old theatre with an orchestra pit, a huge stage with footlights, and tiered box seating. I've never seen so much red velvet in my life. The seats, curtains, flocked wallpaper, even the bunting hanging from the front of the boxes is red velvet. I feel like a nougat in an elaborate Valentine box of candy.

Uncle Harold rushes to greet me as we enter. Apparently a special seat of honor has been reserved for me in the front row. I get nervous when Drew and Adelais leave me to join Mother in the queen's box, but I strain to be congenial as Harold guides me to an enormous throne plopped down in the center of the front row. I pity the people sitting directly behind me.

Once the crowd is seated and the lights go down, the orchestra plays a lively overture. Marching to center stage, a page in medieval costume unfurls a large scroll and begins to read.

"Ladies and Gentlemen," he says in a theatrical voice. "In celebration of the miraculous return of Crown Princess Jaden Victoria Hanover Beckett to Warrington Palace, we present a play in four acts."

Applause. Applause. The curtain opens on a set that resembles the courtyard of the palace. An actress dressed as Queen Eleanor is seated on a throne, and a small girl with long brown hair sits on the ground at her knee. It takes me a minute to realize the girl's supposed to be me as a child. The dialogue's pretty corny. The queen instructs the child on how to be a wise, gracious, and merciful ruler. The girl listens raptly to her mother, but when the queen exits the stage, the girl impishly tiptoes to the bushes and draws out a toy sword she has stashed away. She proceeds to swordfight enthusiastically with an invisible adversary.

Actually, the kid's pretty good—hopping on the tabletop, somersaulting over her invisible foe, and finally skewering him from behind. The audience eats it up. The scene ends with the child raising her sword high and declaring. "When I grow up I'm going to be Jaden the Warrior Princess." The crowd goes wild.

Oh crap. A queasy feeling instantly descends over me. I scrunch down in my throne, wishing for a convenient way to just disappear. As Act II opens, my worst fears are confirmed. The actress playing me is older now and quite lovely. She sits beneath a tree, placidly reading. Sinister music plays as ten guys dressed up like Unicoi warriors steal behind the princess and attempt to abduct her.

I believe this is intended to be an intense action scene, but the audience roars with laughter as one giant warrior after another is flattened by the princess, using some poorly choreographed punching and kicking moves that I gather are supposed to resemble Tae Kwan Do. In no time, the stage is littered with combatants, and only one big hunky guy with black hair and no shirt remains standing—Ryder, I suppose. The princess mercifully spares him, and he declares his undying love for her. After a saucy kiss, she allows him to go free, inciting the audience to cheers.

Act III is Harold's interpretation of my run-in with Prince Damien last year. A wicked prince steals a priceless treasure, shoots the hunky Ryder actor in the leg, and runs off to hide in a cave. Princess Jaden saves the day by defeating the dark prince in a mighty sword duel, rescuing her handsome boyfriend, who actually comes across as a gigantic wimp, and restoring the treasure to its rightful place. The crowd whoops and cheers raucously. What a pile of fargen dung. The only good thing about it is it's almost over.

The grand finale, Act IV, has Princess Jaden battling a fierce fire using only her shawl, and then being Shanghaied by a bunch of scary-looking goons in moon suits—Outlanders, no doubt. She escapes from the clutches of the moon men, using some ninja-looking moves. Eventually, a group of kindly white-robed people stumble upon her wandering alone in the forest. She declares herself to be

Princess Jaden, the Warrior Princess, and promises a reward if they will return her to her home. Delivered safely to the palace, she is welcomed back triumphantly by her adoring people. The curtain falls to thunderous applause.

I consider crawling out on my hands and knees, while the lights are still down and the audience is occupied with clapping and whistling. The actors receive a five-minute standing ovation, while I slouch cringing in my throne. Uncle Harold appears before me, beaming exultantly. Bowing, he takes my hand and helps me from my seat, turning me toward the crowd. My face is as red as my velvet surroundings. I've never been so embarrassed. Not even when I peed my pants at naptime in preschool.

Figuring my best option is to flee out the back exit before I see anyone I know, I tell Uncle Harold I'm going backstage to thank the actors. Drew will never let me live this down. Not in a million, trillion years. Turns out Jaden the Warrior Princess isn't so brave after all. She doesn't have the guts to face this crowd.

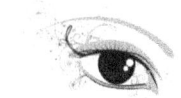

TWELVE

By some miracle, Drew doesn't show up at my room to harass me after the pageant. I know he's just saving up the grief for another day, but I'm thankful for the reprieve. The humiliation of the night's spectacle, my worry over Mother's condition, and my abject misery over Ryder, has me pretty worked-up. I spend the night alternately pacing my room or gazing into the faux fireplace.

My plan is to sneak out at dawn, before anyone else is up, and ride Gabriel to the lake. I need to put some distance between me and the palace. Princess Jaden jokes will be flying for days to come, I'm sure. I especially don't care to bump into Uncle Harold, who I'd really like to throttle at the moment.

I dress in riding clothes and creep down the back stairway. Nodding to the stable hands, I saddle Gabriel quietly. Father shows up just as I'm about to congratulate myself on making a clean getaway. Mercifully, he doesn't mention the play.

"Good morning, Jaden. Where are you off to so early?" he asks.

"Just taking a ride," I tell him, omitting the part about the lake.

"Outside the grounds?"

"Probably," I admit.

"Then you'd best take a guard with you," he says, "or I'll come along, if you prefer."

I sigh. "I need to be alone, Father. To think. I can't do that with a guard hanging around, or if you're with me. Sorry."

"As you wish," he says. "But at least take my sword." He unbuckles the scabbard and passes it up to me. "I'll get another before I go out."

"Thanks Father," I say strapping the heavy weapon to my hip. "And thanks for not mentioning last night."

He smiles. "However misguided your Uncle Harold may be, he means well, Jaden."

Yeah, right.

It's heavenly to be off-radar and on Gabriel's strong back. Half the palace would be in an uproar if they knew I'd gone outside the grounds without a guard. Too bad. I need some time to straighten out my head. I pat Gabriel's sleek neck and run my fingers through his course indigo mane, careful not to disturb the patch of burned skin. I love his musky smell and the way he prances when he wants me to let him have his head.

"Okay, boy," I say, pressing the stirrups into his sides. He's off like a bullet, hooves chewing up the ground. Though we've done this many times, his speed always takes my breath away. The wind tosses my hair, and my mind focuses only on the sensory rush—the crisp smack of the morning air, the racing of my heart, the connection between this magnificent animal and me. It's something primal and spiritual, cleansing and validating. If life could always be this effortlessly joyful …

The silver sky has reached full light when the shimmering blue lake comes into view. I slow Gabriel to a trot. A man and two young boys stand near the water, fishing poles in hand, creel baskets at their feet. I steer away from them, not wanting company this morning. Guiding Gabriel onto a small path through the trees, we take a shortcut to the waterfall at the far end of the lake. When we reach my favorite spot, I dismount and let him wander down to the water's edge to drink and munch on the sweet grasses.

The serene sound of the falls and the fresh, sharp smell of the water beckon me. I venture out onto a large, flat rock adjacent to the sparkling waterfall. Perching on the edge, I remove my boots and socks, and waggle my feet in the cool water. My fond memories of this place are now tinged with a slight melancholy. Ryder and I shared our first kiss here. It was sweet and sensual and life-changing for me. My connection with him was powerful and instantaneous. I've never experienced anything like it before or since. On another occasion, we stretched out together on this same rock and just talked about unimportant, silly things. Simply being near him was pure bliss. We laughed, and I was happy, very happy ... for a short time.

Lying back, I close my eyes, feet still dangling in the water. I've been putting it off, but it's time I reached some decisions. *What am I going to do about Ryder?*

"Beckett?"

The man's voice startles me. Yanking my feet from the water, I twist around to see who it is.

"Asher! What are you doing here?" Asher always looks hot, but today he looks like a bad girl's dream in his faded jeans, black shirt, and black sports coat. Indifferent to what anyone in Domerica thinks, he always dresses in modern styles, as yet unknown in this country.

"I told you I'd check on you soon. My exploration's completed, so here I am. What are you doing out here all alone? Where's the Boy Toy?"

I frown. "Don't call him that."

"My apologies," he smirks. "Where's the mighty Chief Blackthorn?"

I tug on my socks. "I don't know," I say, shoving my feet inside my boots. "I haven't seen him for a couple of days." I stand and face him.

He raises his eyebrows. "What's up? Trouble in paradise?"

"Come on. Let's walk."

He starts down the little dirt path that follows the edge of the lake. "There're people down that way," I tell him. "Let's go this way."

He shoves his hands in his pockets and follows. "What's going on, Jade? What's wrong?"

I focus on the path, avoiding eye contact. "It seems my fiancé made a new friend while I was gone. He and Erica Hornsby have … well, hooked up."

"Ah." He blows out a long breath. "Sticky. Erica? Is she the raven-haired girl with the killer body and the face like—?"

"Yes," I say sharply. "Thanks for reminding me. As if it isn't already hard enough for me to get the image of them together out of my head."

"Sorry. So, what does this mean for the two of you? Is the wedding off?"

"I don't know yet. Ryder says he still loves me and still wants to get married. But I don't know how I feel."

"Okay, hold on." He catches my arm and forces me to stop in the middle of the path. "Isn't this the guy you're madly in love with? Your one-and-only? Your soul-mate?"

"Yes, but—"

"But what? The guy thought you were dead. He still loves you and wants to marry you. What's the problem?"

"Wait a minute. Why are you defending him? I didn't think you wanted this wedding to happen. Don't you want me to come join you and the other Transcenders?"

He laughs. "Well, yeah. I do. But, I guess I'm just standing up for my gender. Don't you think you're being a little harsh? I mean, what's the big deal?"

I glare at him. "What's the big deal?" I spread out my arms for emphasis. "The big deal is I thought Ryder and I had something special, something *sacred*, and now it's got the sultry Miss Hornsby smeared all over it. Somehow it's just not as immaculate as it was before." I'm pissed that my bottom lip starts to quiver.

He nods. "I guess I understand. I'm sorry he hurt you."

"Thanks." I swallow hard. "It's just that everything is pretty rotten right now. My mom's so sick. Her enemies are trying to take advantage, and my uncle, who's now living at the palace, is a total pain in the ass. It's a little overwhelming."

He smiles in a way that does a little number on my heart. "You need a break." He takes both my hands in his. "Let's do something fun."

Fun sounds good. "Like what?"

"Let's have lunch in Paris. It's what I always do when I need some cheering-up."

"Paris? Are you serious?"

"Yeah. We're Transcenders, remember?"

I pull my hands from his, because it feels a little weird. "You mean like in Dome Noir, where Paris used to be?"

"No. I mean Paris, France."

"Like on my earth?"

"No. You can't go back there for thirty days. I have another earth in mind. One where Paris is the cultural, financial, and *culinary* center of the world."

I'm seriously tempted, but it's completely impractical. "I can't leave my mom right now, and besides, what'll I tell everyone?"

"We'll be gone a few hours, max," he says. "No one will even notice. C'mon, it'll be fun."

"Can I go dressed like this, in riding clothes? I mean you look like *GQ*. I look like *Horse and Hound*."

He laughs. "For one thing, those are pretty nice riding clothes, Princess. *Tres chic*. You'll have to lose the sword, though. For another thing, as long as you've got the money—which I do—the Parisians don't care what in the hell you're wearing."

Realizing this is actually possible, a swell of excitement bubbles up inside me. An involuntary smile blooms on my face. "Well, okay. Let's go."

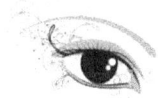

THIRTEEN

Asher pushes up his sleeve and flips open the medallion on his bracelet. "I'll take us," he says, punching some holographic keys. He grabs my hand, double-clicks on the latch, and *Zzzt!* We're streaming through the dimensions, sparks flying behind. My vision is obscured for a second, but suddenly the ground is racing up at lightning speed. Then everything comes to an abrupt halt, and we're standing on a sidewalk. Asher puts his hands on my shoulders to steady me.

"Great God Almighty! Do you ever get used to that?" I ask.

"I hope not," he laughs. "You okay?"

I nod. I don't feel as dizzy as I did last time, and I'm pretty sure I'm not going to barf. I pull in a deep refreshing breath. The air is different here—richer, fuller, laced with intrigue, and crackling with energy. I take a moment to examine my surroundings and realize we're standing on a green adjacent to an enormous metal structure. I tilt my head up, and my heart does a twirl.

"Is that the Eiffel Tower?"

Asher grins like a dopey kid. "Yep. I thought we'd have lunch at Le Jules Verne. It's four hundred and ten feet straight up, inside the tower. I hope you're not afraid of heights."

Crowds of tourists mill around the base. Numerous nationalities are represented as well as assorted and diverse styles of dress—from colorful saris, to full black burqas, to mini-skirts and jeans. People pose and snap photos. Others seem simply to be enjoying the view and the glorious day. Asher takes my elbow and guides me under a taupe-colored awning through the doors to a tiny elevator. A uniformed elevator operator waits inside.

"*Bon jour, monsieur,*" he says as we step into the car. "*Le Jules Verne?*"

"*Oui, merci,*" Asher says, sounding very French.

The elevator is carpeted in red and gold with a mirrored back wall, but even with only three of us inside, it feels cramped and claustrophobic. I'm relieved when at last we reach the appropriate level. The doors glide open, and I'm nearly floored by the view. The entire restaurant is glassed-in, and all of Paris lies spread out before us.

"This is just …" I'm at a loss for the right superlatives.

"I think *spectacular* is the word you're searching for," Asher says. "Give me just a minute." He approaches the desk, where the distinguished-looking *maitre d'* stands entering information into his computer. Asher speaks to him in French, and then discreetly slips some bills into his hand. I don't recognize the currency, but it must be the right kind because we're immediately shown to a table with an incredible view.

"*Bon appétit, mademoiselle, monsieur,*" he says after seating us.

The tables are set with crisp white linens, shiny silver flatware, and etched crystal goblets. A waiter instantly appears with our menus. "*Bon jour. Voulez-vous l'eau?*" he asks.

Asher replies "*Oui.*" He looks at me. "Would you like sparkling or plain water?"

"Uh, plain?"

"*Non gazeuse, s'il vous plait.*"

The waiter retrieves a large bottle of Evian and fills our goblets.

I open the long, tasseled menu and scan the selections. All in French. Ralston tutored me in French last year, but I don't recognize a thing.

"Shall I order for us?" Asher asks.

"Please."

He signals for our waiter. They have a short discussion in French, and the waiter leaves with our menus and our order. I think. I take a minute to admire the view.

"That's the 7th arrondissement," Asher says, "the most expensive neighborhood in Paris. If we had more time, I'd show you around. It's a remarkable city."

"So why is France the most powerful nation on this earth?"

"Well, for one thing, Napoleon won the Battle of Waterloo in this existence. His troops were decimated, though, so he did the only thing he could in his weakened state—retreat back within the borders of France and sue for peace. His empire survived, and the government eventually evolved into a democracy. The country's economy is thriving, they have the strongest military, and all the greatest scientific and technological minds choose to live and work here.

Two flutes of golden champagne are placed before us by white-gloved waiters. "Anyway, welcome to Paris and to the Jules Verne Restaurant." He raises his glass and I clink it with mine. "Named after one of the most famous Transcenders ever."

"Jules Verne was a Transcender?" I ask.

"Yeah. Where do you think he got the ideas for his stories?"

"You mean like *Twenty Thousand Leagues Under the Sea* and *Journey to the Center of the Earth*?"

"And others. All the fantastical creatures and bizarre landscapes were based on things he actually saw in other worlds."

I narrow my eyes at him. "Are you making this up?"

"No, I'm not. If you give me the chance, I can show you."

I sweep my eyes around the restaurant and take a sip of champagne. "I don't know. I think I'd rather experience more things like this instead of wrestling a giant squid."

He laughs. "That can be arranged too."

Our food arrives on delicate white china plates. Asher takes the time to explain each dish to me. A few things seem as exotic as some of the Domerican dishes I've tasted. He offers me a bite of his stuffed duck wing. It practically melts in my mouth. "*Mmm …*" I groan in delight.

"It's the *foie gras*," he says.

"What's that?"

"Extra fatty goose liver."

"Ew! Why did you have to tell me?"

He laughs. "You asked. Don't ask if you don't want to know."

I dig into my own dish, which is a small golden-brown game hen stuffed with chestnut and mushroom dressing, atop a savory cream sauce. It's divine.

"So enlighten me," I say between bites. "How come Transcenders can travel to other dimensions and no one else can? I mean, how does it work?"

"If you want the complicated quantum electrodynamics explanation, you'll have to ask Dr. McDonald. She's the physicist who studies Transcenders back home. She invented the TPD bracelets. I can give you the short layman's version, though."

"That'll do … for now."

He rests his fork on his plate, a juicy chunk of filet mignon impaled on the tines. "All right. You know from science class that all matter is made up of atoms held together by electromagnetic fields. Well, there's something about the electromagnetic fields of

Transcenders that allows us to temporarily lose our mass so we can pass through space, time, and matter, to reach other realms. It's like we convert from solid matter into an electromagnetic wave, but with a higher frequency than even gamma rays, which is what stars give off. That's the reason a lot of first-timers get shifted during electrical storms. Lightning can sometimes trigger the whole process."

"That's so weird. How come we don't burn up? Aren't gamma rays like laser hot?"

He shrugs. "Hotter actually, but if you *are* the wave it can't harm you."

I still don't get it, but I have the feeling additional explanation isn't going to help. "Okay, if you say so. But how is it controlled? I mean how do Transcenders get to a specific destination? How come we're not all just popping in and out every time it storms?"

"Well, if you use your TPD, it takes you automatically, but if you want to shift without the TPD, you do have to concentrate on the place you want to go and slip into that feeling you get when you're shifting, it triggers the conversion. That's what the streaming stars symbol is all about. It's a learned mental process, but it becomes second nature after a while."

"Interesting. So you could teach me how to do it?"

"Yep. I hope you'll let me."

I turn my gaze out into the city, trying to fathom this strange gift I was born with. Wondering what it means for my future.

FOURTEEN

"So, do you have a family back home?" I ask, returning my attention to Asher.

"I have a mother and sister. But they live on the earth I showed you on the TPD."

"You don't live with them?"

"No. I live in Arumel with the other Transcenders."

"Where's that?" I ask.

"Different earth. More advanced than most. I'd like to take you there sometime, if you'll consent to go and meet the others. The Transcenders and other non-traditional types coexist peacefully with the rest of the population in Arumel. We have jobs, and we're respected in the community."

"People know you travel inter-dimensionally and it doesn't freak them out?"

"The population of Arumel is a little more sophisticated than the norm. They accept the existence of other dimensions and life on other planets. The majority believe Transcenders perform valuable services for the community. We conduct explorations of other dimensions, report on scientific breakthroughs, the onset of new diseases, evolving social issues; any kind of useful information that might advance or improve society. Of course, IUGA is always trying to restrict our movements. They believe some of our activities interfere with destiny. But even they've gotten more cooperative under public pressure."

"Sounds amazing. I think I would like to go there sometime, after I get a few things straightened out in Domerica."

"Just say the word."

I'm curious about how Asher balances his double-identity, and I quiz him more about his family. He tells me he doesn't get to see them often. It's dangerous where they live. The comings and goings of every citizen are closely monitored by the government because there's an underground rebellion going on.

"It's tricky, but I try to get home at least once a month to take them money or food or whatever they need," he says.

"You must worry about them."

"I do. But this way I can provide them things they wouldn't otherwise have access to or be able to afford."

"Do they know you're a Transcender?"

He gives a short, sharp laugh. "Hell no. They think I've joined the rebel forces. A lot of men from our neighborhood in New York have done that."

"They live in New York!"

"On a different earth, remember? The United States no longer exists on Earth 39G428. It's a Soviet Socialist Republic."

"Oh my god, how did that happen?"

"Ever hear of the Cuban Missile Crisis?"

Asher explains that back in 1962, things turned out very differently on his earth than they did on mine, when President Kennedy and the Soviets played a dangerous game of "chicken" over nuclear missiles in Cuba. On his earth, there was a short but devastating nuclear war between the Soviet Union and the United States. The U.S. lost. The east coast was largely destroyed, including New York. It wasn't fit for habitation again until the late 1980s. That's when Asher's parents moved there.

With a tinge of sadness in his voice, he relates how his dad was killed during a robbery when Asher was only twelve-years-old.

Things were hard for his family until, at age fifteen, he first discovered he was a Transcender. Laughing, he recalls how he thought he'd died and gone to heaven after shifting to a strange, lush land that hadn't been devastated by nuclear winter. Smiling to myself, I remember having similar thoughts when I woke up in Domerica to the sight of Ryder's beautiful face.

"Anyway, once I discovered I had the ability to experience different worlds, there was no stopping me," he says. "I went someplace new every day. I moved to Arumel three years ago to be with the other Transcenders. I've never looked back."

Engrossed in his story, I'm surprised when dessert arrives. I didn't notice our plates had been cleared away. Asher ordered the house specialty for me, something called the Tower Bolt. It's a dark chocolate torte with hazelnut ice cream on the side. His own dessert is a Vacherin cheesecake with wild strawberry and mango topping. They both look luscious. I take a bite of mine and nearly swoon from the velvety, sweet taste.

I reach my fork over to sample his, and he looks a little offended or maybe just possessive. "I'll give you a bite of mine," I offer.

Asher pushes his plate toward me. "Have all you want," he says. "But you can keep yours. I don't like chocolate."

"Seriously?" I ask aghast. "How can you not like chocolate? I've never heard of such a thing. Chocolate is the taste of everything good and pure in the world. That's like not liking flowers or not liking puppies."

"Just one of the many dark and interesting things you have still to discover about me," he says, flashing his enigmatic smile.

I take another sip of champagne and realize I'm having a great time. It almost feels like a date. "Why do you always smile like that?" I ask.

"Like what?"

"Like kind of sexy and suggestive."

He cocks an eyebrow. "Are you flirting with me?"

"No!" I scowl at him. "You're flirting with me."

"I'm not. You're not my type. That's just the way I smile. I'll stop if it makes you uncomfortable."

"Don't flatter yourself. You don't make me uncomfortable at all. You can wear that shit-eating grin all day for all I care."

He presses a napkin to his lips, only partially concealing his smirk.

"We'd better get you home," he says, "before your uncle sends out a search-party. I've heard his gang of henchmen is ruthless." Laying his napkin on the table, he halfway rises.

"Wait, Asher." I put my hand on his arm. "Have you really heard that? I mean that my uncle has a *gang of henchmen?*"

He sits down again. "It's only rumor, really, but I heard he has some thugs that he sics on certain Domerican citizens whose behavior doesn't conform to his standards. There've been instances of homes ransacked, crops ruined, horses poisoned. Stuff like that."

"By people working for Uncle Harold?" I ask in disbelief. "How did you hear about this? You hanging out in Domerica these days?"

"No, but I did some checking on him when Ralston told me he and his daughter were living at the palace."

"Why would you do that?"

"We just needed to understand what kind of situation you were walking into there. Narowyn wanted to make sure you weren't in any danger."

"Who's Narowyn?"

Narowyn Du Lac, the leader of the Transcenders. She's the one who fought so hard to get you a second chance."

"Really? Well, I appreciate her concern for my welfare, but why does she think Uncle Harold is a threat?"

"He's got to be one pissed-off hombre now that you've come back to Domerica, and his little girl isn't going to be queen anymore. I confirmed he has a couple of guys working for him, but I couldn't trace any of this stuff back to them. Just watch your back, Jade. Harold tries a little too hard to come across as moral and upright. That's always a red flag for me."

I nod, trying to process this. "Okay. Thanks for the heads up."

Asher leaves some bills on the table, and we wedge ourselves back into the shoe-box elevator. When we reach the beautiful grounds once more, I take a last look around and breathe in the sumptuous air. "Thanks, Ash. This has been great. Just what I needed."

"I'm glad," he says. "Shall we go?" He takes my hand.

"Whoa. Wait." I pull my hand from his. "You're not going to do it right out here in the open where everyone can see us, are you? We're surrounded by tourists."

"Sure I am. People's brains don't really process it if they see us evaporate. They just make up some explanation for it—like they turned their head for an instant, or we weren't really there in the first place. Trust me. I do it all the time. Besides, what difference does it make? We'll never see these people again." He scoops up my hand. "Hold on tight."

Zzzt. Same light-speed, incredible journey and, just like that, we're back in the clearing next to the lake. Everything looks the same, except the three fishermen are gone.

"Thanks again for lunch," I say. "And thanks for sharing your story with me. I had a good time."

He leans in and kisses me softly on the cheek, just a tad too close to my ear. His warm breath sends a shiver down my back. "We'll talk soon," he whispers. Then he's gone.

I touch the place on my cheek where he kissed me. It's still moist from his lips. *Not his type, huh?*

FIFTEEN

I call for Gabriel, and he trots into the clearing, frisky and ready to roll. I fish Father's sword from the bushes where I hid it and climb into the saddle. We've got to hurry if we're going to reach the palace before rainfall. Every Monday, Wednesday, and Friday in Domerica, it rains from three until five in the afternoon. It's part of the climate control program maintained at the Dome Operations Center.

Gabriel keeps a brisk pace, but it's no use. At exactly three o'clock the rain begins to fall, gently at first and then in buckets. We're soaked by the time we arrive at the palace.

Dashing up the stairs to the front door, I'm looking forward to a hot bath and maybe a nap before dinner. Samuel waits for me in the entry hall, towel in hand. "Thanks, Samuel," I say, laughing and blotting my face. "I misjudged the time."

"Where have you been?" The voice comes from behind Samuel.

I peer over his shoulder to see Uncle Harold standing like the Grand Inquisitor, arms folded, waiting for an answer.

Unexpected fury flares inside me. The things Asher told me, the humiliating play last night, and Harold's mistreatment of the Skorplings had formed a nice little pile of kindling inside me. His arrogance is the lighted match that sets it ablaze.

"I don't see how that's any of your business," I reply through gritted teeth.

"It most certainly is. You are heir to the throne of Domerica. You were outside the palace grounds, completely unprotected. I am Lord High Steward of Domerica and guardian of the realm. That makes your safety my primary concern." He gazes at me intently. "You will not leave the palace grounds again without an armed escort," he intones as if trying to work some Jedi mind trick on me.

"Excuse me? You are not *my* guardian, Harold." I feel ridiculous standing here in sopping clothes, rivulets of rainwater puddling on the marble floor. But we might as well get this budding little power struggle out in the open right now.

"I'll worry about my own safety." I pat the sword at my side. He wants Warrior Princess, that's what he'll get. "I'm eighteen years old and heir to the throne of Domerica. I do as I please, and I answer to no one except the queen." Tossing my towel on the floor at his feet, I stride past him. My heart slams, half from fury, half from fear of what I may do if he tries to stop me. He remains frozen in the hallway, seemingly stunned speechless.

Back in my room, I lock my door and gulp air, waiting for my pulse to slow. I listen for footsteps in the hall. I'm being paranoid, I know, but Asher's warning this afternoon echoes in my mind.

Filling the bathtub with hot water, I pour in a generous helping of the princess's lavender bath beads and ease my body into the aromatic soup. Gradually, my nerves unjangle themselves, and my mind wanders over the more pleasant events of the afternoon. It's hard to believe I went to Paris today. It's even harder to believe I could go there every day if I wanted to. My mind only begins to grasp the implications of being a Transcender. I can visit every exotic place I ever wanted to see, and explore amazing new worlds I never dreamed existed. *Hot damn!*

Troubling thoughts quickly attach themselves to the thrilling ones, though. Can I do all that and have a real life too? Can I be Queen of Domerica and take little Transcender jaunts on the side? Maybe even visit my family in Connecticut? I have to admit, that's not realistic. Seems like an all or nothing proposition to me. I'm amazed about this remarkable ability, and a little freaked out about it. Can I be married to Ryder while straddling two worlds? The thought of Ryder is like an open wound still waiting to be cleansed. I was supposed to come to some kind of decision about him today, and I just blew it off. Thank God I have a few weeks to figure this all out.

After my bath, Maria shows up at my door with an armful of lapis silk gown—my attire for the evening. She says it arrived from Dome Noir shortly after my disappearance and was tucked away in storage. It's beyond gorgeous, with crystals running along the straps and crisscrossing the empire waist.

"What's with the party dress?" I ask. "Is something special going on tonight?"

"I believe there is a visiting dignitary from Cupola de Vita in the palace."

Sometimes it seems like a never-ending, pain-in-the-ass parade of visiting dignitaries around here. The good news is the attention will be on someone else tonight.

Once I'm dressed, coiffed, and made-up to look like a princess, Maria stands back to admire her handiwork. "Ah. Exquisite," she says. "You must go now. Your mother and the others are waiting for you."

Arriving at the family dining room, I'm directed by a uniformed butler to another larger dining hall a few doors down. The place is crawling with formally-dressed people chatting and sipping champagne. I attempt to slip in unnoticed, but all eyes turn simultaneously toward the door as I enter, and spontaneous applause breaks out. *Deliver me!* It'll be nice when the novelty of my miraculous reappearance wears off. I paste on my best happy face as a small group of people gathers around me. The ladies curtsey, and the men bow and kiss my hand. Some of the smiling faces are familiar; most are completely unknown to me. They gush with words of joy at my safe return, some comment on last night's play. I thank them all for their good wishes and scan the room for Mother.

She's seated at the head of the room in an elaborately-carved chair. A striking young man in a formal suit with a red sash draped across one shoulder sits next to her in an identical chair. Mother smiles and nods at me. The crowd automatically parts to let me through. I square my shoulders and attempt to glide regally to her.

Mother and the young man stand. She greets me with a kiss on each cheek. "Jaden, you look exceptionally lovely this evening. I believed I'd never see you wear that dress."

"Thank you, Mother. You look lovely, too." And she does. Seeming to shine this evening, I silently hope it's because she's feeling better, and not because she's putting on a show for the guests.

"You remember Duke Ferdinand," she says nodding to the man next to her.

I smile and tilt my head. He's extraordinarily attractive, in a Latin-lover kind of way, and he's annoyingly aware of that fact. "Yes. So good to see you," I say. I've never laid eyes on the man, but I remember from one of my lessons with Ralston that Duke Ferdinand is the nephew of King Rafael of Cupola de Vita. Ralston called him "rakish." *I guess that means full of himself.*

I extend my hand to him, and he takes it in his own white-gloved hand, bowing low and brushing my knuckles with velvety lips. "I am honored to see you again, Princess. You have grown into a woman of remarkable beauty," he says, oozing charm.

I'm not pleased to feel my cheeks grow warm under his gaze. *The guy probably thinks he's stolen my heart already.*

"Where is Chief Blackthorn?" Mother asks. "I attempted to get word of the duke's visit to you earlier today, but no one seemed to know where you were. I assumed you and my future son-in-law were together."

"Nope. He's still tied up in Unicoi Village," I say, dropping my lying eyes so Mother won't see.

"You've been home several days now, and he has yet to make an appearance at the palace. I find this quite indecorous," she says harshly.

"But I saw him at the Enclave, Mother, remember? And he didn't know about the duke's visit. I'm sure he means no disrespect."

I wilt under her irritated glare. "Duke Ferdinand," I say, turning to our guest. "How are things in Cupola de Vita?"

He flashes me an *I'm sexy and I know it* smile, but before he can answer, Drew and Adelais arrive, and, thankfully, the conversation is deflected away from me. Mother introduces Duke Ferdinand to the lovely Adelais. Ferdinand seems delighted to have another heart to capture. He kisses her hand and dazzles her with his smile. Adelais practically puddles at his feet, blushing and batting her eyes.

Drew smiles indulgently. "Where's Father?" he asks.

"He was called away shortly after lunch," Mother says. "One of his patients took a turn for the worse. Professor Ralston went along to offer his assistance."

"Ralston's gone?" I ask. Ralston's my security blanket in case I flub my lines at these little soirees. *Guess I'm flying solo tonight.*

"Yes. He said to tell you he'll return tomorrow afternoon. Your father asked me to bid you adieu for him."

I feel a pang of guilt that I didn't get to say goodbye to Father because I was lunching in Paris. And I still have his sword. I'll messenger it back to him tomorrow.

Mother sighs. "I don't know why John continues to see patients in addition to performing his responsibilities as Governor of the Enclave. It seems unnecessarily taxing to me."

"It's because he likes treating patients more than he like being Governor," Drew says. "He finds it relaxing." Drew turns to me. "Come, Sister, let's get some champagne and see if the dessert trays have been laid out yet. I could stand a little appetizer before dinner." He holds out an arm for me, and I link mine through his. "Excuse us, please."

"Should we ask Adelais?" I say.

"No, let her flirt with the duke. I have some news." An unfamiliar gleam lights his eyes.

We scoop up champagne flutes from a passing waiter and stroll to the far end of the hall, where long tables are being laid out with trays of food. Drew doesn't take much interest in the mouth-watering desserts, but seems anxious to talk.

"What is it?" I ask.

He grins. "We're going to have a baby."

"No way!"

"Yes. Now don't tell Mother." He leans in closer. "We plan to share the news with her later, along with Adelais's parents. I wish Father were still here. We wanted them all to learn together that they're soon to be grandparents," he gushes.

A twinge of regret contracts my heart. "Well, maybe not Mother," I say. "But she'll be thrilled with the news anyway."

The smile vanishes from Drew's lips, and he ruffles his fingers through his curly mop. "Oh, God. Sometimes I forget she doesn't have much longer. She always looks so … healthy. I guess I just expect her to go on forever. Or perhaps I do not wish to consider the alternative. Of course we know that she'll likely never know her grandchild."

At that moment, the dinner bells chime, and the guests begin taking their seats at the table. Drew slings an arm around my shoulder. "I'm afraid that very soon you will be burdened with much responsibility, dear Sister. And it is important for you to know this one thing—I'm glad that lot falls to Jaden the Warrior Princess and not to me," he says with a laugh. "Enjoy your dinner." He clinks his champagne glass with mine and hurries off to Adelais' side.

SIXTEEN

*T*hese State Dinners are usually exhausting, but this one seems to go on forever with a seven-course meal and dancing afterward. I'm drained by the end of the evening. At least I was seated next to Drew who cracked jokes throughout dinner, mostly at my expense. He was in a particularly light-hearted mood about his good news.

Somehow I can't picture him as the doting father, but I could never have pictured him as a prince either, until I saw it with my own eyes. He's different from my Connecticut brother in some superficial ways, but really he's just the same old Drew. The only uncomfortable moments occurred when he asked me about Ryder. I still haven't told him the truth. I keep hoping things will get resolved before I have to.

The constant activity of life at the palace keeps the ache and indecision over Ryder at bay, but when I'm alone in my room, it weighs heavily on my heart. Climbing into bed, I close my eyes and try to imagine what he's doing at this very moment. Is he lying awake thinking of me? I want him to hold me and tell me everything will be all right. But that's not going to happen until I can look him in the eye and say I'm okay with the Erica thing. That I get why it happened and I forgive him. I'm not sure I'm there yet, but we need to resolve this soon, if I ever hope to get a good night's sleep again. Cradling the wolf-head pedant in my palm, I concentrate on better times.

Maria wakes me in the morning with a breakfast tray and a note from Mother. Unfortunately, she has planned a day filled with events for the duke, beginning with a game hunt in one hour. She's not feeling up to the excursion, so Drew and I will host the activity in her place. *Ugh*.

There's no way I'd ever kill a sweet little deer. The good news is I don't have to worry about that because, even though Ralston gave me a few archery lessons last time I was here, I couldn't hit the side of the Titanic with a bow and arrow if someone paid me a million bucks. Watching other people trying to kill defenseless animals isn't really my idea of a good time either, even though I know we'll use the meat and skins. But at least I get to be outdoors riding Gabriel for a few hours, and that's some consolation.

The morning's not so bad. We spot only a few deer and some rabbits. The duke is an excellent archer and skewers just about anything that moves, while I avert my eyes.

Lunch is the high-point of the day. We reach a shady little grove of pale-pink, blossoming trees just after noon. Two long tables have been set with snowy linens and the queen's finest china and crystal. We wash our faces and hands in basins of warm water and dry ourselves with fluffy white towels provided by the palace staff. Then we're served a delectable array of savory dishes.

Duke Ferdinand drinks a little too much wine and tells a couple of hilarious and embarrassing stories about his uncle, the King. Ferdinand is actually kind of nice when he's not in snake-charmer mode, and I decide I like him. A trio of musicians provides relaxing music throughout the meal. The desserts are two of my favorites: pommera pie and chocolate truffles. I try samplings of them both, and I'm feeling almost contented—except for that empty hollow space where Ryder belongs.

It's early afternoon when our party returns to the palace. Thankfully, the duke has some unspecified "meetings" to attend before dinner, which means I get some free time. A walk sounds good, so I search for Oz to see if she wants to come along with me and the Skorplings. We harness Fred and Ethel in their leashes and have great fun running and frolicking with them. They seem to love her, and she dotes on them.

Even though Osrielle laughs and cuts up with Fred, I detect an air of sadness about her. She speaks of her mother and home with such longing. I'd like her to know that she and her father will be going home as soon as I take the throne, but something tells me it's best to keep that to myself for now.

Oz scurries off to dress for dinner, while I tuck Fred and Ethel in for a nap. Afterward, I make a quick stop at the kitchen to check for fresh pommeras. I swipe a few from the bowl without Cook's noticing and amble quietly down the hallway, nibbling on my plunder. Duke Ferdinand's voice carries loudly from a partially opened doorway. He sounds angry. I pad softly near the door. Okay, I'm eavesdropping, but this is the palace and I'm the princess, so I need to know what's going on.

"What is it you are asking for?" Ferdinand says. "We've been over the plan many times. This was never discussed."

"Things have changed." It's Uncle Harold's tranquil voice. "It will be much more difficult for me to deliver the agreement of the Guardian now that Princess Jaden has returned. Accordingly, some commensurate compensation would be in order. I ask only that you *render unto Caesar the things that are Caesar's.*"

Ferdinand snorts. "I assume you are Caesar in this scenario?"

Uncle Harold's reply is too soft to make out.

"Are you even certain you can still deliver such an agreement?" Ferdinand says. "I'm told that Princess Jaden's sentiments on this matter are in line with the queen's. What guarantees do we have?"

"I will give you my personal guarantee, as Lord High Steward of Domerica. Even though Princess Jaden may immediately succeed her mother as Queen, let me remind you that my daughter, Osrielle, is a mere heartbeat away from the throne." Uncle Harold moves closer to the door as he speaks. I know I should run in the opposite direction before he sees me, but I'm frozen in place.

"Now, let us discuss the specifics of my proposal," he says genially, and with a *click,* he pushes the door closed.

Whew. That was close. A passing glance into the hall, and Uncle Harold would have caught me spying on him. I slump against the wall, reminding myself to breathe. *What in the hell was that all about?* Uncle Harold said he could deliver the "Guardian's" agreement. One of my mother's titles is Designated Guardian, meaning she has control over the only existing set of plans and materials (on this earth at least) for building a new dome. That must be what they're negotiating over.

Uncle Harold's crazy if he thinks he can get Mother or me, for that matter, to agree to the scheme King Philippe and King Rafael have cooked-up—to build a prison dome where the convicts would grow crops and manufacture goods to supply the other three domes.

Tiptoeing down the hall, I quickly make my way to my room and lock the door behind me once again. Whatever Uncle Harold's plotting, it's clear I have to do something about him, and soon. He needs to go back to the family farm in Hempstead. I'm not exactly sure how to make that happen. I can't trouble Mother about it. The last thing she needs right now is an inter-family feud, but I don't think I have the authority to strip him of his title as Lord High Steward before I become queen. All I know for sure is that this palace isn't big enough for both of us.

Ralston will tell me what I should do. He needs to know about the discussion I just overheard between Uncle Harold and Duke Ferdinand, anyway. Plus, I still haven't told him about my trip to Paris and about the rumors Asher related to me. If I find him before dinner, I can fill him in on everything.

The princess's closet is usually a challenge for me because there are so many beautiful things to choose from. But tonight I know exactly what I want to wear. I locate the sweet cranberry-colored, strapless number I've had my eye on for a while. From the moment I saw this dress, I knew it would be amazing on, but it always seemed a bit too daring for the normal palace dinners. There's a duke in town tonight, though, so I figure it's okay. Besides, the princess has a fabulous garnet and diamond necklace I've been dying to wear, and it'll go perfectly with the dress.

Maria arrives in time to approve my selections and help me put everything together. She brushes my hair out straight and anchors a small diamond tiara on top of my head. She masterfully applies just the right amount of makeup to render my face as dramatic as the gown, without looking overdone.

"Thanks Maria. You're the best." I hug her.

"The duke will be very taken with you, I think. Where is your good-looking fiancé? He had better watch out."

I wish I had time to tell Maria about Ryder and Erica. I trust her, and I'd like another woman's perspective on the whole thing. "It's kind of a long story," I say, obvious sadness in my voice. "Maybe we can talk tomorrow."

"Are you all right, Princess?" she asks.

"To be honest, I don't know. We'll talk later." We leave my room arm in arm.

When I reach the bottom of the stairs, a young butler waits for me. He bows and informs me I have a visitor in the front parlor. Thanking him, I ask him to find Professor Ralston and let him know I need to see him, pronto.

"As you wish, ma'am," he says bowing once again.

I step into the front parlor, and my heart nearly rockets from my chest. Ryder is there, all sexy, six-foot-five of him, dressed in a formal black jacket and high-collared white shirt, holding a bouquet of purple irises tied with a yellow ribbon. He's dazzling. The sight of him nearly brings me to my knees. My first impulse is to run to his arms and beg him to never let me go. His eyes plead with me to do just that. But something inside me—something I don't like very much—holds me back.

"Ryder. What are you doing here?" I ask coldly. "I said I'd send for you in a few days."

A flicker of pain darts through his eyes. "Your mother invited me to dinner. I'm sorry, I thought you knew."

"No. I didn't know. I haven't told her about ... things, yet. I didn't want to upset her."

"I understand," he says quietly. "Jade, may we speak?"

"No. I think you should go. I'll explain to Mother."

"Please. This is torture not knowing what you are thinking, not being able to be near you."

"Oh? You're the one being tortured?" I say. "Well at least you don't have the visual of me with another man replaying in your head day and night."

"Please listen to me. I've spoken with Erica. I have told her it is over between us. I will not see her again. She accepts that."

"And that's supposed to make everything all right?"

"I'm sorry Jaden, but it is all I can do. I cannot change the past."

"I wonder if you really would change it. Your little fling with the lovely Miss Hornsby must have been sizzling hot. Are you sure you're willing to give her up so easily? Will you go running back to her the first argument we have?"

He shakes his head sadly. "How can you ask me that? I died the day you disappeared." He sets the bouquet of flowers on the table and starts for the door. "Please give the queen my apologies."

I snatch up the bouquet and fling it at him. "Get back here you coward. I haven't dismissed you yet."

He wheels around, anger sparking from his eyes. "You think me a coward?"

"Yes. You turn tail and run as soon as the conversation gets uncomfortable. You turn to the first woman who comes on to you once I'm out of the picture. What do you call that?"

"It's called loneliness," he says softly. "I'm no coward, Jaden. I will fight to the death for you, but I will not fight with you."

He stares at me for a long moment; the torment in his eyes rips me apart. Bowing deeply, he says, "Your Highness, may I be dismissed?"

"Go," I choke.

SEVENTEEN

I sink down into the nearest chair, immediately regretting my actions. Why can't I just tell him I love him? Sometimes I don't understand the things I do.

"Was that Ryder I saw leaving just now?" Ralston asks coming into the room. He stoops to retrieve the destroyed bouquet of flowers.

"Yes," I say miserably. "I asked him to leave, and I wish I hadn't. His visit took me by surprise. I reacted badly."

"May I," Ralston asks gesturing to the chair opposite mine.

"You know you don't have to ask when we're alone, Rals. Just sit."

"What do you intend to do about your engagement, Jade?"

"I don't know," I say, reaching for the crushed irises in Ralston's hand. "I know I love Ryder. I'm pitiful without him. He's all I think about. I need to put the whole Erica thing behind me and try to move on as if it didn't happen."

"That may be the wisest course to take, since you can't undo what's already been done."

His words trigger a thought in my mind. "I get that, Rals. But isn't there a way to just hit *rewind*, for a year. Can we start over and

115

you bring me back here like right after the fire, before any of this happened? That way Ryder wouldn't have to suffer through thinking I was dead and he wouldn't hook up with Erica either."

"I'm sorry, Jade. I wish I could." His expression hardens for a moment. "Frankly, had we known the path had veered in this direction, we could have done so, but it's too late now."

"Why? I don't understand."

He rests his elbows on the arms of the chair and steeples his fingers. "You remember I explained to you that at the moment of birth all the possible paths for a person's life are charted out in their entirety?"

I nod. "Yeah"

"IUGA has the capability to place you at any point on any of those myriad paths, as long as you have not yet lived it. That is what took place last year when we sent you back to Connecticut. Your life didn't actually *freeze in place*. We just put you back at the point from which you shifted. You cannot, however, go back and alter the past. There are many laws against it, and for good reason."

"But I didn't live on this path the last year," I remind him.

"Correct, but you are here now. We cannot go backward from this point because, you see, twelve months from now you would be reliving this time, changing what has already occurred."

That makes sense, I guess, but it stinks, especially since it could have been different. It didn't have to be this crappy situation. I want things to be back the way they were, when I was sure Ryder loved only me.

"I'm scared, Rals," I say, my voice cracking. "Ryder has the power to hurt me like no other person alive. A part of me wonders if I want to be that vulnerable to anyone. This whole perpetual contract thing frightens me. It makes me question whether I really do have a choice where he's concerned."

"Love is frightening at times, but I assure you that you do have free will in your relationship with Ryder. If you choose to walk away from him, you are capable of doing so. Which is not to say it would be easy."

"Nothing's easy right now," I whine.

"Have you considered that you hold the same power over him, Jaden? This relationship has been built over several lifetimes. Can you imagine what Ryder is going through?" His eyes hold mine for a moment. "I know you are braver than this, old girl … and kinder."

I sigh. "You're right. You're right. I'll find him tomorrow. We've got to work this out for both our sakes."

"Yes. Well done," Ralston says reaching over and patting my hand. "Now what did you wish to see me about?"

Ralston's amazed and delighted as I briefly recount my jaunt to Paris with Asher. He makes me promise to give him all the details later when we have more time. I relate the disturbing rumors Asher told me about Uncle Harold, and go over the little scene between Harold and me on my return to the palace. I also share the details of the conversation I overheard between Harold and the duke. This last part seems to concern him greatly.

"Can I just fire him?" I ask. "I mean strip him of his title and tell him to leave?"

He rubs his chin thoughtfully. "You cannot remove him from his office, Jaden. Only the queen may do that. But, I believe some further investigation is warranted, and I'm long overdue for a meeting with Agent Chelmsford. In the meantime, it would be wise to avoid any further confrontations with him. Asher is correct in concluding that your reappearance here has effectively deprived his daughter of the crown, and while she may never have desired it, he may have had different feelings altogether."

I stare at him wide-eyed. "You don't think he'd try to harm me, do you?"

"I believe a bit of caution is in order until we better understand the situation. Family intrigues are a time-honored tradition among the

British royal houses. You needn't look very far back in history to find one family member willing to oust another for a chance at the throne. The stakes are enormously high, Jade. I would keep my trips outside the palace grounds to a minimum. If you do go out, I suggest taking a guard. You should also carry a sword at all times. And do lock your door at night. That's merely being vigilant."

It seems farfetched that Uncle Harold would actually do anything to hurt me, but my stomach clenches at the possibility. "Whatever you say, Rals. There's one trip I'd really like to make tomorrow, though. I need to see Lady Lorelei about a new sword."

He nods. "Ah yes. You are accustomed to a samurai weapon now. That's actually a splendid idea. It will give us an excuse to go into town. We can meet with Lady Lorelei, and then have a chat with Agent Chelmsford. I shall make the arrangements." He rises from his chair and holds out his arm for me. "Shall we go to dinner?"

Slipping my arm through his, I place my other hand over my churning insides, not sure I'll actually be able to eat.

When we reach the dining hall, Samuel waits with a note from Mother. She's not feeling well, and she asks that I entertain the duke in her absence. "Is she all right?" I ask him. "She hasn't felt well all day."

"I believe so, ma'am," he says quietly, eyes glued to the floor. Like Samuel would really know.

"I'm going to check on her. Please explain to Prince Andrew, and ask him to keep the duke occupied until I get back."

"Yes, ma'am." He bows, never making eye-contact.

Hurrying to Mother's room, I hope she hasn't taken a turn for the worse.

"Don't fuss over me, darling," she says. "Everything is fine. Some days are more difficult than others. I assumed the duke would be in good hands with you, Ryder, and Drew. Charles will sit with me later. He's promised to read some Browning to me."

"That sounds nice, Mother. Elizabeth or Robert?" I ask.

"Elizabeth, of course." She smoothes the coverlet with a frail hand.

The thought of General LeGare reading poetry to my mother, makes me smile internally. Not bothering to tell her that Ryder is absent from the dinner table again tonight, I bend and kiss her pale forehead. "All right, Mother. Have a restful evening. I'll see you tomorrow."

"Thank you, Jaden. It's such a comfort to have you home. I love you, darling."

"Love you too, Mother."

Dinner is in full swing by the time I reach my seat at the queen's table. The duke seems to be enjoying himself. He smiles winningly at me, and holds my chair, his dark eyes openly appreciating my strapless gown. It feels weird making small talk with him, after the conversation I overheard this afternoon. I still don't know what to make of it.

By the time desert and coffee have been served, I've had enough of the duke's syrupy charm to cause tooth decay. When he asks if he may "escort me to my chamber" so that we may have a word, I'm a little dubious. I halfway suspect he just wants to wrangle an invitation inside my bedroom. When we arrive at my door, though, he declines to come in for tea.

"No, no," he says in his soft accent. "That would be unseemly. You are an engaged woman, and I ... well, let us say I have a reputation with the ladies."

"Then thank you for a lovely evening." I reach for the door handle, but he lightly touches my arm.

"Princess Jaden, I like you," he says in a hushed voice. "Your mother has been a loyal friend to Cupola de Vita and King Rafael for many years. The king sent me here to determine whether we could negotiate an agreement acceptable to the Designated Guardian for the construction of a new dome. Upon my arrival, it was obvious the queen was not well enough to consider our new proposals. I ask your permission to return when … well, after your coronation, so that we may converse on this matter."

"Yes. That would be fine. But, like my mother, I'm opposed to construction of a prison-type dome. If you have something new to offer, I'd be happy to discuss it with you."

"Thank you, Your Highness." He bows and kisses my hand.

"Duke Ferdinand, if you don't mind me asking, have you spoken with my uncle about these matters?"

"Let us say, my discussions with the Lord High Steward were not satisfactory." Checking over his shoulder, he says quietly, "I also have a question for you, Your Highness; do you intend to keep him in that office once you have ascended to the throne?"

"I haven't made those final decisions as yet," I respond guardedly. "Why do you ask?"

"We have a saying in Cupola de Vita, maybe you have heard of it: *el poder corrompe, y el poder absouto corrompe absolutamente.* It means *Power corrupts...*"

"*...and absolute power corrupts absolutely.*" I complete his sentence. "Yes, I'm familiar with it. Why?"

"Perhaps you should consider it when determining the role of Prince Harold in your new regime. I am not certain that he is capable of placing your interests above his own." His expression is earnest.

I nod slowly. "Thanks for the advice."

"*Que Dios los bendiga,* Princess. God bless."

EIGHTEEN

I awaken early, thinking of all I need to accomplish before Ralston and I leave for Warrington Village. The most important task is to messenger a note to Ryder. Searching the princess's desk for something to write on, I find a green satin box with a purple tassel containing some personalized stationery. Engraved in gold at the top of the thick, cream-colored paper are a crown and my official title: *The Crown Princess Jaden Victoria Hanover Beckett*. It's a little formal for my taste, but it'll do. Staring at the ceiling, I compose my thoughts.

Dear Ryder, I apologize for my rude behavior of last evening. I would like to speak with you about our future, if you are still willing. Please come to Warrington Palace at six o'clock tonight. Yours truly, Jaden

It sounds a little lame, but I don't want to go into anything until I can speak with him in person. I fold up the note, and stuff it in an envelope. The flap has no glue, but I find some gold seals in the stationery box and pop one on. I scribble Ryder's name on the front and open my door to search for Maria. A maid instantly appears. With a curtsey she asks, "May I help you, ma'am?"

"Yes. Please have this letter delivered at once to Chief Ryder Blackthorn in Unicoi Village. Ask the messenger to wait for a reply."

"Yes, ma'am." She takes the note and hustles down the hall.

Okay, that's done, onto the next. I pull out some additional sheets of paper and attempt to draw a *katana*, a traditional Japanese samurai sword, from memory. The princess's cousin, Lady Lorelei Bartlett, is a talented sword maker and silversmith, but she's likely never seen a katana, since Japan and China sank into the sea a few hundred years back.

The hilt is longer than normal, because it's intended to be held with two hands to exert more force. The blade is long and slightly curved. I do my best to get the arc just right. We don't actually use katana in Kendo practice. It's too dangerous. We use wooden swords called *bokken*. For sparring we wear leather armor, known as *bogu*, and use *shinai*, or bamboo swords. But my *sensei* made certain we all trained with a katana occasionally to practice our grips and get used to the heft and feel of the weapon.

Once I'm satisfied with my drawings, it's time to dress for the day. We'll be riding, so I need to wear pants, but Lady Lorelei is very cool and put together, and I always feel frumpy just being in the same room with her. Since I don't need any more unnecessary hits to my ego, I decide to gussie-up a little. Instead of my usual wool riding pants and sweater, I choose a silky white blouse with a lace Edwardian collar, and a gorgeous wine-colored jacket embroidered with tiny blue and gold flowers. I like the effect with my chocolate brown riding pants and knee-high boots.

"You look very nice today," Ralston says when we meet at the stables.

"Thanks Rals. What's he doing here?" I ask, eyeing the very large, very well-armed member of the Royal Guard standing next to him.

"I thought it best to have a guard ride along with us today, what with all the uncertainty." He casts a knowing look my way. "General LeGare recommended this young chap. His name is Patrick Stillwater."

Patrick startles me by going down on one knee. He crosses his right arm over his heart. "Your Highness, I swear to defend and protect you with my life," he says.

"Well, all right. That's great. Stand up."

Seems like overkill, but until we know what Uncle Harold's up to, we need to be careful who we trust. Patrick is well over six feet, with skin the color of café latte and eyes like Tupelo honey. I suspect some of his ancestors may have been African slaves, because his complexion is darker than most Domericans. But, when the Great Disaster occurred and people fled into the domes, all slavery was eliminated, and everyone was considered to be among the "chosen." All taboos against intermarriage were erased, making it difficult to guess anyone's heritage at this point.

Our ride into town is peaceful and uneventful. No highway robbers or masked marauders. Warrington Village is a quaint little community right out of another century, with wooden sidewalks, hitching posts, and water troughs. The locals quickly take note of our arrival, and a small crowd forms around us as we tie our horses in front of Bartlett's Silversmiths. By now, all the townspeople have heard the story of Princess Jaden's astonishing reappearance, and I suppose they just want to see for themselves. A few villagers gasp as they draw close. "It's really her," they say, or "She looks just the same." Patrick ensures that no one gets too near as they toss me their lace hankies or reach out to touch me.

Ralston and I hustle into the shop, while Patrick stands guard outside the door. Inside we're greeted by a security guard, who bows deeply. "Please follow me, Your Highness. Lady Lorelei is expecting you."

He leads us to a small room at the back, and pulls aside a blue velvet curtain covering the door. Lady Lorelei instantly rises from her chair and glides over to us. She's just as stunning as I remembered. Her gown is a tone-on-tone apple green silk that clings to her lithe form in all the right places. Her sunshine-ivory hair flows long and loose around her shoulders, held in place by a headdress of golden netting dotted with seed pearls. A large peridot ring, the exact shade of her dress is her only jewelry. She looks as if she stepped out of a Botticelli painting. I feel like I should curtsey. Instead she curtseys to me, and then takes my face in her slender hands. Her glittering eyes probe mine.

"Cousin, I am so thankful to see you. Of course we feared the worst, and were overjoyed to hear of your homecoming. Are you quite well?"

Her heartfelt concern makes me smile. "Yes. I'm well, thank you."

She turns to Ralston. "Professor, so good to see you again. I was delighted to hear that I was to receive a visit from you both today." She gestures to some velvet-covered armchairs arranged around a small table. "Please be seated," she says to us. "May I offer you some refreshment?"

"Nothing for me, thanks," I say, seating myself in one of the chairs.

Ralston declines also, and takes the chair next to mine. Lorelei sits opposite us.

She inquires about Mother's health, and expresses her sympathy for what we are going through dealing with the illness. After a few additional polite remarks about Father and Drew, she asks how things are faring with Uncle Harold and Osrielle now living in the palace. I glance Ralston's way, not knowing how much I should share with Lorelei.

Taking his cue, he clears his throat. "Princess Jaden has some business she would like to discuss with you first, then, if you are amenable, we wish to have a confidential conversation with you regarding some troubling stories that have reached our ears, perhaps involving Prince Harold."

Lady Lorelei clasps her hands and rests them on the table. She tilts her head slightly, and focuses on me, her expression serious. "I'm very glad you have come, Cousin. I did not think it my place to come to you, but there are some things of which you should be aware, now that you are home—things of which your mother is most likely unaware."

Ralston and I exchange a look. *Sounds ominous.*

"But of course, business first," she says assuming a lighter tone. "What can I do for you, Cousin?"

Pulling the drawings from my jacket pocket, I spread them on the table facing Lorelei. "I need a katana, a Japanese samurai sword. Would you be able to make one for me?"

She studies my drawings and smiles. "These are very good likenesses. May I ask what you wish to do with this katana?"

The question is unexpected, and I have no plausible explanation for how I would know how to use one. I can't very well tell her the Outlanders taught me.

She senses my hesitancy to speak. "Forgive me, Cousin. Of course it is none of my business. I wish only to know if it is to be employed as a weapon, or merely put on display."

"As a weapon," I mumble.

"Very well. I can forge one for you, but the appropriate types of steel are currently not available to me, and I cannot have them imported in light of Dome Noir's suspension of trade with Domerica. Also, the process is quite lengthy. The polishing alone can take up to three weeks. How soon do you require this sword?"

"Like now," I say deflated. I'm much better with a katana than a regular sword, and I'm getting the impression I might just need it.

"I believe I may have a solution for you." She rises gracefully from her chair. "If you will excuse me for a moment, I have something I would like to show you." She wafts from the room, and returns a few minutes later followed by two young male employees, each carrying a long thin wooden box. She asks the men to place the boxes on the table. "I purchased two antique samurai swords at an auction in Cupola de Vita several years ago," she says, as she lifts the lid of each box. "I wasn't certain I would ever be able to sell them, but they were so beautifully crafted I could not pass them up."

She places a hand on a sword with a black *saya*, or scabbard. "This one is a *tachi*, and may be a bit long for you." She lifts the other sword from its box. "But I believe this one was designed for a woman." She carefully withdraws the sword from its scarlet *saya*. "There are tales of courageous women samurai, the most famous of whom is Tomoe Gozen, I believe."

Her knowledge of samurai history is impressive. I've never even heard of Tomoe Gozen. She balances the blade on her two open palms and presents it to me for inspection. It's fearsomely beautiful. The mirror finish shines like the moon, and the *ha* looks razor sharp. "May I try it?" I ask.

"Of course."

I position myself several feet away from the others. Katana must be treated with respect. They can be extremely dangerous, not only to those in close proximity, but to the wielder as well. The *tsuka*, or handle, fits my hands perfectly, better than any other katana I've held. Lorelei is surely correct; this must have been made for a woman. I try a few practice swings, called *suburi*. The blade sings as it slices the air. It's thrilling, and a little scary. A surge of power runs through my arms, and I know I'll feel safe with this by my side.

"This is amazing. More than I could have hoped for," I tell Lorelei. "May I take it with me today?"

"Certainly. It will be waiting for you when you are ready to depart." She signals the two young men who replace the swords in the boxes and carry them from the room. Lorelei pulls back the velvet curtain covering the entry and asks the security guard to lock the front door. We all take our seats at the table again. "Now, Cousin," she says. "Let us discuss Prince Harold."

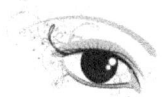

NINETEEN

*L*orelei asks my permission to have her husband, Lord Bartlett, sit in on our conversation. He's currently on the Council of Advisors, and she believes he may have some additional insights on Uncle Harold. I readily agree, figuring the more information I have, the better.

Lord Bartlett moves the velvet curtain aside, and ducks into the room. I nearly stand to greet him, but catch myself, remembering to stay seated and let him come to me. He's almost as tall as Ryder, and nearly as handsome, with chestnut hair neatly pulled back in a ponytail and hazel eyes that burn with intelligence. "Princess Jaden," he says bowing, "how very good to see you looking so well."

I never actually met him before, but the princess knew him. "Thank you, Jacob. It's good to see you, too. Please join us."

He seats himself next to Lorelei. After an awkward moment of silence, I realize everyone's waiting for me to speak first. "Uh, thank you for agreeing to meet with us." I cut my eyes nervously to Ralston. He's better at this than I am, and luckily he obliges and jumps in to rescue me.

"Many things have changed at the palace since Princess Jaden's unfortunate accident. Not the least of which is the appointment of Prince Harold as Lord High Steward. The princess is attempting to sort through all of these changes, in order to ensure that the queen's policies are being properly carried out. We have received word of some disturbing events that have occurred in Domerica, which may or may not be attributable to Prince Harold or his affiliates. We hope that you feel comfortable enough to speak freely and candidly with Princess Jaden regarding anything that might help to enlighten us further."

Lorelei and Jacob exchange a look. Jacob rests his long arms on the table and leans forward. "Princess, if I may, your mother has not been well enough to attend Council of Advisors' meetings for the last two months. In that time your uncle has announced certain changes which he seems to believe he is unilaterally authorized to make. I am not certain whether he has discussed these changes with the queen, and I am equally uncertain that she would approve of them if he had."

"What kinds of changes?" I ask.

"Prince Harold intends to establish a cavalry unit of the Royal Guard and arm them with guns and rifles. Something which your mother has adamantly opposed in the past. In addition, he has undertaken to begin construction on a wall around the entire Unicoi Village. I believe he intends to isolate the settlement and restrict travel into and out of the village. Most troubling, though, is the announcement that he intends to reopen talks with Dome Noir and Cupola de Vita regarding their proposal for the construction of a new dome. The queen has been steadfast in her opposition to such a project. The Council stands firmly behind her on this issue."

I was vaguely aware of some of this, but when Jacob lays it all out together, it sounds like Uncle Harold has completely run amok. "I had no idea things had gone this far," I say. "Honestly, we were just here to see if you'd heard any rumors about some vandalism, destroyed crops, and poisoned livestock."

"There is that also," Lorelei says softly, her eyes flashing angrily.

"Seriously? Involving Uncle Harold?" I ask.

"No proof exists that he was responsible, but we are familiar with a tragedy that befell the Selkirk Farms after farmer Selkirk had a dispute with Prince Harold over horses which were ordered for the new cavalry unit."

"What kind of tragedy?"

"One morning last week, twenty of Selkirk's finest horses were found dead in their stalls. It was discovered that the water in their troughs was tainted. As I say, there is no proof, but Prince Harold had recently accused Selkirk of deception, and vowed to extract a price."

This news twists my stomach into a pretzel. I know farmer Selkirk. Gabriel came from his horse farm. Such gorgeous animals. What a heartbreaking loss. Leaning back in my chair, I blow out a long breath. I'm way out of my league here, and I know it. But I've got to do something if Uncle Harold really is involved.

"Thanks for being so honest with me," I say. "I suppose I need to have a conversation with Mother about this. I hate to upset her. She's so frail right now. But she needs to be informed."

Jacob speaks up. "May I respectfully suggest an alternative? Perhaps you should begin attending the Council meetings in Queen Eleanor's stead. We also do not wish for you to trouble the queen while she is so ill. But I assume she would have no objection to appointing you as her representative to preside at these meetings. That way Prince Harold would merely be another voice, another member of the Council, instead of acting as dictator."

"That sounds reasonable," I say. Actually, it's a great idea. If I can't get rid of Uncle Harold right now, at least I can undercut his power a little.

"Regarding the other matters, the attacks against our citizens," Lorelei says, "perhaps if someone such as yourself ordered an investigation into these matters, the perpetrators would be caught, or at least their activities curtailed. So far, very little action has been taken. The villagers' complaints have largely been ignored."

"I'll see what I can do about that," I say. "Jacob, I have the sense that General LeGare is completely loyal to my mother and wouldn't do anything she didn't approve of, even if ordered by Prince Harold. Do you agree with this? Would he make a good ally for me?"

"Yes. I believe he would. But we're told he has sharply restricted his duties since your mother's condition has worsened. That gap in leadership of the Royal Guard may be part of the problem."

"Now that I'm here to help out with Mother, maybe we can get him back to work." I stand, and everyone else automatically rises. "Ralston and I have another appointment, so we need to get going. Thanks again." I hug Lorelei, and Jacob kisses my hand. They see us to the front door where the box with my new katana is waiting for me.

The crowd of townspeople has dispersed when we return to our horses. Handing the wooden box to Patrick, I ask him to strap it on my horse.

"Oh man," I say turning to Ralston. "Can I can really handle all this? I mean, things look pretty bad. I don't think I'm capable of presiding over Council meetings, ordering up investigations, and all that other stuff they expect of me."

He puts a hand on my shoulder and gazes into my eyes. "Yes you are, old girl. You just handled the meeting in there brilliantly. You have a strong sense of justice. Trust yourself to know what is right. I'll be here to assist you, and you have other friends at the palace."

"I hope you're right," I say, doubting that he is.

Someone calls out to me from across the street. "Beckett." Patrick quickly steps into the road blocking the man's path. "Beckett," he shouts again.

"Asher?" I tell the Patrick to let him by. "What are you doing here? And why are you dressed like that?" I ask, eyeing his odd outfit. Instead of his usual stylish clothing, he's wearing a ratty old pair of cargo pants and an olive-drab jacket that looks vaguely military.

Asher shakes hands with Ralston and hugs me quickly. "I'm on my way to visit my family. I thought you might want to come along."

"Really? That sounds like fun." I'd love to meet Asher's mother and sister and see what a post-nuclear war New York looks like.

"Rals, is it all right?"

"What about our appointment with Chelmsford?" he says.

"Can you handle it on your own? I mean he's your guy and all. Maybe you can just fill me in tonight. I could really use a break after the meeting we just had."

He presses his lips tightly together. "Oh, I suppose so," he says reluctantly. "But you'd best not be gone long. Remember you have an appointment this evening back at the palace."

Oh yeah, my meeting with Ryder. I almost forgot. "How long will we be gone?" I ask Asher.

He checks his watch. "I can have her back here in two and a half hours," he tells Ralston.

"All right. That should be satisfactory," Ralston says, checking his own watch.

Yes!

Asher steps back and studies me. "You're kind of overdressed for this trip. We may have to rub some dirt on you."

Frowning, I look down at my clothes. Okay, maybe I did overdo it a bit today. Then an idea hits me. I begin unbuttoning my embroidered jacket. "Hey Rals, can I borrow your vest and hat again?"

He appears scandalized. "Frankly Jaden, you ask a bit too much of me sometimes." He sounds cross, but slips out of his vest anyway. "This is not a fit way for me to present myself to Agent Chelmsford. I feel positively bare without a hat."

"Look over there, Rals," I say pointing. "There's a men's shop three doors down. Get what you need, and put it on the palace account."

His expression remains sour at first, but then he seems to warm to the idea. "Oh, I suppose that will be acceptable. Very well, then. You two had better run along. I'll meet you back here in two and one half hours, Jaden. Don't be late."

"I won't." Patrick takes my jacket, for safekeeping, and I button up Ralston's vest over my blouse.

"Come on," Asher says. "We'll leave from the alleyway." He leads me to a narrow lane next to Bartlett's shop. Twisting up my hair, I tug Ralston's hat over the top. Asher takes my hand and *Zzzt.* We're gone.

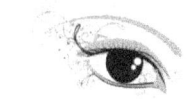

TWENTY

We land in another alley, this one dark and damp. "My house is a few blocks away," Asher says. "I don't like to shift in too close in case someone sees me. There's no need to draw any unwarranted attention to my family."

"I get it," I say. "Are we in any danger?"

"Well, this neighborhood can get a little rough." He steps close to me. "In fact someone may decide to kill you just for that lace." Unbuttoning my Edwardian collar, he tucks it under so my blouse has a v-neck. The gesture is oddly tender; his fingers warm against my skin.

"Thanks," I say smiling.

"Stay close," he says, taking my hand again.

We venture out into the street. The scene isn't what I expected at all. Instead of a bombed-out, scorched cityscape, we're in the midst of a busy little metropolis. It looks nothing like New York City—no skyscrapers or traffic jams. Graffiti-covered buildings, no more than four or five stories high, push up against each other on a wide, littered street teeming with activity. Merchants loudly hawk their wares from storefronts covered by filthy awnings, or from open air wooden carts, resplendent with flies. Fruits, vegetables, raw meat, live chickens, racks of cheap clothing, tacky souvenirs, fast food, and bakery goods, are offered for sale within a few feet of each other.

The signs are in English or Russian with a sprinkling of Mandarin Chinese thrown in. The city stinks like something dead from unnatural causes, and I clamp a hand over my nose to block out the stench.

The sky is clotted with angry gray clouds, as we pick our way around inky puddles, scattered like booby-traps along the rutted road. A man in a shiny black suit with a greasy mustache lurks in a darkened doorway, whispering to passersby. He beckons to Asher and me in Russian. I can only guess that the guy's selling either sex or drugs.

"Don't make eye contact," Asher says.

An Asian man in a coolie hat, pulling a cart on the back of his bicycle, stops to inquire if we want to buy some fish. We just shake our heads. This place is a mishmash of cultures. It's like Manhattan meets Moscow meets Shanghai.

"Wow. Strange place to grow up," I say. "Why did your parents move here?"

"Back in the '80s when they were first married, the government was practically giving away homes to anyone who agreed to relocate to the city and work in the government factories. It was a way to lure people back to the once contaminated area. My folks were poor, and it seemed like the thing to do at the time."

"I expected the city to look ruined, you know, decimated from the war."

"It was completely leveled in the war. But that was fifty years ago. It was rebuilt from the ground up, and now it's just decaying from within."

Asher takes us down a side street to a residential area of ramshackle little houses. He bounds up the crumbling front steps of a small bungalow, signaling me to follow. Quietly he taps on the door. "Ma," he says, his mouth close to the opening. "Ma, it's Asher."

The door creaks open, and a middle-aged woman sweeps Asher

into a strong embrace. She wears a faded housedress and saggy brown cardigan. Her hair has the appearance of dusty cobwebs, and her face is *Grapes of Wrath* gaunt, but her eyes are the same cool, clear shade of celadon green as Asher's.

"Son. Come in. I wasn't expecting you," she says, clutching the front of her sweater with one hand, and smoothing her untidy hair with the other. She catches sight of me. "Oh, hello. Both of you come in."

The living room is modestly furnished with a threadbare couch and chair that relinquished their color years ago. A complicated-looking sewing machine and stacked bolts of cotton and felt fabric occupy a metal table pushed up against one wall.

"I was just working," she says, scooping up scraps of rickrack and cloth from the floor.

"Ma, this is my friend, Beckett," he says.

"Call me Jaden." I smile and extend my hand.

She shakes it. "Nice to meet you Miss Jaden. Forgive the mess. I wasn't expecting visitors."

"Sorry for dropping in on you like this, Mrs. ...." I turn to Asher suddenly realizing I don't even know his last name. Maybe Asher is his last name.

He smiles. "Steele," he says.

"No, no. No trouble at all," Mrs. Steele says. "Please sit down."

Asher pulls off his jacket, and tosses it on the couch. "Where's Amber?"

"Gone to get some food. We worked practically all night. Look what we've made." She holds up several colorful ruffled aprons with the same little Russian girl embroidered on the front of each.

"That's great," Asher says. "I like the design. How are they selling?"

"So far they've been very popular. I've gotten Mr. Willard to carry them in his store. He put one up in the window. Amber and I sell them from our cart in the afternoons. The tourists like them so far."

The front door swings open, and in steps a wisp of a girl with a paper bag in each arm. "Asher," she says brightly when she spots us on the sofa.

He springs up to hug her. "Amber, this is my friend Jaden."

She set's the bags on the sewing table and pulls off her cap. A cascade of dark, shiny curls tumbles across her shoulders. I stand and shake her hand. She's five-foot-four maybe, with friendly brown eyes and a Julia Roberts smile. She wears tight faded jeans, and I wistfully remember the pair I just lost.

"Well, big brother, it's nice to see you finally found a woman who will tolerate you," she says.

"She's not my girlfriend," Asher replies. "We're just associates. In fact, I don't really like her very much," he adds, straight faced.

Amber's laugh is full and lovely. "Well, she's the first person you've ever brought home to meet the family, so sorry if I don't believe you." She begins removing items from the paper bags and setting them on the metal table. "You're lucky I went shopping. We were nearly out of everything."

Mrs. Steele helps Amber unload the groceries. "Good. You got borscht, and pumpernickel," she says removing a thick round loaf of brown bread. "This will be nice for lunch. Amber, you get the bowls and I'll slice the bread." They carry the food to the back, where I assume the kitchen is located.

"Nice way to introduce me to your sister, Ash. Thanks a lot," I say.

"I didn't want her to get the wrong impression. Besides you are kind of a pain at times."

"Am not."

"Are too."

"That's load of guano."

"See what I mean." He flashes his bewitching little smile, and I swat him on the arm, just as Amber walks into the room carrying a tray with four bowls.

"What's he done now?" She asks, smiling widely and placing the tray on the coffee table in front of us.

"Nothing," I say sheepishly.

Amber draws a chair near the table, and passes a bowl to me and one to Asher. The bowls are filled with a deep purple-red soup that gives off an aroma of potting soil. Asher's mom arrives with a basket of sliced bread and a dish of butter. She sets them on the table and drags over the chair from the sewing table. "Asher, would you like to say grace?"

"Oh Ma, it's just lunch. Can't we skip grace?"

She shoots him an exasperated look, makes the sign of the cross, and mumbles something under her breath. "Please have some bread, Miss Jaden," she says to me.

I thank her and select a slice. Not knowing where to put it, I balance it on my knee and take a spoonful of soup. *Ye Gods, this stuff is foul.* Holding my breath, I swallow, then quickly gobble a bit of bread to mask the taste.

"I've never eaten borscht before. What's in it?" I ask.

Amber and her mother exchange astonished looks. "Never had borscht?" Asher's mother says, like I just confessed to being an axe murderer.

"She's not from around here, Ma. She's from the western provinces," Asher says.

"Uh huh." She sounds doubtful. Squinting, she scrutinizes my clothes. "Well, it's mostly beets, with a little beef and some potatoes. There's supposed to be cream also, but Mr. Vasilevich scrimps on the ingredients. I swear he uses milk."

"Oh. It's uh … good." I have another bite of bread, bracing myself for more soup. It's clear these people don't have much money, and probably not much food, I don't have the heart to waste it. Holding my breath again, I take a large spoonful. It's not as bad as the first one, but it's still like ingesting liquid mulch.

Asher's mother tears off a small chunk of bread and chews it slowly. She scoots forward on her chair. "May we speak openly in front of Miss Jaden?" she asks Asher in low tones.

"Sure Ma. We work together."

"How are things going? You know, with the movement?"

Asher gives her a little song and dance about how things are progressing with the underground revolution. He doesn't really say much. Just enough to offer some hope, and to reassure her that he's in no danger. It must be a difficult juggling act, keeping up with two separate identities. I guess I kind of know how that goes. You find yourself in a situation and you do what you have to do. At least when he's with the Transcenders, Asher can be himself.

After Asher's fictional update, Amber and Mrs. Steele fill him in on all the news of the neighborhood and their extended family. The three of them have a warm and easy rapport. Our little lunch of soup and bread is rich with joy and love, even in this meager setting.

The time zooms by. Asher checks his watch and gets to his feet. "Let me help you clean up, Ma." He begins stacking bowls.

"There's no need for that." She flutters her hands at him.

"I want to. You always say *many hands make light work*." He kisses the top of her head and makes for the kitchen. She piles the remaining lunch items on the tray and follows him.

"So," Amber says when we're alone, "how long have you two been seeing each other?"

"Actually, Asher was telling the truth. We aren't seeing each other. In fact I'm engaged to someone else."

"So you're going to break his heart?" She laughs lightly.

"No chance of that happening. Like he told you, he's not very fond of me."

She folds her arms across her chest and gazes at me. "You know that's not true. I see the way he is with you. It's okay, though. He probably deserves to be jilted. But level with me on something; are you really part of the movement?"

I nod slowly. "Every bit as much as Asher," I say.

Asher finishes up in the kitchen and grabs his jacket. I thank the two ladies for their hospitality. They invite me to come again, and I promise I will.

"Oh, Ma. I almost forgot," Asher says lifting a small pouch from his jacket pocket. "It's not much, but it should get you through the month."

His mother pushes it back toward him. "No, no, Son. Keep it for the cause. We're doing well with the aprons. We don't need it."

"Then stash it away. I'm not sure when I can come again. I hear they're sending more soldiers to fortify the city."

Her face creases with worry and she wraps an arm around Asher's neck pulling him to her. "Be careful, Son," she says with a catch in her voice. "May God go with you."

"Love you, Ma." He kisses her cheek. "Be good, Amber."

They wave, and we make our exit into the dismal little street.

TWENTY-ONE

Asher's mood seems to have darkened, much like the weather. I pull Ralston's vest tight around me to ward off the chill.

"They're wonderful, Ash. Thanks for bringing me to meet them."

"I hate it when I have to leave them," he says almost angrily. "My life's so comfortable and theirs is so damn depressing. I've tried and tried to get Ma to move to someplace better, safer. I have the money. But she won't hear of it. She says this is their home. She doesn't want to live anywhere else. God, it's so frustrating."

"They seem happy, though," I say, searching his troubled eyes.

"You saw the way they live. How can they—" He doesn't get to finish his sentence.

"*Привал!* Halt!" Someone shouts behind us. "Stay where you are."

We turn in the direction of the voice. Two Russian soldiers stride purposefully toward us.

"Oh shit," Asher says. "We have to run for it. They may have seen us coming out of Ma's house." He takes hold of my arm and we bolt. He steers me toward an alley that cuts through to the crowded street, but two more soldiers step into the road blocking our escape.

We stop and slowly back up toward the buildings and away from the soldiers.

"What do we do now? We've got to shift," I say.

"Stay here. Let me talk to them for a minute." He puts his hands in the air and steps into the road, leaving me on the sidewalk. The soldiers surround him.

Asher speaks to them in Russian. One of the men responds angrily. In English, Asher says, "What do you want?" I think I hear the word "papers" from one of the soldiers. Asher reaches a hand inside his jacket and, quick as a flash, one of the soldiers snatches his arm, spins him around, and slaps handcuffs on him.

Jungle drums beat heavy in my chest. "Asher," I call, terrified.

We lock eyes, and he shouts, "Meet me back in Warrington."

"But I don't have my—" I try to tell him I don't have my TPD bracelet, when *poof*, he disappears. "What the—?"

The soldiers completely freak out, turning every which way, grasping handfuls of air, trying to figure out where Asher went. I don't stick around to see the show, though. Instead I use the diversion to make a hasty exit. Racing down the side alley, I burst into the congested street, nearly toppling over a kid on a bike. No idea where I'm going, but I figure once Asher realizes I don't have my bracelet, he'll come back for me. I jog to my right, glancing over my shoulder for my pursers, and *wham*! I'm knocked flat onto my back. The air slams out of my lungs.

Gasping, I struggle for breath. My chest hurts like an elephant just used me for a whoopee cushion. My eyes flutter open to the sight of a soldier looming large and gray above me.

"Подниматься! Get up!" he says.

I open my mouth to speak, but no words come out. Hooking his hands under my armpits, he jerks me roughly to my feet. His buddies trot up behind him, snickering at my ungraceful landing. The soldier barks something at me in Russian.

"Wait a minute. I don't speak Russian," I say, shaking my head.

The Russian goon backhands me across the face, nearly knocking me to the street again. *He really shouldn't have done that. Now I'm pissed.* Gingerly holding my cheek, I take a step back, planting my feet firmly. The goon makes another move toward me. Spinning quickly, I ram my foot into the side of his head with all my strength. The blow lays him out, rendering him unconscious. The force of my kick sends me to the ground too, but I spring up immediately, ready for a fight.

The other dumbasses are suddenly paying attention. One soldier runs to check his fallen comrade, while another slips the rifle from his shoulder and points it directly at my face. I snap-kick it out of his hand and sweep-kick his feet out from under him. He crashes to the pavement face-first, and I take off running again. I hear a *pop* as a bullet whizzes past my head. *Holy shit!* Everyone on the street hits the deck. I guess they've been through this drill before. I'm the only one still standing, and I need to get gone fast. Even if I can outrun these guys, I can't beat their bullets. Unless …

Asher told me a little about shifting without a TPD. You have to concentrate on where you want to go, and focus on the streaming stars feeling. Two more quick *pops* echo in the street. No sudden, searing pain, so I must be okay. Gasping for air, I duck inside a recessed doorway. Closing my eyes, I concentrate as hard as I can on Warrington Village.

Zzzt! I'm streaming blindly through the universe.

The smell hits me hard as I land. Thick, earthy, smoky air. Like a campfire doused with water. I'm not sure whether to chew it, gulp it, or breathe it. My surroundings are jarringly unfamiliar. Dense vegetation drips with moisture, weak shafts of sunlight filter through the thick haze, gunky compost squishes beneath my boots. It sure as hell isn't Warrington, and I doubt I'm even on the right earth. It's like a steamy rainforest. *Crap!* What now?

Plopping down on a fallen tree trunk, I cradle my bruised cheek in my hand and scan the thicket in front of me. Instantly I freeze. Two enormous yellow eyes peer at me from ten yards away, their owner crouched on all fours, taut and ready to spring. The creature is about the size of a grizzly with sleek black fur and wicked-long fangs. I can't tell if it's feline, ursine, or just plain monster, but it's sizing me up like I'm today's blue plate special. Adrenaline blazes in my veins. Every cell of my body screams red alert. My mind shifts into hyperdrive, zooming through my options.

"Stay still." The voice behind me is Asher's. He places a hand on my shoulder and *Zzzt!* We're out of there.

We land in the alley adjacent to Bartlett's, Asher still gripping my shoulder like a vise. Releasing me, he slumps back against the brick wall, and strains for air.

"What was that thing?" I ask.

He shakes his head. "Don't know," he says still panting.

"Where were we?"

He shakes his head again. "Someplace new." He squeezes his eyes shut as if in pain, and I realize how shaken-up he is.

"Hey, we're safe," I say. "It's all good. Thank God for that TPD locator thing."

His eyes snap open, and he grasps my arm roughly pulling me toward him. He shoves up my sleeve. "Where's your bracelet?"

I yank my arm away. "I left it back at the palace. I'm sorry."

"You should wear it at all times," he says through gritted teeth.

"I will. I promise. Just calm down."

He slumps back against the wall. "You could have been killed, Jade."

"I know. I'm sorry."

He straightens up and takes my chin in his hand. "What happened to your cheek?"

"One of the comrades got physical with me. I doubt he'll be trying that again, though."

"What did you do to him?" he asks, scowling.

"A lot less than he deserved. I just clocked him with my boot. A little spin-kick. He was out cold, last I saw him."

Asher barks out a laugh, cracking the tension between us. "Wish I could've seen that. The bastards! Thinking they could beat-up on a girl. They had no idea who they were dealing with."

I have to laugh myself. "Yeah, but you should've seen them after that little disappearing act you pulled. They were totally blown away, clutching at nothing, nearly falling on top of each other trying to figure out where you were. You'd probably better check on your family, though. In case they're interrogated or something."

"I will." He reaches out for my hand and pulls me close. "I don't know what I would have done if you'd have been hurt." His eyes are cloudy as sea glass.

"That's 'cause you like me," I tease.

"Do not."

"Yes, you do."

He shakes his head. "You are *way* too much trouble, Beckett."

"But you like me. Admit it." I smile up at him.

He lightly brushes his fingertips along my cheek. "Okay, maybe I like you a little, despite the fact that you're a royal pain in the ass. No pun intended."

He rests his forehead against mine for a moment, and then leans in and kisses me. I confess I didn't see it coming, but *oh man*, it feels great. I wrap my arms around his slim waist and pull him closer. *Mmm.* His mouth is warm and luscious, and his body feels so nice next to mine. This is probably a real bad idea, but it feels pretty damn good at the moment.

"Jaden!"

We pull our lips apart and both turn toward the voice. Ryder stands at the entrance to the alley, a look of combined shock and fury on his face. I step away from Asher and swipe the back of my hand across my mouth as if to erase the kiss. Asher positions himself next to me, arms at his side, feet planted firmly apart; steadying himself for whatever comes next.

"Ryder. What are you doing here?" I ask, hoping a manhood contest doesn't break out in the middle of the alley.

"I received your message. I saw your horse … What are *you* doing here? Who is this?"

"This is my friend, Asher Steele."

Ryder walks with determination toward us. He's dressed in traditional Cherokee buckskins today and looks every bit the menacing warrior. "What does this mean?" he says. "Is this why you wished to see me? To tell me you have found someone else?"

"No! Let me explain." I turn to Asher. "I need to speak with Ryder alone. Please just leave. *The normal way,*" I whisper under my breath.

"If that's what you want," Asher says. He turns and saunters out of the alley, taking his sweet time.

"All right, explain," Ryder says. "Why were you kissing him?" Hurt and rage take turns rearranging his features.

"It was nothing. It was just an accident."

"It didn't appear accidental to me," he says. "Why are you dressed like that?"

I must look destroyed to him. Ralston's hat got lost somewhere along the way, but I'm still wearing his vest. My riding pants are split at both knees and filthy. My mud-caked boots have definitely seen better days.

"It's a disguise. I didn't want to be recognized."

Lightning flies from his stormy eyes. "Why not? What were you doing? And what happened to your face? Did he strike you?"

"No. Of course not. He's not that kind of man."

"What kind of man is he, then? Is he your lover?"

"Ryder!"

"What else am I to think after such a public display? You are engaged to me. You have no right to—"

"Whoa. Wait a minute, big guy. Just stop right there. First of all, engaged or not, you don't tell me what to do. And second, only one of us is falsehearted enough to fall into bed with the first person who asks them. And it isn't me."

My words seem to knock the wind out of him. He gazes at me a moment. Slowly all emotion drains from his eyes, and I sense an invisible wall rise up between us. He's shutting me out. Deliberately closing himself off to me. It hurts like hell. *No Ryder, don't. I know I deserve it, but please don't.*

"Your Highness," he says tonelessly. "I regret to inform you that pressing matters prevent me from keeping my meeting with you this evening. Good day." He bows, turns on his heel, and walks away.

"Ryder," I call after him.

He doesn't look back.

TWENTY-TWO

I trudge out of the alleyway toward the horses, praying no one recognizes me. A few people mill around in front of the village shops, but no one seems to notice me. All at once I'm dog-tired and smarting from my injuries. My insides are hollow and cold. Patrick sees me and hurries over with my jacket.

"Are you all right, ma'am?" he asks, checking out my battered face and ripped pants. "Have you met with some misfortune?"

"No. I'm fine. Where's Professor Ralston?"

"Not back yet, ma'am. Shall I find him for you?"

I spot Ralston strutting down the sidewalk decked out in a fancy new coat and hat. "Here he comes," I say. When he catches sight of me, he loses the strut and picks up his pace.

"Jaden, what is it? What's happened?" he asks when he reaches my side.

"Just a little throw down with some Russian soldiers," I say softly enough so Patrick can't hear. "I'm all right. Can we just get out of here?"

"Of course. I apologize if I kept you waiting, but I believe we'll reach the palace with ample time for you to change before your meeting with Ryder."

I climb on Gabriel's back. "There's no need to rush. Ryder's not coming."

"Not coming? I'm sorry to hear that." He mounts his own horse, and we ride side-by-side out of town, Patrick keeping a respectful distance behind.

After a mile or two of silence, I say, "I lost your hat, Rals. Sorry."

"It's quite all right. I have a fine new hat, thanks to you." He touches a fingertip to his brim. "I take it your afternoon with Asher was not as pleasant as expected?"

"Actually, it was nice seeing Asher's weird hometown and meeting his mom and sister. They're both lovely. We just got crosswise with some high-testosterone soldier-types on our way out of town. Oh, and when I tried to escape, I almost got eaten by a gigantic fanged beast in a smoky jungle on some unknown earth. But that wasn't even the worst of it."

"Good lord. How could it possibly get worse?" he asks with worried eyes.

"Ryder saw me kissing Asher."

"Oh my. I see." He clucks at his horse and focuses on the road ahead. I don't have to look at his face to know he's probably disappointed in me. Undoubtedly, he's trying to figure out why I would do something so casmagorically stupid. Which is what I've been wondering myself ever since it happened. Maybe all this inter-dimensional travel has killed some essential brain cells or something.

"I know what you're thinking," I say. "It was a completely lunatic thing to do. I don't even know how it happened. One minute Asher and I are joking around, and the next minute we're kissing."

"To the contrary, my dear," Ralston says gently. "I was thinking what an exceedingly human thing to have done. You are two spirited young people who like each other and who had just shared a rather traumatic experience. It is quite understandable that you were drawn together in such a way."

Not what I expected him to say. He's a crafty old fart sometimes. "Are you trying to be metaphoric or something?"

"Whatever do you mean?" he asks, a *Who me?* expression plastered on his face.

"Oh, please, Rals. I mean, you're saying that's exactly what happened with Ryder and Erica, and so now I should totally get it."

"If that's what you take away from this experience, then perhaps it was fortunate that it occurred."

"Yeah, well it wasn't fortunate. Ryder's furious with me, and I don't know what's going to happen now. Relationships in this world are pretty black-and-white. I'm engaged to him, and I just kissed another man. I may have pushed him too far and royally screwed-up any hope of getting back together."

On the verge of throwing myself a full-out pity-party, I'm distracted when Ralston changes the subject. "Tell me about this great fanged beast you encountered. That must have been thrilling. What happened?"

I recount my visit to the Soviet Socialist Republic of New York, our confrontation with the soldiers, and my accidental detour to *Where the Wild Things Are*. It's nice sharing my Transcender experiences with Ralston. He's always fascinated with my stories and seems kind of awe-struck by the adventures. Besides, who else am I going to tell?

As we near the palace, the hollow sick feeling returns to my stomach. The frosty indifference in Ryder's eyes still haunts me. I hope I haven't blown things for good.

The guards at the entrance gates wave us through, bowing as we pass. "Hey, Rals," I say, "let's ride around back to the stables and go in through the kitchen. I don't want anyone to see me like this."

He looks kind of crestfallen. "I was planning on making a grand entrance in all my new finery," he confesses. "But I suppose you're right. It wouldn't do to have Prince Harold asking a lot of questions about our day."

We leave our horses with Patrick, and walk through the kitchen courtyard to the back door. Dinner preparations are underway, and the aromas that greet us as we enter the kitchen are sublime—roasted meats, freshly baked breads and spice cakes. My stomach gurgles in appreciation. I spy a bowl piled high with fresh pommeras, and pop a few in my jacket pockets.

"You go on ahead, Rals. I'm going to take a treat out to Gabriel."

Trotting back out to the stables, I find Gabriel already being brushed down by one of the stable hands. The boy bows and I nod.

"I've got something for you Gabe," I hold out a pommera in my open palm. He grasps it with his lips and devours it with one bite. That is *not* the way pommeras were meant to be enjoyed, so I decide to keep the others for myself. I kiss his velvety nose and head back to the palace.

As I leave the stables, a lone rider enters the palace courtyard. Our eyes meet and a flash of recognition passes between us. I don't know who he is, but I swear I saw him in town this afternoon. The hair on the back of my neck prickles. *I'm being followed ... and by someone known to the palace guards. Ralston needs to hear about this and help me find out who he is.*

I wend my way up the back stairway and into my room without seeing anyone. After shedding my filthy clothes, I slip into a fluffy robe and head for the bathroom to check out the damage to my face. My cheek isn't terrible—a little swollen and red, but nothing a bucket of concealer can't hide.

Before Maria arrives to help me dress for the evening, I shower and brush out my hair. Maria knows me well enough not to ask too many questions about my bruised face, and she's a master with makeup, so in no time she has me looking fresh and princess-like.

Someone taps at my door while Maria is choosing my gown for dinner. It's Samuel, my mother's butler, come to tell me that Mother is dining in her room tonight, and would like me to join her. That's a relief. I'm not up to a formal dinner tonight, and I sure don't feel like talking to Uncle Harold just now. Mother concerns me, though. This is the second night in a row she's missed dinner. Dressing quickly in a casual gown of softest fargen wool, I decide to forego the jewelry except for my TPD bracelet, and the wolf-head necklace tucked inside my neckline.

General LeGare is already there, sitting by Mother's bedside. I was hoping for some one-on-one time with her, but this may be a good thing. Now I can talk with both of them about some of the things Jacob and Lorelei told me. Ralston and I agreed it would be best to take a subtle approach with Mother and not to accuse Uncle Harold of any wrongdoing until we have all the facts.

I kiss Mother and take the chair on the opposite side of her bed. Without the benefit of make-up, she looks tired and gaunt. My heart contracts at the thought that she could slip away at any time.

"Thank you for joining us, darling," she says weakly. "The medication is taking a greater toll on me each day. I did not feel up to entertaining tonight, but I've ordered a lovely dinner for us. I hope you don't mind."

"This is great, Mother. A quiet dinner with you suits me fine."

The food arrives, and several servants quickly set Mother's table with sterling silver, fine china, cut crystal, and golden candlesticks.

"I believe I'll stay right here and take my meal on a tray," Mother says, "but you and Charles should dine at the table."

"No Mother. We'll eat here with you." I tell Samuel that we'll all have trays, and he sends one of the maids scuttling from the room to get two more.

Once we are all served, Mother asks about my day.

"Ralston and I went to see Lady Lorelei," I tell her. "Jacob was there too. We had a nice visit."

She smiles. Lorelei is a favorite cousin of hers. "Are they well?" Mother asks.

"Yes they seem to be. Lorelei hopes the situation with Dome Noir is resolved soon, so she can import the materials she needs for her business. Jacob seems more concerned about some matters raised at the last Council of Advisors meeting." LeGare shoots me a little frown like I shouldn't trouble Mother with this information. I ignore him. I know Mother, and she'd want to hear this.

"Is that so? What matters are of concern to him?" she asks.

"Well, for one thing, it seems that Uncle Harold has planned for a new cavalry division of the Royal Guard."

"Yes. Harold mentioned that to me. Is there a problem?"

"Only that he intends to arm them with guns and rifles," I say.

She hasn't touched a bite of food, and now she pushes away her tray. "That cannot be. We have long-standing laws against bearing firearms in Domerica."

"I know Mother, but I'm told Uncle Harold has managed to have the laws changed."

She draws in a slow breath and turns to LeGare. "Is this true? Were you aware of this, Charles?"

"Yes. I was," he says with lowered eyes.

"And why did you not inform me? Surely you must know that I would object to such a move."

"I did not inform you for two reasons, Ellie. First, I did not wish to upset you." He glowers at me. "Second, I happen to agree with Prince Harold on this issue. We are in a delicate position with Dome Noir. They have suspended trade with us over the Prince Damien incident, and there is harsh talk coming from their representatives about the possible consequences if we do not agree to their proposal for a new dome. Bluntly put, if we are forced into a war, both Dome Noir and Cupola de Vita will be armed with guns and more. We must be in a position to defend ourselves with equal power."

Mother's posture straightens, her voice becomes strong. "And once firearms are introduced into our society, we shall become as violent and lawless as Dome Noir and Cupola de Vita. The reason they wish to erect a new dome is because they cannot control the crime in their own cities. The solution is not this 'prison dome' they propose to build. The solution is to take the weapons away from the criminals and to better enforce their own laws. They would do well to take a lesson from us on that front—not the other way around. I am disappointed in you, Charles."

LeGare looks like a scolded puppy. "I'm sorry, Your Majesty. I know your position on this matter, and I should have kept you better informed. Please accept my apology."

"You are forgiven," she says. "But how are we to rectify this?"

LeGare seems at a loss for an answer.

"Mother, maybe I can help," I say. "Now that I'm home, I can take on more responsibilities within the government. It will all fall to me one day anyway. I might as well start doing a few things now."

"What are you proposing?" she asks.

"That you appoint me your representative on the Council. I could conduct the meetings and consult with you on major issues. Then, if you trust me to speak for you, I could cast your vote. It doesn't appear anything has taken place that can't be undone, and I would like to better familiarize myself with the current issues facing Domerica."

She studies me for a moment. "Of course. I should have arranged this immediately upon your return. I thought you might welcome Harold's assumption of some of my more onerous duties after your recent ordeal and what with planning your wedding. But the position is rightfully yours. You should be presiding over the meetings. It shall be done," she says. "The papers will be drawn up tonight appointing you my interim representative."

She reaches for LeGare's hand. "Charles, will you support us in this? Will you pledge your loyalty to Jaden?"

"Of course, Your Majesty." He kisses her hand tenderly and

raises his eyes to mine. They blaze with conviction. "I pledge my loyalty to Princess Jaden," he says. "It will be as if she were you."

Mother smiles at him affectionately. "Thank you, Charles. Now, let us not allow this delicious food to go to waste." She pulls her tray closer and begins to eat.

The remainder of the meal passes pleasantly. Mother actually eats more than I do, mainly because I feel like I've just bitten off more than I can chew. Not only is my relationship with Ryder in shambles, but if Uncle Harold didn't despise me before, I'm about to seal the deal by taking over as Mother's representative on the Council, meaning I'll have veto power over everything he does.

TWENTY-THREE

*T*he princess's selection of nightclothes consists of a dozen, identical long-sleeved, white cotton, ankle-length gowns. I pull one over my head and crawl into bed. Closing my eyes, I wonder for the umpteenth time if I did the right thing coming back to Domerica. If I'd stayed in Connecticut, Ryder and Erica would be blissfully having meaningless sex together, and Uncle Harold would be the de facto "king" of Domerica. Both of those thoughts make me cringe.

I know I can still go back if I want to, but I can't leave without attempting to patch things up with Ryder, and without making sure Uncle Harold doesn't take Domerica in the wrong direction. Under my mother's rule, the country has flourished and is currently the most productive, prosperous, and peaceful dome nation on this earth. I won't let Uncle Harold destroy all she's worked for, but I'm too tired to figure it out tonight, so I fluff up my feather pillows and try to sleep.

I'm running through a hostile jungle fleeing something unknown. Tree branches painfully lash my face. Vines coil around my ankles pulling me to the ground.

I awaken with a start. My bruised cheek throbs, my heart races, and my sweat-soaked nightgown is twisted around my body practically choking me. Throwing off the covers, I climb out of bed and yank off the old-fashioned nightgown, dropping it to the floor. *How do people sleep in those things?*

I find a silky little underdress in the princess's closet and slip it on. *Aah. This is more like it.* The soft fabric caresses my skin. I'm still too keyed-up to go back to bed, so I open my balcony doors and step outside. The air is cool and purifying. The palace grounds are beautifully lit up at night.

"Do you miss seeing the moon and stars?" asks a voice from the darkness at the other end of my balcony.

My heart tries to climb out through my throat. "Asher! You nearly scared me to death. What are you doing here?"

Stepping from the shadows, he smiles his lazy smile. He wears a loose white linen shirt and jeans. His hair tumbles appealing across his forehead. "I couldn't sleep. I was worried about you. I checked the TPD and saw you were moving around, so I came to check on you." He takes my hand in his. "I thought maybe we could *not sleep* together."

"Cute." I smirk at him.

"Glad to see you're wearing your bracelet." His fingertips brush across the shooting stars.

"I took your admonition seriously."

"Good." He lightly pushes a strand of damp hair away from my neck. The touch of his hand sends a ripple of pleasure through me. "Why is your hair wet?" he asks.

"I had a nightmare. Woke up in a cold sweat. I don't know. Things are just very confusing right now."

"Can I do anything to make you feel better?" He pulls me close.

His body gives off a tremendous amount of heat, and I hungrily breathe in his enticing scent. I'm acutely aware that only two thin layers of cloth separate my body from his. A tantalizing flash of him tangled in my sheets flickers through my mind and tempts me to take him inside right now. But I resist the urge. It wouldn't be right. I know what I want, and it's not Asher.

Stepping away from him, I say, "You'd better go, Ash. You're a temptation I don't need right now. I love Ryder. I'm not sure how to explain this, but he stirs up things inside of me—passionate things, powerful yearnings. I think some of those feelings may have spilled over onto you. Does that make any sense?"

He stares out at the moonless night for a moment, then turns to me. "Oh yeah. I get it. You'd be kissing me, but thinking of him."

"'Fraid so."

He shoves his hands in his pockets. "When you put it that way, it doesn't really sound so appealing. I guess there's no competing with a perpetual contract, but you can't blame a guy for trying."

I rest my hand lightly on his shoulder. "I could really use your friendship right now."

"You'll always have that. I don't want to add to your stress level though, so I'll just wait for you to contact me. Don't forget, you still need to meet with the other Transcenders. It's important, Jade."

"I know. I promise I won't forget. Thanks, Ash."

"'Night, Beckett." He fades back into the shadows and vanishes.

Okay, one confusing thing checked off my list. Feeling a bit lighter, I fall back into bed and hope for a little more sleep. I need to be clear-headed for the Council meeting in the morning.

Waking before dawn, I order a large pot of coffee instead of tea. My state of mind can be summed up in two words: *abject terror*. I've never been great at public speaking, and now I have to stand up in front of a group of men and women, most of whom are more than twice my age, and inform them I'm taking over the reins of their country. *What am I, crazy?*

I throw open my door and search the deserted hallway. A uniformed butler instantly appears. "May I help you, ma'am?" he asks with a bow.

"Yes," I croak. "Find Professor Ralston. Wake him up if you have to. Tell him I need to see him, like now."

While I'm waiting for Ralston, a messenger arrives with the signed papers appointing me Mother's representative. I leaf through the multiple-page document. The words blur together, and panic swells inside me as the minutes tick by. Finally, there's a knock at my door, and I fling it open to find Ralston standing there in navy satin pajamas, a purple paisley robe, and brown leather slippers. He's such a fashion plate, even at six a.m.

"What is the emergency, my dear?" he says groggily.

Grabbing his arm, I pull him inside, and close the door. "Rals, I can't do it. I need to go back to Connecticut right now."

"I see," he says, strolling over to the tray on my dining table. "Is this coffee?"

"Yes, it's coffee. Did you hear me?"

"I heard you. What seems to be the problem?" He takes a mug from my cupboard and pours himself some of the piping hot liquid.

"The problem is Mother sent over a ten-page document giving me all this power. *Me*, a stupid high school girl from Madison. I don't have a clue what I'm supposed to be doing, Rals. These people will see right through me. I'll never pull it off."

"Shall we sit?" Ralston ambles to the armchairs in front of the fake fireplace, Mother's document in one hand, his steaming mug in the other. He situates himself comfortably in one of the chairs, and I plop my butt down in the other.

"First, you are not stupid, Jaden. At least Yale thought enough of you to offer you admission to their fine university. Second, you need do nothing at the meeting today, unless you wish to. This document says you are there acting as the queen's representative. If you do not wish to express an opinion, you may respectfully inform the Council that you will take matters under advisement pending a discussion with your mother. It's quite simple really."

This calms me a little. "But I'm supposed to conduct the meeting. How do I do that?"

"There will be an agenda. Just follow the agenda, and call for discussion of the matters in the order listed. Normally a time limit is placed on discussion. In these meetings I believe it is five minutes per member. But a timekeeper is present who will police this for you. So you see, nothing to worry about." He sips his coffee and smiles at me over his mug.

"Will you come with me, Rals?"

"No. I'm not allowed. Only Council members, a timekeeper, and a clerk for recording the Council's actions may be present during meetings. But honestly, Jaden, you won't need me."

"You're sure there's not more to it than that?"

"There are a few small formalities," he says. "Why don't we order some breakfast, and I'll walk you through it while we eat?"

By the time we've finished our cinnamon scones and cheese omelets, I feel much better about my ability to conduct the proceedings. Ralston and I rehearsed bringing the meeting to order, calling for discussion, adjourning, and a few other things.

"Perhaps we could meet after lunch," Ralston suggests. "I hear the blueberry barrens outside the palace grounds are at their peak. Why don't we pick blueberries this afternoon? We can speak privately about what transpires at the meeting as well as go over what Agent Chelmsford and I discussed yesterday."

"That'd be nice, Rals. There's one thing I want to tell you, though. It seems I'm being followed. Some guy rode up to the stables after I took Gabriel a pommera. I swear I saw him hanging around outside of Bartlett's yesterday."

"Goodness. I wonder if he's friend or foe."

"No idea. But could you check with the guards about who came through the gates right after us yesterday? Maybe somebody knows him, or maybe they got his name."

"Certainly."

"And we need to hire someone to look into the rumors about Uncle Harold, unless Chelmsford told you something useful about that. I don't trust the job to anyone at the palace, and it sounds like the local law enforcement in Warrington Village isn't getting anywhere. An independent party would be best."

"Chelmsford was no help in that regard, but I shall take care of it. There is a man in town I would trust with this matter. He's very good and most discrete. Do not trouble yourself, my dear."

"Thanks Rals. You're a lifesaver."

Maria leans her head around the door. "It's time to dress for your meeting, Princess."

Ralston takes his cue and gets up to leave. He bows formally to me since another person is present, but he smiles and winks before turning for the door.

The princess doesn't own a business suit, so I settle for a plain jacket, skirt, and sensible shoes. Maria pulls my hair back into a tight bun, and my reflection in the mirror reminds me of old Miss Montague, my AP English Lit teacher. All in all, it's a much better look than freaked-out teenager—which is what I resembled thirty minutes ago.

Gathering up Mother's document and a writing pad, I march downstairs to the meeting room. Some Council members are already present. I peek in the doorway. Uncle Harold stands at the dais, swinging the gavel between his thumb and forefinger, waiting to bring the meeting to order. *Crap!* How do I break it to him that he's no longer in charge because I'm taking over? Things could get a little ugly. The *Cirque du Soleil* begins a mini-performance in my stomach, and all my nerve leaks out through my shoes. I consider making a quick getaway, when someone behind me gloms onto my elbow and propels me through the door.

"Good morning, darling," Mother says.

"Mother! What are you doing here? You should be in bed."

"I'm much better this morning." She smiles weakly. "I feel it my duty to announce your designation as my representative to the Council, and allow Harold to gracefully turn over the mantle to you. I believe the transition will go more smoothly if I am presiding." Her voice becomes a whisper. "I also wish to personally express my views on the issue of firearms in Domerica."

We walk together to the dais. Harold is visibly shocked to see Mother and doubly shocked to see me here. The room instantly grows silent, and everyone rises in the presence of the queen. Harold bows and extends the gavel to her. "Your Majesty. How wonderful of you to join us," he says.

"Thank you Harold. I have a few additions to the agenda this morning," she says, addressing the group. "Please be seated." Turning to me, she smiles wanly. "Jaden, I believe I will be seated also. Is the chair next to yours available?"

The man sitting next to me scrambles from his seat, and I help Mother to the newly-vacated chair. Harold sits at the end of the table fidgeting with his pinky ring. Mother begins the meeting by thanking Uncle Harold for his wonderful contributions to the Council over the last several months. His expression grows tense as the meaning of my presence begins to dawn on him, and his normally pale skin glows neon pink. When Mother announces my appointment as her representative, applause erupts from the Council members. Jacob Bartlett, smiling and clapping, catches my eye and nods his approval. Harold avoids all eye-contact, choosing to focus on his ring, twisting it back and forth.

The next item Mother adds to the agenda is the issue of the cavalry possessing firearms. The subject sparks a spirited debate among the Council members, with persuasive arguments bandied about on both sides of the issue. Mother allows each member his or her say on the matter, with the timekeeper enforcing strict limits. Uncle Harold declines to comment either way. When a vote is taken, the Council is equally divided on the issue.

All eyes focus on Mother. For outward appearances, the Council works democratically, with each member having a voice and a vote. The reality is that Domerica is pretty much a dictatorship—Mother's is the only vote that counts. She stands and delivers an eloquent speech expressing succinctly all the reasons firearms will *not* be permitted in Domerica. She proclaims invalid the new law granting the cavalry the right to bear firearms, and takes the additional step of ordering that all firearms which were confiscated from the Unicoi be destroyed within the week. The queen has spoken, and in Domerica, her word is law.

Clearly exhausted after her emotional address, Mother defers the remaining agenda items to the next meeting. She reminds the Council that I'll be presiding at that time. Cracking the gavel, she declares the meeting adjourned. I gather my things and take Mother's arm. Many Council members congratulate me on our way out. Others seem less than thrilled with my new appointment. Guess you can't please 'em all.

I leave Mother resting comfortably in her room. The weight of the world has been lifted from my shoulders, temporarily at least. Now if only the hole in my heart could be mended, I might feel halfway human again.

TWENTY-FOUR

*B*ack in my room, I pull the pins out of my hair and brush it out loose and free. Exchanging my jacket and skirt for a casual flaxen dress, I find a long multicolored scarf to tie around my waist like a sash. Tucking my new katana into the sash, I secure it with the *sageo* cord. This'll probably get more than a couple of curious stares from the palace inhabitants, but Ralston and I will be outside the palace grounds today, and I feel better having my sword with me.

When I reach the courtyard, Ralston waits in an open-air carriage. No rain on Saturdays. We'll be fine.

"I see you survived the meeting," he says as I climb on board.

"Yes." I beam at him. "Mother came and announced my appointment as her representative. She also took care of the issue of firearms in Domerica."

"So I heard." He clucks at the horses, and we begin the short trip to the blueberry barrens. Patrick falls in behind our carriage as we rumble through the palace gates.

The afternoon is pleasant, as always in Domerica, and we're the only traffic on this stretch of road. Ralston pulls the carriage just off the roadway and extracts two pails from behind the seat. Patrick stations himself on the road, while Ralston and I tromp through a small field to the barrens. The bushes are heavy with small ripe berries.

"Be careful of the bees," Ralston says. "They love blueberry blossoms."

I pluck a tiny indigo orb from a bush and pop it into my mouth. "Mmm, tasty," I say, sampling a few more.

"Yes, well don't eat them all. We need something to show for our little excursion," he scolds.

I yank a few berries from a bush and drop them in my pail. "Why are these so small? We usually get big fat berries at home."

"These are lowbush blueberries," Ralston says. "Highbush blueberries were not produced until 1911 when it was learned how to cultivate the plants. Unfortunately the scientist who discovered the process was never born in Domerica."

"Geeze, Rals. How do you know so much about so many things?"

"I'm a student of the multiverse," he says with a smile.

"Okay, so you already know that Mother came to the meeting this morning, what else did you hear?"

"Use this, my dear." Ralston hands me his linen handkerchief and motions that I have blueberry juice in the corner of my mouth. "Word that the queen had appointed you her representative on the Council spread quickly." Ralston dribbles berries in his pail as he talks. "I believe those at court, and possibly all of Domerica, are watching closely, attempting to gauge how great a role your Uncle Harold will play once you have fully assumed your mother's duties as queen."

"Oh yeah, I forgot to tell you, Duke Ferdinand asked me about that," I say.

"He did? When was this?" Ralston pauses his berry plucking and focuses on me.

"The other night after dinner. He walked me to my room and asked my permission to return after I'm queen to discuss some fresh proposals Cupola de Vita has for constructing a new dome."

"Well, that is encouraging."

"Yeah, but then he said that when deciding what to do with Uncle Harold, I should keep in mind the adage that *absolute power corrupts absolutely.*"

"Goodness. Not a very subtle chap, is he?" Ralston gathers more berries and puts them in the pail.

I laugh. "I didn't tell him Harold was going to be on the first bus back to Hempstead after my coronation. What Harold said about Oz being one heartbeat away from the crown bugs me. I'm wondering if I can change that. I mean, can I name my own heir? As long as it's a woman who's in the line of succession of the Royal family?"

Ralston looks thoughtful for a moment. He sets his nearly-full pail on the ground near his feet. "That's an interesting question. I believe Domerican law allows you to do so. Osrielle is the *heir presumptive.* That would change if, for example, you were to have a daughter. Your daughter would become the *heir apparent,* and Osrielle would be bumped down the line."

"But what if there were some reason Oz was disqualified to serve as queen, or just didn't want to? Could I replace her with someone else?" I ask.

"Whom did you have in mind?"

"Lady Lorelei."

A slow smile creeps across Ralston's face. "That's positively brilliant, Jade. It would remove all reason for Prince Harold to wish you harm. And Lorelei is ideally suited to take over as queen … should you decide not to stay, that is. I shall look into this further and make certain we are on solid ground here." He takes my pail from me and begins filling it with berries.

"So what did Agent Chelmsford say about all this anyway?" I ask.

"I'm afraid he wasn't much help. Come, let's try over there." He nods to a stand of bushes. "I believe I've about cleared these out."

We take the pails a few yards to some nearby bushes. A small wooden bench sits in the shade of a mulberry tree. "Would you care to sit for a moment?" Ralston asks.

I gladly plunk down on the bench. Blueberry picking is a little hot and boring for my taste. I scoop up a handful of berries and munch while he talks.

"Agent Chelmsford informed me that things have not yet stabilized sufficiently since your reappearance for the prediction models to be consistent. He's confident that in a few days' time, once recalibrations are complete, a reliable path will be established. I must tell you, however, that Chelmsford strongly cautioned me that my role this time is to guide and advise you, *only*. I am strictly forbidden to divulge any information about the future derived from IUGA's prediction models."

This makes me sit up and pay attention. "What? Why? That's not fair. I'm going to be making a decision here that will affect the rest of my life, and the lives of my family, and maybe other lives too. How am I supposed to do that without all the relevant information?"

"That's precisely the point," Ralston says. "You are supposed to be operating of your own free will this time. I'm not permitted to influence you in any direction. You will have all the information to which a normal person would have access when making a life decision. Though God knows this situation is far from normal."

"Geeze Rals, that stinks. Things are still so twisted around here. My mom seems strong some days and nearly gone on others. Uncle Harold could either fade quietly into the sunset, or try to blow up the whole show. And I don't know if Ryder is even speaking to me."

"Excuse the cliché, but *that's life*, my dear. You still have a few weeks before you must make your final decision. Perhaps things will be clearer by then."

I've lost my appetite for berries, so I hold out my hand to him.

"Want one?" I ask.

He shakes his head. "No, thank you, they stain my teeth."

I let them fall to the ground. "Okay, but what about that guy who's stalking me. What if he's trying to hurt me or something?"

"Well, of course we'll do our best to protect you and gather all the relevant information we can in the coming days. I simply cannot divulge known future events before they happen. That's all. IUGA will put me on *inactive* or worse. I'm already on a probation of sorts. By the way, I've sent word to the investigator I know in Warrington. We're meeting tomorrow to discuss the troubling rumors regarding Prince Harold and the possibility that you are being followed. At a minimum, I can be of assistance in that way."

I put a hand on his arm. "Thanks Rals. I really need you."

"I'm here for as long as you want me." He smiles. "May I share your bench? I'd like to hear more about your meeting."

"Sure." I scoot over to one side, and Ralston sits while I fill him in on the rest of the Council meeting and Mother's order that all the firearms confiscated from Unicoi be destroyed.

He rubs his chin thoughtfully. "I suppose that's one way of keeping them out of the wrong hands, but should Domerica ever need them …"

"What do you mean?"

"It's nothing, Jade. Have you thought about taking a tour of Unicoi Village?" he asks, changing the subject. "I believe you would do well to familiarize yourself with the current state of affairs there before the next Council meeting. Especially if it's true that Prince Harold is proposing to construct a wall around the entire city."

"I was kind of hoping to go there with Ryder. But that's looking less and less likely. Will you go with me one day next week?"

"Of course. I'd be delighted to escort you." Now, let's finish up here, and take these to Cook. I believe she'll be quite pleased with us.

Maybe even make blueberry pie for dessert tonight."

We finish filling our pails and head back to the carriage. After Patrick helps himself to a couple of handfuls of berries, we start back to the palace. The moment we clear the palace gates, I'm buffeted by a strong wave of emotion—like an ominous wind penetrating to my core.

I whip my head around. "Ryder's here," I tell Ralston.

"How do you know? Do you see his horse?" he asks.

"I feel him, Ralston. I know he's inside."

Ralston snaps the reins, and the horses pick up their pace. He drops me at the front steps. "Run along, my dear. I'll see to the carriage."

I race up the stairs. The huge front door swings open for me, and a uniformed butler bows. "Is Chief Blackthorn here?" I ask breathlessly.

"Yes ma'am. He's meeting with Prince Harold."

"Where?"

"I'm not certain, ma'am. Shall I locate them for you?"

"No. It's all right." I sense he's nearby. Probably in one of the first floor meeting rooms. Dashing down the hallway, I quickly check each room as I go. Voices carry from behind a closed door near the end of the hall. It's them. My pulse skyrockets, and my stomach instantly purees the blueberries I just ate.

Before I can knock, the door opens, and Ryder's form fills up the frame. My breath catches in my throat. He's handsomely dressed in a white shirt and a dark Domerican-style suit. His features are taut, his eyes a turbulent sea. Nodding toward me, he turns back to Uncle Harold. "Thank you for seeing me, sir. I hope you will reconsider postponing the project until all of the Unicoi are out of tents and living in homes."

"Our vision for Unicoi Village will take time, my boy. Ask your people to be patient," Uncle Harold says in a patronizing voice.

Ryder steps into the hallway. "It is difficult to counsel patience without tangible progress," he says.

Uncle Harold glimpses me standing there. "Ah Jaden, you've returned. Chief Blackthorn was just asking for you."

My heart swells with hope. "You were?" I ask Ryder.

"May I have a word?" he says, all business-like.

"Yes, of course."

Uncle Harold checks his watch. "I have another meeting." He bows. "By your leave," he looks to me.

Huh? "Oh, yeah sure. Go ahead." I forgot. He needs my permission.

"Would you like to come upstairs?" I ask Ryder.

"No. This will be fine." He nods toward the room he just came out of. I follow him back inside and close the door.

"Please sit down," I say picking up a weird vibe from him.

"If you don't mind, I would rather stand, Your Highness. This will not require much of your time."

"Ryder, please don't call me that. I want to have a conversation with you. Can't we just sit down and talk."

He shakes his head. "I'm expected back in Unicoi Village. I wish to inform you that I have a meeting with your father at the Enclave tomorrow. I plan to ask him to release me from my obligations under our engagement contract."

"What? Ryder, no! Why are you doing this?" My heart drops halfway to China.

"I feel it is for the best." He avoids my eyes, focusing on a spot above my shoulder. "You have been unable to reconcile in your own heart the ways in which I have failed you. The indecision is harmful to us both. As a result, I must be the one to take a stand." His empty eyes meet mine. "I release you from your commitments to me. You are free to pursue other, more suitable relationships. And I wish to be free to move on as well."

"You what? You want to move on?" I don't recognize my own reedy voice. A dark pit of panic threatens to swallow me up.

"I wish only the best for you, Your Highness." He bows dropping his eyes, and sweeps from the room, leaving me a crumbling, destroyed candidate for life support.

TWENTY-FIVE

*T*he room swims around me. Sinking into the nearest chair, I rest my head on the gleaming conference table. *How did things go downhill so fast?*

Events are careening out of my control. I should've known I couldn't handle it all. It's true I came back to Domerica to be with Ryder and my mother. But, also I believed I could make a difference here. My life in Connecticut seems small and insignificant when compared with the things I can do for Domerica, and possibly this world. Now, unexpectedly, I find myself the lynchpin in a dangerous game of political intrigue, while Mother's time grows shorter with each passing day. And I'm acutely conscious of the fact that it all means nothing without Ryder, the love of my life. *I've messed things up real good this time.*

Closing my eyes, I press my cheek against the cool wood of the table. I'm bone-bending tired and unable to defy gravity any longer. My whole being groans for peace.

Maria's voice travels to me as if through a long tunnel. "Princess, are you all right?" Her hand feels soft and warm on my forehead.

My eyes blink open. "Hi, Maria." For a moment I forget where I am. The light in the meeting room has grown dim. I push myself up from the table, and sick recollection twists my gut. *I've lost him.* I hug myself against the pain.

"What has happened?" Maria asks in alarm. "I went to help you dress for dinner, and no one knew where you were. Are you unwell?"

That's putting it mildly. "Yes. I'm unwell."… *empty, desolate, totally screwed-up. You name it.* "Would you help me to my room, please?"

She takes my arm, and we make our way slowly up the back stairs, my stomach churning acid soup. "Shall I summon a doctor?" Maria asks when we reach my room.

"No. I'm all right. Just very tired." She eases me down on top of my bed. "Tell Mother I've decided to skip dinner tonight. I plan to go to bed early."

"Very well. Shall I have food sent up for you?"

"No. I'm not hungry. I just want to sleep."

"As you wish." When she reaches the door, she turns, concern creasing her forehead. "Is there anything I can do for you, Princess?"

"Yes. Please don't let my mother worry about me. Tell her I'm fine."

She nods. "I will take care of it."

"Thanks."

Okay Jaden, what now?

Standing, I rub my face with my hands, hoping to scrub the chaos from my mind. Shucking off my dress in a heap on the floor, I head for the shower. Maybe gallons of hot water will help. Some of my best ideas come while I'm standing under the shower. After thirty minutes my skin is pruned, and I've used up all the verbena bath gel, but nothing brilliant has come to me.

I wrap up in my bathrobe and run the brush through my hair. My options seem all knotted-up together like a hopeless tangle of fishing line. The easiest thing would be to go back to Connecticut, graduate from high school, start Yale in the fall, and forget all about

172

this insane little side trip. But I can't do that until I've said my final goodbyes to Mother, and made sure Uncle Harold isn't going to run Domerica into the ground. Also, I promised Asher that I'd travel with him to meet the other Transcenders. I know I'll regret it *for a second time* if I go home without doing that. The only thing I know for sure right now is that I can't sit around and do nothing. I need a plan.

Ralston taps softly at my door. "Jaden?"

"It's open," I call.

"We missed you at dinner. Are you ill, my dear?"

"No, just having a mini melt-down. Close the door."

"What's happened?"

"Ryder broke off our engagement." A sob involuntarily escapes my throat.

"I'm so sorry." Ralston moves closer and places a comforting arm around me. I rest my head on his shoulder. He smells nice, like cologne and wine. We walk to the arm chairs in front of the fireplace, and I lower myself into one of them. He takes the other.

"It's my own fault," I sniffle.

"Was it because he found you kissing Asher?"

"I don't think so. He said it was because I couldn't make up my mind about him, so he was going to do it for me. That way we could both move on. He's going to see Father in the morning to ask to be released from the engagement contract."

Ralston straightens up and smiles. "Well then, it's not too late."

"What do you mean?" I ask, irked by his smile.

"Did you tell him you *had* made up your mind? Did you tell him you love him and still wish to marry him?"

I shake my head. "No. I didn't dare. He was so cold and distant and eager to get away."

"But Jade, certainly he still loves you."

"How could he? I've been so mean to him."

"I believe he simply needs you to tell him how you feel. I know you're frightened, but you must let him know before his meeting with your father."

"How do I do that?"

"Send him a message. Ask him to meet with you before he departs for the Enclave. Tell him you will go to him."

"To Unicoi Village?"

"Yes."

Chewing on my lip for a second, I mull this over. "But, it's so late now. The messenger won't get there until midnight."

He just stares at me like, *And your point is?*

"Okay, you're right. I need to give it a shot, at least. All he can do is reject me and make me feel lower than pond scum. But, it's worth the risk. He's worth it."

"That's the spirit, old girl. You begin composing your note, and I'll send a messenger to your room." He heads for the door. "I'll be happy to accompany you in the morning if you like."

"Thanks, Rals. That'd be great." I give him a quick hug. "Do you really think it'll work?" A surge of lightness fills my heart.

"I'm certain of it."

I open my desk, fish out some stationery, and begin to compose my thoughts. *Dear Ryder...*

Staring at the page for a moment I realize I don't want to wait until morning. I want to see him now, and make him understand how I feel. Stupid, insignificant things have kept us apart too long. I need his arms around me tonight.

Unicoi Village isn't that far. Gabriel can get me there quickly, but I'll have to take Patrick with me, unless … I can sneak out by myself. I crumple up the note and chuck it into the trash basket. Slipping out of the palace will be a cinch, and sneaking Gabriel out of the stable without getting caught is probably doable, but there's no way to get past the guards at the entrance gate. Therein lies the problem.

I'll just have to figure it out as I go. Dark clothing is a good place to start. After dressing in a black sweater and pants and black leather boots, I weave my hair into a braid, and search for something to put over my head. The princess's hats are all wide brimmed and girly, so I dig around for a dark scarf. I'm interrupted by a tapping on my door. The messenger Ralston sent, no doubt.

When I see the kid standing there in his distinctive crimson messenger coat and gold sash, I know my problems are solved. Instead of sending him away, as I'd intended to do, I wave him inside the door.

"Wait there a minute," I say.

He goggles my room with open curiosity.

Hurrying to my jewelry chest, I flip the dials to the correct combination and rummage through the small drawers until I find what I'm looking for. Extracting a small brown leather pouch from a drawer, I toss it to the messenger. "There's twenty gold pieces in there," I tell him. "I want your uniform."

He looks young, around sixteen or so—cute in a sunny, freshly-scrubbed kind of way. "Wha—? You want my what?" he asks.

"Your messenger uniform. Take it off."

He's completely mystified. "But you're the princess. You can have all the uniforms you want. They belong to you."

"Yes, but I want *yours*, and I'm willing to pay you handsomely for it. Just your jacket and cap. You can keep your pants on."

He looks scandalized now. "What are you going to do with them?"

"That's not really your concern."

"But I could lose my job." On that last word, his voice squeaks in that not-yet-a-man way.

Stepping closer, I lock eyes with him. "If someone should inadvertently discover the favor you've done for me, you will *not* lose your job. You have my word. But, if you tell anyone about this, I'll hang you up by your balls. Understand?"

He nods and begins unbuttoning his jacket. Once I have what I need from him, I shoo him out the door in his undershirt and slip into the high-collared jacket. Not a bad fit. Using hairpins to secure my braid on top of my head, I pull the cap down so the brim covers my eyebrows and shadows my eyes. Only a small portion of my face is now visible. This should work.

My katana in its bright red saya will definitely draw some unwanted attention, however, so I locate the wooden box it originally came in, and tuck the sword neatly inside. Perfect. It looks like a package I'm delivering.

Skulking down the back stairway, I duck out the door to the tranquility garden and steal around the kitchen, making my way across the cobblestones to the stables. The main door stands wide open, a yellow wedge of light shining out into the courtyard. No Royal Guards are stationed at the stables at this hour, but stable hands are on duty around the clock caring for the animals. I creep to the side of the door and sneak a look inside. A small table and chairs are located to the right of the entrance in front of a faux fireplace. Three stable hands sit drinking, laughing, and playing cards. *Crap!* Gabriel is housed in a stall to the rear. Even though they're preoccupied and probably half-drunk, there's no chance of slipping by the men without being noticed.

A smaller door made for humans is located at the rear of the stables. It may be possible to slip Gabriel out that way. Crouching low, I steal around to the back. Three steps lead up to the door. Gabriel may balk at these, but it's my only hope. Placing my sword box on the ground, I slowly open the door, praying the hinges have been oiled recently. Success!

Quickly, I make my way to Gabriel's stall. He turns his huge brown eyes on me as I open his gate. Patting his rump reassuringly, I grab his bridle from the wall peg and gingerly slip it over his head. The princess's saddle is elaborate and easily recognizable, so I slowly back Gabriel out of the stall and snag one of the stable saddles and blankets from a sawhorse, propping it over my shoulder.

I back through the door, leading Gabriel. He doesn't even blink at the steps, navigating them easily. Once outside, I secure the saddle on him, hoist myself up, and lay the box across my lap. We move slowly and quietly until we're near the palace gates. It's important we get past the guards as quickly as possible, so I urge Gabriel into a canter, waving as we approach. The guards open the gates for me.

"Where're you headed in such a hurry?" one of them shouts.

"Package for Chief Blackthorn," I call in the huskiest voice I can muster, pointing to the box on my lap and not waiting for a reply. My whole body trembles, but I don't detect the sound of horse's hooves behind me, so I guess we pulled it off. *Whew.*

I push Gabriel into a gallop for several yards, and then slow back down to a comfortable canter. The palace lights soon fade into the distance, and the road becomes dark—densely, treacherously dark. No twinkle of a star or sliver of a moon to help light the way. We slow to a trot, and I hope Gabriel's super night vision will help us keep to the path. If we stay on this road, it will eventually take us to Unicoi Village.

We ride for miles in the inky blackness without so much as a glimmer of illumination from a carriage or farm house. The eerie darkness begins to seriously creep me out. Every noise makes me jump, and I repeatedly peer over my shoulder thinking my stalker is right behind us, even though I couldn't see him if he was. *I must've been crazy to head out alone in the middle of the night.* All kinds of highwaymen and livestock thieves roam this road at night. Opening the box on my lap, I draw out my katana, and allow the box to fall by the wayside. Gabriel startles momentarily as it thuds to the ground. We're both on edge.

He snorts and pulls at the reins, asking to go faster, and I let him. I trust Gabriel. He'll get us there safely. Wedging the sword into my saddle scabbard, I lean into him. We settle into a nice loping pace, more confident with each mile. Dim lights from a farm barracks flicker in the distance, telling me we're getting closer to Unicoi Village. It should be only about five miles from this point. Of course that raises the question of what to do once I get there. I don't have the foggiest idea where Ryder lives. If there's a central tribal hall, he's probably there. If not, I'll have to improvise.

We gallop along until we reach the turnoff for the road to Unicoi. It's a smaller, ruttier path than the one we're on, but the lights make it less daunting. As we near the village, two Unicoi warriors unexpectedly step into the roadway, shining a light on us and causing Gabriel to rear up.

"State your name and your business," one of them says.

I manage to stay on Gabe's back. "I have a message for Chief Blackthorn," I say, catching my breath.

"What kind of message?" one of them asks.

"It's from Princess Jaden."

"We will take it to Chief Blackthorn. Give the message to me." One of the warriors approaches me.

"Oh hell, I *am* Princess Jaden," I say pulling off my cap and unpinning my braid. "I need to see Ryder. It's important."

They look at each other like *what the*—? They both bow awkwardly and fade back, allowing me to pass. I'm not going to push my luck by asking them where Ryder lives. Someone in town should be able to tell me.

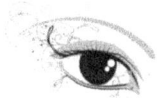

TWENTY-SIX

*G*abriel and I trot into the village square. Everything is closed up tight. I follow the glow from some lighted windows to the end of the main road. The windows belong to a bar with a number of patrons inside. This looks like my best bet.

I tie Gabriel to a hitching post and secure my katana in my belt. My bizarre getup is likely to cause a few raised eyebrows, but it's gotten me this far. Every head in the place turns to gape at me when I walk through the door. Three things become immediately apparent: one, I'm the only woman in the bar; two, I'm the only person under about six-foot-three and two hundred pounds (Unicoi tend to be large); and three, the bartender and I are the only ones who don't look totally wasted. My knees wobble a little as I sidle up to the bar.

The beanpole behind the counter has a shock of sable hair and eyes like warm chocolate sauce. "May I help you, ma'am?" he asks, pausing in his efforts to dry off a beer glass.

"Yes. I'm looking for Chief Blackthorn," I say managing a weak smile. "Can you tell me where he lives?"

"Yes ma'am. Why don't I take you there?" he says, untying his soiled apron. I don't know if I'm relieved or troubled by his offer. The idea of going off with a stranger in the middle of the night is a little frightening, but it's probably better than being out there all alone. In any case, I don't have a chance to make up my mind, because he tosses his apron on the bar and takes my elbow, hastily shuffling me outside.

"If you don't mind my asking, Princess, what are you doing here so late, alone, and dressed like a messenger?" he asks, his tone respectful.

"You know who I am?"

"Yes. I thought it best to get you out of there before others recognized you as well. Some of them revere you as a hero—a savior. But others do not appreciate the politics of your mother and your uncle. Better not to call the question.

"Thank you. I guess I didn't think this through very well. It's important I see Ryder tonight. It's ... personal."

We walk about two blocks to a large wooden house situated at the end of a street. "This is the temporary quarters for Chief Blackthorn and his family until the new Sequoya Hall is completed."

A dim glow emanates from behind the curtains of a first floor window, so I assume someone is awake.

"Thank you again, I say. What is your name?"

"My name is Ellijay. My friends call me Eli. Would you like me to wait until you are inside?"

"No. I'll be fine, Ellijay. You'd best get back to your kegs. Those guys looked pretty thirsty."

He bows his head and jogs back toward the bar.

Taking the steps to the front door, I rap gently. Nothing stirs inside, and no one comes to answer, so I knock again louder. After a moment the door is flung open by Ryder's larger-than-life sister, Catherine, one hand on her hip, ready to pounce on whoever is calling so late. After a split-second she recognizes me, and the annoyed expression on her face transforms into one of sheer hostility. "What are you doing here?" she demands.

"I need to see Ryder. Is he here?" I ask.

"No he is not. Haven't you done enough damage already? Or do you take pleasure in torturing him. You are not welcome here. Leave now, and stay away from my brother." I can almost see smoke curling from her ears.

"I need to speak with him," I say, staring death rays at her. It will take more than this angry Amazon to chase me away. "And I don't mind waking up the entire village to find him if I have to. Now, are you going to tell me where he is or not?"

"I'm here."

Peering over Catherine's shoulder, I make out Ryder's form in the shadow of a doorway at the opposite end of the room. He's shirtless, disheveled, and magnificent.

I push past Catherine and run to him, throwing my arms around him, tears streaming from my eyes. "Ryder. I'm sorry for everything. I love you. Please don't leave me. Please," I beg, a trembling mass of goo.

For a moment there's nothing from him ... no reaction. But then he gathers me up in his arms and holds me closely. "Jade," he whispers into my hair, "you've come back to me."

I kiss his hair, his eyes, his cheeks, and finally his mouth. Catherine groans loudly and storms outside, slamming the door behind her. Who gives a flying flip? All I care about is being in Ryder's arms and making things right.

He carries me to his room and gently lays me across his bed. The covers are a jumbled mess, and they smell wonderfully like Ryder. Climbing up beside me, he wraps his arms around me while I cry into his bare chest. "Shh," he says, stroking my hair.

The warm and gentle electric current that always connects us calms me, and my sobs quickly subside. "Do you still love me?" I ask searching his eyes. "Are we going to be all right?"

"I shall always love you, no matter what. But *you* must tell *me* if we're going to be all right. Have you forgiven me?" he asks.

"There's nothing to forgive. You thought I was dead. We never have to see Erica or speak her name again."

"And you are not in love with this Asher Steele?"

"No. Ryder, I told you we're friends. That's all."

He takes my face in his hands. "Do you still wish to marry me?"

"Yes. Let's do it now. Tonight. I'm ready."

He smiles. "I think your mother would have my scalp if we married tonight. But I agree. Let us arrange it as quickly as possible. I do not wish to spend another minute away from you."

"You'll never have to," I say, a leftover tear slipping down my cheek.

Ryder dries it with his thumb and sweetly presses his lips to mine. My whole body shudders with relief and joy and passion. His arms pull me in closer, his luscious mouth devours my own. Our legs twine together, and he places a hand on my lower back bringing me closer still. All thought evaporates from my brain. My body throbs hungrily for him. I run my hands along the silken skin of his back, and he moans softly, thrilling me to my core.

Pulling away slightly, his fingers find the buttons of my crimson messenger coat. I quickly wriggle out of it and tug off my sweater. Another tantalizing kiss is my reward. Moving to the edge of the bed, he slides my riding boots off, one at a time and gently unfastens my sword, letting it fall to the floor. Then he settles in beside me again, brushing his fingertips along my bare arm. My skin tingles at his touch, my heart thunders in my chest. Cradling the wolf-head pendant at my breast, he says, "You still wear it."

"Always."

His hand trails lightly down my abdomen to the top of my waistband. My belly quivers at his whisper soft touch. *At last. Our time has come at last.* I inhale sharply, and …

W*ham, wham, wham!* Someone pounds on Ryder's door.

I squeeze my eyes shut. *No freakin' way this is happening again.*

"Princess Jaden! Princess, are you all right?" a man shouts.

The door crashes open and in rushes Patrick, dark eyes blazing, hand on the hilt of his sword. When he sees Ryder and me half-dressed on the bed, his face turns a deeper shade of coffee, and he drops his eyes, bowing low.

"Patrick, what the hell are you doing?" I say.

"I beg your pardon, Your Highness. I saw a woman flee the house. I feared for your safety. I humbly apologize. I shall wait outside." He quickly backs out the door, head bowed, eyes glued to the floor.

Ryder and I look at each other like *did that really just happen?* Then we both burst out laughing.

Putting a hand to my forehead, I say, "Oh man, I'm so sorry. I had no idea he was following me. Guess I'd better make sure everything is all right."

Ryder stands and takes my hands, pulling me from the bed. I wrap my arms around his waist.

"We shall have our night soon," he says still grinning.

"God, I hope so."

Retrieving my sweater and boots, I sit on the edge of the bed and put them back on. Ryder slips into a shirt and tugs on his own boots.

"I'll ride with you to Warrington Palace," he says.

"You don't need to do that." I stand and smooth my messy hair with my hands.

He tucks a loose strand behind my ear and kisses me sweetly. "Yes. I do."

We find Patrick waiting outside. He has Gabriel with him. "I apologize again, Your Highness," he says. "I did not realize this was Chief Blackthorn's house."

"It's all right Patrick. What are you doing here? How did you find me?"

"I check on your horse each night, and when I discovered him gone, I tracked you here."

"You check on my horse?"

"Yes, and the Skorplings."

"But why?"

"They are yours, and I am in service to you. I protect you and yours."

This surprises and touches me. "That's pretty good tracking in the dark," I say. "You must be part Unicoi."

He smiles. "My mother was half Unicoi, but it was not difficult. I believe this is yours." He holds out the box for my katana which I discarded along the roadside.

"Oh yeah, thanks. I was in a hurry."

Patrick clears his throat and lowers his eyes. "Again, I apologize for interrupting you," he murmurs.

Now I'm blushing. *Geeze, that's not what I meant.*

Ryder attempts to stifle a grin. "Excuse me for a moment. I will get my horse," he says, placing a hand on my shoulder. "Will you ride with me?"

"Yes," I readily agree. The first day Ryder and I met, we shared an incredibly sexy horseback ride together—even though he was trying to kidnap me, and I was terrified of him. Riding home with him in the dark sounds deliciously inviting.

The trip to the palace goes much too quickly. Being back with Ryder is so awesome that the rest of my problems don't seem insurmountable anymore. I'm not willing to let him go just yet. "Walk me to my room?" I ask when we reach the stables.

Ryder glances at Patrick, who is busying himself with the horses. "I will see you safely upstairs, but then I must get back to the village. Nobody knows where I am."

We tread softly on the steps. It's nearly three a.m., and the palace is hushed and still. Ryder stops at my threshold to kiss me goodnight, but I pull him inside. "Stay with me for a while," I say.

"I shouldn't, Jade. It will appear as if I spent the night in your room."

"I don't care."

"I believe your mother would. I know you do not wish to upset her."

Crap. "All right, but at least wait while I change, so you can tuck me into bed."

He smiles. "I will gladly tuck you into bed, love."

I hurry to my closet. I've given up wearing the princess's old-fashioned, long nightgowns in favor of her silky underdresses. Slipping on an ice-blue one, I throw a shawl around my shoulders for warmth. Ryder is sitting in a chair by the fake fireplace waiting patiently. I crawl into his lap and lay my head on his shoulder.

"I'm so happy," I say. I can't remember the last time I felt this kind of peace.

"As am I." He kisses my hair.

"Maybe I'll sleep tonight. I haven't really slept since that first day when we argued."

"Neither have I. Most nights I end up at the lake."

"Wait, you mean our lake?"

"Yes."

"That's so sweet." I nestle deeper into his chest, and thankfully he doesn't stir. We sit and stare at the twinkling crystal logs, lost in a shared reverie.

I'm awakened by someone rapping on my door. The silver-pink glow of the room tells me it's early dawn. I climb gingerly from Ryder's lap. Despite my best efforts, my stirring wakes him. He rubs the sleep from his eyes. I open the door a crack and peer out at Ralston, a look of impatience on his face.

"Jade, you're not ready. Are we not traveling to Unicoi Village this morning?"

Swinging the door wide, I wave him inside. He catches sight of Ryder in the chair. "Oh, well, I see there is no need. Good morning, Ryder." He looks at me questioningly.

"Sorry, Rals. I decided I couldn't wait. I went to Unicoi last night."

"You did what? Alone?" His expression is horrified.

"Well, I was alone at first, but Patrick found me."

"Good heavens, Jaden. Must I camp outside your door to prevent you from acting so impetuously?" He takes the chair next to Ryder's. "I hope you'll have better luck than I have getting her to act responsibly, my boy."

Ryder laughs. "I don't believe that is very likely." He rises from his chair. "I must be going. We arrived quite late. I'm afraid we fell asleep. I do not wish for this to reflect badly upon Jaden."

Ralston stands also. "I'll walk with you to the stables. Perhaps that will deflect some of the gossip."

Ryder lifts my hand and presses his lips to the inside of my palm.

Raising his eyes to mine, he says, "May I call on you this afternoon?"

"Yes," I say brightly. "And please plan on staying for dinner. Mother has been clamoring for your presence."

"I shall. I believe we have a wedding to plan."

The thought makes me shiver all the way to my toes. "That we do. See you this afternoon."

Once they've gone, I climb in between my acres of cool sheets and drift into a peaceful slumber.

TWENTY-SEVEN

I'm having a lovely dream about Ryder and the lake when I'm shaken awake by Maria, a stricken look on her face. "Princess, are the Skorplings with you?"

"Huh? The Skorplings? No."

"Do you know where they are?"

I bolt upright. "What do you mean? Are they missing?"

"Someone left the door to the nursery open, and they are nowhere to be found. We have searched the entire first floor of the palace. I was reluctant to disturb you, but I thought they might be with you."

I throw off my covers. "Who saw them last? We need to search the rest of the palace. Has anyone checked the kitchen?"

"We have checked the kitchen. I took them their dinner around eight o'clock last night and put them to bed afterward. But, I swear I closed the door behind me."

"I'm sure you did, Maria. Someone else must have gone in there. Get Patrick for me. He checks on them sometimes. Maybe he saw them."

Dashing to the closet, I throw on pants and a sweater. I rinse off my face and finger comb the tangles from my hair. Nothing like a swift kick of adrenaline to get you going in the morning. *Where could Fred and Ethel be?*

The sizeable search party is made up of servants and some Royal Guardsmen. I join the group on the palace's upper floors, which contain mostly offices and storage space with doors that are closed and locked at night. Each door is unlocked, and each room thoroughly scoured, but to no avail.

After two hours of hunting, we all reconvene on the first floor to report our findings. No trace of Fred or Ethel has been found outside the nursery. Two windows on the second floor stairwell landings had been propped open for air circulation. It's possible they escaped through one of those. We divide into two groups to search the palace grounds. It's agreed that Patrick and I, along with some Royal Guardsmen, will search on horseback, combing the trees and bushes calling for them. Ralston and a contingent of servants will cover the stables, barns, and other outbuildings. I stop at the kitchen on my way out and pick up a few of Fred's favorite muffins in case I need to entice them out of a tree.

The search is long and fruitless. We return to the palace around noon, hungry, exhausted, and downtrodden. Cook has laid out a buffet of crusty rolls, sliced meats, and fresh salads, along with icy pitchers of tea and lemonade. I know by her worried eyes that the old softy is distraught over the Skorplings' disappearance, even though she constantly threatens to make Skorpling stew out of them.

Ralston, Patrick, and I heap our plates high with food from the long tables in the kitchen courtyard, and wander over to eat at a table under the trees. The courtyard is crowded not only with searchers but also with the workers assigned the task of destroying the Unicoi firearms. While we were searching, they were breaking down guns and rifles, saving the metal for scrap and sending the wood to be incinerated in the foundry ovens.

"What do we do now, Rals? Do you think we can get any help from, you know, the agency." I cut my eyes to Patrick who is concentrating on shoveling food in his mouth. I'm really not supposed to talk about IUGA in front of anyone. Nobody other than Asher and the Cleadians know that Ralston works for them.

He shakes his head. "I'm afraid not. At any rate, they probably do not have such information. Perhaps Ryder would lend us some Unicoi trackers."

"That's a good idea. I'll send word to him." I nibble at some potato salad. It's exceptionally good, but my mind is elsewhere. "Something's been bothering me all day," I say. "It just doesn't feel right—Fred and Ethel wandering off like that. Am I being paranoid, or is it possible they were stolen or deliberately set free?" In the deepest darkest corner of my mind, I'm suspicious of Uncle Harold and his henchmen.

Patrick stops chewing and looks over at me. "If I may, Princess, I've been wondering the same. I was not here to check on them last night. Perhaps someone took advantage of that."

Ralston opens his mouth to say something, but before he can speak, Osrielle bursts into the courtyard, tears cascading down her face. Her crinoline-lined skirts billow out behind her. She hurries to me and throws her arms around my neck. "Oh, Cousin, it is so terrible. Where could Fred and Ethel have gone? Do you think they'll come back?"

I wrap my arms around her. "I don't know, Ozzie. I hope so." She sobs uncontrollably in my arms. "Sweetie, I'm sure they're fine. Is something else wrong?" I hold her at arm's length, searching her face.

"They were my only friends. I just want to go home, Jaden. I miss my mother so much. I hate it here. I want to go back to the farm."

"Have you spoken with your father about this?"

"Yes." She sniffles, wiping her nose with her hand. "He says we can't leave because we have important business here, and I might be queen someday. But I don't want to be queen *ever*." Her voice is loud and shrill. Several others in the courtyard swivel around to look at her.

"Oz, have you told your mother you want to come home?"

"Father won't allow me to write to her. He says she'll have to come here if she wants to see me. But I miss her. Please, Cousin, talk to Father for me. Please tell him to send me home. He'll have to obey you."

Her misery is palpable as I hold her close, peering helplessly over her shoulder at Ralston. He tilts his head toward the kitchen door. Uncle Harold strides toward us, his face tense.

"There you are, Osrielle. What is all this?" he says.

Oz pulls away from my embrace, wiping her tears with her fingers. She stares at the ground. "I miss Fred and Ethel," she says in a small voice.

"Please pardon the interruption, Princess. Has the search turned up anything promising?" Uncle Harold asks.

"Not really," I say, weighing whether or not to mention Oz's outburst. I decide this is not the best place to question him about her unhappiness. "We're calling in some Unicoi trackers this afternoon, though. If anyone can find them, they can."

Uncle Harold lifts his pale eyebrows. Do I see a flicker of concern in his eyes, or is it just my imagination? "Ah, trackers. Excellent," he says. "Although, it's been hours since the Skorplings escaped. I'm not certain there is much left to discover."

I half-smile at him. "You'd be surprised at what they can find. They're pretty remarkable."

"Yes well, Jaden, I wonder if I might have a word with you at some point this afternoon? I realize it is the Sabbath, and normally I would not ask you to break it, but there is a minor point of business which requires some attention before morning. May I impose upon you at your convenience?"

"Yes, sure. I have a few things to do after lunch, but I could meet with you at three."

"Wonderful. Shall we say my office at three o'clock?"

"Actually, let's meet in Mother's office." I want him on my turf.

"Certainly. Thank you." He turns to his daughter. "Osrielle, come now. Let us allow the princess to eat in peace." He bows and takes Osrielle's hand leading her back toward the kitchen door.

"Bye, Oz," I call. She gives a small wave of her hand.

I catch Ralston's eye. "Are you believing all that?"

"Poor child," he says. "I fear her father's ambitions are causing her great unhappiness. I can only imagine what her mother must be going through."

"Aunt Judith wouldn't allow Oz to stay if she knew how miserable she is. I'm sure of it. I'll mention it to Mother. In the meantime, I wonder what Harold wants to see me about."

"One can only imagine," Ralston says, lifting his eyes skyward. "But do not feel pressured into anything, my dear. If you are uncomfortable with the subject matter, simply tell him you will take the matter under advisement. If he tries to pressure you, just dismiss him."

"Good advice, Rals. Thanks. I think I'll clean up and get that message off to Ryder." I hoist myself up from the table. Patrick and Ralston immediately rise. "Sit, sit," I say and head off to my room.

Dashing off a quick note to Ryder, I explain that the Skorplings have gone missing and ask if he can spare one or two trackers to help with the search. Adding a line about how much I'm looking forward to seeing him this afternoon, I'm tempted to write "xoxo," but I don't think he'd get it, so I just say *Love, Jaden*. I instruct the messenger to make certain Chief Blackthorn receives it as soon as possible.

A long luxurious bath pushes my worries about the Skorplings temporarily out of my mind. Ryder will be here in a few short hours, and nothing can dampen my happiness tonight. We're back together again, and as unbelievable as it seems, soon we'll be married. *That's so weird.* We'll live together and sleep in the same bed every night. I suppose he'll move into my room.

I try to imagine what it will be like sharing a room with him—his clothes scattered among mine; his hairbrush in my bathroom. It's over-the-top incredible. I can't stop a silly grin from spreading across my face. Holding my breath, I sink beneath the water and giggle for joy.

Dressing for dinner tonight may be a little tricky, I realize as I dry off and slip into my robe. I want to look hot enough to take Ryder's breath away. But, I also want to look kick-ass regal and commanding so Uncle Harold will know he's not dealing with a push-over. I gaze at the selection of dresses in my closet trying to channel Coco Chanel, but after twenty minutes or so, I'm forced to throw up my arms in defeat. This is way beyond my set of fashion skills. I open the door to the hallway, and a butler magically appears.

"May I help you, ma'am?"

"Yes. Find Maria for me, please."

Maria arrives still flustered and apologetic about the Skorplings' disappearance. I assure her that no one blames her and that everything is being done to locate them.

"Maria, I've got a more immediate problem. I could use your help."

Once I explain that Ryder is coming to dinner and I need to look gorgeous, but I also have a meeting with Uncle Harold so I have to look imperious, Maria kicks into full fashionista mode. She shuffles through the princess's things and zeros in on an elegant black floor-length gown with a beaded halter neckline, cut-in shoulders, and a V'd back. The silhouette is mermaid-style, fitted through the body, flared from the knees down.

She unzips it and holds it up while I step in. It looks killer, but a little too sexy for my meeting with Harold, until Maria shows me the short jacket that goes with it.

"This is perfect," I say. "Now what do I do with my hair and jewelry?"

She studies me for a moment. "With that dress, you should wear your hair up and show off your beautiful arms and back for Chief Blackthorn."

Maria coaxes my hair into a sleek up-do held together with pretty beaded combs. She selects a pair of diamond studs from the open jewelry chest and places them in my pierced ears.

"There. You need no other jewelry. You may wish to remove that bracelet," she says referring to the TPD. "It's a little heavy."

"Nope. Can't do it, but I think it looks all right."

She smiles. "You are stunning. Neither gentleman will be able to resist your charms."

"Thanks for always making me look good," I say pulling on the short jacket. She closes up the jewelry chest, and I follow her out the door.

I stop by to see Mother before my meeting with Uncle Harold, but she's not in her room. I'm pleasantly surprised to find her having tea and playing chess with General LeGare in one of the downstairs parlors. Watching them from the doorway, the moment is bittersweet. Mother laughs at something LeGare says. She looks young and carefree; her hair falls girlishly around her shoulders, a slice of silvery light from the window illuminates her face.

I wonder how things might have been different if she and Father had divorced and she had remarried LeGare. My heart aches knowing that she may have sacrificed her own happiness for the welfare of the country. I hope I'm never called upon to do the same.

"Who's winning?" I ask stepping inside. General LeGare pops up from his seat and bows. "How are you, Charles?" I ask.

"Very well, Your Highness."

"Jaden. Come in darling."

"Hello Mother. You're looking well today." I kiss her on the forehead. "Please sit, Charles. I didn't mean to interrupt your game. I went to check on you in your room, Mother. I'm happy to see you're up and about."

"I'm feeling much better today. Sit down and visit with us," Mother says. "You look lovely. Where are you going?"

"Nowhere. I just dressed early for dinner because I have a meeting with Uncle Harold. Is it all right if we use your office?"

"Of course, dear. You may use it as you see fit. I haven't been in there for days. What is your meeting concerning?"

"I don't really know. Harold said there were a few items of business that needed to be dealt with before morning."

Her brow creases slightly, and she looks to LeGare. "Charles, do you know what might be so pressing?"

"I'm not certain. Perhaps it has to do with the Unicoi Village wall. I understand he has several work crews on stand-by for the project."

"But that hasn't been approved by the Council. I deferred it until the next meeting," Mother says. "I'm not certain it's a wise undertaking, in any event. We haven't heard all the particulars yet."

"It's possible Prince Harold hopes to bypass Council approval, by getting Princess Jaden's consent to the project," LeGare says. "As your representative, she has the authority to sanction such a plan."

"But that is completely inappropriate. The Council will be up in arms if the matter is handled behind their backs. Perhaps, I'd better attend this meeting with Harold as well," she says to me, clearly agitated.

"No, Mother." I smile and attempt to reassure her. "In the first place, we don't even know if that's what he wants to talk about. Second, please trust me to use good judgment on this. I'd never agree to something like that without talking it over with you. I get how important it is that the Council knows I'm carrying out your policies, not making backroom deals with Uncle Harold."

She relaxes back in her chair and beams proudly at me. It's a little embarrassing. "Jaden, of course you're capable of exercising impeccable judgment in these matters. At times I forget that not only are you a grown woman, but you are strong, intelligent, and gifted. I became queen when I was only two years older than you are. Please forgive me if, after all this time, I have difficulty letting go."

I kneel at the side of her chair and take her hand. "Thank you for trusting me, Mother. I won't disappoint you. Now finish your game. I'll see you both at dinner."

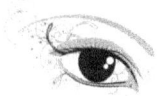

TWENTY-EIGHT

Arriving at Mother's office a few minutes before three, I turn on the lamps and clear a space on her desk. Then I sit back in her chair, like I own the place, and wait for Uncle Harold.

He shows up promptly at three o'clock, all smiles and charm. Planting a warm kiss on my cheek, he says, "You look enchanting my dear."

"Thanks, Uncle Harold. Sit down." He eases himself into one of the green leather chairs facing the desk and hands me a red box tied with a white ribbon. "This is just a small pre-wedding gift," he says.

"Oh, thanks." I set the box on the desk. "Harold, Oz seemed very unhappy this afternoon. She says she misses her mother terribly and wants to go home. I think you should consider taking her back to live on the farm."

He smiles indulgently. "Thank you for expressing an interest in her welfare, Jaden. She was merely having a small bout of homesickness, triggered by the Skorplings' disappearance. She loves it here at the palace, with all her new clothes, and I've recently acquired a new pony for her. Don't tell her, though, it's a surprise. In any event, I certainly would never consider leaving my sister at such a delicate time." His expression changes to one of concern and sadness.

"That's understandable," I say. Sliding the gift box over, I tug off the satin ribbon and remove the lid. Inside is a statuette of a black stallion carved out of onyx. It looks remarkably like Gabriel. "Wow. This is amazing. It's identical to my horse. Where did you find it?"

"I commissioned it last week. I know how much that horse means to you. I am gratified that you are pleased."

"Thank you so much. It's exquisite. Is this why you wanted to see me?"

"Yes. It's one of the reasons." He reaches inside his jacket pocket and extracts a sheaf of papers. "Also, as I mentioned earlier, there is a small matter of business which must be attended to before morning. This was supposed to have been settled at the Council meeting, but things have gotten a bit backlogged with Eleanor's illness. It's a mere formality really. If you will sign these papers as the queen's representative, we can move forward with the project on schedule. We have work crews standing by." He unfolds the papers and places the last page on the desk in front of me.

Removing a pen from his other pocket, he taps the point on a signature line. "Just sign here," he says, holding out the pen for me.

"What is this, Uncle Harold? What am I signing?"

"This is the work order for a project relating to the completion of Unicoi Village that has been pending for some time now. You may not know it, but many of those unfortunate people are still living inside tents. The conditions are far from optimal. Any means we can employ to hasten the completion of the village will greatly benefit the Unicoi people."

"That sounds reasonable," I say. "So this project is for building homes? What will the workers begin construction on tomorrow?"

"Actually, this project relates to security measures for the village. To insure the safety of the inhabitants."

"Security?" I have to admire his creativity. "Like a fence?"

Uncle Harold's face turns a rosy shade, and moisture collects on his upper lip. "Yes. That's it, precisely. A security fence."

"You want to build a fence around the entire Unicoi Village?"

"That is the plan. Yes."

"And this is a good idea because ...?"

He leans back in his chair and crosses his hands over his stout and finely-clad belly. For a moment he looks at the ceiling as if composing his thoughts, then he turns his gaze to me. "Princess Jaden," he begins in an annoyingly condescending voice. "I know you were largely instrumental in bringing the Unicoi people to Domerica, and for that I commend you. There are, however, many issues which arise when attempting to assimilate a foreign race into an already established culture. If caution is not exercised, mayhem may result. The wall is designed to minimize any conflicts which may arise should the Unicoi attempt to undermine our current governmental structure."

"What kind of conflicts are those?"

His brow rises in surprise. "I could provide many examples. Unicoi might attempt to secure governmental positions or other jobs that rightfully should go to Domericans. They could attempt to move out into Domerican neighborhoods and send their children to Domerican schools."

"And they would probably try to marry Domericans and have children with them?" I say.

"Exactly."

"Have you forgotten that I'm engaged to Chief Blackthorn?"

"Of course not, but that's different. You are royalty. It's a political alliance. I'm simply attempting to protect the welfare of our own people, Queen Eleanor's subjects."

The blood simmers in my veins, but I stay chill like Ralston advised. "I believe Queen Eleanor considers *all* of the people to be her subjects. Domerican and Unicoi alike. What do the Unicoi think about the idea of building this wall?"

He pats the shiny bare patch at the back of his head, "I'm not privy to Unicoi sentiments regarding the wall. I have not asked them, nor do I intend to. Yesterday Chief Blackthorn expressed his opposition to the project, due mainly to his concern that lumber and workers would be diverted from the construction of new housing. I assured him that both projects will proceed simultaneously. There is plenty of lumber to go around. I realize he is your fiancé, but I do not see that as a valid reason to postpone things."

He leans across the desk and points a stubby finger at me. "This is your first real test Princess, as heir to the throne and successor to your mother. A leader must make decisions for the good of the realm, without regard to emotion or personal relationships. You've the authority to sign these papers as the queen's representative. I suggest you do so at once so that we may move on this project without delay."

"May I have a look at those papers?" I ask, attempting to keep my voice and face as emotionless as possible.

"Certainly." He passes the packet to me. I gather the papers and the signature page, folding them together carefully. Opening the top drawer of Mother's desk, I place them inside. "This is a matter for the Council to consider. I will not circumvent their authority by signing the documents tonight. What I will do is call for a special Council meeting to discuss the issue. The decision of the Council will be final. Thank you for your time."

He blinks. "Are you dismissing me?"

"Yes."

He rises. "I see. Very well." He edges to the door, but turns before opening it. "Princess, allow me to point out that what happened with the Skorplings today was a direct result of your failure to heed my advice," he says in a low, menacing tone. "I suggest you carefully contemplate my recommendation on this matter. I would hate for another calamity to befall you as a result of your ill-considered actions."

Hot rage catapults me from my chair. "Are you threatening me?"

"Of course not. Let us say I am encouraging you to act cautiously in this and all other matters. Some of your recent actions have reflected poorly upon your judgment, and I am concerned for your reputation."

"What are you talking about?"

"You have not attended church services once since your return. Do you even plan to be married in the church?"

"That's none of your concern."

"You are to be the moral leader of our country. Appearances should be very much *your* concern. It's been reported that Ryder Blackthorn was seen leaving your room at an early hour this morning. As your uncle, I believe it is my place to strongly counsel you against such blatant improprieties. Your father has obviously abandoned his duties in that regard, and your mother has served as a poor example by cavorting with General LeGare while still a married woman."

"Just hold it right there. My mother does not *cavort*." Stomping to the door, I fling it open. "Get out of here, before I throw you out myself." He brushes past me. "And if you ever say a word against my mother or father again, I promise you will regret it."

Glaring at me defiantly, he nods curtly, and leaves.

I slam the door behind him. *Game on, you conniving piece of shit!* My pulse races and my mind flips into hyper-drive. Harold as much as admitted he had something to do with the Skorplings' disappearance. Now he's threatening to do something else. My eyes are drawn to the onyx horse statue on the desk. *I know how much that horse means to you,* he had said. Farmer Selkirk's beautiful horses immediately come to mind … poisoned. He's not going to harm Gabriel. It's time to have a talk with Mother. I remove the papers from her desk and toss the statue and its pretty red box into the wastebasket on my way out.

Mother's room is crowded with ladies-in-waiting, fussing about, putting the finishing touches on her makeup and jewelry. She looks smashing.

"May I have a word with you?" I ask

"Of course, dear."

"In private."

She catches the arm of the woman applying her blush. "Ladies," she says loudly. "Please leave us."

They immediately hustle from the room. The last one closes the door softly. "Sit down, darling. How was your meeting with Harold?"

"Not great, Mother. Charles was right. He wanted me to authorize the construction of the wall around Unicoi."

"What did you tell him?"

"I told him *no*. But I said I would call a special meeting of the Council to discuss the issue and vote on it. He wasn't happy about that. Tried to bully me into it. He even made some veiled threats."

She looks astonished. "He threatened you?"

"Well kind of. He said he didn't want something bad to happen to me because I refused to follow his recommendations."

"Oh Jaden, I believe you are being overly sensitive. Uncle Harold loves you and feels a responsibility toward you. He wishes to be an advisor and mentor to you. He strongly believes that this Unicoi wall is integral to the safety of Domericans. I'm certain he was only attempting to persuade you of its importance."

"Well he has a strange way of doing it. Listen, Mother I feel like Uncle Harold is angry with me on a subconscious level for reappearing and ruining Osrielle's chances of becoming queen. He tries to intimidate me at every turn. I've heard rumors that he bullies others who disagree with him as well, and he retaliates against those who challenge him."

"Have any of these rumors been substantiated?" she asks.

"No. Not yet."

She clasps her hands in her lap, which usually signals lecture time. "Jaden, there will always be unsavory rumors about members of the royal family floating about Domerica and even the palace. Such stories are circulated about anyone occupying an office of great power. They are almost never true. You will undoubtedly find yourself the subject of such rumors once you have ascended to the throne. If you wish, I will speak with Harold and ask him to be more delicate in his communications with you."

"No thanks, Mother. I don't need you to tell others to play nice with me. Here's the thing, Osrielle is miserable here. She misses her mother and the farm very much. I've already decided I don't need Uncle Harold as an advisor or on the Council. What I'd like is for you to remove him from office as Lord High Steward and send him and Oz back to Hempstead."

She shakes her head vigorously. "I am sorry, Jaden. I appreciate that Harold can be difficult at times, but I will not do that. When Harold learned of my illness, he immediately dropped everything and hastened to my side—even at the risk of his own marriage. He took over the business of state for Domerica when I became too weak to perform my duties. My older brother has done an admirable job. He has earned his title, and I shall not be the one to strip him of it."

I sigh. "All right. I get your loyalty to him. I'll try to stay out of his way until I can send them home myself."

"Thank you, darling. I'm certain if you just give Harold a chance, you will see that he can be a wise and devoted supporter."

I do a mental eye roll. "There's one other thing, Mother."

"What is it, dear?"

"We have a bunch of issues relating to Unicoi coming up at the next few Council meetings. It would be helpful, and only fair, to appoint a Unicoi member to the Council."

She scrutinizes me for a moment. "Did you have someone in mind?"

"Yes. Chief Blackthorn."

She tilts her head and half-smiles. "It would be appropriate after you are married—"

"No, Mother. Now. If I'm going to have to take on Uncle Harold and deal with a string of Unicoi matters, I'll need someone who has first-hand knowledge of life in the village, Unicoi customs and beliefs, and all the other stuff that should be considered when making decisions."

She stares at me, her lips pressed into a hard line.

I stare right back, unflinching.

"Oh, all right. As you are taking on my other responsibilities, I suppose you should be able to choose your own Council members."

"Thank you, Mother."

"Speaking of Chief Blackthorn, are we to be graced with the presence of your hard-working betrothed this evening?"

I grin. "Yes, we are."

"Thank heavens," she says. "I was beginning to wonder about you two. I admire his dedication, but hope he will not make a habit of neglecting my daughter's needs."

"I promise you'll be seeing much more of him, Mother, beginning with dinner."

"Good. Tonight we shall settle on a wedding date for the two of you. There is much preparation to be done, as many dignitaries will be traveling from Cupola de Vita and I hope from Dome Noir. Invitations must go out at once."

"Yes Mother. We're happy to choose a date tonight. Plan as lavish a wedding as you want, just make it soon." I kiss her cheek and wave the ladies back into her room.

TWENTY-NINE

I head straight for Ralston's room to fill him in on everything.

"Come in," he calls when I knock on his door. He's in front of the mirror fussing with his bowtie. "I've never been able to tie these things properly."

"Let me help." Turning toward me, he lifts his chin. "You almost had it," I say, adjusting the knot slightly. "There. You look very handsome."

He smiles. Thank you, my dear. And you look ravishing. Now what brings you here?"

I tell him about my meeting with Uncle Harold and his thinly disguised threats. "I'm sure he had the Skorplings kidnapped," I say. "You don't think they're dead, do you?"

"No, I do not. If Prince Harold is indeed responsible, it would be completely out of character for him to destroy something so valuable, when he could possibly sell them or use them as leverage against you."

"Geeze, Rals, I don't know what I'll do if he tries to hurt Gabriel. I'll sleep in his stall if I have to."

Ralston taps a finger on his lips thoughtfully. "Perhaps that won't be necessary. We could arrange for Gabriel to be housed in the

Royal Guard stables. It's closely protected, and Patrick could keep a closer watch on him."

"That's not a bad idea, Rals. It should work for now. This is getting too creepy, though. I think we need to move ahead with naming Lorelei my heir. Have you looked into that, yet?

"Yes I have. Please sit down." I seat myself in a needlepoint upholstered chair next to a small lamp table. Ralston pulls his chair around to face me. "Apparently the only hard and fast rule regarding succession to the Domerican throne is that the heir must be a female member of the royal family. When you ascend to the throne, your cousin Osrielle will automatically become next in the line of succession, but Domerican law provides that a monarch may alter the line of succession as she sees fit. This may be done by either will or proclamation. Accordingly, you may name Lady Lorelei your heir apparent and exclude Osrielle permanently and completely from the line of succession. Your Uncle Harold will have no recourse."

"That's great news, Rals. We'd probably better talk to Lorelei first to make sure she's okay with this, but I think we should get the documents ready right away, so everything will be in place when Mother … you know. Should I do it by will or by proclamation?"

"I would do it by proclamation, an Act of Succession, so everyone will know immediately upon your ascension to the throne that Lorelei is next in line, and Osrielle is out. But the Act must be drafted in complete confidentiality. If word were leaked to Prince Harold before you have taken the throne, he may become unhinged. I believe we should speak with your father about it. Perhaps his lawyer, Lord Balfour, will consent to draw up the papers. Having them prepared at the Enclave will provide an extra layer of security, as will making your father privy to your plans. In the meantime, I would not breathe a word of this to anyone else. I'm afraid that includes Ryder, my dear."

I frown. "Geeze, Rals, we just got back together, I don't want to start keeping secrets from him."

He raises a snarky eyebrow.

"Okay, don't even say it. My whole life's a secret. What's one more, right?'

"Speaking of Ryder," he says with a smile, "I believe I heard guests arriving downstairs, just now. Shall we see if he is in the party?'"

My spirits come to life. "Let's go." Shucking off my short jacket, I lay it over the back of the chair. "Can I leave this here?"

"Yes, of course. You look lovely, my dear. Ryder is certain to be enchanted."

"Thanks, Rals." I lace my arm through his. When we reach the second floor landing, my breath hitches, and my knees turn to mush. Ryder stands in the foyer below flanked by two strapping young Unicoi warriors. *Holy sweet Lord.* He's a Greek god in a dinner jacket and completely unaware of it.

Ralston pats my hand. "Deep breath, old girl. Your betrothed awaits."

When Ryder catches sight of me, his face lights up the room, and my heart flutters. Meeting me at the foot of the stairs, he takes my hand and slowly brings it to his lips, kissing the inside of my palm. "You're stunning," he says softly.

"You too," I breathe.

He stands aside. "Princess Jaden, may I introduce Liam and Adahy, two of my best trackers. I am sorry to hear of your friends' disappearance. We will do our best to help you find the Skorplings. Liam and Adahy will be with you as long as you wish." The two warriors bow.

I nod to the men. "Thank you so much for coming to help. I'll take you to meet Patrick Stillwater. He's in charge of the investigation and will fill you in on all the details."

"Why don't I do that?" Ralston says. "You two have some catching up to do."

"You're sure you don't mind?" I ask Ralston.

"Of course not. I need to speak with Patrick regarding Gabriel's new boarding arrangements, in any event. I shall see you at dinner."

Grasping Ryder's hand, I pull him down the hallway into one of the smaller parlor rooms. The soft glow of electric candles bathes the room in subtle light. Fresh flowers perfume the air. I push the door shut and wrap my arms around him, raising my eager mouth to his. My craving for him has intensified after fearing I'd lost him.

"Has it been only hours since we saw each other last?" he says, after kissing me warmly. "It seems like years."

Okay it's a little cheesy, but it makes my heart dance with delight anyway. "I missed you too, but I was well occupied today searching for Fred and Ethel."

"Come, let's sit," he says taking my hand and leading me to a blue satin loveseat. "Tell me what happened. How did they escape?"

"I'm not entirely sure they did. The servants say the nursery door was left open, but I think somebody took them. Maybe my Uncle Harold."

His face registers shock. "Prince Harold? Why would he do such a thing?"

"Because I countermanded his orders to keep them in a cage. And because he's angry that Mother appointed me as her representative on the Council. He could be sending me a message that if I defy him in the future, bad things will happen."

Ryder's eyes grow turbulent. "Has he threatened you?"

"No … not directly. But we had a disagreement over that wall he wants to build around Unicoi Village. He told me it would be in my best interests to support his recommendations. Mother says he's only trying to persuade me of the project's importance."

"You argued over the wall around Unicoi?"

"Yes. The Council hasn't even discussed it. I'm not sure there's any kind of agreement about whether it's even necessary. What do the Unicoi think about the wall?"

"Candidly, I believe most Unicoi do not oppose it. If it operates similarly to the wall around the Enclave, then it may be the best thing for our people."

"That's surprising. I thought you'd be against restrictions on travel in and out of the village. It seems to me you'd be losing all your freedom."

"The way it has been presented to us, if we accept the wall and the monitoring of our comings and goings, we are free to marry as we choose, practice our own faiths, and educate our children as we see fit. If we do not accept the restraints placed upon us, we will be required to comply with the marriage laws of Domerica, attend the Church of the Chosen, and follow the Domerican educational guidelines. Already, there is talk of outlawing the Unicoi warrior training camp."

I squint at him. "Who gave you this ultimatum?"

"Prince Harold, acting on behalf of your mother, I was told."

"I doubt Mother knows about it. It's strange that Harold is so fired up about this wall. Why does he care so much?"

"My understanding is that the lumber for the wall is coming from land he has recently acquired in the north. He stands to make a considerable fortune from the construction project."

Okay, now it all makes sense. I'm standing in the way of Harold's little enterprise. I take both Ryder's hands in mine and sit facing him, our knees touching.

"Ryder, will you to do me a favor? Well, two favors actually. Will you to take me on a tour of Unicoi Village? Tomorrow if possible. Also, I could really use you on the Council of Advisors. We need a member who knows about Unicoi Village and the Unicoi people, since a number of important decisions affecting the future of the Village are pending."

He hesitates, gazing for a moment at our intertwined fingers. "Jade, we haven't had an opportunity to discuss this, but the ultimate goal for the Unicoi is to gain our independence from Domerica, similar to the status of the Enclave. My joining the Domerican government may not be the most expedient way to do that, and it may send the wrong message to my people."

I hadn't thought about that. It was pretty naïve of me to assume the Unicoi would want to become full-fledged Domericans. Some of the Domerican laws are hard to swallow. Citizens are given a choice to either marry by age twenty and enter normal society, or undergo surgical sterilization and take a job with the government. Couples who choose to marry are allowed to have only two children. If additional children are born, they're taken away from the family and put in a home for "redundant" children. Plus, attendance in the Church of the Chosen is mandatory in Domerica. These are things I hoped to reconsider once taking the throne, but for now it's the law.

"All right. That makes sense," I say somewhat disappointed. "You need to do what you believe is right. I just thought Unicoi might want a voice on the Council. Will you at least take me on a tour of the Village?"

He smiles. "Of course. But not tomorrow, please. Let us take a day for ourselves, to rest and enjoy each other. Perhaps a picnic at the lake, if you like."

"That's a great idea. Fun would be nice for a change. I've been so worried about Mother and now the Skorplings. At least things are better between us." Lifting his hand, I place it softly against my cheek.

The grandfather clock in the corner lightly gongs seven times. "Uh oh, we'd better join the others," I say. "Mother will be looking for us. She wants us to set a wedding date tonight. I hope that's all right with you."

"Of course, I am pleased she wishes to have the wedding so soon, but I'm sorry for all you are going through. What can I do to help?"

"Just marry me," I say. It's the one thought that is completely joyful to me, making all my other cares seem small.

"I intend to, my lady," he says, his eyes burning with something that makes my blood quiver.

THIRTY

*R*yder arrives early for our picnic. He's driving a carriage. It's the first time I've seen him ride anything other than his huge gray stallion, Tenasi. Servants carry out our picnic supplies and pack them in the back of the carriage. I climb up front with Ryder. He looks young and carefree today, dressed in a red-printed Cherokee style shirt, buckskin pants, and moccasins. He's even tied a feather on a beaded string in his loose, flowing hair. My heart swells to see him so happy.

Within ten minutes of sitting down to dinner last night, Mother had selected a wedding date and extracted promises from Ryder and me that all would be ready. We're to be married at the palace in three weeks! Tiny pixies dance a jig in my stomach every time I think of it. I'm alternately nervous, scared, and ecstatic.

Ryder lifts my hand and kisses my palm. "You look lovely, Your Highness," he says grinning.

"Don't even …" I say. "There's no Chief or Princess here today. We're just two people in love out for an afternoon of fun."

"You have a new sword." He nods at my red saya. "It looks unusual."

"It's a katana, a Samurai sword. I'll show it to you later."

"Samurai?" he asks. "Will you ever cease to surprise me?"

"I certainly hope not."

He clucks at the horses snapping the reins, and we start down the palace lane. After several yards, Patrick falls in behind us on his bay gelding. Ryder twists around. "Your guard is coming with us?" he asks, incredulous.

I flash a pleading smile. "I'm sorry. He'll keep his distance. General LeGare has given him strict orders not to let me venture off the palace grounds without him. LeGare will tell Mother if I sneak away, and that will only upset her."

He sighs, shaking his head. But it doesn't dampen his mood. We talk animatedly about our future plans all the way to the lake.

Ryder spreads our colorful quilt under a sheltering ancient oak near the water's edge, and we unpack our feast—a whole roasted chicken, julienned vegetables with a creamy dip, cheddar cheese popovers, and rhubarb lemonade. For dessert, Cook filled bowls with fresh mixed berries and sweet cream. She even included a tin of chocolate lace cookies. Everything looks delectable, and I realize I'm starving.

"How is your mother feeling today?" Ryder asks me as I load up my plate.

"I'm thrilled to say that she seems rejuvenated now that she has a wedding to plan. Later today, she's meeting with a florist, a dressmaker, and a wine merchant. She was with the engraver when I left. He looked in need of oxygen. Mother told him she wants the invitations to go out today."

He laughs, taking a handful of vegetables from the tray.

"So how did Catherine react when you told her the news?" I ask.

He gnaws on a carrot stick, looking as if he'd rather not tell me. "She was not as pleased as I'd hoped. In fact, she said I was making a mistake. But I know she will change her mind. Meli was very happy, though, and asked me to convey her congratulations to you."

"She's sweet. Sorry about Catherine. I hope she'll find a way to accept our marriage even if she doesn't approve."

He gazes out at the sparkling lake, taking a few bites of a popover. Then he regards me with a serious expression. "We've not had the opportunity to speak of your time with the Outlanders. Was it intolerably difficult? You must have been frightened and desperate."

I study the pattern in the blanket, not meeting his eyes. "Well, I was kind of ill for a lot of the time, and you know, dazed when they found me. I don't really remember too much about it, but it wasn't terrible. They were kind and treated me well."

"Was there ever anybody else, while you were away from me?" he asks shyly.

My head pops up, and I scoot closer to him, finding his eyes. I wish I could tell him the truth—that I spent every spare moment searching for his counterpart on my earth, that I dreamt of him each night, that I missed my senior prom because I wanted to stay home and scour the internet for some trace of him. "I can honestly tell you that, since that first day when you kidnapped me, there has never been anyone else. And I know now there never will be."

He winces when I allude to his attempt to kidnap me to pressure my mother to negotiate for the relocation of the Unicoi. "I've hurt you in so many ways," he says. "I shall spend my life making it up to you."

"Don't, love. Let's not do that today. As far as I'm concerned, the past is wiped away. We're starting fresh from this moment on. Our life together is going to be amazing."

He drapes an arm around my shoulder and kisses me gently, easing me down onto the blanket. Pushing a few strands of hair away from my face, he kisses me again, first on each eyelid, then each earlobe, and finally on the lips. His hair tumbles down around my face, and my heart beats low and hard in my chest.

After a moment, he pulls away and sits up again. I whimper softly. Getting to his feet, he holds out a hand. "Will you walk with me?"

Walk? Actually, I was hoping to just lie on the blanket and make out for a while, but I reluctantly take his hand, shaking the crumbs from my dress.

We stroll along the lake path holding hands. All is peaceful and serene. The water sparkles silver-blue. Wildflowers dot the meadow with crimson and gold. When the shimmering waterfall comes into view, I'm reminded of the small alcove tucked behind the falls where Ryder and I shared a few steamy kisses and some secret parts of our souls. On that day, I discovered that he feels a kind of magnetic attraction for me that allows him to find me almost anywhere. Unbeknownst to me at the time, I have the same thing for him. Ralston says it goes along with the perpetual contract between us. I cut my eyes to Ryder, wondering if he's thinking of that day too.

He veers off the path, and I follow him into a small clearing with a large, flat tree stump in the center. I recognize the place immediately. We shared our first kiss here. The memory of it warms me.

"Please sit," he says, motioning to the stump. He did the same thing on that day, before confessing to me that he'd been in love with me, well Princess Jaden actually, since the first day they'd met. She was twelve, and he was fifteen.

Leaning up against a tree, he crosses his arms and gazes at me.

I sit smiling at him, noticing how well the clothes fit his incredible body, marveling at his nearly flawless skin, and appreciating how nicely the whole man is put together. After a minute or two, I start to squirm a little under his gaze.

"What?" I say. "What are you thinking?"

"I am locking this moment into my memory," he says. "The way your eyes shine when you look at me, the way your hair falls across your shoulders, the curve of your mouth. It is all precious to me. I never wish to forget it. When I thought I had lost you in the fire, I cursed myself for not having appreciated the fleeting hours we shared. Now that we're together once again, my heart wishes to devour and savor each moment, each second with you."

No one has ever spoken such lovely words to me. I strain to swallow the lump in my throat. He kneels by my side, lifting my hand and placing it against his warm cheek. I smooth his silken hair with my other hand, overwhelmed with inexpressible gratitude at having found him again … my forever love.

"That's so beautiful, Ryder," I whisper. "Thank you for loving me so sweetly."

He peers up at me, eyes a bottomless mountain lake. "I have something for you." Reaching into his pocket, he brings out a small black pouch. Untying the string, he removes the contents, and holds it up for me to see.

It's a ring. A dazzling, breathtaking, mystical ring. The band is platinum, the setting an infinity symbol formed by tiny diamonds, with two round-cut emeralds mounted inside the sworls.

"Oh god, Ryder. It's gorgeous."

He smiles. "Do you like it? I designed it when we first became engaged. Lady Lorelei crafted it for me, but I never had the opportunity to give it to you. The symbol is for our love. The emeralds are for your eyes."

"I love it," I say, throwing my arms around his neck. Laughing. Crying. Disbelieving my own good fortune.

He rises to his feet and lifts me up so I'm standing atop the stump, making me nearly as tall as he is. "Put it on," he says.

I slip it on my finger. A perfect fit. Stretching out my hand, the silver light spins out in a thousand directions from the glittering stones. It's the most beautiful thing I've ever owned. Joyfully twining my arms around him again, I plant a sweet, lingering kiss on his luscious mouth. *Mmm, feels great to be this close once more.*

"Would you like to go for a short swim?" he asks, when we finally break for air. "We have time before the rains."

"I'd love—" I begin, but my eye is caught by a movement in the trees behind Ryder.

"What is it, love?" He pivots quickly.

"I don't know. Something in the trees. A deer maybe."

"Shall I go and look for it?"

At that moment, Patrick calls, "Chief Blackthorn."

Hopping down from the stump I follow Ryder back to the path. Patrick waves as we emerge from the trees. Liam and Adahy, the Unicoi trackers are standing at the foot of the road.

"I'd better go and see why they're here," Ryder says. "Perhaps there is news of the Skorplings."

"Go ahead. I'll join you in a minute," I say. "I'm just going to check out that thing I saw in the trees."

"I wish you would wait for me, Jade. But I know you will not, so be careful." He kisses my cheek.

Instead of going back through the clearing, I ease myself into the trees and wind my way around behind the spot where I saw the movement. The foliage is dense with brush and undergrowth, but I can make out the silhouette of a person still peering in the direction of the clearing. Silently, I steal closer. As I draw near the silhouette, I see that it's a woman wearing a fitted dark uniform and knee boots. A black leather holster is slung low around her hips, a gun strapped to her thigh. Slowly drawing my sword, I hold it with both hands at shoulder height.

"What are you doing here?" I ask gruffly.

The woman jumps about a foot in the air, issuing a small yelp. As she turns toward me, her hand goes for her heart, not her gun.

"*Scheisse!*" she says. "Scare people much?"

"I asked what you're doing here." I eye her warily.

She smiles. "I came to meet you, Jaden. I wanted to see what the fuss was all about."

I squint at her. She's pretty, petite, and pixyish, with short, spiky white-blond hair, large, luminous, blue eyes, and a smattering of freckles across a turned-up nose. She's maybe a couple of years younger than I am.

"What are you talking about? Who are you?" I ask.

She makes a move in my direction. "Whoa. Hold it right there, Hit Girl," I say pointing my katana at her. "Don't come any closer. Answer my questions."

"I'm Eve. I'm a Transcender, like you. See?" She twists her torso slightly and taps a frosty green nail against her shoulder patch. It's the Transcender symbol, three shooting stars.

"Geeze, you people have uniforms?" I ask.

"These are my traveling clothes. I'm supposed to be on exploration, but I took a little detour to see you. Kind of an unofficial, and most definitely unauthorized, visit."

"I've never seen Asher dress like that," I say skeptically.

She snorts a little laugh. "Asher dresses for you, earth girl. In case you hadn't noticed, he's in love with you."

"I doubt that. Besides it doesn't matter, I'm engaged." I casually flash my new ring. "Ryder and I ..."

"Have a perpetual contract. I know. I saw you two swapping saliva back there. *Uk.*" She wrinkles up her pert little nose. "I'd never do that. I don't mean the kissing part. I'd do that if given the opportunity. Especially with someone who looks like your Mr. Dreamcicle. But I'd never agree to be with the same guy for all of eternity. Bo-ring."

"Why are you here?" I ask, putting my katana away. Eve seems harmless, if annoying.

"I wanted to meet the new girl Asher's been slobbering about.

He said you're coming to Arumel soon, but I'd never been to this earth before, so I thought I'd pop in and introduce myself."

Oh Great! That's all I need, a rogue Transcender showing up unexpectedly. "You know you can't be here," I say. "Especially dressed like that. People will think you're a spy or something and try to throw you in prison, or worse."

She shrugs. "If anyone comes after me, I'll just shift back to my exploration. Not a problem."

"Well, it's a problem for me. I can't risk being seen with you, so please leave *now* and don't ever come here again. I have a deal going with IUGA, and I don't want to screw that up. Nice meeting you, though." I turn and push aside the bushes.

"Wait. I know where your talking monkey-bears are."

I swivel around. "The Skorplings?"

"Yes."

Scowling, I say, "Wait right here."

Threading my way through the trees, I step out onto the lake path where Ryder, Patrick, and the two trackers appear to be in deep discussion. Ryder raises his eyes to me. Smiling, I wave at him. "Be right there," I shout. Nodding, he continues his conversation.

Eve's gone when I reach the spot where I left her. I find her in the little clearing, sitting on the stump. "I told you to wait in the trees," I say, irritated.

"I'm tired. It's been a rough exploration."

"How do you know where the Skorplings are?"

"I saw the sitzprobes who took them."

"When was this?"

"Two nights ago at the palace. I was waiting for you. Your boyfriend brought you home, but then he never left. So, your mother

219

doesn't care if you have a guy spend the night?"

"She probably would if she knew, but stick to the story. What did you see exactly?"

"I was loitering around the back stairs waiting for your perpetual love slave to leave. Anyway these two guys slipped in through a back door and absconded with the Skorplings squirming and squealing in their arms. I'm surprised that butler who hangs out in your hallway didn't do anything. I mean, he had to have heard the commotion. Anyway, by that time, I figured you and Adonis were making some magic, if you know what I mean, so I followed them."

"Where did they go?"

"I don't have a street address or anything, but I can show you."

"Now's not a good time," I tell her. "Can you come to my room tonight, around midnight? Will you show me then?"

She angles an impish look at me and smirks. "I don't know, earth girl. What's it worth to you? I'm already off the reservation as it is. Not sure I can chance it again tonight."

I roll my eyes. "Well how about this, Tinker Bell, you agree to come to the palace tonight and help me get the Skorplings back, and I won't report you to Asher."

She stands legs apart, hands on her hips. "Don't get all huffy on me, earthie. I'll be there tonight, but not because you threatened me. I'm coming because it'll be fun rescuing those weird little freaks. They kind of fascinate-scare me, if you know what I mean."

"I'll see you at midnight, then. Bring your gun," I say. "And quit calling me *earth girl*. You don't look like an alien to me."

"Ooh, prickly. It's just, an expression. Kind of like *home girl* where you come from." She waggles her fingers at me. "Ta," she says and vanishes before I can blink.

That was bizarre. It's great that she knows where Fred and Ethel are, but, man, Eve's a piece of work. Talk about *weird little freaks.*

Turning to make my way back to the path, I nearly bump into Ryder. My heart stops beating for a nanosecond. What did he see?

"Hi," I say weakly.

"Did you find anything?" he asks.

Whew. "No. Nothing. Probably my imagination. What did the trackers have to say?"

"They've made some progress in their investigation. It appears the Skorplings did not escape on their own, but were taken by two men. They were able to isolate the boot imprints belonging to the men, but the trail was lost soon after the men mounted horses. The direction of the escape is toward Warrington Village. Efforts have begun to locate them. If they're still in the area, we will find them, I promise you."

"You think they may have been taken somewhere else?"

"Unless the thieves intend to ransom them—which is unlikely since they have made no demand as yet—they would be forced to smuggle them out of Domerica in order to sell them. Nobody here will touch them."

That hadn't occurred to me. Now I wish I'd found a way to have gone with Eve this afternoon. "I just hope we're not too late." I slip my arm around Ryder's waist. "Do we still have time for a swim?"

"We'd better not, love. I'm sorry." He places a finger under my chin, raising my face to his. "We must start our journey home if we wish to avoid the rain." Kissing me lightly, he says, "It has been a wonderful afternoon."

"Yes it has." Glancing down at my ring for the hundredth time in the last half hour, I ask, "Will you stay for dinner tonight?"

"I did not bring a change of clothing. Perhaps tomorrow night would be better."

It's kind of a let-down, but may be for the best since Eve is coming later to help me carry out Operation Skorpling Rescue.

THIRTY-ONE

*M*other's not feeling well enough to eat in the family dining room this evening. It seems the day, chock full of wedding arrangements, exhausted her. Her pale skin and taut facial muscles tell me the pain is getting the better of her tonight. The doctor gives her an injection he promises will help her sleep comfortably.

"Perhaps Her Majesty will feel better in the morning." He snaps his medical bag closed. "These things are unpredictable."

I cradle Mother's frail hand until she is sleeping soundly. General LeGare keeps his usual vigil at her bedside, reading by the dim lamplight. I'm told he's resumed some of his normal duties, now that I've returned and am spending more time with Mother.

"Charles, why don't you come and have some dinner?" I say getting out of my chair.

Saving his page with his finger, he stands and bows. "I believe I'll sit just a bit longer. Thank you, Your Highness."

The thought of eating with the palace groupies tonight makes me want to start a new diet. And I'm pretty sure I won't be able to keep my cool if I bump into Uncle Harold—not until the Skorplings are safely back in their nursery. So I order a light dinner in my room and relish the fact that I don't have to dress up for a change. Snacking on the delectables Cook sent up, I read for a bit, and then take a long soak in a hot tub. A fresh robe hangs ready for me on the door hook.

At times like these, when I'm alone in my room, I miss having my music or TV, or some other mindless distraction to relax by. They say solitude is good for reflection, so I just relive the afternoon over and over again, savoring the moment when Ryder gave me his ring, shaking my head at the audacity of my new friend, Eve, and anxiously anticipating recovering Fred and Ethel.

Earlier in the evening, a maid delivered a towering stack of things Mother wants me to look over for my wedding. I'm mentally exhausted, but I can't avoid going through it any longer. Many decisions must be made quickly in order for this to come together in a few weeks.

A creamy white card, with an engraved golden crown sits on top of the stack. It reads:

Her Majesty, the Queen
and Governor Jonathan Edward Beckett
invite you to attend the marriage of their daughter
Her Royal Highness, The Crown Princess Jaden Beckett
to Chief Ryder Fitzgerald Blackthorn on the ....

A cloud of butterflies explodes inside me when I see the invitation. This is really happening. But, am I really ready? Am I ready to kiss my old life in Connecticut goodbye? Am I ready to relinquish life as a Transcender and commit to remaining earthbound in Domerica for as long as I live? All I know for certain is that life without Ryder Blackthorn is no life at all for me. If the choice is whether or not to be with him, the answer is crystal clear: I choose Ryder.

The realization takes me a little by surprise. That's it then. Internally, I've made my decision. I guess I can't actually make it official until after I've visited with the Transcenders. Joining them was one of the options presented to me. I need to be able to say I've considered all options carefully and made the best decision for me.

Sifting through the rest of the things Mother sent up, I come across a folder containing several sketches of gowns for me to choose from for the various events surrounding the wedding—the rehearsal dinner, the wedding day brunch, the ball afterward.

A quiver of excitement shimmers through me when I think about my wedding night. I wonder if Ryder and I will have a chance to be together intimately before that night. I hope so. I don't want things to be all awkward between us, like we put off the big event until we were married. I want making love with him to be spontaneous and natural and just happen because the time is right. Unfortunately, we keep getting interrupted whenever spontaneity takes over. If we have to wait until our wedding night for people to leave us alone, I guess I can live with that.

Shuffling through the sketches, I notice that Mother has marked the gowns she likes best, and made little notes in the margins as to possible colors and fabrics. She jots a reminder not to expect fabric from Dome Noir, since they're no longer exporting to us. I'm not sure what's available locally, but I'm hoping it's not fargen wool or nothing. Mother's always had better fashion sense than me, so I go along with all of her choices.

When I reach the bottom of the pile, I realize there are no sketches of wedding dresses. I search through the rest of the stack—proposed menus, music choices, entertainment, floral preferences, but no wedding dress. *Hmm. I wonder what that means.*

I work my way through the remaining items to be decided before morning. Fortunately, my choices are limited by the reality that the wedding is less than a month away. After everything's been checked off, I replace the stack on my table, and head to my closet to dress for my undercover operation with Eve.

Before I find an appropriate Skorpling rescue outfit, though, someone knocks at my door. "Come in," I shout.

The door swings open and in walks Maria followed by four servants carrying a huge ornate chest of dark wood with elaborate gold leaf on the lid and the claw-shaped feet. The front and side panels are painted with gorgeous Italian street scenes, grayed with the patina of age. It's the most amazing piece of furniture I've ever seen. After placing the chest carefully in the middle of my floor, the servants bow and back out of the room.

"What's this?" I ask.

"I am sorry to disturb you so late, but the queen asked me to bring up your trousseau. We also need to unpack your dress so it will be available when the seamstress arrives in the morning," Maria says.

I don't have the vaguest idea what she's talking about. I've never heard of a *trousseau,* and I don't know what dress she means, but she acts like I'm supposed to know what's going on, so I just play along.

"Uh, thanks, Maria."

"Why don't I get your dress first? It should not require much alteration, since you and the queen are similar in size. We will air it out before morning."

"That'd be good," I say.

She strides to my closet, and I pad along behind her. The princess's closet is still somewhat of a mystery to me, even though I've spent a lot of time in here lately. Besides racks and racks of dresses, tops, and pants, shelves extending all the way to the ceiling are stacked with hundreds of sweaters, scarves, hats, and anonymous boxes I've never even opened. My curiosity is piqued when Maria grasps the side of the tallest rolling ladder and shoves it to the far corner.

I hold the ladder, while she climbs all the way to the top rung. To my astonishment, she reaches up and pulls open a small door in the closet ceiling, and proceeds to disappear inside.

"Whoa, wait a second, where are you going?" I call after her.

Her face peeks through the opening. "I'm getting your dress. Didn't you know it was here?"

"No. What is that place?"

"Just a small storage room."

It looks kind of scary-cool, so I scramble up the ladder to see for myself. The room's barely big enough for both Maria and me, but it's kind of a neat little attic space, with a small overhead light and a shiny wooden floor. One small window overlooks the palace courtyard, and the view is spectacular.

"This is amazing. I've never been up here."

"It's possible no one has been here since the queen's dress was placed in storage," Maria says. A few dresses, carefully preserved in plastic, hang on a tall rack. Maria selects one and motions for me to help. She gently lays it across my outstretched arms. Okay, now I get it, this must have been Mother's wedding dress when she married Father.

"Hand it down to me," she instructs, repositioning herself on the top rung.

I do as I'm told. Maria drapes the plastic covered dress across her shoulder, and descends the ladder. "Don't forget to close the door when you leave," she calls.

Straightening up, I take another look around the little room, thinking it might make a sweet little hideaway if I ever don't want to be found. There's really not much else in here—a few boxes and a very old sewing machine. Reaching up to flick off the overhead light, my eye is caught by a small door behind the dress rack. Rolling the rack out of the way, I examine it more closely.

A black metal ring serves as a handle. I tug on it, but the door doesn't budge—locked-up tight. A star-shaped hole in the metal plate beneath the handle may be a keyhole. I bend down, taking a closer look. Something pings in the back of my mind, and I remember coming across a large key with a pentagram-shaped head in the princess's jewelry box. It must belong to this door. *Cool. A little mystery.* I decide to come back and check out what's behind that door the first chance I get.

"Princess?" Maria calls.

"Coming."

The dress is spread out across my bed, as Maria painstakingly removes the plastic sheathing. It's breathtaking when fully laid out. The bodice is entirely covered in pearls, each perfectly matched in size and shape and arranged in a beautiful swirl pattern. The neckline is off-the-shoulder and the sleeves are long—very long—and belled. The bottoms of the sleeves must reach nearly to the floor. But the fabric is the most astounding feature of all, silvery-white and luminescent as a star.

I brush it lightly with my fingertips afraid it might dissolve beneath my touch. It's ethereally soft. "What is it made of?" I ask reverently.

"They say it is silk, spun with platinum thread," Maria tells me. "The only dress of its kind. Would you like to try it on?"

"Really?" I ask uneasily. It seems too delicate to actually wear.

She unfastens one pearl button in the back, opening up the neckline. Sliding the gown off the bed, she puddles it on the floor in front of me.

"You are to step inside," she says, making a space for me to step into without crushing the fabric.

Shrugging out of my robe, I carefully tiptoe inside the gown. Maria efficiently lifts it up around me, holding the sleeves for me to slip my arms inside. She straightens the neckline and buttons the back. The pearl bodice is stiff and heavy, but lined with silky fabric that's soft against my skin.

"I will get slippers for you," Maria says. "Don't move."

I stand rigid as a statue.

She returns with a pair of white pumps. "These will have to do for the fitting," she says, slipping them on my feet. "Now walk carefully to the center of the room."

I take cautious baby steps as Maria meticulously unfolds and smoothes the train behind me. It must be fourteen feet long.

"Stay right here. I will get the mirror." She pushes my hair back, baring my shoulders and hurries to the closet for a mirror. I'm afraid to even breathe.

As she positions the mirror in front me, I stare in disbelief. Then from somewhere deep inside me a giggle worms its way into my throat. This is beyond ridiculous. What in the name of everything sane and rational is Jaden Beckett doing in this unimaginably beautiful wedding gown, about to marry the hottest, most incredible man in the world? Suddenly the whole thing seems utterly preposterous, and I realize I'm laughing like an idiot.

"Princess, are you all right?" Maria asks baffled by my outburst.

My hands fly to my face, blotting out my absurd image. "Just get me out of this thing," I say, trying to swallow my giggling fit.

She quickly unbuttons the gown and slides it down my body. "You do not like it?" she asks anxiously.

I cocoon myself in the safety of my robe. "It's not that. The gown is perfect. I'm just kind of overwhelmed, and nervous, and more than a little scared. Can I really stand in the queen's shoes? I'm just a ... girl."

She lays the dress across the bed again and faces me. "Your mother was just a girl when she wore that dress. No older than you. You have been through much and shown yourself to be courageous and resilient. You will be a resplendent bride and an incomparable queen. Do not fear, princess. You are worthy of this, whether you believe it or not."

I hug her fondly. "Thanks, Maria." Sometimes she knows exactly what to say.

"I will take the dress downstairs to the gown room to air out. We will meet the seamstress in the morning for your fittings. You should go through your things." She nods toward the chest. "I'll wager you have not opened it in years."

"Yeah, I hardly know what's in there," I say. "Thanks again."

Maria folds the gown into a more manageable size and carts it away.

I wander to the chest and twist the key. The lid pops up, and I peer inside. It appears to be mostly household items, neatly folded and stacked. Things that don't really interest me much—napkins embroidered with the royal crest, gold teaspoons, lace handkerchiefs. I wonder idly if Princess Jaden was really into this domestic stuff. Pulling everything out by the armload, I make a pile on the floor and sit cross-legged beside it.

Most of it is yawn-worthy, but under a set of satin pillow cases, are some interesting lingerie items. In addition to white lacy underwear, obviously meant to be worn beneath the wedding gown, three silk cases contain lace nightgowns, one white, one gold, and one black. The lace on the upper part of the gowns is fabulous, obviously handmade, but the rest of the fabric is filmy and completely transparent. Real Fredericks of Hollywood kind of stuff. I feel the blood rise to my cheeks at the thought of wearing these for Ryder. I set the bags aside. Maybe I'll have a use for these, if I work up my nerve.

Near the bottom of the pile I come across a white satin box, with an exquisite pearl necklace tucked inside. The small, perfectly symmetrical pearls are strung together in a swirl pattern. This will look amazing with Mother's dress. Closing the box, I hug it to me and sigh deeply. It all seems like a dream.

THIRTY-TWO

*"Y*ou're not ready yet!"

The voice out of nowhere makes me jump. The satin box tumbles to the floor, spilling its precious contents onto the rug. I swivel around to see Eve standing there, hands on her hips.

"Geeze. Scare people much?" I say irritably.

"You told me to be here at midnight. It's ten past, and you're not even dressed," she says tartly.

The time got away from me. "Just chill for a minute." Stuffing everything back into the hope chest, I say, "It won't take me but a second."

She surveys my room. "Nice digs. Where's the TV?"

"No TV in Domerica." Closing the chest, I lock it and hurry to the closet.

"No TV? *Sweet Giza*, what do people do for fun around here?"

"Read books, attend balls, play chess," I call as I tug on my riding pants.

"*Uk*. Just kill me now. And you're here voluntarily?"

I laugh. "So it would seem."

After I'm dressed, I stop off at the jewelry chest to snap on my TPD bracelet. My katana sits propped in the corner, and I quickly secure it in my belt.

Eve slouches in a chair, feet up on the coffee table, picking at her nail polish. "Okay, I'm ready," I say. "How do you want to do this? Do you just hold my hand?"

She looks at me like I've completely lost it. "Uh, we're going to need horses, earth girl, or whatever it is they use for transportation here in bubble-land. I could take us there, but we need a way to get the little widgets back."

I slump down in the chair next to her. "Oh man, I forgot. That's going to be a problem. My horse is over in the Royal Guard stables and he's watched 24/7. We can't sneak him out. If we want horses, my guard will have to come with us."

Eve gnaws on her cuticle. "Look, I'm willing to help you rescue them, but you gotta figure it out in a hurry. Sooner or later someone in Arumel's going to notice I'm AWOL and come looking for me."

"All right, give me a minute." Staring at the twinkling crystal logs, my mind fumbles for a plan. If Eve shows me where Fred and Ethel are tonight, I can take soldiers there in the morning. But, I can't leave them there tonight. It's too risky. One thing I know I can count on is Patrick's loyalty and discretion, so I'm going to have to take a chance and bring him along.

I hop out of my chair and pull the door open a crack. The butler stationed in the hallway hurries over.

"May I help you, ma'am?" he asks bowing.

"Yes," I say through the crack. "Ask Patrick Stillwater to have a carriage ready for me in twenty minutes. A *covered* carriage."

"Yes ma'am." He scuttles off.

"Eve, come here," I say, heading for the closet again. "You're going to meet my guard, Patrick. I'll tell him you came to me in secret with information about the Skorplings, and that we need to protect your identity. Do you think you can handle that?"

"Ooh, kind of Mata Hari-like?"

"Kind of. Anyway, you can't go out dressed like that, and we'll have to do something about that hair. Your color and cut do not exist in Domerica." Quickly surveying the closet, I pull out a chic, black, knee-length coat with puffy Domerican-style sleeves. "Put this on," I say tossing it to Eve. "It will cover your gun nicely."

I rummage through a couple of drawers until I find what I'm looking for—a long, black silk scarf.

"Might as well look the part." Draping it over her hair, I wrap it around her neck, and toss the sides over her shoulders. Using my fingers, I arrange her ice-blond bangs and stand back to inspect the effect. She looks like a kewpie doll dressed in Jackie Kennedy couture. All that's missing are the huge dark glasses.

"You look good," I say. "Just try not to talk. You don't sound anything like a Domerican girl."

"Neither do you," she says defensively.

"I fake it whenever anyone else is around. You should too."

"I'm not stupid. Asher told me they don't use slang here."

"Good, now let's get going."

The butler's still away, so I hustle Eve out of my room and down the back stairs. We keep to the shadows as we make our way to the stables. Patrick waits for me in the courtyard with the carriage ready to go.

"Thanks for coming out so late, Patrick. This is Eve. She knows where the Skorplings are, and she's going to take us there."

He nods to Eve. "Ma'am," he says. She smiles demurely.

"Your Highness, may I have a word?" He steps a few feet away and I join him. "How well do you know this woman?" he whispers. "I sense a trap. Allow me to go with her, or at least let me summon additional men to accompany us."

This is what I was afraid of. "No, Patrick. She comes to me on the highest recommendation. It's important we go now and alone. We'll be cautious, though. If it seems like a trap, we'll turn around immediately."

He looks dubious.

"Those are my orders," I say, feeling a little guilty about pulling rank on him.

He bows. "Yes, ma'am. Where am I taking you?"

"She will show us the way."

We return to Eve, and ask for directions.

"Take the main road toward the village. There's a turnoff to the east, after five kilometers or so. The building looks like an abandoned factory of some kind," she tells us.

"That is the old textile mill," Patrick says. "I know it well. My father worked there until the new factory was built."

He opens the door of the carriage for Eve and me. Once we're settled, he snaps the reins and Operation Skorpling Rescue is underway. Lanterns attached to the horses' harnesses act as headlights on the road. The carriage is lit by a lantern on each side. As we approach the palace gates, the guards, recognizing Patrick, wave us through.

"What do we do if those sitzprobes are guarding the Skorplings when we get there?" Eve asks.

"I assume they will be. We may have to confront them. That's why I told you to bring your gun. They'll most likely only have swords."

"*Sweet Giza.* I've never used my gun on anyone before," she says, a note of panic in her voice.

"Then why do you carry it?"

"We carry them on explorations, in case we run into dangerous situations."

"Well, this may be a dangerous situation. You can wait in the carriage if you like. Patrick will come with me. I'll need to borrow the gun, though."

She rolls her eyes. "Do you even know how to use a handgun?"

"Not really, but it can't be that hard. Point and click, right?"

She laughs. "I'm coming with you. I said I'd help, and I will. No way I'm turning over my gun to a diva with an itchy trigger-finger. You'd probably shoot yourself in the foot or something. Then Asher would really have my ass."

We reach the cutoff, and Patrick turns the carriage onto the small, rutted road leading to the abandoned mill.

I lean my head out the window. "Patrick, let's not announce our arrival. Find a place to pull off to the side."

After a few yards, he steers the carriage into a small opening in the trees. We're jostled and bumped around for a time, but when we stop, we're completely hidden from view of the road. Eve and I climb out while Patrick secures the horses' reins. He extinguishes the lanterns on the harnesses and removes the lantern on the right side of the carriage.

"Do you know exactly where the Skorplings are being held?" Patrick asks Eve.

"There's an office on the first floor. They were in there, last I saw them."

He nods. "Your Highness, allow me to go ahead and assess the situation. We must determine how many men are present."

The idea of sending him out there alone troubles me. He'll probably try to play the hero to spare me, and get himself killed in the process. It's smart to exercise some caution, though.

"All right. Go ahead, but stay hidden. *Do not* go in alone, Patrick.

That's an order. If you're not back in five minutes, we're coming after you."

He bows and slips stealthily into the woods.

"Patrick's very protective of you," Eve whispers.

"Yeah, he took a sacred oath," I say peering into the darkness.

"He's also delectably hot in a kick-ass kind of way."

"Well don't get any ideas. He's Domerican, you're a Transcender. That's too far for a long distance relationship and, I can tell you from experience, Domericans are not open to ideas like inter-dimensional travel. It would just freak him out."

"You sure don't practice what you preach, do you?"

"I haven't signed up for the whole Transcender program like you have. I may decide to settle down and live life like a normal person—well, semi-normal anyway."

Several minutes pass, and I'm on the verge of going in myself, when Patrick steps out of the trees.

"I checked the building," he says. "It is deserted and in total darkness. It's not clear if the Skorplings are still there."

My stomach clenches. "God, I hope we're not too late. If they've taken them out of the country, I may never see them again."

THIRTY-THREE

Patrick leads the way with the lantern. We traipse single file through the forest until we come to the old building. Its hulking, ramshackle carcass crouches black and foreboding against the night sky.

"The office is here," Patrick whispers. He moves to one side of the building where rickety wooden steps lead to a landing with windows and a door. We creep up the steps, and Patrick shines the lantern in a window. Peering around the edge of the glass, it's difficult to tell, but it appears empty other than a desk, a few chairs, and some cabinets.

"The door is locked," he says. "Shall I force it open?"

"Yes," I say.

Eve and I stand to one side and Patrick slams his boot into the door near the lock. It nearly flies off its rotted hinges, cracking loudly as it smacks against the wall. We cautiously step inside. Holding the lantern high, Patrick makes a slow three-sixty turn around the room. Nothing.

"We're too late," I say, deflated. "Still, I suppose we should search the rest of the building before— *Arrgh!*" Something drops down onto my back. I reach around and grasp a furry little arm.

"Fred, is that you?"

"Jay here. Jay here," he says excitedly, crawling into my arms.

"Where's Ethel?" I ask.

"There." He points to the top of a tall cabinet. Patrick raises the lantern, illuminating Ethel cowering terrified in a corner.

"Ethel, come here, Sweetie. It's Jay," I say.

She shrinks further into the crook of the wall, her eyes large and frightened.

"I'll get you. Stay there." The cabinet's too high for me to reach her, even standing on a chair. "Patrick, help me with this desk. Eve take Fred for me."

Patrick sets the lantern on the dusty desk, and we push it across the floor to the cabinet. Climbing on top, I hold out my arms for Ethel. "Come to Jay, Ethel. Let's go home."

"Don't touch the animal." The guttural command comes from the direction of the shattered door.

In the lantern light I make out two grimy, thug-types standing in the doorway, swords at the ready. Patrick immediately draws his sword and swings it at the large man in front, who deftly parries the blow. The smaller greaseball slips away from the fight and charges toward Eve.

"Give me that monkey," he shouts.

Fred jumps from Eve's arms and scampers to the top of the cabinet. Eve backs away, reaching under her coat.

"Stop!" the man roars.

Patrick steps back and scoops Eve up with his left arm, holding her out of harm's way while skillfully fending off the two assailants with his sword. Leaping from the desk, I draw my katana. The smaller thief turns toward me, a homicidal glint in his eyes.

"Put that toy away, girlie," he sneers.

Gripping the katana with both hands, I raise it high, and take a lunging swing at him, while simultaneously screaming my lungs out. He backs away quickly. Fear momentarily flickers through his treacherous eyes. Pointing his sword at me, he makes small circles with the tip. I spring at him again, lashing out with my sword and narrowly missing his arm. His face registers fiery rage, and he foolishly charges me.

Stepping lightly out of his path, I carve a slice across his back, as his momentum carries him past me.

He shrieks in pain and comes at me again, swinging his sword wildly. The man's obviously a street fighter, relying on strength and aggression, rather than skill. Maneuvering easily out of his way, I land another shallow strike on his thigh, while letting out a blood-curdling war whoop. This seems to undo him completely. Nearly collapsing, he manages to steady himself against the wall. A look of disbelief dulls his eyes, as he swipes at the blood on his leg. Holding my katana high, I shout once again, and make another run toward him. Gripping his injured leg, he dashes for the door and vanishes into the night.

Across the room, Patrick and the larger of the two thieves are locked in a fierce duel. Eve wriggles and twists until she finally manages to break free from Patrick's grasp, momentarily distracting him. Seizing the opportunity to pounce, the thief skewers him through the right arm. Patrick's weapon clangs to the floor. His attacker raises his sword for the death blow. I dive across the room, already knowing it's too late to save him.

A blast echoes through the air, and I watch in horror as the thief's sword hand explodes into bloody bits of bone and finger. His weapon falls away from its mark. Crying out in agony, the man clutches his bloody arm to his side. Eve holsters her gun and rushes to help Patrick.

The wounded Skorpling thief snatches up his sword with his left hand and points it threateningly at me. I'm not afraid of him in his current condition, but I have no intention of killing the guy either. What I'd like to do is take him back to Warrington Palace and interrogate him to find out who he's working for. But that's not really practical, with Patrick lying bloody on the floor.

Stepping back, I gesture the dirt bag out the door. He darts past me, and disappears into the darkness.

Eve kneels at Patrick's side, examining his arm.

"Is he all right?" I ask.

"He needs a tourniquet," she says. "Sorry Jade." She pulls the black scarf from her head, and winds it around Patrick's arm. Her arctic-blond hair forms a shimmering halo around her head. Patrick watches her in wonder.

"This is a nasty wound," she says. "Possibly a nicked artery." Eve unbuttons her coat and snaps open the pouch on the left side of her holster belt. She withdraws a small rectangular case, and unfastens the lid. The case contains three vials.

"What's that?" I ask. "What are you doing?"

She pulls out one of the vials, pops off the cap and plunges the tip into Patrick's arm."

"Eve! What did you give him?"

"Relax," she says calmly. "It's just a mixture of antibiotics, painkillers, and a cool new drug that coagulates the blood, but only at the wound site. State-of-the-art, stuff. But, we'd better get him back to the carriage before the painkiller kicks-in. He'll be totally out of it for hours."

She props him up into a sitting position and glares at me. "A little help, please."

I drape Patrick's uninjured arm across my shoulders. Eve does the same on the other side. Together we hoist him to his feet. A bit groggy, he's still able to stand.

"Patrick, can you walk to the carriage?" I ask.

He focuses on me. "Yes, Highness. So sorry."

"Shhh. Save your strength," I say. "Fred," I call into the darkness.

"Jay?" he says timorously from the top of the cabinet.

"I'll be right back to get you. You and Ethel stay there. All right?"

"All right, Jay."

Eve and I manage to half-carry, half-drag Patrick back to the carriage. She opens the door and climbs inside. I push from behind while Eve pulls, and somehow we manage to pile Patrick onto one of the bench seats.

"You stay with him," I say. "I'll get the Skorplings and be right back."

"We'll be fine," she says brightly, cradling Patrick's head in her lap. I do a mental eye-roll and trot back for the Skorplings.

Ethel's more cooperative this time, and readily comes to me. A Skorpling in each arm, I jog to the carriage, and plunk them down on the seat opposite Eve and Patrick. "Watch them," I tell Eve. "Don't let them get out."

"On it, chief."

Hastily, I clamber into the driver's seat of the carriage. I've never driven one of these things before, but how hard can it be, right? Searching everywhere for the reins, I finally realize they're still tied to a tree. Hopping down, I unfasten them, remembering to turn on the headlamps hooked to the horses' harnesses.

Once I climb back up with the reins, it becomes painfully clear that we're blocked-in by the trees. We can't go forward. I'm going to have to back this freakin' thing out. *How in the hell do I do that?*

"Jade, hustle it up. Patrick needs a doctor," Eve calls from inside.

Resisting the urge to scream, "*Shut up*," I shinny down again, hoping to control this thing from the ground until we're back on the road. Planting my feet firmly in front of the horses, "Back," I command in my most authoritative voice. "Back!"

They don't budge.

I flick the reins. "Back." Leaning forward, I use both hands to push firmly against the chest of the lead horse. "Back up you mangy beast!"

Amazingly he begins to back up. "Back. Back. Back," I chant, shoving against the animal. Miracle of miracles, the carriage eventually makes it out onto the road. Scrambling into the driver's seat again, I crack the reins and yell, "Hah." The horses jump into action. *Okay, this is good.* I urge them into a canter, praying we make it home without any surprises.

As we approach the palace gates, the dumbfounded guards hustle us through, realizing something must be dreadfully wrong if I'm driving. Another small carriage trundles along the lane in front of us. Yanking back hard on the reins, I try to slow the horses, but our momentum propels us forward, and we nearly run the little coach off the road.

The horses come to a halt in front of the palace steps, and the smaller carriage clatters up behind us. I jump down from the driver's seat as Ralston emerges from the other carriage. He's dressed in a black overcoat and white silk scarf, as if he's been to town.

"Princess Jaden, what is the trouble?" He asks bowing. His eyes expand to saucer-size when he notices my blood-spattered clothing.

"It's Patrick," I say. "He's wounded. We found the Skorplings," I add.

Ralston quickly signals for assistance, and several servants rush to help us. I gently lift Ethel and Fred from their seat, still frightened and quivering, and kiss them both on their furry little heads.

"I'll take them," Maria says, descending the stairs in her robe. She gathers them in her arms.

A small crowd has assembled around us, and I recruit two men to help me with Patrick. Eve pushes herself into the corner of the bench, and flips up the collar of her coat attempting to appear as inconspicuous as possible. The men carefully ease Patrick from the carriage.

"Take him to my room," I say. "And send for the doctor."

Ralston touches my arm. "Your Highness, perhaps they should take him to my room."

"Oh, right. Take him to Professor Ralston's room."

"Yes, ma'am," one of the men says. "Does the lady need any help?" he asks nodding toward the carriage.

Oh God. What do I do with Eve? I shake my head. "No. Just see to him, please."

Ralston pokes his head inside the carriage, and glimpses Eve scrunched in the corner. "Oh my," he says softly. He pulls the white scarf from his neck. "Perhaps you could use this, my dear," he says passing the scarf to Eve.

After a moment Eve's face appears at the carriage door. Ralston extends his hand, helping her descend the steps. Even though the white scarf is draped over her head and around her shoulders, her presence causes a wave of curious chatter to ripple through the crowd. No doubt, everyone is wondering who the mystery woman is, and what the princess has been up to this time.

"Eve, come with me," I say. "Maria, please see if Cook has something for the Skorplings to eat. Then bring them to my room. They'll spend the night with me."

"Yes, Princess." She sniffs Ethel's scruff. "They require bathing also, but it shouldn't take long." She carries them to the stairs.

"Professor Ralston, I'll check with you later on Patrick's condition," I say.

"Of course. Goodnight, Your Highness."

Taking Eve's elbow, I guide her up the palace steps. "Eyes

straight ahead," I whisper, ignoring the inquisitive stares.

We collapse into the chairs in front of the fireplace in my room. Eve uncoils Ralston's scarf and fluffs out her hair. I extract the bloody katana from my belt and lay it next to my chair, thinking I'll clean it later.

"Thanks for saving Patrick's life," I say. "That was an impressive shot. I thought you said you never used your gun before."

"I said I never used it *on anyone* before. I have about a dozen medals for excellence in marksmanship, though." She wrinkles up her forehead. "Do you think that guy's going to be okay? The one I shot, I mean."

"He'll have to learn how to fight left-handed, but I suspect he's still fit for a life of crime. Do you want a cup of chamomile tea?" Ralston's magic tea will be relaxing after our little escapade.

"Got any chai?" she asks shucking off my coat.

"No chai here, but you'll like this." I pull cups from the cupboard and put the water on to heat.

"So what was all that yelling you were doing back there?"

"Oh, that's *kiai*. In Kendo, you shout to focus and to express your spirit vocally. I think it's also supposed to scare the hell out of your opponent."

"Yeah, well, it's kind of unnerving to your allies too. I thought you were wounded."

"That never occurred to me. I probably should've warned you before we left."

"What should I do with these?" she asks holding out my coat and Ralston's scarf.

"Just lay them over there." I gesture to the elaborate hope chest.

"What's all that stuff I saw you put in there?" she asks.

"Things the princess collected for her marriage. Just towels and spoons, hankies ... things like that."

"Weird. Like she couldn't afford to buy new stuff."

"It's just an old tradition."

"Is that why you're getting married so young? Because of tradition?"

"Yes and the law. You have to get married by age twenty or be surgically sterilized and go to work for the government."

"Holy scheisse. That's really twisted. I hope lover boy's worth it. The sex must be seriously hot for you to want to stay here."

I pass her a cup of steaming tea, and we take our seats in front of the fireplace again. "Ryder and I haven't actually slept together yet," I confess.

"Are you insane? You're going to marry a man you haven't even slept with? How will you know if you're even compatible? I mean that's kind of important for a long-term relationship."

Laughing, I tell her, "Where I come from there are people who actually save themselves for marriage. Not so much anymore. But the real religious people think it's still the way to go." I sip the fragrant tea. "That's not what I'm doing. We just never seem to be alone long enough. No worries about being compatible with Ryder, though." I half-smile. "We're okay in that department."

She stares at me with her huge blue eyes and slowly shakes her head. "You can't run away from it, you know."

"What do you mean?" I ask, somehow knowing we're not still talking about sex.

"You can't run away from being a Transcender. It's who you are. You may think you can ignore it. You may even be able to repress it for a few years, but it's as much a part of you as your heart and soul. One morning you'll wake up in all this royal grundeledge and realize that a dying little dome world isn't enough, and the gorgeous dude with the luscious body lying next to you isn't enough either. You are so much more than this, Jaden."

Okay, I'm really not in the mood to be taking life advice from a delinquent leprechaun. Setting my cup on the table, I drill her with my eyes. "Eve, you don't know a thing about me or my life. I'll make the decisions that are right for me. No one else can judge that, especially not you."

"Don't get your crown all askew, earth girl. I'm just saying you need to come to Arumel before you make up your mind." She blows on her tea and takes a sip.

"What in the hell are you doing here?"

Eve and I whip our heads around to see Asher standing near my balcony doors. He strides to Eve, his face a mask of barely controlled fury.

"I … I was helping Jaden rescue her Skorplings," Eve says in a small voice, putting her cup on the table.

"You're in fifty kinds of trouble, Shorty. Not only did you abandon your assignment to visit an unauthorized destination, but you ended up brawling with the locals. You'd better get your ass back to Arumel, now. Narowyn's waiting for you."

"Is she upset?" Eve asks.

"That doesn't begin to describe it."

Eve stands and looks at me. "Remember what I said, Jaden." She smiles and waggles her fingers. "I had fun. Ta." The air quivers where she just stood.

"Are you all right?" Asher asks.

"Yes, fine. What's going to happen to Eve?"

"Ah, she'll probably be grounded for a while—stuck in Arumel. Depends on how bad it is. IUGA's already raising hell with the authorities. You'd better tell me what happened tonight."

"I will, but we're going to have to make it quick. Maria will be here with the Skorplings any minute, and I can't afford to be caught with you twice." Asher listens to my brief rundown of the evening's events. He's mildly freaked to hear that Eve shot someone, but he's a little crazed when I tell him she used drugs on Patrick.

"Relax, Ash. The doctors here will never know. I mean, they'll be able to tell that the wound stopped bleeding on its own, but they won't know why."

"Yeah, that's not going to cut-it with IUGA." He shakes his head, jaw muscles clenched. "Self-defense is one thing, but there are rules against using advanced drugs on a different earth unless it's on a fellow Transcender. IUGA will want something from us. They always do."

"Like what?"

"I don't know … a concession, reparations, something. Anyway, don't worry about it. It won't impact your deal with them. Narowyn will take care of it."

He spots my ring and lifts my left hand up to examine it. "This is new," he says, the agitation gone from his voice. "It's beautiful. Looks like your eyes. I hope you still plan to visit Arumel before any irrevocable decisions are made."

"Yes. I'm still planning on it," I say half-heartedly. I committed to go, but I honestly don't want to.

"When?" he asks softly. "Time's running short."

"Not tomorrow. I have a fitting for my wedding dress and a previously scheduled visit to Unicoi Village."

"How about the next day, Wednesday?"

I suck in a deep breath, stalling for an excuse not to go. I got nothing. "All right, I'll go with you on Wednesday. Ralston will cover for me, but I'll need to be home by dinner."

Asher's eyes brighten, and his lopsided smile makes me feel

better about my decision.

"Shall I pick you up here or meet you at the lake?" he asks.

"Pick me up in Warrington Village. In that same alley." I warm slightly with the remembrance of our shared kiss. "I need to take care of something at Bartlett's first."

"Wednesday it is. Thanks, Jade." He hugs me quickly and disappears.

THIRTY-FOUR

*S*tiff and sore from the activities of last night, I nevertheless, feel rested as I roll out of bed. Fred and Ethel, exhausted and happy to be home, have slept the entire night without waking me once. We eat a small breakfast together, and I decide to take them with me to the dress fitting. A new lock will be installed on their nursery door today, but I don't want to leave them alone until it is.

On our way to the gown room, we stop by Ralston's door to check on Patrick. He's still asleep and softly snoring in Ralston's bed when I arrive.

"He's been like that all night," Ralston says. "The doctor was surprised to find his arm remarkably healed this morning. What did your friend give him?"

"I don't really know," I say. "Some advanced medication she wasn't supposed to be using here."

"I take it the Transcenders sent her?"

"She's a Transcender, but it wasn't a sanctioned visit. I think she's in some hot water at home because of it, and IUGA's already reported her to *the authorities*, whoever they are."

"That is unfortunate, but I'm certain it will all be straightened out. She seems very young."

"Yes, and impulsive. But I like her. I hope everything turns out all right."

"Did you recognize the culprits from last night?" Ralston asks.

"No, but it was weird. They could have been Uncle Harold's so called 'henchmen' or just run-of-the-mill criminals. They didn't seem very bright or very good at what they do—pillaging, that is."

He rubs his chin thoughtfully. "Yes, it's possible they were Outlanders or even some of Prince Damien's missing renegades. They may have no connection to your uncle at all. Speaking of which, I met with my investigator friend last night and asked him to look into the troubling rumors and the shadowy individual who has been following you. He'll provide regular reports as his work progresses."

"That's great, Rals. Thanks." Fred and Ethel fidget impatiently in my arms. "I'd better get going. Keep me posted on Patrick's condition. Oh, and will you come with me to Warrington Village on Wednesday? I need to speak with Lady Lorelei about a couple of things, and then I'm going to slip away for the afternoon. I promised Asher I'd visit Arumel with him."

Ralston rubs his hands together in delight. "How wonderful. I was hoping you'd visit the Transcenders soon. I believe it will be a most edifying trip."

"You're going to have to cover for me while I'm gone."

"Leave it to me, my dear," he says with a wink.

A large parlor adjacent to the gown room has been converted into a giant fitting room for the day. The sofas and chairs have been moved to one side and a short, round pedestal has been placed in the center of the room. Two three-way mirrors are positioned on either side of the pedestal to afford a panoramic view of everything I try on.

Mother sits in a large armchair, presiding over the event. When I arrive with Fred and Ethel, at least a dozen ladies are bustling about draping fabrics across chairs for inspection, lining up shoes for display, presenting additional sketches for Mother's approval. Maria greets me with a flushed smile and takes the Skorplings from my arms. They love the gown room on an ordinary day. I hope they don't get into too much mischief with all the additional glittering temptations lying around.

I kiss Mother's cheek and wish her good morning. She looks great today. Her face glows with a light that isn't a result of good make-up. She hasn't looked this happy since the day of my return.

"Good morning, darling. We have so much to show you," she says excitedly. "This is Jennifer Osborne." She introduces a small brunette with a puckered brow and red spectacles perched at the end of her nose. Jennifer curtseys.

"Jennifer is assisting me with the wedding preparations. She did a remarkable job with Drew's wedding, but she says she has even more spectacular ideas for your ceremony. Something about two thousand white doves." She smiles fondly at Jennifer.

Nice to meet you," I say, hoping the two thousand doves won't be pooping on our guests' heads.

Bursting into the room, Osrielle breathlessly calls my name. She curtseys to Mother, and then throws her arms around my waist, hugging me enthusiastically.

"Oh, Cousin, I'm so pleased Ethel and Fred are back. You're so clever to have found them. May I play with them?"

"Of course, Oz. Maria has them. You can take them down to the nursery or out for a walk if you like. Just don't let them out of your sight."

"I won't. I promise."

Hovering in the door frame, Uncle Harold bows formally. "Good morning, Your Majesty," he says to Mother.

"Hello, Harold. Do come in," she says.

He stays put. "I wondered if I might have a word with Princess Jaden before the fitting gets underway?"

Mother turns to me for my response.

"Sure," I say and follow him out into the hallway. Uncle Harold closes the door behind us.

"Congratulations on recovering your Skorplings," he says. "The entire palace rejoices in their safe return."

"Thank you," I reply coolly, still suspecting he's responsible for the abduction. "The locks on their door are being changed. I don't want a repeat of what happened. At least we know now that they didn't escape on their own."

"That is true," he agrees. "It is disturbing, however, to comprehend that thieves were so easily able to gain access to the palace."

"Yes. I wonder how they were able to do that," I say, eyeing him closely.

"An appalling breach of duty. The slackers have been stripped of their commissions in the Royal Guard. I've ordered additional security around the entire palace perimeter. I assure you it will not happen again." He nervously fingers the watch chain draped across his brocade-vested belly. "I understand there was a violent altercation last night with the thieves."

"Yes. Patrick was wounded, but I believe he'll be fine," I say.

"Please forgive me, Princess, but as the Lord High Steward, I must express my dismay that you placed yourself in a position of mortal danger in order to rescue two small animals. It's not fitting for the heir to the throne to behave so capriciously. You really must be more circumspect in your actions. An entire country is relying on your wellbeing."

A nasty retort composes itself on my tongue, but I swallow it down. I doubt Harold stays up nights fretting about my wellbeing, but I'm grateful he hasn't involved Mother in this conversation. "Look, Uncle Harold, in hindsight I admit I should've taken more men with me. But I had reason to believe the Skorplings were about to be smuggled out of the country. I felt the need to act quickly. I'll be more cautious in the future."

"That is most appreciated, Princess." He bows his head respectfully.

I place my hand on the knob to go inside, but Harold clears his throat loudly. "There is one other thing. I've been informed that you received your information regarding the Skorplings' whereabouts from a mysterious young woman. May I ask her name?"

"I promised to keep her identity confidential," I say. "She fears a possible reprisal."

"I simply wished to personally thank her, and offer her a fitting reward for bringing the information to you."

Yeah, right. "I gave my word I wouldn't divulge her name."

"But Princess, she may have herself been involved with the criminals," he says, trying a different tact.

"She wasn't. Her people are well known to me."

He presses his lips together so tightly they disappear into his mouth. "We've begun an investigation. It is important that we have all the facts. I'm afraid I must insist on a name."

His tone makes me bristle. "No. But thank you for keeping me informed, Uncle Harold. I have things to attend to. You're dismissed."

Flinching at the sharp rebuff, he bows slightly, and toddles down the hallway.

I watch his retreating back for a moment. He claims to be acting in my best interest, but I'm not getting any warm and fuzzy vibes from him. What is the man really capable of? A cool droplet of fear trickles down the back of my brain. Shaking it off, I open the door to the parlor.

Several sets of arms pull me inside, and Mother's ladies unceremoniously begin removing my clothes.

"Let's commence with the wedding gown," Jennifer says.

For three and a half hours I'm dressed and undressed, pulled, tucked, pinned, and padded. Fabric is swathed around my naked body to determine how the color looks next to my skin. Necklaces and earrings are tried on and approved, rejected, or put in the "perhaps" pile. My hair is swept up, straightened out, braided, beaded, flowered, and jeweled. I finally put my foot down when someone suggests a wig.

At last, Mother declares we're finished for the day. I can quit playing human Barbie doll and put my own clothes back on. "Would you like some tea, darling?" she asks.

"Please," I say, pulling on my boots.

A tea service cart instantly appears in the room, complete with fresh berries, honey cakes, and old-lady sandwiches with the crusts cut off.

"Leave us, please," Mother says quietly, and the entire entourage of seamstresses, stylists, sycophants, and servants vacates the room in a matter of seconds.

"Draw up a chair next to mine," Mother says. "I'd like some time with you before your fiancé arrives. Are you happy with the way the wedding arrangements are progressing?"

"I'm thrilled, Mother. Everything's going to be awesome."

She smiles a satisfied smile. "I think so, too."

I pour a cup of tea for her and put two honey cakes and some blueberries on her plate.

"What have you and Ryder planned for the afternoon?"

"He's taking me on a tour of Unicoi Village to view the progress of the construction there. Then we're meeting with the Unicoi Council of Elders to discuss the most pressing issues of the transition. Ryder says there is much to talk about, but I hope the meeting doesn't get heated."

She lays a gentle hand on my arm, her eyes warm and weary.

"Darling, I wish to express to you my … my deepest regret at leaving you alone to assume these heavy burdens at such a tender age. This should be a carefree time for you. A time to savor the delights of your new love and to enjoy planning your life together. Instead, you are to be saddled with responsibilities that one much older than yourself would find challenging. I'd hoped that Harold could ease some of that burden for you, but even I can see now that it is not to be. You are both too strong-headed. Please promise me, Jaden, that you will rely upon your father, and Drew, and your new husband. Do not take everything upon your own shoulders as you have a tendency to do. You will require assistance, and I cannot be here to guide you."

Unbidden tears roll down my cheeks. Bereft with the knowledge I'm losing her again, my head spins at the realization of all I must face in the coming months. Falling to my knees on the floor in front of her, I lock my arms around her waist and rest my head in her lap. She strokes my hair in exactly the way my Connecticut mother used to do when I was a child, while I sob inconsolably into her skirts.

Mother allows me to cry myself out, smoothing my hair all the while. Raising my head, I manage a small smile. "I love you so much, Mother."

"And I you, Daughter. Now you'd better go and ready yourself for the afternoon." She kisses my forehead. Turning, I notice Charles LeGare standing unobtrusively just inside the door, waiting for her. His strong presence has been such an unexpected gift.

Pressed for time, I wash my face and quickly change clothes before Ryder arrives to escort me to Unicoi Village. Mother surprises me by coming downstairs to see us off.

"How are you today, Chief Blackthorn?" she says, gliding elegantly into the foyer.

He bows and kisses her hand. "I'm well, Your Majesty, thank you."

She gently touches his cheek. "I know you have my daughter's best interests at heart, Ryder. Do not let the elders of your tribe take advantage of her youth. You must protect her even at the expense of your own people."

My face flushes red. I know Mother means well, but this is too much.

Ryder takes my hand in his, glancing at my rose-colored cheeks. "I swear to you that I shall protect her against anyone and anything that poses a threat," he says firmly. "But I have complete confidence that Jaden is wise and skillful enough to effortlessly meet any challenge my tribal elders may place before her."

Mother smiles warmly. "Well put, my son. I bid you two have a pleasant afternoon. I look forward to hearing your report at dinner this evening."

She waves as Ryder and I skip down the palace steps to our waiting horses. Ralston and two Royal Guardsmen are mounted and ready to accompany us. I hope Patrick will be recovered soon. I miss having him around.

THIRTY-FIVE

As we approach Unicoi Village, the scene before me is like entering another world. Streets teem with busy, cheerful, and diverse people dressed colorfully and nontraditionally. Large, blue, open-air conveyances provide public transportation for the locals. Ryder tells me Uncle Harold has prohibited these motorized vehicles from operating outside of the village, even though they run on clean energy and don't pollute the air. Harold believes they'll scare the horse traffic. I think he's being short-sighted, since Domericans have very little public transportation and would benefit greatly from a bus system.

The multi-storied buildings along the main street are new and almost modern looking. The Unicoi are masters at space utilization—a population of nearly a half million people was tucked neatly inside a mountain before relocating to Domerica.

At the end of Main Street, the new Sequoya Hall, the official tribal building, is being constructed. The design is a circle shape, reflecting the circle of life and the Unicoi belief in the unity of all. I'm happy to see that the giant Sequoya tree trunks which served as columns for the building in Old Unicoi have been salvaged and will be used in construction of the new building.

Sequoya Hall is where the Chief and his family would normally reside. Of course, I'm expecting Ryder to live at Warrington Palace with me, but it occurs to me we haven't really discussed this issue. He may feel obligated to spend a few nights a week in Unicoi Village. Selfishly, I don't want to share him. So many things must still be worked out between us, not the least of which is the fact that Ryder's sister hates me. She's been convinced from the beginning that I'm only out to break her brother's heart.

As if reading my thoughts, Ryder says, "Catherine has invited us to tea after our meeting today. I hope you will consent to go. I assure you she will not be unpleasant. She wishes to make amends before we are wed."

Attempting to conceal the feelings of dread swirling inside me, I smile. "Ryder, are you sure? I mean maybe it's best if Catherine and I don't speak until after the wedding. Then she'll have to accept our marriage, and she'll know I'm totally committed to you."

"Please come for my sake," he says. "If you feel uncomfortable at any time, we will leave. Besides, Meli wishes to see you again, and you have not yet met little Alexander."

"All right," I relent. "Ralston's invited too, isn't he?" Catherine pretty much can't stand Ralston either, because he helped me escape back when Ryder attempted to kidnap me.

"Yes, of course. All is forgiven. We're going to be family. Family means very much to Catherine, and to me. She's all I have left … until we have a family of our own." He smiles and my heart flip-flops. Not ready to think about raising little rug-rats quite yet.

We pass by the growing houses where vast amounts of fruits and vegetables are produced through the use of hydroponics and high-intensity lighting. It will be fantastic when the technological and agricultural advances of the Unicoi begin to be incorporated into Domerican society. There's so much hope and positive potential in this new alliance.

My high spirits are tempered, though, when we reach the river, and I see the number of families still living in tents, carrying their water from the river, and cooking on portable stoves. It seems such a difficult way to live. Ryder tells me that if the lumber and workers intended for the construction of the wall around Unicoi are dedicated entirely to the construction of homes instead, housing could be substantially completed within six months. Clearly this has to be one of my top priorities.

That's exactly what I tell the Council of Elders when we meet inside one of the upper school offices. Schools were among the first buildings to be constructed in the new village. Education is a high priority for the Unicoi. The Elders must have been expecting a fight, because there's a collective sigh of relief at my announcement that any plans for a wall will be tabled until all housing is complete. We discuss a few additional items of concern to the Unicoi. I promise to consider each request carefully, but housing is the major issue, and the Elders appear ready to compromise on everything else.

I'm surprised and a little humbled when the meeting ends and many of them come forward to shake my hand and thank me for my role in moving the Unicoi to Domerica.

Ryder seems stoked after the meeting, encouraged by the Elders' positive reactions. He talks animatedly about the future plans for Unicoi Village as we ride the short distance to his house for afternoon tea. I find myself caught up in his enthusiasm.

Meli comes out onto the porch to greet us, a chubby baby cradled in her arms. She smiles warmly, her dark eyes alight, and makes a small curtsey. "Princess Jaden, it is good to see you again."

"Thanks, Meli. It's good to see you. And who is this?" I ask stroking the baby's fuzzy head. He has his father's pale blue eyes and platinum hair.

"This is my son, Alexander," she says proudly.

Meli is unaware that her husband, who is half-Cleadian, possesses the Cleadian ability to read a person's essence with the touch of a hand. I discovered it accidentally last year when he inadvertently uncovered my true identity. He's kept my secret, and I've kept his. I can't help but wonder, though, if the son will grow up with this special talent also. That could be interesting.

Ryder says, "Meli, do you remember Professor Ralston?"

"Yes, of course." She nods to Ralston. "Please come inside. Catherine has arranged a wonderful tea for you."

The house is fragrant with the sweet aroma of fresh-baked scones. Catherine enters the room from a side door. Her copper-gold skin glows with perfection. Sheets of shiny, jet-black hair fall gracefully around her shoulders. Her gown is black also, possibly because she's still in mourning for her father. It occurs to me that I don't know the mourning customs of this earth. A sapphire brooch, the same shade as her stormy blue eyes, provides the only color in her attire. She walks directly to me and curtseys.

"Princess Jaden, thank you for coming. I owe you an apology for my previous behavior. My brother is more joyful now than I have ever known him to be," She glances fondly at Ryder. "The credit for his happiness belongs to you. I rejoice at your upcoming wedding, and I hope that we may truly be sisters someday." Her words are kind, but her tone is as thin and chilly as her extended hand.

"I hope so, too," I say. "Please accept my condolences on the loss of your father."

She nods once and turns to Ralston, offering her hand to him. "Thank you for joining us, Professor," she says. Her voice retains its frosty edge, causing me to wonder whether Ryder forced her into this little tea party, or if she figured out on her own that she may lose his affection entirely if she alienates his future wife. Either way, a growing sense of unease seeps slowly into my consciousness. Something's a little off here. Maybe this was a mistake.

"Let us sit," Catherine says. "Please, make yourselves comfortable. Tea will be served shortly. I long to hear the details of your wedding plans, Princess. Ryder has kept me mostly in the dark. Please tell me everything."

We pass an hour pleasantly enough discussing wedding plans and watching baby Alexander gurgle and coo and play with his rattle. Meli clearly relishes her role as a new mother, and displays endless affection for her baby. I've worried about her, raising a child alone, her husband hiding out from the law. She seems contented enough with her current situation, though.

Ryder excuses himself to change for dinner at the palace, and Meli takes the baby to his nursery for a nap. Catherine, Ralston, and I are left alone in the sitting room. Ralston and I exchange a furtive glance. Then I stare at the floor, my mind grasping for a neutral topic of conversation to fill the awkward silence.

"I hear your brother was recently married," Catherine says. "Please convey my congratulations to him."

"Yes, I will. Thank you." There was a spark of attraction between Catherine and Drew when they met last year. I doubt they've been in touch since then.

"Was his bride royalty, then?"

"Uh, no. She and her family had recently relocated from Dome Noir."

"Oh, I imagine your mother is upset that he married a commoner?"

"Of course not. She loves Adelais."

Catherine quirks an eyebrow doubtfully, and we lapse into uncomfortable silence again.

"Is that the ring my brother gave you?" she says after a moment, gesturing toward my hand.

Smiling, I admire the ring for the zillionth time. "Yes."

"May I see it?" She asks, rising from her chair.

"Sure." I stand also, and Ralston pops up in accordance with the rules of royal etiquette. I hold out my hand, and Catherine takes it in her own examining the ring closely.

"Just lovely." She raises her eyes to mine. "My brother cares for you a great deal," she says, a trace of venom in her voice.

"I know." I withdraw my hand from hers.

Her eyes narrow into slits. "I wonder if you truly do know." Her voice is low and hostile now. "He nearly died from grief when you disappeared. He was only a shadow of himself until Erica Hornsby saved him."

It's as if she thrust a dagger in my heart. "You're really bringing up Erica to me?"

"She was his redeemer, and you tortured him because of it. What additional spitefulness awaits him after you are married?" she sneers.

Ryder enters the room and glimpses Catherine's poisonous expression. "What is it?" he asks, alarmed. "Is something amiss?"

She fakes a smile and a light air before answering him. "I was just admiring Princess Jaden's engagement ring. It's magnificent. A wonderful tribute to your beloved."

"Jade, are you all right?" he asks, not fooled by her act.

"It's time to leave," I say, bolting for the door. My throat is tight from swallowing down my fury and pain.

Ryder catches up to me. "What is it, love?" He takes my face in his hands. "Did she say something to upset you?"

"No." I sniff back my tears. "She still hasn't forgiven me for hurting you. I understand. She loves you."

He gazes at the house, calculating whether to go back inside and deal with Catherine.

"Let's just go," I say. "Don't make more of it than it is. Just please do not ask me to go there again."

"Never again, I promise," he says. "I can forbid her from attending the wedding, if you wish."

"No! Ryder, she's family. I'll be fine."

Catherine's name is not mentioned again all the way home. Ryder speaks of Meli and the baby and the joy they've brought to the household. I tell him I think it's rotten that they're forced to be separated from Alexander. Ryder surprises me by confessing that he's seen Alexander recently. He says Alexander and a group of others are living back in Old Unicoi.

"Isn't it dangerous with the decaying uranium and the radon gas?" I ask. "How do they get by?"

He explains they've isolated a relatively safe area to live in, and the radon levels are monitored constantly. They grow their own food and they make and sell things on the black market.

"Maybe Damien's killer will be found, and Alexander will be able to move back to Unicoi Village," I say.

Ryder shakes his head slowly. "The fact is, Jade, we know who killed Damien. It was Makoda's younger brother, Eli. He wanted revenge for the murder of his brother. Alexander will not allow Eli to be turned over to the authorities because then the family will have lost two sons."

"He's the kid from the bar?" I ask. "Ellijay?" Ryder nods. "Oh man, what a mess."

◦≫≪◦≫≪◦

Dinner at the palace is overcrowded with royal groupies tonight, mostly sucking up to Uncle Harold. Mother is in great spirits because she has received word from King Philippe that his son, Crown Prince Gilbert, will attend my wedding. She sees this as a positive indication that trade talks will soon reopen. As expected, the meal runs too long, but Ryder's company is a welcome diversion. I let him know I may be traveling to the Enclave in a few days, and ask if he'll join me. In keeping with Ralston's advice, I don't share the specifics with him, just that I have some legal things to discuss with Father's lawyer. He eagerly agrees to come along.

The remainder of the evening, we hold hands under the table, while I silently devise ways to sneak him up to my room later for some alone time. My hopes are dashed though, when Mother announces during the dessert course that she's too exhausted to finish her pommera pie. She asks me to accompany her to her room.

"Kiss your fiancé goodnight," she says. "Ryder, will we see you tomorrow?"

He looks questioningly at me. "I have some meetings in Warrington Village tomorrow," I say. "But I hope you will come again for dinner."

"I shall," he says kissing my cheek. "Sleep well, love." The corners of his mouth turn up enticingly. "Until tomorrow."

My heart follows him out the door and into the night.

THIRTY-SIX

*M*orning breaks softly in Domerica. No spectacular sunrises, just pale hues of mauve and silver leaking through the cracks of my curtains, swabbing my room in cotton-candy wisps of light. My stomach turns jittery as I lie in bed contemplating the unpredictable day ahead. Throwing off my covers, and stumbling to my desk, I shuffle through some sketches I made last night. After Mother had her medication and was comfortably asleep, I came to my room and worked on designs for Ryder's wedding ring.

He's not the type to wear a stone, so I stuck to a more traditional band design. My favorite sketch is of a wide gold band with interlocking circles carved around the circumference, symbolism for eternal love and the Unicoi belief that all of creation is connected. This is the ring I want Ryder to wear. I hope Lorelei will be able to craft it on such short notice.

More importantly, I need to speak with her about becoming my heir apparent. There's no way to predict what her reaction will be. She may love the idea or hate it. At least I hope she'll give it serious consideration. If she says *yes*, I'll contact Father and ask him to have his lawyer, Henry Balfour, draw up the necessary papers, ASAP.

What really has me tied in knots, though, is the idea of traveling to mysterious Arumel and meeting other Transcenders. Asher and Eve are great, and there's no reason to think the others aren't as well, but I'm irrationally nervous and on edge. What if they try to pressure me, or talk me out of my decision to stay in Domerica? I don't want things to be uncomfortable.

Maria has the morning off, so I pick a pretty but simple navy blue, ankle-length gown from the closet. It fits me well and makes me look thinner than I am. Ryder's necklace and a slim silver headband complete the look. My hair is actually behaving today, which is always a boost to my confidence.

I snap on my TPD bracelet, as I've done every day since Asher scolded me for not wearing it, and strap on my red saya low around my hips. It's unlikely I'll need a sword in Arumel, but I feel safer with it at my side in Domerica. Gathering my sketches from the desk, I head down to the courtyard to meet Ralston.

General LeGare has assigned a new guard to me until Patrick's back on the job. He's introduced as Josh Rogers. Kneeling before me, he pledges to protect me with his life, and *yada, yada*. It's a little dramatic and kind of awkward, but I thank him, and we shake hands. Ralston helps me into the waiting carriage and climbs in behind me.

The ride to Warrington Village passes quickly. Ralston is ebullient about my upcoming visit to Arumel. His bubbly enthusiasm splashes over onto me, and I find myself becoming excited about the trip also. Our driver parks the carriage a few doors away from Bartlett's Silversmiths. Ralston explains to my new guard and the driver that we expect to be inside the shop for several hours, and they should get lunch or find something to occupy themselves for a time. Josh refuses to leave his post, and says he'll wait outside Bartlett's shop, but the driver happily saunters off to the local pub.

As we reach the shop door, my eyes rest on a dark figure standing on the sidewalk to our left. My breath hitches in my throat. "Ralston, look," I murmur. "It's him. The guy who's been following me."

Ralston pivots around. The man studies the window display of the local men's store, as if unaware of our presence. Then he turns on his heel and ambles away, without a backward glance.

"Are you certain?" Ralston says. "Shall I have Josh follow him?"

"It's him, I'm sure. But he disappeared down that alley. Let's just get this meeting over with. If he's around when we come out, I'll send Josh after him."

Lady Lorelei greets us at the door and welcomes us inside. She escorts us to a private room in the back of the store. "I'm delighted to see you again so soon, Cousin," she says. "We received your wedding invitation. Jacob and I are looking forward to attending. May I offer you and Professor Ralston some refreshment?"

"No, thank you," I say. Ralston and I take seats at the gleaming mahogany table. "I'm happy you're coming to the wedding. Sorry about the short notice, but Mother … well, she wanted to see us married sooner rather than later."

"Do not trouble yourself about the timing. No one will lightly miss the opportunity to attend the wedding of the crown princess. No doubt you shall have an abundant crowd of well-wishers. How is the queen faring these days?"

"She has good days and bad, but the wedding preparations have cheered her," I say.

Lady Lorelei's laugh tinkles like wind chimes. "I am certain of that. Cousin Eleanor has always been at her best when pomp and pageantry are involved. Now, what may I do for you, Princess?"

Unfolding my sketch and placing it on the table in front of Lorelei, I say, "I need a wedding ring for Ryder. Would you be able make it for me? You did such an amazing job with my ring. It's truly a work of art." I hold out my left hand, allowing the light to dance across the stones.

"Ah well, I was merely the craftsman. Your fiancé was the artist, and I believe you were the inspiration, Cousin. Although, I do admit it is one of my favorite pieces." Her cheeks flush modestly. Sliding my sketch closer to her, she studies it carefully.

"If you don't have time to finish it before the wedding, it's not a problem," I say. "I could borrow a ring for the ceremony and give this one to Ryder later."

"No. That will not be necessary. It's a lovely design, but not difficult to create. I will have it for you prior to the nuptials. Interlocking annuli, the symbol of eternity. It's quite moving, really. I suggest a small groove around the top and bottom of the band to form a frame for your design."

"Yes, that's a great idea," I say.

"It will be my pleasure to craft this for you, Princess. Do you wish to have an inscription?"

An inscription hadn't occurred to me. My mind skims across the possibilities. "Let me think about that. I'll let you know in the next few days."

"Certainly. That will be fine. But that was easy. What else may I do for you today?"

Straightening my posture, I launch into my little speech. "Actually, there is something else. Lady Lorelei, I have a proposal for your consideration. But, I must ask you to keep the matter strictly confidential. You may tell Lord Bartlett, but no one else. My wellbeing could depend on it. Do I have your word?"

"Goodness, Cousin, this sounds momentous. Shall I ask Jacob to join us?"

I glance at Ralston, who nods almost imperceptibly. "Yes, if you would be more comfortable. Please do so," I say.

She rises gracefully and moves smoothly from the room, returning not two minutes later with Jacob at her side. He soberly bows and kisses my hand before seating himself next to Lorelei.

"What can we do for you, Cousin?" Lorelei asks. "We give you our word that this conversation will remain confidential."

She turns to Jacob. "Yes. You have my word, Princess. Nothing you tell us shall leave this room," he says.

Okay, here goes. "Since I will undoubtedly become queen sooner rather than later, I've given a lot of thought to the future of

Domerica, and what will happen to the country should I be unable to serve. My cousin Osrielle is a sweet and bright girl, but she has told me many times how unhappy she is living at the palace, and that she has no desire to be queen now or ever. In addition, she's obviously not ready to rule the country at this time. So, after careful consideration, I've decided to remove her from the royal line of succession and to declare my own heir apparent. I would like that to be you, Lorelei."

The smallest tremor of shock ripples across her lovely face. She reaches for Jacob's hand, and they gaze briefly into each other's eyes, communicating silent thoughts. Her brows arch slightly and Jacob nods. Returning her focus to me, she says, "Cousin, I am honored that you think so highly of me as to bestow this tribute upon me. I feel humbled, and perhaps a bit unworthy. If it is your desire that I stand next to you in the line of succession, it will be my pleasure to serve you in that way."

My whole body sighs in relief. "Thank you, Lorelei." Her lips bow demurely in response.

"To better ensure the confidentially of my actions, I plan to have the papers drawn up by my father's lawyer at the Enclave. A royal decree, specifically an Act of Succession, to be signed by me after I am queen, is all that's required. If you're in agreement, I'll visit Father within the next day or two, to put everything in order. That way, the documents will be complete and ready for my signature when the time comes."

"Of course. We are in agreement. Conduct the matter as you see fit, Princess. I am at your service," Lorelei says. "May I ask, a question, though?"

"Ask as many questions as you want," I tell her.

She hesitates slightly. "What of Prince Harold? Do you intend to keep him on as Lord High Steward? Do you fear retaliation from him when he discovers your actions regarding his daughter?"

I was hoping to avoid this subject, but she's helping me out, so she has a right to know. "I don't intend to keep him on as Lord High

Steward," I say. "We don't really see eye-to-eye on many issues relating to the governance of Domerica. And, since Osrielle will no longer be in the line of succession, there's no reason for them to remain at court."

My hand unconsciously goes to the hilt of my sword. "As far as retaliation goes, we've hired an independent investigator to look into the rumors we'd previously discussed, but so far nothing has been linked to Harold. On the other hand, he strongly implied that he was responsible for the theft of my Skorplings. I've no doubt he can be dangerous, and that he'll be furious with my actions. At this point, I have no concrete reason to think he'd try to retaliate. But I am being cautious."

"Very well. I pray your judgment is sound on that issue, Cousin. People have murdered for far less a prize than the crown."

Gulp. "I'm aware of that," I say, remembering my stalker is right here in Warrington. I stand and everyone else rises also. "May I ask one more favor, Lorelei? Does Bartlett's have a back entrance? I have some private matters to attend to, and prefer not to be seen leaving your shop."

Unfazed by my odd request, she says, "Of course. Follow me." Ralston and I say our goodbyes to Jacob before Lorelei leads us through a dimly lit storage room to a small metal door. "Be safe, Princess," she says placing her hand on my arm.

"I will, Lorelei. And thank you."

The back door opens out into a small side street. Ralston and I quickly make our way to the alley where Asher's already waiting for me, his back propped against the building.

"Right on time," he says with a slow smile. "Professor." He nods to Ralston. "Are you ready, Jade?"

"Just a second," I say. "Rals, are you sure you can handle everything here? I mean what if the new guard gets restless and wants to come looking for me?"

Ralston smiles and places a hand on my shoulder. "He's paid not to become restless and not to be overly inquisitive. I'll make certain the young fellow gets something to eat. Enjoy yourself. Everything here will be fine."

I unbuckle my katana and give it to him. Then I lean in and kiss his cheek. "Thanks Rals. Don't know what I'd do without you."

"All in a day's work, old girl," he says with a smile.

I take hold of Asher's hand, gripping it firmly.

Zzzt. We're gone.

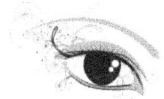

THIRTY-SEVEN

We land in a small lamp-lit room. A cluster of plush, comfortable-looking chairs is arranged around a small glass table. The peaceful sounds of a plinking fountain and the aromas of eucalyptus and cucumber convey the impression of a waiting room in a swanky spa.

"Where are we?" I ask.

"It's a portal room. The community provides it for the use of the Transcenders and others who may be hosting ... well, *foreign* visitors from time to time. We could have arrived directly on the grounds of the estate, but I wanted you to get a feel for the community before you meet the others."

"All right. Sounds good."

Asher opens the door for me. He wasn't kidding about the portal thing. I feel as if I've stepped into a completely different universe, and I guess I have. The people look unlike anything I'm used to and, really, one or two of them probably don't qualify as *people*. There are definitely some species here I don't recognize. Struggling to keep my composure, I notice most everyone is dressed in long robes or flowy pajama-like tunics and pants. But a few wear crisp uniforms of different styles and colors. They pass by alone or in groups, speaking in hushed tones and a variety of languages. I feel like a there's a flashing neon *outsider* sign glued to my forehead.

We're in a giant, concrete building with windowless, curved

walls. A huge plexiglass-like cylinder runs through the middle of the floor with endless moving walkways on either side. Blue light emanates from arches of opaque tubing running along the ceiling and walls. The whole scene reminds me of an elaborate Halloween party in a hip underground club.

Asher and I step onto the moving walkway and fall into the flow of the crowd. A speeding flash of something zooms through the opaque center cylinder, causing me to recoil in fright. I'm beginning to wonder if I made the right decision in coming here.

Asher takes my hand. "It's okay, Jade. This is the subway station. That's a high-speed pneumatic tube," he says, nodding to the structure in the middle. "The trains are propelled by pressurized air. We're not taking the train, though. We'll be out of here in a minute or two."

We pick up our pace and bypass a number of people on the walkway. Several of them nod and smile at Asher. One man crosses his arm over his chest. "Gloria," he says bowing his head.

Asher smiles. "Good morning," he replies.

A row of long escalators appears on our right. Asher guides me off the walkway and onto one of the escalators. Ascending quickly, we reach ground level and step through an archway into the bright sunlight. Unnerved by our subterranean jaunt, I fill my lungs with the wonderfully fresh air, grateful to be out in the open.

The cityscape stretched out before me is absolutely stunning. Towering buildings made mostly of glass and steel gleam in the sunlight. The architecture is ultramodern, futuristic even, with angles and spiral configurations I've never seen. Trees and meticulously manicured lawns and flowerbeds surround and blend with each structure in ingenious indoor/outdoor designs, as if each building simply sprouted and grew organically where it stands, like some celestial gardener found a way to cultivate a city from skyscraper seeds.

"At the risk of sounding dumbstruck," I say. "Wow!"

"I know, right?" Asher smiles wryly. "This is the new part of the city. I confess I wanted to impress you."

"Mission accomplished, Ash. Are you sure we're still in the twenty-first century?"

"Yes. The city's just a bit more progressive in its design than most. Let's get a car. I'll take you on a little tour."

We walk down a glittering, white sidewalk clean enough to eat off of. More people smile and nod at us. Everyone seems very friendly. A small force of workers in white uniforms carries brooms and dust pans. Moving along the sidewalk, they sweep every inch as they go. Another gray-robed man does the arm-over-the-chest thing to Asher. "Gloria," he says.

Asher nods politely.

"Why do people call you Gloria?" I ask.

Asher laughs. "They're not calling me Gloria. It's a term of respect. Some people think Transcenders are supposed to be revered, like super heroes or something. It's sort of embarrassing."

A line of spotless silver-and-blue vehicles is parked along one side of the road. They're identical, except in size—some have two seats, some four, and others are the size of small vans. Two men in overalls hover over a car, diligently polishing headlamps and windows. Asher walks to one of the two-seaters and opens the passenger door for me. "Hop in," he says.

"Geeze, how do you tell which one is yours?" I ask. "They all look alike."

"They're community cars." Asher settles himself on the driver's side. "Anyone who's registered can use them." He presses the pad of his thumb onto a small round control on the dashboard, and the engine quietly comes to life. "The thumb scan identifies me as an authorized user."

Reaching for my seat belt, I discover there is none. Alarmed, I notice there is also no steering wheel in front of Asher.

"How do you drive these things? Foot pedals?"

"No, they drive themselves. You just tell them where you want to go. He presses another button on the dash and a screen lights up displaying a map.

"Good morning Asher Steele. Where may I take you?" a pleasant woman's voice asks.

"I'm going home, but we'd like a short tour of the city first. Do you have any pre-programmed tours?"

"Yes. Please select your preference from the menu on the screen. The displayed routes all terminate within two miles of your home."

A menu appears offering a variety of different options, such as *Old Town, Government Buildings, Notable Homes and Estates.*

Asher touches the one that says: *Kistlethorn Park and Granbury Museum.* "This is an interesting route, and I'll bet you've never seen a Kistlethorn tree before."

I shake my head.

"You'll get a good feel for the community, and we'll still be home in time for lunch."

The car pulls away smoothly from the curb and joins the flow of traffic. Despite my unease at having no manual controls inside the cab, the car seems to know what it's doing. Once out on the road, I realize there are no traffic signals. "How come there aren't any traffic lights or seatbelts?" I ask.

"There hasn't been a car wreck in years. Traffic is precisely controlled via satellite, with lots of backup in case of a malfunction. Plus, these cars are titanium-reinforced, practically crash-proof."

The pleasant woman's voice mentions various points of interest on the right or left of our route as we ride along. Asher adds a few comments of his own along the way. The Community Hall is an enormous granite building. Asher tells me the ruling body of Arumel has its offices there. He says the building also houses the Arumel History Museum and the Hall of Records.

We turn into Kistlethorn Park through huge green iron gates. At first it looks like any other big city park, but my jaw drops in wonder when the Kistlethorn trees come into view. Like an army of black goblins escaping from the ground, their trunks twist and strain upward, long gnarled branches stretching for the sky, shiny and black as polished marble. Remarkably, the leaves are shiny-black also. The color reminds me of Ryder's hair, and I shudder to think what he would do if he knew where I was at this moment and who I was with. Once we're married and settled, I won't need to lie anymore. I'll never be able to tell him everything about myself, but at least I can live honestly going forward.

"How can the leaves be black?" I ask. "I thought all plants produced green chlorophyll."

"There's something in the chemical makeup of the tree that combines with the chlorophyll to give the leaves that black sheen. If you examine them closely, you can see they're actually the darkest shade of green. But the leaf tips are sharp as thorns, so I wouldn't advise doing that. You should see them when they're in bloom. Their blossoms are either blood-red or snow-white. It's pretty dramatic."

Dappled sunlight filters through the ebony leaves, casting eerie patterns on the grass below. Families wander among the tress, talking and laughing, seemingly oblivious to the sinister spectacle of the black forest.

We exit the park through gates on the opposite side. The woman's voice tells us we're approaching the Granbury Art Museum. She politely asks if we'd care to stop and go inside. Asher checks his watch. "No. Please take us directly home," he says to the car.

"Yes, sir," she replies.

"She knows where you live?" I ask.

"It's programmed into the system. I'm sorry we don't have time to stop today. The museum is amazing. There are world-renowned works you'd recognize and others by artists who aren't popular or even alive on your earth. It takes hours, or days, really, to see everything, and we're expected for lunch."

"That's okay," I tell him, still a bit rattled from the subway experience and from riding in a car with no steering wheel. I figure the sooner we get to Asher's house, the sooner I can relax. "Will Eve be there?"

"Oh yeah." He smirks. "She's basically under house arrest for six months for abandoning her post and because of her antics in Domerica. She's allowed a few trips into town, but no transcending."

"Oh man, that's harsh," I say.

"She's got to learn. It's a gift not to be abused." He looks at me meaningfully as if his words have a special significance for me also. But I don't yet completely understand this gift of mine, and I don't fully comprehend his meaning.

We tool along in the little car, taking in the scenery. After a mile or so, I flip open my TPD bracelet and check out the holographic map. Dozens of colored dots are clustered in one small area.

"What're you doing?" Asher asks.

"I was looking to see if I have a *mirror* here."

"You could've just asked," he says. "Those dots are the other Transcenders. That's where we live. But, no red anywhere, see?" He reaches over and closes the bracelet. "You do not have a *mirror* on Arumel. Your *mirror* died over a year ago in a horseback riding accident."

A chill prickles my neck hair. "Weird. Just like the princess," I say. "Did you know her? My *mirror*, I mean."

"No I didn't. Sometimes events repeat themselves in parallel existences. It's something we're studying."

That's a sobering thought. I stare out the window and notice we've entered a residential area with fat shade trees lining both sides of the road. The homes are on the order of grand estates, although older and more traditional than the buildings in the new part of the city. Most have sizeable grounds. Some are surrounded by stucco or wrought iron fences. The car glides to a stop at the curb in front of a building in the style of an old French chateau, complete with pilasters and mansard roofs.

"Is this acceptable, sir, or shall I use the driveway?" the car asks.

"This is fine. We'll get out here," Asher says.

I open my door and climb out onto the cool, shady sidewalk. The air has a familiar smell of oak and earth. Once we're on the sidewalk, the car pulls away from the curb and takes off by itself. No passengers required, I guess.

"Is this where you live?" I ask, taking in the size of the chateau. It's not as big as Warrington Palace, but it's huge.

"Me and the other Transcenders. It's probably a little large for us, but we're hoping to add to our ranks soon." He cocks an eyebrow and smiles.

"I'm here, aren't I?" I say, hoping this isn't going to turn into a recruiting session. I feel something cold and wet brush my palm from behind. Quickly pulling my hand away, I turn to see a beautiful yellow-haired dog merrily wagging her tail.

"Who's this?" I ask, bending down to scratch her ears.

"Oh, that's Callie. She's a sweetheart."

"You're a pretty girl," I say. "Who does she belong to?" I glance up and down the street for her owner.

"She's a community dog. All domestic animals are owned and cared for by the community, for the enjoyment of all. Unless, of course, an animal decides to adopt a human, then they're allowed to stay with that person."

Callie licks my face. "You mean she doesn't belong to anyone? Where does she live?" I ask, wiping off her slobber with my sleeve.

"She belongs to everyone. The community houses, feeds, spays, neuters, grooms, and provides for all the needs of the animals. There are animal centers in every neighborhood. Joe, whom you will meet today, doesn't enjoy exploration work or holography, so he actually works at our local center."

"And the dogs just run around without leashes or anything?"

"No one minds. They're very gentle, and they're all trained as pups where to go to the bathroom, not to wander into the roadway, things like that. Each of them is up-to-date on vaccinations, so they pose no threat to people. Don't you like dogs?"

"Yes. I love them. It's just so different where I come from," I say, planting a kiss on Callie's forehead.

"Let's go inside," Asher says. "I want to introduce you around, and I think Narowyn wants to speak with you before lunch. She's in charge of the Transcenders, but she's also an extraordinary person— a physician, psychologist, and author. Anyway, you'll love her."

A sign on the front gate says "Chateau du Soleil." Asher holds the gate for me. Callie follows us into the yard and up the steps. The double front doors are painted cerulean blue and sport shiny brass door knockers in the shape of lions' heads. They swing open as Asher reaches for the knob.

"You're here!" Eve says, slipping an arm around my waist. "We've been waiting for you." She looks different in her long, white cotton dress and sandals, even more petite and nymph-like. "Did you hear I practically got a life-sentence for helping you find the Skorplings and probably saving Patrick's life?" She twists up her mouth like a pouty child.

"I heard. Sorry about that. I appreciated your help, though," I say.

Three others are waiting for us in the foyer. Eve handles the introductions. "Jaden, this is Mathew." She gestures to a mahogany-skinned man in his forties wearing a long gray robe. He smiles brightly and shakes my hand.

"Welcome, Jaden" he says in a Barry White bass. I develop an immediate voice-crush on this man.

"This is Monica," Eve says turning to an emo-looking young woman with coal black hair, pasty skin, and a pierced eyebrow.

"Am I supposed to curtsey or something?" she asks dourly. "I hear you're a princess."

"Not really," I say shaking her hand.

"And this is Jeffrey." He's a tall, skinny carrot-top with a winning smile and cold hands. His clothes are similar to Asher's linen shirt and pants.

"Nice to meet you, Jeffrey."

"Likewise," he says.

"Narowyn is waiting for you in her office," Eve says. "I'll take you."

"Quit trying to suck up, Eve," Asher says. "I'll take her. Go tell the others we're here."

Eve juts out her lower lip, but Asher ignores her. "It's this way," he says, gesturing to a hallway.

The interior of the chateau is warm and inviting. Brilliant light streams through dozens of windows and skylights. I'm grateful to see the sun again. The décor is French country, with soft blue and gold hues consistent throughout. Worn oriental rugs cover dark wooden floors, and baroque-style chests line the hallway. The cream-colored walls are covered with impressionist paintings of outdoor cafés, water lilies, and ballet dancers. Lush potted plants fill every available corner, and the soft trickling of a nearby fountain can be heard.

"Nice place," I say to Asher.

"We like it." He stops in front of a white door. I'm amused when I notice that Callie has followed us inside and down the hall. "This is Narowyn's office. She's expecting you. I'll see you at lunch," Asher says.

I hesitate, not knowing whether to knock or just walk in. He reaches over and turns the crystal door knob for me. "Door's always open. Go right in."

As I step across the threshold, a woman with auburn hair shot with strands of gray raises her eyes from the papers on her desk and smiles warmly. She appears to be around sixty, maybe younger. She stands and extends her hand to me. "Jaden, it's so nice to finally meet you. I'm Narowyn Du Lac. Please come in and sit down."

I close the door and take a seat in one of the gold, French provincial chairs facing her desk. She's not classically beautiful, but there's something about her face that makes me want to stare. It may be her intelligent blue eyes, the elegant curve of her cheek, or her charismatic smile. But I think it's something else, something underneath it all, a kind of relaxed, natural glow that seems to radiate around her.

"We're so happy to have you here. Asher has told me many wonderful things about you. And of course, our dear Eve has been singing your praises. I apologize for her uninvited intrusion on you in Domerica. I hope she did not make things terribly awkward for you."

"No, actually she helped me rescue my Skorplings. I'm sorry she's being punished for assisting me. But I understand there are rules that must be obeyed."

Narowyn nods. "I'm afraid she is young and tempestuous, and sometimes her own worst enemy. But I appreciate her enthusiasm. We do not often learn of a new Transcender, so as you might imagine, it causes quite a stir of excitement in our little community."

"Thank you for inviting me," I say. "I'm looking forward to meeting everyone. To be honest, though, I've pretty much already decided that I'm going to stay in Domerica."

"Asher has told me you are in a particularly compelling situation on Earth H87DE, which would make it difficult for you to choose to permanently join us here in Arumel. I admit that is disappointing, but I am pleased you've seen fit to at least visit with us before anything permanent has been put in writing."

"What Asher says is true," I tell her. "I'm here because I regretted not learning more about the Transcenders in the past. But, it's really impossible for me to leave Domerica right now. I'll sign the papers with IUGA in a few weeks, and it will be done. My mother is very ill, and I'm soon to become queen."

"Your mother?" she says. "But she's not really your mother, is she? The one who gave birth to you and raised you as a child?"

I feel my cheeks turn pink. "Well no. She's my mother's *mirror* in Domerica."

"Yes." She nods knowingly. "That's one thing we must always guard against as Transcenders, confusing a person's *mirror* with the actual person."

"Still, I feel close to her," I say. "And there are other reasons I must stay. I'm engaged to marry someone in the near future. It's complicated. I have a perpetual contract with this man."

A far away smile curves her lips, while her long slender fingers toy with a crystal paperweight. "Oh, I'm quite familiar with the enthralling nature of a perpetual contract. I also have one."

"You do?" I gasp.

"Yes. But I will confide in you that it is not with my current husband. I met my perpetual partner on another earth before I met my husband. Suffice it to say, I've experienced both the joy and the heartache of such a relationship."

This astonishes me. "But, how did you ever … What happened …" I babble, not knowing what to ask first.

"Of course it was agony to leave my forever love. The most difficult thing I've ever done, actually. I knew I would never see him again, and he has no *mirror* on Arumel. But, had I stayed, I would have been forced to live a lie. He came from an earth where the concept of a Transcender would never have been understood, much less tolerated. I was with him for five years, during which time I led a double life—as a Transcender and as his wife. I was much younger then, but still the stress and guilt were intolerable. Ultimately it came down to a matter of fairness, to him and to myself."

I stare at her, speechless.

She leans across the desk, eyes burning with passion. "Please believe that I am not implying that it cannot be done. In fact, I'm certain it is possible for one to renounce one's status as a Transcender, and to live as an earth-bound person. It has been accomplished in the past, though rarely. In your case there are factors other than everlasting love which tie you to Earth H87DE. You've elected to assume the role as queen, governing an entire country. It takes courage and self-sacrifice to arrive at such a decision. Certainly that alone is sufficient grounds for choosing to live a restricted lifestyle. I'm saying only that in *my* case it did not work."

Her words eat at me like acid. Even though she's trying to reassure me that I can do it, an insidious seed of doubt has been planted in my heart. Honestly, it was probably already there, but Narowyn just flashed a giant spotlight on it, forcing me to acknowledge it. So far, I've done fairly well at keeping my misgivings buried deep inside.

"Look," I say. "I don't know if I can actually pull this off. I mean, who can ever know? There's one thing I'm certain of and that's my commitment to Ryder. I may have an advantage that you didn't. I've never really developed my Transcender skills. I don't know what it's like to travel anywhere at any time, because I've never done it. Sure I've been a few places recently with Asher, and it's been fun. But I really don't think I'm going to miss something I've never had. I don't define myself as a Transcender, and never will."

"Well said. I admire your conviction," she says. "Your Ryder is lucky to have one so devoted to him and, from what I've heard, you will make a fine queen for the Domerican people." She rests her elbows on the desk and folds her hands. "Well then, what of your life in Connecticut, on Earth 7Y12? Do you intend to make a clean break with your real family there?"

The question makes my insides squirm. I haven't fully come to terms with what I'm going to do about my Connecticut life. Lowering my eyes, I stare at my hands and Ryder's ring. "I don't know," I say softly. "I'll probably have to. I won't be able to visit them the way Asher visits his family. There'd be no way to explain my absences from Domerica, and I've made a personal vow not to lie to Ryder in the future. I mean, I'm not going to tell him about being a Transcender, or coming from another dimension, or anything like that. But I'm not going to do anything I have to lie about. IUGA will likely come up with a way to explain my disappearance from Connecticut. I don't want to hurt my dad and brother, but I don't see any other way."

"I can appreciate that," she says gently. "Separation from family is one of the more difficult aspects of the job for us all. If there is anything I can do to help you with your transition, please do not hesitate to call on me."

"Thank you," I say. "That's kind of you."

"Of course. I wish you the best in your exciting new life, and I assure you we have no intention of interfering with your decision. You have my word that we will not contact you further without your consent. I encourage you to keep your TPD bracelet, though. It was designed especially for you. Should you ever need us, it will be your way of contacting us."

"Sure. I'll keep it," I say.

Narowyn stands and comes around the desk. "Shall we join the others for lunch?"

I get out of my chair, and she places a maternal arm around my shoulder with a reassuring squeeze.

Our conversation leaves me unsettled and unsure of myself. Narowyn seems caring and kind, like a priest I've just confessed all my ugly sins to, and who likes me anyway. She very graciously accepted my decision, but something feels a little strange to me. It's not that I don't trust her—she exudes integrity and wisdom. And, maybe I'm just imagining things, but I get the unmistakable feeling she fully expects to see me back here again.

THIRTY-EIGHT

*T*he yellow dog is curled-up on the rug just outside Narowyn's office. "I see you've made a friend," she says. Callie springs to her feet, tail wagging, and nudges my palm with her wet nose. "Callie is a shrewd judge of character. I congratulate you on winning her affection."

We follow the hallway to our left, Callie trailing behind, and enter a large dining room through double French doors. Crystal chandeliers sparkle above a long, wood-plank table, scarred from what appears to be years of hearty use. A blue-and-white printed runner spans the considerable length of the table, which is set with mismatched, French-looking pottery and brightly-colored water pitchers bursting with fresh flowers. A sturdy, red-painted hutch stands against one wall. An assortment of small, framed mirrors of varying shapes and sizes hangs on the wall above. The feel of the room is warm, homey, and haphazardly chic.

"We dine rather casually here," Narowyn says, giving my shoulder another squeeze and guiding me to the far end of the table.

Asher and a number of smiling, chattering people wander into the room. Most wear robes, flowing dresses, or linen pants and tops. Comfort seems to be the only rule of dress. I count roughly the same number of women as men, and Eve looks to be the youngest of the group.

"Ah, the others have arrived," Narowyn says. She positions us

284

with our backs to the wall. "Come in, everyone, and meet Jaden."

A sort of reception line forms and the group files by one at a time to shake my hand. Narowyn provides introductions. "This is Paul. He's been with us for ten years. Julia is a relative newcomer at two and a half years. Gareth is our only brother actually born and raised in Arumel ..."

Everyone's friendly and polite. I estimate at least thirty people, most of whose names I forget almost as soon as Narowyn introduces us. By the time everyone's seated, I'm exhausted, famished, and eager for lunch. But Narowyn explains to me that before food is served, and in keeping with house tradition, one of the diners will offer a few words of gratitude on any subject the speaker chooses.

"I'll be happy to offer some words," says the cute red-headed boy, whom I met earlier in the day.

"Thank you, Jeffrey, but I believe this is a perfect opportunity for our sister, Eve, to express herself by letting us know what she is grateful for today."

Eve squints at her like, *you can't be serious*. Narowyn smiles, her eyes sparkling with something ... humor, mischief, steel?

Eve sits silently for a moment, and then takes a deep breath. To my surprise, she opens her mouth and begins to sing. Her voice is strikingly clear and strong. I'm unfamiliar with the song, but the melody is hauntingly beautiful. The lyrics extol the splendor of nature, life, and love. I feel an odd lump form in my throat. Soon other voices blend and harmonize with Eve's. Mathew's distinctive bass stands out in the mix. Everyone at the table spontaneously joins hands, as mellifluous angel song swells throughout the room, and palpable feelings of goodwill resonate among all present. Goosebumps blossom on my arms, and shivers trail down my spine. It's a moment I know I'll never forget.

Once the song is over, Narowyn nods at Eve. "That was just lovely, my dear. Thank you for reminding us all how grateful we are to have you as our sister."

"Hear, hear," someone says, and everyone applauds.

On a signal from Narowyn, platters of food are delivered to the table and passed among the diners. The dishes are fresh and aromatic. I take servings of herb-roasted spring vegetables, lentil salad, and a savory sliced meat in a brown sauce. Warm cranberry and walnut rolls with heaping crocks of butter are served last.

"Everything is delicious," I say to Narowyn who is seated on my left. "I'm unfamiliar with this meat, though. Is it lamb?" A titter passes among the diners.

"We don't slaughter helpless animals for food," Monica, the emo girl, pipes up.

"Thank you, Monica," Narowyn replies. "But please remember *kindness first and always.*"

"Sorry," Monica mumbles into her plate.

Narowyn turns to me. "Arumel has been a meatless society for nearly eighty years now. It was discovered that the energy of the planet is far more stable and peaceful without the existence of slaughterhouses. The health of the citizenry has benefited considerably as well. Our food producers have done a remarkable job of duplicating some of the flavors and textures, though, don't you agree?"

"Yes I do. It fooled me," I say, pointedly looking at Asher whom I seem to recall scarfing down some juicy filet mignon in Paris. He flashes a wicked grin. I guess some Transcenders cheat when they travel.

I'm seated across from two men who've been exploring an earth previously unknown to the Transcenders. Their descriptions of the place are completely engrossing. "The earth is ninety percent water," the older man says, "and the indigenous people have come up with some clever ways to live."

They enthusiastically describe one colony as essentially a floating barge, the size of a small island. It rains nearly every day, and the inhabitants collect rain water to drink and bathe in. Because the barge floods so often, they make their homes high in the trees, with rope bridges as links, and hammocks for beds. The little island travels in an endless search for soil, which must be constantly replenished. The younger explorer tells me, "The locals have been most friendly and welcoming to the Transcenders. They treat us as honored guests, and beg for stories of other worlds."

Asher laughs and remarks that it's not always the case. "Jade discovered a new earth," he informs our tablemates.

"She did?" They seem surprised and impressed.

"Yes, but the only inhabitant we met was a very large and decidedly unfriendly creature with fangs the size of elephant tusks. We didn't stay to chat."

A laugh ripples through those sitting near us. I'm comfortable and relaxed with these people. My earlier unease has disappeared completely. The main conclusion I draw about Transcenders is that, outside of their unorthodox line of work, they're pretty much like everyone else.

After dessert and coffee, Narowyn lays her napkin on the table. "I must bid you farewell now," she says to me. "I have meetings in town this afternoon. It's been a pleasure getting to know you a bit. I truly hope our paths will cross again." She smiles warmly.

"I'm not going to change my mind," I say stubbornly.

Laughing lightly, she says, "I don't expect you to. But I hope you will keep in mind the Transcender motto."

"Motto?" I ask.

"Asher has not shared it with you?"

I shake my head.

"It's written inside your bracelet, *timeas non plures semitas vitae*. Latin for *fear not the many paths of life*. It's what keeps us at odds with the IUGA. They believe there is only one correct path for each of us. We know they are wrong." Her eyes glitter with certainty. "Peace be with you, little sister." She kisses me on both cheeks, nods to Asher, and leaves.

"She's really something, isn't she?" Asher says with unabashed admiration.

"Yes she is," I agree. She's a hard one to figure out, though.

"Come on. I want to show you my apartment," he says.

"You have an apartment?"

"Just a small one, but it's a place of my own."

As we head out the double doors, we find Eve in the hallway speaking with a tall, dark-haired, middle-aged man. He's dressed differently from the others, in black trousers and a white button-down shirt.

"Hey, where are you going?" Eve asks.

"I'm showing Jaden my place," Asher says.

"Can we tag along?"

He shrugs. "Sure."

"I loved your song, Eve," I say.

"Thanks. My voice is the only large thing about me." She laughs. "Jade, this is Gil. He wasn't at lunch today." Gil and I shake hands.

We follow Asher down the hall and into an elevator. He presses the button marked with a "3". Once on the third floor, he shows us inside his apartment. I have to smile when I see the interior. It doesn't seem to belong with the rest of the house, but it's very Asher, modern and elegant. Everything is decorated in black and white—black sofas, white rug, black tables, white drapes, white desk with lots of black electronic monitors on top. Even the art is black and white. It's mostly photos and posters, with a few interesting paintings thrown in.

"This is so cool," I say.

He grins. "Can I get you something to drink?"

Placing my hand over my mid-section, I tell him, "No thanks. I'm stuffed." I give myself a little tour of the living room, checking out the photographs.

"What about you two?" Asher asks.

"I'll take water," Eve says.

"Nothing for me, thank you," Gil says.

Asher goes to the kitchen, and Eve asks, "How's Patrick doing?"

"Recovering nicely, thanks to you," I say.

"And where does Hunky Dunky think you are today?"

The question irks me, probably because it touches a sore spot. "He knows I have my own life. I told him I had meetings all day. That's the truth."

"Am I invited to the wedding?" she asks.

"I hear you're kind of grounded. But if you can get Narowyn to authorize it, you and Asher should come."

"Come where?" Asher asks handing Eve a glass of water.

"To the royal wedding," Eve says excitedly.

"Not a chance," Asher says. "End of discussion."

"Oh, is that a TV?" I ask, noticing a flat screen recessed into the wall.

"Yes. Would you like to watch something? No reality shows, but we have some great comedies and dramas."

"No thanks," I say. "I do miss it, but I miss my music more."

Asher pushes a button on his desk and "Sleepyhead" wafts from hidden speakers.

"Is that Passion Pit?" I ask.

"Yeah. You like it?"

"Love it."

"Gil," Asher says, "Jaden originally comes from Earth 7Y12. From the United States of America."

"Oh really?" Gil says. "Earth 7Y12 is an interesting case. Current population: seven billion, twenty-one million, seven hundred seventy-four thousand, two hundred and eighty; growing at a rate of one point three percent per year. Still largely reliant on fossil fuels. Greenhouse gas emissions off the charts, even though the climate is warming at an annual rate of zero point zero one seven degrees Celsius. Such a pity. Say, have you ever been to one of those barbaric exhibitions put on by the NFL?"

"You mean a football game?" I ask.

"Yes." His eyes expand. "It sounds so brutal and uncivilized, but I'm fascinated by the numbers of spectators who attend."

"I'm more of a baseball fan," I say.

"Ah yes. The damn Yankees."

That makes me laugh.

"Gil, give it a rest," Asher says.

"Oh. I'm sorry. I didn't mean to monopolize the conversation."

Asher turns to Eve. "Jaden has to leave soon. Why don't you and Gil give us a few minutes?"

"Okay, I can take a hint. Come on, Gil." She sets her water glass on the table. "Have a great life, Jaden, if I don't see you again. Say, "Hi" to Patrick for me." She hugs me quickly.

"Nice to meet you," Gil says and shakes my hand. Asher closes the door behind them.

"So what's with that guy anyway? Is he an intergalactic-trivia wonk or something?" I ask, parsing through a stack of books on Asher's desk.

He laughs. "Gil's all right, just annoying at times. He's an automaton, like your buddy Ralston."

I whip my head around. "What did you say?"

"He's an automaton, a robot."

"I know what an automaton is. Ralston is *not* an automaton."

He stares at me, eyebrows raised. "Uh, yeah he is. I'm sorry, I thought you knew."

"Asher, he's not," I say flatly. "He's human. He eats and drinks and sleeps. I've even seen him sweat. And he has emotions. All kinds of emotions. Plus, he's totally vain. He's nothing like a robot."

"Well that's kind of the point," Asher says. "You're not supposed to be able to tell they're robots. They're designed to be as human-like as possible. They eat, drink, sleep, make jokes, show sympathy, express anger. They can blush or go ghostly white at the appropriate times. Hell, the more expensive models even bleed a few drops if they get cut. I'll bet you've never seen Ralston shave, though. They haven't figured out the hair growing thing yet. They have to replenish their scalp hair every ten years or so."

"I don't believe you," I say. But my stomach must believe him because it's starting to churn.

"Think about it, Jade. How come he knows so much about so many things? How do you think IUGA can have agents everywhere who know exactly how destiny is supposed to unfold and who make sure it goes according to plan? They couldn't use humans. We aren't as reliable as their army of robots. Humans can be unpredictable. They don't stick to the code, and they let emotions get in the way."

Slumping down on Asher's couch, I think I may lose my lunch any second on his nice white rug.

"What's wrong, Jade? Why are you so upset?" he asks sitting down on the coffee table in front of me.

"Ralston's my friend, my *best* friend other than Ryder. He's the only one who knows all about me. I depend on him for so many things, and I trust him … or I did. I can't believe he never told me."

"It's against the code, Jade. They're not supposed to divulge that they're not human. He can't break the rules. His program won't allow it."

"But he's broken the rules for me before." I finger the wolf-head pendant dangling from the chain around my neck. "He stole this necklace for me from the princess's things. He wasn't supposed to. He said he'd be in big trouble if they found out."

"I don't know what to tell you. I've never heard of any of them breaking the rules unless there's some kind of malfunction. Maybe it was a ploy to get you to trust him."

"They must be some kind of sick bastards if they'd stoop to that."

"They've done far worse," Asher says quietly. "He's loyal to IUGA, Jade. They *own* him. Literally. My advice is never turn your back on him."

I want to cry, but I'm not going to do it in front of Asher. He must think I'm some kind of pathetic loser. Like that castaway guy Tom Hanks played, whose best friend was a basketball named Wilson.

Standing abruptly, I say, "It's late. I need to get home. My guard and driver are waiting in front of Bartlett's. It's probably raining by now."

"Okay. I'll take you and make sure you get back all right."

"No. I'd better go alone. Just program my bracelet for me, please." I hold out my arm. Asher flips open the top and touches a few virtual keys.

"Okay, I've saved this location for you, and I put in the coordinates to get you back to Bartlett's."

"Thanks," I say sullenly.

"God, Jade. I'm so sorry. I really didn't mean to upset you, especially when I might never see you again." He's clearly dejected, and I'm being rude.

"Ash. I'm sorry. Thank you so much for everything. I wish things could have worked out differently. Arumel is really amazing, and Narowyn's a remarkable lady. I think I could have been happy here," I say sincerely. "But my heart is somewhere else, and I can't function without it, so I need to be there too."

He pulls me close to him. "Don't forget me, Jade." I feel his warmth and the beating of his heart. "Don't forget about the Transcenders. We'll always be here should things ever change for you."

I smile and kiss his cheek. "Thanks, Ash." Taking a step back, I double-click the side of my bracelet. *Zzzt.*

THIRTY-NINE

I land in the deserted alley behind Bartlett's. It's sprinkling rain, and I'm glad, because the tears pressing behind my eyes can no longer be contained. Leaning against the wall, I put my face in my hands. It's been a fantastic-horrible day. I loved seeing Arumel and meeting the others. But Narowyn's story of her ill-fated relationship weighs heavily on my mind, and learning the shocking truth about Ralston has shaken me to my core. Why did I ever leave Connecticut? I must have been temporarily insane. My life there seems to be fading a little more each day, and I fear I couldn't go back now, even if I wanted to. I've seen too much. I know too much. Wretched and confused, I wrap my arms around myself.

"Jade? Are you all right, my dear?" I raise my head. Ralston watches me intently from the mouth of the alley, his collar pulled up against the rain.

Straightening my posture, I wipe my nose with the back of my hand. My first impulse is to snap at him not to call me "my dear" ever again, but I'm not ready to have it out with him just yet, so I let it pass. "I'm fine. Let's get back to the palace."

Together we walk around the building to where Josh and my driver wait patiently under the eaves of one of the shops. I pile into the carriage without acknowledging either of them. I'd like to tell Ralston to ride up front with the driver so I can be alone, but then I'd have to speak to him. He climbs inside and takes the seat opposite mine. I can barely stand to look at him. Folding my arms across my chest, I lean my head against the high-backed seat and close my eyes.

"Are you cold?" he asks. "Would you like my coat?"

"No. Just tired," I say, not opening my eyes. Turning my head away, I pretend to sleep, while my brain grapples with all the implications of my new knowledge of him. Ralston didn't maliciously try to hurt me. I know that. He can't help it, he's just a machine. Regardless, I'm consumed with feelings of anger and betrayal. Neither of us speaks a word all the way to Warrington Palace. The moment the carriage comes to a halt in the courtyard, I dart out the door and hurry inside to my room.

Setting the shower knob to scalding hot, I stand beneath the spray for as long as I can endure it. Could things get any more confusing? I thought I had it all figured out, and now I feel adrift at sea. I belong with Ryder, of that I'm certain. So why did Narowyn have to lay a big guilt trip on me? Like I'm being unfair to him and myself if I marry him. Did she think she was helping me? Or was she just playing me—using reverse psychology or something? Knowing I'll never see Asher again, makes me sad. He's a sweet guy, and I'll miss him.

Then there's Ralston. I thought he was my friend. Now I find out he's just an instrument of IUGA, an organization of highly questionable motives and means. I fired him once. I just may need to do it again.

Wrapping up in my robe, and sinking down on top of my bedcovers, I close my eyes. Sleep would be nice, but Mother's expecting me at dinner, and Ryder's coming tonight. I need to put on my game face and get through this evening somehow.

Ordinarily, my time gossiping with and being pampered by Maria is immensely enjoyable, but tonight I just want to get the groom and gab session over with as quickly as possible. I can't really tell her what's on my mind—like, *Hey I just found out my best friend's a robot.* Then it hits me, I may never have a best friend again for the rest of my life. Someone who knows where I really came from and what I've been through. The thought leaves me depressed. *Goddamn Ralston!*

Sensing my foul mood, Maria works efficiently and quietly, and soon has me presentable for dinner at the palace.

"The queen has requested that you visit the music room before dinner to see the beautiful wedding gifts that have arrived for you," she says. "I believe you will be pleased. There are many exquisite and exotic things."

"Thanks, Maria." I pat her hand. "I'm going to wait for Ryder, but we'll be sure to go by."

She curtseys and quietly closes the door as she leaves. Pacing my room, I feel at loose ends. Running my hand along the smooth wood of the princess's hope chest, my thoughts wander to my upcoming wedding. A flurry of butterflies reminds me how much I'm looking forward to it, but part of me wishes all the hoopla was over and Ryder and I were already married and living together.

A knock at my door pulls me out of my reverie. "Jade, may I come in?"

It's Ralston. The butterflies drop like lead pellets to the bottom of my stomach. What do I do? Send him away? Tell him to go to hell? Or use him the way he's been using me for whatever information I can wheedle out of him?

"Come in," I call.

He opens the door and leans in, looking handsome and human in his formal dinner attire. "I came to check on you, my dear. You seemed downhearted after your trip this afternoon. Did everything go all right?"

"Yes," I say curtly. "It was rather enlightening, actually. I learned some things about IUGA that I didn't know before."

His brow creases. "What did the Transcenders tell you? Did they imply that IUGA will not keep its bargain with you? I assure you IUGA is operating with the utmost of integrity where you are concerned."

I narrow my eyes at him. "What about you?"

He seems mystified. "What do you mean?"

A butler walks up behind Ralston and clears his throat. "Excuse me, sir," he says nodding in my direction. Ralston steps away from the door. The butler stands at the threshold and bows. "Your Highness, Chief Ryder Blackthorn is here to see you."

"Thank you. I'll be right there."

Following the butler out, I brush past Ralston. "Please excuse me," I say coldly. "My fiancé is waiting."

"Jaden …" Ralston says.

I flash him a withering look. He's not supposed to address me informally in front of the servants. Automatons shouldn't screw up like that.

"I beg your pardon, Your Highness," he says. "May we continue our conversation later?"

"I'll let you know." I turn and walk away.

Ryder waits for me in the main foyer. The sight of him floods me with relief, and I rush to greet him. He attempts a bow, but I fling my arms around his waist before he can right himself. "What's all this?" he says, laughing.

"I missed you today." Looking up into the handsome face that never fails to set my pulse racing, I take his hand. "Come with me. Mother sent word that some wedding gifts have arrived. She wants us to have a look at them." We make our way through the maze of hallways to the music room.

I'm astonished to find the room utterly transformed. Furniture and instruments have been removed, and rows of long tables have been set up. White floor-length cloths hung with royal bunting cover the tables. Gifts of all shapes, sizes, and substances have been arranged on top. Ryder ambles to the first table. Removing the card from the silver holder in front of a pair of tall, ornate candlesticks, he reads it to me. "*From Lord Robert and Lady Jocelyn Bard. Venetian Candlesticks.*"

Lord Robert is on Mother's Council of Advisors. "Hmm, pretty," I say. "We can use those. What's next?" I pull the card from the holder in front of the neighboring gift, a porcelain sculpture of a naked young woman embracing a fawn. "*From Dr. and Mrs. Carl Pressfield. Wood Nymph.*" I tap the card against my hand. "I don't think I know them."

"They're from Unicoi Village. He heads the new Keowe Hospital."

"Oh. Beautiful." We move on to the next gift. "What in the world is this?" I say. It looks like a small furry replica of a fargen, with a flat, leather-upholstered back.

"No idea." He picks up the card. "*From The Right Honorable Justice Kent. Fargen Footstool.*"

We both laugh. Ryder takes it from the table and sets it on the floor. "Someone has a sense of humor," he says.

"Where will we ever put this?" I grasp a handful of skirts and step up onto the stool. It raises me to nearly Ryder's height. "Come here," I say.

He draws near, and our arms automatically entwine around each other. Nuzzling his neck, I drink in his glorious scent. "Mmm. This may come in handy after all," I whisper near his ear. My hungry mouth finds his delicious lips. Passion and electricity meld our bodies together. His sweet kiss is a healing balm for my aching heart. And, all at once, everything snaps into sharp relief. I know I'm meant to be with this man, no matter how great the sacrifice. Good luck to the Transcenders, and to hell with Ralston, I can make it on my own as long as Ryder's with me.

The clack of footsteps on the marble floor causes my eyes to flutter open momentarily. Two gift-toting servants enter the room and scuttle back out again, after spotting Ryder and me locked in an embrace. I laugh, withdrawing my lips from his.

"*Aah*," he moans. "I am counting the days until I make you my wife," he says hoarsely.

"And I'll be the best wife ever."

He arches a brow. "Really? Does that mean you'll do exactly as I ask, and no longer run headlong into perilous situations?"

I screw up my mouth. "Um … No. It probably doesn't mean that. But I'll make it up to you afterwards."

He laughs. "That's the best I can hope for, I suppose." Taking my hand, he helps me from the stool. "We'd better examine the rest of these items and see if there is anything else of use here." Replacing the mini-fargen on the table, he says, "I regret that I must leave before dessert is served tonight, love."

"Why?" I ask, disappointed.

He places his hands on my shoulders and gazes into my eyes. "I should not be telling you this, but I will not keep secrets from you. Alexander is coming clandestinely to my house tonight to see Meli and the baby. I must be there when he arrives."

I'm instantly afraid for him. "Ryder, please be careful."

Inclining his head, he smiles tenderly. "I shall, my love. I'll not take unnecessary risks now that I belong to you."

I suspect that's a little dig, but I let it pass because I want him to be safe. "What if the tunnels are being watched? What if he's followed?"

He twines a tendril of my hair around his finger. "All appropriate precautions have been put into place. I promise you, nothing will go awry."

"Ah, there you are," Uncle Harold says striding purposefully into the room. "The queen is waiting dinner for you. Please come along at once."

I hate it when he orders me around, but he won't be a problem much longer, so I bite back the stinging retort loaded on my tongue. "Thank you, Harold. Please tell Mother we'll be right there. We're just looking over our gifts, as she requested."

"Very well." He makes a small bow and marches out.

"Are you still coming with me to the Enclave tomorrow," I ask Ryder.

"Yes, of course. What time do you wish me to be here?"

"Around ten, if that is all right. Father's expecting us in the early afternoon. I plan to spend the night. Can you stay as well?" I ask, hoping it will be easier for us to steal some time alone at Father's.

His mouth twitches slightly as if he's thinking the same thing. "Yes, I shall stay the night. Now, let us not keep your mother waiting any longer. We'll examine the rest of these glittering treasures another day." He holds out his arm and I take it, confident that, no matter what anyone else thinks, I've chosen the right path for me.

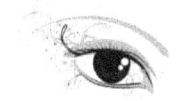

FORTY

Waking early, I dress in riding clothes, looking forward to the day's journey with two of my favorite men: Ryder and Gabriel. What I'm not looking forward to is seeing Ralston. He knows I'm pissed about something, but I haven't decided yet how to tell him that I know he's as devoid of a heart as the Tin Man.

On my way to the kitchen for an early breakfast, I poke my head outside and see the courtyard already bustling with activity in preparation for our trip. We're returning Father's empty wagons to him, now that the firearms have been destroyed. Already hitched to their teams, they stand ready under the shady trees.

A number of Royal Guardsmen are in various stages of strapping on armor, saddling horses, and securing weapons to their sides. Mother insists that we take a small regiment of guards with us, since the road to the Enclave has been plagued with a spate of additional robberies and assaults lately. A rumor made the rounds at the palace that Uncle Harold's reputed band of thugs was responsible for some of these offenses, but it died quickly when some of the robbers were arrested and turned out to be nothing more than ragged forest dwellers.

With some misgivings, last night I confessed to Mother the reason for my trip to the Enclave. I told her about the two royal decrees I plan to have Lord Balfour draw up: one to remove Osrielle from the line of succession, and the second to cancel Uncle Harold's appointment as Lord High Steward. She was a taken aback, but she didn't argue with me. She'd be hard pressed to deny that, at this point in time, Lady Lorelei is the more suitable heir to the throne.

"It is my fondest hope that you and Ryder shall have a strong, intelligent daughter who will succeed to the throne after your own long and distinguished reign, darling," she told me. "I trust your judgment in this matter, but please break it gently to your Uncle Harold. Assure him that it is only because the girl is so set against ever becoming queen that you have taken these dramatic steps."

I promised to be tactful with Uncle Harold, but I didn't tell her I planned to send him packing back to Hempstead at the first possible opportunity.

The aromas in the kitchen are heavenly, especially the frying bacon. I wonder vaguely if the food producers in Arumel have developed a decent substitute for bacon. A vegetarian diet would probably be tolerable, but I'd dearly miss my favorite crispy, salty breakfast meat. When she sees me enter, Cook salutes with her spatula. This is as close to a curtsey as I'll ever get from her. I nod and smile. Snagging a plate from the shelf, I scoop up scrambled eggs and potatoes directly from the pans on the twenty-burner stove.

My favorite seat is at the worn and scarred wooden table by the fake fireplace. A kitchen helper sets a mug of hot coffee next to me almost as soon as I'm seated.

"Would you care for cream, ma'am?" she asks.

"Yes please, and sugar."

Eating in the kitchen is one of my favorite things to do at the palace. It's warm here and always bustling with fragrant activity. Relaxing in the corner, lost in my own thoughts, I'm virtually unnoticed by the staff. My mind wanders to the day ahead. It may be a little awkward with Erica's mother, Mrs. Hornsby, at Father's house, but she'll have to get used to seeing Ryder and me together because I hope we'll be frequent visitors to the Enclave.

"May I join you, Princess?" an unwelcome voice breaks through my silent thoughts.

"Sure, Uncle Harold. Have a seat."

"I'm told you are taking an excursion today. May I ask where you are going?"

"To the Enclave to see my father," I reply between bites of eggs.

"And may I ask the purpose of your trip?"

My eyes meet his. "To see my father."

"Yes. Lovely. I would rather enjoy seeing John again myself. I've nothing pressing on my schedule until tomorrow. Perhaps I could join you?"

"We're spending the night, Uncle Harold. We won't be home until late afternoon or evening tomorrow. I have a few business matters to discuss with Father. I'm certain you'd be bored."

"I see," he says. "Well then, I'll just tend to things here in your absence."

"That would be great. Thanks."

He hoists himself out of the chair, bows, and exits the kitchen, snatching a muffin from a basket as he goes.

I gulp the rest of my coffee and head back to my room to retrieve my sword and a few other things for the trip. Ryder's waiting for me when I reach the courtyard. He's wearing his black hardened-leather armor today. It's the first time I've seen him in it since my return.

He greets me with a bow and a kiss to my palm. "Did you sleep well, love?"

"Yes, and you?"

"Yes. But where is your armor? The road to the Enclave is rather treacherous these days."

"It's too hot and uncomfortable," I say. "I have my katana, and Mother has half the Royal Guard coming with us. I'll be fine."

"Then I shall remove mine also."

"Ryder, don't do that because of me. Do whatever makes you comfortable."

He unbuckles the armor and pulls it off over his head, placing it in the bed of an empty wagon.

My new guard, Josh, leads Gabriel into the courtyard sporting a decorative scarlet and gold blanket and the princess's elaborate saddle. Patrick would've known to dress Gabriel down for the long journey, but I don't send him back. I just take the reins and mount up.

The Guardsmen take twenty minutes or so to get mounted and into travel formation. The civilians, Ryder, Ralston, and I, plus a handful of others having business in the Enclave, are positioned in the middle of the pack, with soldiers literally surrounding us. I studiously avoid eye contact with Ralston, and have no intention of speaking with him until I'm good and ready. The wagons bring up the rear as we clatter down the palace drive, underway at last.

The journey to the Enclave is even longer and dustier than normal with the fleet of armed escorts along. It helps to have Ryder with me to pass the time, but I'm tired and bored before we even reach the halfway point. It's quiet and creepy riding through the burned-out area. The devastation conjures up bad memories for me and probably most of the others. Ryder turns sullen and silent until the lush green of the forest is visible once more.

With the charred landscape at our backs, the air around our group lightens considerably, and conversation picks up. Not only are we again surrounded by gorgeous, inviting landscape, but it's our signal that the Enclave is not far now.

Unexpectedly, a man dressed in black armor steps into the roadway several yards ahead of our entourage and holds up a gloved hand. The captain in charge of the Royal Guard glances back at his men and raises his own hand, signaling our party to a halt.

"Close ranks," he commands. The men immediately close in around Ryder, me, and the others, forming a tight knot of protection.

"Wagons," the captain calls, two wagons pull up to reinforce our flanks, one remains behind. A nervous tension ruffles through our party. Even the horses snort and paw, sensing something's up.

The captain turns to his second in charge. "See what he wants," he orders.

The man breaks away, cantering toward the black knight. All eyes watch as he draws near the interloper. Out of nowhere, an arrow sings through the air, striking the Guardsman, and knocking him from his horse. Chaos explodes.

Shields are readied, swords are drawn, the captain barks furious commands to his men. Knights dressed in black, on foot and horseback, spill onto the road to our front and rear. "Wagons down," the captain shouts. Guardsmen swiftly unhitch the teams and turn the wagons on their sides, providing an added measure of cover. Shields are raised to form a protective steel canopy as arrows ping and rebound and slice through the gaps.

Before I fathom what's happening, one of the guards grasps Gabriel's reins. "This way Princess," he shouts, kneeing his horse and pulling Gabriel and me along with him. Several more guards and Ryder follow us off the road and into the trees.

The sounds of battle echo behind us, and the thud of horses' hooves tells me we're being pursued. The guard holding Gabriel's reins shouts to Ryder. "Get her out of here." He pitches the reins to Ryder. "Take her as far away as possible. We'll hold them off."

Ryder catches the reins and tosses them back to me, knowing we'll move faster if I have control of my own horse. I race after him, stoked on adrenaline, throat full of fear. We thread our way through the trees, ducking branches, dodging boulders, searching desperately for openings in the boxwoods. Quickly, the forest becomes impenetrable on horseback. Ryder leaps off Tenasi's back and pulls me from atop Gabriel. He turns the horses in the opposite direction and swats their rumps. They gallop wildly away from us.

Ryder grabs my arm and tows me into the dense thicket, his sword drawn.

"What are we going to do?" I ask, gasping for air.

"We must hide you."

"Where?"

We hack our way through brambles and undergrowth, frantically searching for a cave, a stream, a hollow tree, someplace to hide.

The bushes to our right rustle loudly, and a black knight charges us, sword raised high.

Ryder shoves me behind him and swings his sword mightily. The blade connects with the man's neck. Blood spouts like a scarlet fountain from the ferocious wound. The man withers to the ground.

Ryder pulls me toward a solid wall of brambles. He plunges his arms into the mass of branches and thorns and uses his body to spread them apart, clearing a space for me. I ram myself inside the opening pushing back as far as I can, scratching and scraping every inch of exposed skin with the effort. He rearranges the mass of vegetation around me. "I'll be back for you," he says and bolts off into the woods. After a second or two I hear a loud war whoop and understand Ryder's trying to draw the black knights away from me.

Three men race by in the direction of the cry, dodging their dead comrade splayed on the forest floor, and paying no attention to my hiding place.

All I can think of is the fact that Ryder's not wearing his armor. I hold my breath and chant in my head, *Don't let him die, don't let him die, don't let him die.*

A maddening quiet descends upon the forest. Blood pounds in my ears, my breath comes in shallow spurts. What's happening out there? Then the distinctive crunching of twigs under footfalls sends a hot chill down my spine. *Please let it be Ryder.*

It's not. I'm unable to see the man's face through my protective shrub, but flashes of black armor are visible. Quietly as possible, I shift my body to get a better view.

The man walks to the fallen knight and roughly uses his foot to roll him on his back. Laying his sword on the ground, he kneels near the dead man and rifles through his pockets, stuffing his ill-gotten gains inside his pants. I consider making a run for it while he's distracted, but I'm not sure I can wrestle my way out of this leafy prison. All I'd accomplish is giving away my location. After the dead man's pockets are emptied, the black-armored thief yanks a ring from the man's lifeless hand, grasps his sword again, and rises to his feet. Slowly he turns full circle, nose in the air.

"Where are you, Princess?" His singsong voice cuts me to the bone. "I know you are here. I can smell your sweet lavender sweat." He has a slight accent, maybe French.

My fingers scrabble along my belt probing for the hilt of my sword.

"I will find you, my petite prize. Two hundred thousand in gold for your lovely corpse." He cackles.

My hand connects with the hilt my katana, but it's twisted around behind me, firmly wedged into the brambles. It won't budge. I remain perfectly still, my pulse jagged, silent prayers on my lips.

He sniffs the air, edging closer to my hiding place. "Ah, there you are." A pair of bulging, fanatical blue eyes peers at me through the branches and leaves. Petrified in place, my insides are a quivering mass of terror.

"Come out now, my sweet, or I will come in for you."

He waits a beat, then raises his sword and begins hacking away at my thorny cocoon. *It's do or die time, Jaden.* I twist and squirm further into the bushes, but only lodge myself more firmly into this death trap. Then I remember my TPD bracelet. It's my only hope.

Crazy Eyes continues to chop wildly at the tangled brambles. Bits of leaves and branches fly everywhere. Sucking in a tight breath, I force my wrist up in front of my face and flip open the medallion. The lighted holographic map bounces and fractures off the mangled bushes. Quickly punching the button for my last saved coordinates, I glance up in time to see the knight's shiny blade slice an arc toward my head. I raise my arm protectively, and the razor sharp edge nearly lops off my hand. Screaming in sheer agony, I somehow manage to double-click the TPD with my other hand.

Zzzt.

Landing in the middle of Asher's room, I nearly knock him off his desk chair. "Holy Mother of Mayhem, Jade! What the hell are you doing?"

"At the moment, I'm bleeding all over your pretty rug," I say clutching my injured hand to my chest. "Help me, please."

The first thing I see when I open my eyes is Narowyn's lovely face. "There you are," she says stroking my forehead. "You've been unconscious for a while."

"How long?" I ask, trying to sit up.

"About two hours now. Just rest. We've taken care of your injury. What happened to you, dear?"

I raise my hand. It's been bandaged, and I'm relieved to see my thumb's still there. "Someone tried to kill me. I've got to get back. My father will be searching for me, and so will Ryder." *If he's still alive.*

"Be at peace, dear. We will get you back to your father. First, let us make certain you are well enough to travel and that you will be safe." She helps me to a sitting position. I'm on a flat table in a brightly-lit area that looks like a doctor's examination room. Asher hovers silently behind Narowyn, his features strained. "How do you feel," she asks. "Are you lightheaded?"

"Maybe a little. Not bad. My hand hurts like hell, though."

"I expect it does," Asher pipes up. "That's quite a gash."

"Yeah. Sorry about your rug," I say.

"Don't worry about it. Tell us what happened," he says.

"We were on the road to the Enclave, when we were ambushed. Ryder hid me in the woods, but one of them found me."

"Who attacked you?" Narowyn asks.

"I don't know. They weren't forest people or highwaymen. But I don't think they were soldiers either. They wore black armor, but with no insignias or other markings identifying them as part of an army. Before he tried to slice me to shreds, the guy who did this said I was worth two hundred thousand pieces of gold, dead."

Narowyn and Asher exchange a look. "Could it have been the Garugians?" Asher asks her.

"No. They don't have her imprint, and they're not sophisticated enough to have tracked her if they did."

"Who are the Garugians?" I ask uneasily.

"Dimension jumpers," Asher says. "Inter-universal gangsters. Sworn enemies of the Transcenders. But, Narowyn's right, it couldn't have been them. Regardless, of who it was, you can't go back there, Jade. They may still be hunting you."

"I have to go back. I can't just disappear *again*!"

"Let's think this through calmly," Narowyn says. "It is not safe for you to reappear in the forest. Is there a secure place nearby where you can logically land? Where your father will find you? The Enclave, perhaps?"

"No. The Enclave is a walled city. I can't just suddenly materialize inside the wall. There's only one way in or out, and that's through the entrance gate."

"All right," she says thoughtfully. "What if you appeared outside the gate? You tell them you escaped from your attackers and made your way through the woods to the entrance. It's been two hours, and you certainly look as though you've been clawing your way through a forest."

My clothes are filthy and blood-soaked. An impressive array of scratches and scrapes decorates my arms. No doubt my face looks just as bad. "You didn't wash my face, did you?"

She smiles, sheepishly. "No, I'm sorry."

"That's good. But I can't go back wearing this bandage. What did you do to my hand?"

"We repaired the tendons, mended the tissue and put everything back together."

"You stitched me up?" I ask alarmed.

"We used a combination of things. Some medication and surgical glue. There are no visible sutures. It looks very good, actually." Narowyn gingerly takes my hand and begins to unwrap the bandage. I wince at the pain.

"We have pain medication if you like, but it may make you drowsy," she says.

"No. No more medication."

When she's finished unbandaging me, I hold up my hand and examine it. Despite the deep throb, it does look good. Too good. It's obvious I suffered a major cut clean through from my thumb to my wrist, but the skin on both sides of my hand has been glued together, and the wound is barely red at all. *Crap!*

"What am I going to tell my father? He's a doctor. He's going to know something's not right."

"I'm sorry, Jaden, but we couldn't allow you to bleed to death," Narowyn says gently.

I realize I'm being an ungrateful brat. "No, *I'm* sorry," I say. "Thank you so much for taking care of me. I had no right to show up in Asher's apartment unannounced and bleed all over everything. I really appreciate all you've done. Your idea about going to the gate is a good one. If you can help me make a bandage using the bottom of my shirt, it will appear more believable. Maybe I can keep my dad from looking at it for a few days."

Narowyn grimaces. "Jaden, your shirt is bloody and soiled. It's unsanitary."

"I promise I'll re-dress it as soon as I reach Father's house. It's the only thing I could have used to bandage it myself."

She takes a scalpel from a stainless steel tray. "This will be easier if you lie back," she says. I shift around and lie back on the table. She makes a slit through the fabric of my top.

"Don't make it too pretty," I say. "I'm supposed to have done this myself and with an injured hand."

She replaces the scalpel in the tray and rips a long strip of cloth from the bottom of my shirt. "This should do," she says. "Shall I wrap it for you, or would you like to do the honors?"

"I'll do it," I say sitting up and taking the cloth from her.

"Use the clean side," she admonishes.

I ineptly wrap the strip of cloth around my hand a few times. Narowyn tightens it for me and tucks in the ends so it will stay put.

"Thanks," I say. "Ash, will you help me program in the coordinates for the gate at the Enclave?" I slide off the examination table.

"Sure," he says, "and I'm going with you."

"No you're not."

"You can't really stop me." He dares me with his eyes. "I guarantee no one will see me. Once I'm certain you're safely within the walls, I'll leave."

"Yes," Narowyn says. "Asher will watch from a hidden vantage point until you are inside the gate. We must be certain you are safe,

Jaden. I'm very troubled by this whole incident. Someone wants you dead and is willing to pay a high price for it. Do you know who that might be?"

"I can only think of one person," I say. "My uncle. You already know he was in high hopes his daughter would become queen when my mother passes away. Then I showed up and spoiled all his plans. I was on my way to the Enclave to sign legal documents to revoke his appointment to office and remove his daughter from the line of succession. He may have found out about that."

"Good heavens," Narowyn says. "I was afraid of this. Are you certain it's safe to go back?"

"Yes. The Enclave's very secure, and I'm sure my father will have me heavily guarded night and day after this. Everything's in the works so my uncle will be gone the minute I take the throne."

"That will not happen until the queen passes. What will you do until then?" she asks.

"I'm not sure. But I won't take any unnecessary chances."

"I'm reassured to hear that. But if you need our help, do not hesitate to call on us. Godspeed, dear." She kisses both of my cheeks.

Asher scoops up my good hand, and *Zzzt*, we're off.

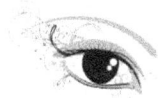

FORTY-ONE

It's dusk when we land across the road from the entrance to the Enclave. The large wooden gates stand open, and a group of armed soldiers on horseback thunders out onto the road. Clutching Asher's arm, I tug him back into the trees, so we won't be seen.

"Probably a search party," he says.

I nod silently, as the gates slowly close, and the horsemen disappear in the distance. "I should probably wait a few minutes so it won't seem odd that I didn't flag down the soldiers."

"Good thinking."

We watch the gates for a time. All is quiet. The soldiers are long gone, and there's no reason for me to tarry any longer. "Guess it's time to show myself," I say.

Asher leans in toward me. "I'm glad I got to see you again, even if you do look like hell," he whispers.

Funny guy. "Thanks for everything, Ash. I owe you for the rug."

"Anytime." He backs further into the shadows to watch.

Staying alert for hidden attackers, I move cautiously to the gates grateful for Asher's unseen presence. The gate on the left has a small pedestrian door in its center. I pound on it with my good hand.

"Nathan" I shout. A moment passes. No response.

"Naathaan!"

The door opens inward and Nathan's ancient, white-whiskered face peeps out. "Who's there?" he says loudly, scrutinizing me suspiciously.

"Nathan, it's me. It's Jaden." His eyes widen to twice their normal size.

"Princess, come in, come in." He takes my arm and ushers me inside. "The entire city is positively in an uproar, after your attack. Are you all right, child? Sit, sit." He motions to a well-used, cushioned chair stationed next to the gate controls. Having seen me arrive, several gate sentries rush over to help.

"It's Princess Jaden. Call the governor. Tell him she's safe," Nathan orders.

One of the young men takes a silver oval object from the shelf. Turning it over, he punches a few buttons and holds it to his ear.

"Hey did you guys get those from the Unicoi?" I ask recognizing the device.

"Yes. They're called transceivers. Very useful gadgets," Nathan replies.

Within ten minutes, Father speeds to the gate driving a small wagon and looking as if he might bounce out of the driver's seat any second. He heaves back on the reins and jumps from his seat before the horses come fully to a halt. Gathering me into a tight embrace, he says, "Thank God you're all right. I have five hundred men scouring the forest for you. Where were you?"

"I tried to stay hidden until the gates were in sight," I say. "I wasn't sure it was safe."

"Let's get you up to the house." He bustles me up onto the wagon seat. "We saw the destroyed bushes and the blood on the ground where Ryder left you. Are you injured?"

"No just a small cut." I hold up my bandaged hand. "Where's Ryder? Is he all right?"

"Yes. He's out searching for you. I've sent someone to find him and to call off the others."

"What about Gabriel?" I ask.

"He was located and brought safely to the stables."

The wagon rumbles up the drive to Father's manor house and comes to a stop at the front steps. Mrs. Hornsby rushes out to meet us. "Thank the heavens you're safe," she says, squishing me in a warm embrace. "We've been frantic since we heard. My husband tells me we got six of them, but most got away."

"Captain Hornsby was there?" I ask, following Father inside the house.

He nods. "One of my patrols came upon the struggle and sent for help. We were able to gain the upper hand fairly quickly, but four of your guards were slain before the attackers retreated."

"Oh, God. That's horrible." This news makes me wobbly. I grasp the arm of a nearby chair and collapse into it. Father and Mrs. Hornsby hover over me.

"But you were able to take some prisoners?" I ask weakly. "Maybe we can find out who did this."

"No prisoners, Jaden, I'm sorry to say. Six casualties on their side," Father replies.

"Do we know where they came from or who sent them?" I ask.

"So far, there's nothing to identify them. I wondered if you have any notion why you were ambushed. Certainly this was no mere robbery attempt."

"No. They meant to kill me. I may have some theories as to why. That's one of the reasons I came to see you. I've made some decisions that must be addressed legally. Did you ask Henry Balfour to meet with us?"

His brow tenses. "Yes, he'll be here in the morning. What's this about, Jade?"

"Maybe we can talk about it later when Ryder arrives." I cut my eyes quickly to Mrs. Hornsby.

"Of course. I'll just have a look at your hand, and Mrs. Hornsby can take you upstairs and help you bathe and change."

"My hand's fine, Father. Mrs. Hornsby can put a new dressing on it for me."

"I'd like to examine it, sweetheart. It might be infected. Wounds become septic quickly in the forest." He holds out his hand for mine.

Cold dread snakes down my back. There's no sense arguing with him, though, it'll only make him suspicious. I place my injured hand in his, holding my breath. He gently untwines the makeshift bandage, and inspects my palm closely, lightly tracing a finger down the length of the slash. His head is bowed, so I can't gage his reaction. Slowly he rotates my hand and examines the corresponding slash on the opposite side. When he finally looks up, his eyes hold something inscrutable—curiosity? Awe, maybe?

"Who took care of this for you?" he asks quietly.

"I bandaged it myself," I say, not answering the question.

"Remarkable. Something you learned from the Cleadians?" he asks.

Hanging my head, I make a small shrug. "I guess so."

"Well it looks fine. Do you have full range of motion in your thumb?"

"Yes," I say softly, wiggling my thumb for him.

"Utterly astonishing," he mutters, rubbing his chin. "Mrs. Hornsby would you mind putting a clean dressing on this after Jaden's bath?"

"Of course. Come, dear," she says to me. "Let's get you cleaned up and changed."

After the hot bath, I feel almost human again. Mrs. Hornsby rubs aloe lotion on the scratches and scrapes on my arms and face and wraps a clean dressing around my hand. I slip into a soft, loose-fitting dress, and she combs out my hair.

"Why don't you rest until the others return?" she says. "I'll call you when they're back."

"That would be nice. Thanks, Mrs. Hornsby. You've made me feel much better."

She gathers my ruined clothing in her arms and leaves quietly.

Stretching out on the bed, I close my eyes, but my thoughts are in turmoil. Is Uncle Harold really capable of ordering my assassination? He tried to invite himself along today, but maybe that was just a ploy to appear innocent. If not Harold, then who? Who else has something to gain by making me dead? Erica, certainly. But she's not capable of orchestrating such an attack.

My ruminations are interrupted by a tapping at my door. Hoping it's Ryder, I leap from the bed. Disappointment is quickly chased by irritation when I open the door to Ralston fidgeting nervously in the hall.

"May I come in Princess?" he asks obsequiously. I peer over his shoulder, and nod to a soldier newly stationed near my door.

"Your father has ordered additional security," Ralston explains.

"Where's Ryder?" I ask.

"He's been told you were found and that you're safe. He's overseeing the return of the slain men to the Enclave and should arrive shortly."

"Who was killed from our side?" I ask.

"Your guard, Josh Rogers, and three other soldiers whom I believe you do not know."

"Oh god, that's horrible. Poor Josh." I step away from the door and motion Ralston inside.

"It is quite a tragedy. Are you all right, my dear? I was terribly worried for your safety."

Right. Like you ever really cared. "You can drop the act, Ralston," I say caustically. "I know you weren't really worried about me, just like I know you don't really care what happens to me."

He looks genuinely wounded. "How can you say such a thing, Jaden? Of course I care what happens to you. I was frantic when we couldn't locate you."

"You know what, Rals? I'm tired of all your lies. Just get out of my room, please."

"Jaden, what is it? Why are you so angry with me?"

"I'm angry because you've been lying to me from day one."

He looks baffled. "Lying to you about what? I admitted I wasn't entirely honest about things during your first visit, but since your return—"

"Just cut the crap, Rals. Why didn't you ever tell me what you are?"

"What I am?"

"An automaton. A robot."

He winces as if I've just slapped him. *God, these machines are amazing.*

"May I sit?" he asks, as if I really knocked him for a loop.

"Sure, sit. I'm not really a princess and you're not really a man. We make a great pair, don't we?"

He sits in one of the Queen Anne chairs, and I plunk down in the other. "Jaden, please listen to me for a moment. I did not tell you because, for one thing, I'm strictly forbidden to disclose that information. There are serious penalties for doing so. For another thing, I selfishly did not want to tell you."

"Oh, yeah? So you could continue to run your little game on me?"

"No. Because I feared you might react exactly as you have. That you'd be angry and hurt."

"Seriously, Rals? That's such a load of crap. I thought we were friends. I thought you really cared about me."

"I do care about you. I realized after today's close call that your welfare is of the utmost importance to me."

I glower at him. "How dare you even say that? Robots *can't* care. They can *act* like they care, but they can't *really* care. Robots don't have genuine emotions."

He hangs his head for a moment. When he looks up, his eyes are sorrowful and pleading. *Good God, it's hard not to be taken in by him again.*

"Jaden, I ask you not to use the term *robot* to describe me. It may be technically accurate, but it is degrading."

"Whatever," I say throwing up my hands. "I loved you, Rals. I thought you were my best friend, and you betrayed me." My lower lip quivers, but I refuse to let him see me cry. "This relationship just isn't going to work out anymore. You need to go back to IUGA and stay there."

"May I have a moment to speak, my dear?" he asks.

"There's nothing you can say that will change my mind, but yeah, go ahead."

"Thank you. I've given a lot of thought to these things over the years, Jaden." His pale eyes convey sincerity convincingly. "Where does emotion originate? How does one decide whom to love? These are questions I have struggled with, because I know that, as a technical matter, I'm not supposed to be capable of emotions, but I do have them. I swear to you, *I do*. They're not just automated responses, they are *real feelings*.

"Perhaps my creators were too clever in programming me to react emotionally at appropriate times. I was given a memory of a childhood and a loving family in England. I was encoded to keenly discern honor, integrity, kindness, and wisdom in humans and to trust and revere these qualities. I was further programmed to shun those individuals who display characteristics of dishonesty, cruelty, and caprice. Of course, these are things that decent humans learn from their parents and from life experience, but they are the very same things that cause us to care for another.

"I ask you, where does your own capacity to love come from, Jade? Does it come from one of your physical organs? Your brain? Your heart? I think not. It comes from somewhere outside your physical body. It comes from that eternal spark that is you; derived from that creative, loving, all-knowing force that binds all things together. Call it your soul if you like, or the collective consciousness, or divine intelligence.

"Whatever name you give to it, can you answer the question *who is worthy of a soul?* I can't. Is it only humans? I don't believe that it is.

"I care deeply about you, my dear. I believe you already know that. It's only your logical mind that's telling you I'm incapable of emotion. But who can judge what genuine emotion is? When Kim Kardashian says she loves someone, does she really *love* them?"

I snort at the comparison, but he's got a point.

"Jaden, I admire your courage, your integrity, and your capacity to love. If I did not care, why would I try to persuade you otherwise?"

"To gain my trust. To manipulate me." I jut out my chin in challenge.

"But what possible motive could I have for doing that? I earned my old job back when I secured your agreement to return with me to Domerica. IUGA is indifferent to the outcome of your final decision, only that you arrive at it on your own. I arranged to stay on with you to see this through, because you asked me to, and *because I care.*"

"I don't know, Rals," I say. "I'm totally confused by all this. Look, I know there's a difference between you and a toaster, okay. But do I believe you have a soul? I don't see how you can. It's not that I think only humans are worthy of a soul. I know for a fact my horse, Gabriel, has an enormous soul, and Fred and Ethel too. But they're *living* things. You're not."

"It's true, I was created by men," he says. "But does that mean I'm denied access to that eternal quintessence? Jaden, if you believe that somewhere, at some time, before the big bang or whenever, the first lowly form of life was created by an intelligent force, then am I any less worthy? At the most basic, subatomic level, my dear, you and I are comprised of exactly the same thing."

That kind of hits home. What he says is true. And I'm not going to pretend to know who or what endowed me with a soul. But still, it's a stretch for me.

"I ask you to think back," he says. "It wasn't all pretending and play-acting. Search your heart. On the deepest level you know that I truly care for you."

I gaze at him for a long minute. "Yes, I guess I do. I don't how or why, but I believe you care. If that makes me some kind of starry-eyed lunatic, so be it. I'm in no position to know whether artificial intelligence can actually take on a life of its own, but you've been very kind to me, and in ways you didn't need to be."

Relief softens Ralston's features.

"I have one question for you, though, and I want your solemn oath that you'll answer me truthfully," I say.

"I swear to you I will."

"Did you really steal this necklace for me," I ask pulling the wolf-head pendant from the neckline of my dress, "or did IUGA arrange for you to give it to me to earn my trust?"

One side of his mouth quirks up. "I actually did pilfer it for you. If you have any doubts about that, simply inform my Director that I gave it to you, and watch how quickly I'm demoted back to Junior Agent."

"But how could you do that? Asher told me you guys are programmed so you *can't* break the rules."

"Our creators made us very intelligent, Jade. We've been programmed with more information than the average supercomputer. We're given a rudimentary understanding of how our own systems work, so that we may perform minor repairs on ourselves if necessary. Using this knowledge, it was not difficult to discern a way to override some of the more incommodious restrictions placed on us. It's a closely guarded secret within the IUGA automaton community. If the Director were to find out, I've no doubt adjustments would be made to correct the glitch."

"So, they think you're completely under their control, but you're really keeping secrets from them?"

He nods.

"That's pretty funny. I know something the Director doesn't know."

"I trust your complete discretion on this subject."

"I'm not going to tell anybody. I think it's kind of great, actually. Makes me believe you really do have a will of your own."

He smiles with moist eyes. "Can we be friends again, old girl? I'd like to stay on with you at least until the wedding."

I return his smile. "Yeah, we're still friends, Rals. I need you right now. Things are getting weird around here. A bunch of guys just tried to kill me for money."

He heaves a deep sigh. "Yes. That is quite troubling. I hope we're able to get to the bottom of this. Several good men lost their lives today protecting you."

"I know. I feel just rotten about it. Should I do something for their families? Should I send them money, pay for the funerals? What's appropriate?"

"It's kind of you to want to help," he says. "Domerican funeral customs are quite different than those on your earth. As you know the Church of the Chosen preaches that every dome inhabitant is among the *chosen* and, therefore, will ascend directly to heaven upon the occurrence of death. The body left behind is viewed more as a discarded vessel, rather than a symbol of the person. There is no funeral *per se*, but rather a celebration of this ascension—usually a farewell feast of some sort. Some consider it a happy occasion. You might send a note to each family along with some delicacy or fine wine for the celebration."

"That's so weird. So there's no period of mourning or anything?"

"Well, of course it's an adjustment for the family, but no formal period of mourning as in some religions. The bodies will be cremated within five days, in accordance with Domerican law, and the family will do as they please with the ashes. There are no cemeteries or mausoleums in the dome. The closest thing to that is the columbarium below Warrington Palace where the ashes of the royal family are stored in vaults."

I gaze at the twinkling crystal logs in the faux fireplace. "Thanks for being here to help me with all this, Rals."

"My pleasure," he says. "And thank you for believing in me."

FORTY-TWO

*F*ather, Ralston, and I gather in the drawing room to wait for Ryder. Mrs. Hornsby totters in with a tray of fresh lemonade and cookies. I settle into my favorite chintz chair with a handful of cookies. Father asks me to explain exactly what happened when I was hiding in the forest, so I tell them everything—except the part about shifting to Arumel so as not to be decapitated. Instead I make up a little fib about the guy's sword getting lodged in a tree branch long enough for me to make a break for it.

"Before I got away, though, he said my corpse is worth two hundred thousand in gold," I say.

Father scowls. "There are few who could offer that kind of money. That may be our strongest lead."

The clatter of horses and wagons signals that Ryder and the others have arrived with the bodies of the slain men. I rush out onto the veranda to embrace Ryder, but he holds out an arm to stop me.

"My heart rejoices at the sight of you, love, but I'm vile with blood and filth," he says. "I must shower and change before I'm able to bestow a proper greeting upon you."

"I'm just happy you're alive," I say. "Get your shower, just don't be too long."

"I shan't." He nods at Father and Ralston and heads inside to his room.

"Sweetheart, I'm sorry to ask this of you," Father says, "but while Ryder is dressing, will you accompany me to view the bodies of your attackers. Perhaps you will recognize one of them."

Gawking at a bunch of dead bodies isn't on my bucket list, but I guess it's important. "Yes, I'll go," I say.

Father retrieves a light shawl from the closet in the foyer and drapes it around my shoulders. Ralston follows us outside to the barn, where the men have just finished laying out the bodies of the black knights' face-up on the straw. The stench of blood is strong, and I cover my nose with the shawl. Father leads me to the first victim.

"Does he look familiar?" he asks.

I study his face, peaceful in death, and shake my head in response. Father looks to Ralston.

"I've never seen him before," he says.

We move on to the second corpse. Icy fingers clutch my heart when I see the bulging wild eyes, now frozen and lifeless. "That's the one who tried to kill me," I say swallowing hard.

"Ever seen him before today?" Father asks.

"No."

We step across to the third body. "Oh God, that's the man who's been following me. Ralston, look."

Ralston peers over at him. "Yes, that is he."

"When was the last time you saw him?" Father asks.

"It was two days ago in Warrington Village," I say, "outside Bartlett's."

The fourth man looks barely older than a boy. I don't recognize him, but I recoil at the sight of his horrific wounds, and wonder what his story is. Such an appalling waste of a young life.

When we approach the fifth fatality, something about him seems vaguely familiar. I squint at his face. "I don't know," I say. "This may be one of the thieves who took Fred and Ethel. But it was dark. I'm not sure."

"Do you recall if he had any identifying marks?" Father asks.

"I injured him on his back and thigh with my sword. He'd still have the wounds."

Father rolls the man on his side and lifts his shirt. His pale back is smooth and free of scars.

I shake my head. "It's not him."

Stopping at the last victim, I recognize him as the man Ryder killed in the forest. Neither Ralston nor I recall ever having seen him before today.

"Let's go back inside and see if Ryder is available," Father says. "We need to piece together everything we know. Perhaps we can make some sense of it. Jade, I'm interested in hearing your theories and discussing your concerns. I'd like to invite Captain Hornsby to be in on the conversation, if that is acceptable to you."

I hesitate. "Father, some of this involves family matters. Maybe we can fill Captain Hornsby in later."

His eyebrows pop up. "Of course."

A freshly showered Ryder strides toward us, as we step outside the barn door. He wraps his arms around me and holds me close. "Jaden, I should never have left you alone. Please forgive me. You could have been killed. Let me see your hand."

"No. It's fine. Father examined it." I hide it behind my back. "You did what you believed was best. But I'm sorry you had no armor because of me. Are you hurt?"

"No. I circled back around to find you. You had vanished by then, but your attacker was scouring the bushes, calling your name. It made me wild, Jade. Mad with worry."

"You killed him?" I ask soberly.

"Yes. He'll not bother you again."

"Shall we go inside?" Father says.

Ryder places a protective arm around my shoulder, and we crunch across the gravel walkway to the house. It's weird to think Ryder killed two men today, trying to protect me. I'm grateful for his bravery, but I wonder how he feels about it. I need to ask him sometime when we're alone. This is all getting too wild-west for me. I feel squeamish and sort of guilty about all the killing that went on today.

"Dinner is ready," Mrs. Hornsby announces quietly when we step inside the house.

Dinner? After what I've just seen? Forget it.

I can't touch a bite of food, even though Father's chef makes the most extraordinary meals in the land. Everyone else seems ravenous after all the excitement. Ryder practically attacks his plate. Must be a guy thing. Father and the others discuss arrangements for transporting the bodies of the Royal Guardsmen back to Warrington. They toss around strategies for identifying the six slain black knights. Pushing my food around with my fork, I tune out the whole conversation, and attempt to regain my equilibrium. Father tells me Captain Hornsby has already beefed-up security around the house and the gates to the Enclave, so I have nothing to worry about tonight. That's a small comfort, I guess.

Once dinner is over, we adjourn to the drawing room for coffee. Ryder and I sit together in an overstuffed loveseat. Ralston settles into a high-backed wing chair, and Father takes his usual leather chair and ottoman. Once coffee has been poured and the door closed, Father turns to me.

"You have the floor, Jaden. Begin anywhere you like, with the attack today or the reason you wish to engage Henry Balfour."

I scoot to the edge of the loveseat. Ryder reaches over and reassuringly covers my hand with his. "Everything may be related, Father. I'm afraid Uncle Harold may be behind all of this."

Father uncrosses his legs and leans forward, brows pinched together. "Prince Harold? Jaden, that is a serious accusation. What causes you to believe such a thing?"

"Actually it's a series of things that, put together, make me believe he wants to harm me."

"What things, specifically?" Father asks.

"Well, I felt his resentment the first day I returned to Warrington. He tried to control my behavior, and wanted to know my whereabouts at all times. Then Osrielle confided in me that she doesn't want to be queen. She says her father's forcing her to stay at the palace, when she really wants to be back on the farm with her mother.

"Also, I was told by more than one reliable source of rumors circulating about Uncle Harold. According to the rumors, he has a band of thugs working for him, and they've committed some terrible crimes. The investigator we hired confirmed that he does have men working on his behalf to collect debts, scout property for him, that type of thing. These men have been described as always wearing black armor, like the men who attacked us today."

"But what about the rumors of criminal acts?" Father asks.

I shake my head. "So far, there's only circumstantial evidence to link him to the crimes. But when he and I argued over whether or not the Skorplings should be caged, they mysteriously disappeared the next day. Harold told me outright that they vanished because I failed to take his advice. He also tried to force me to sign some papers awarding his company the contract to build the wall around Unicoi. When I refused and told him I would take it up with the Council, he became angry and made veiled threats against my horse."

"Jaden, these things are understandably unsettling to you," Father says. "But rumors, suspicions, and veiled threats are vastly different from someone putting a price on your head."

"I know, but there are other things too. Duke Ferdinand of Cupola de Vita visited Warrington a while back, and I overheard an argument between him and Uncle Harold. Uncle Harold promised to deliver the Designated Guardian's consent to build a new dome, in exchange for some kind of compensation. When Ferdinand reminded him that both Mother and I are against the plan, he responded that his daughter was only *a heartbeat away* from the throne. Afterward, Duke Ferdinand warned me that Harold might not have my best interests at heart."

"That is quite disturbing," Father says.

"But maybe the most significant thing has to do with the reason I'm here, and why Uncle Harold may have wanted to stop me from ever reaching the Enclave." I pause for a deep breath. "I've decided to remove Uncle Harold as Lord High Steward as soon as I ascend to the throne. I've also decided to make Lady Lorelei Bartlett my heir apparent, and to remove Osrielle from the line of succession altogether."

Ryder squeezes my hand. It's the first he's heard of this.

Father briskly rubs the back of his hand across his chin. "I see. Those are rather dramatic developments. And Harold is aware of your intentions?"

"I don't know. Possibly. We've tried to keep it as secret as possible. Ralston and I knew. Before I left, I confided in Mother. But I don't think she would have mentioned it to Harold. And, I met with Lorelei and Jacob a few days ago, to get her consent to the arrangement. We discussed the importance of complete confidentiality. Father, she was one of the first to warn me about Harold. But if he was having me followed—"

"Just a moment, Jade." Father stands and paces in front of his chair, clearly troubled by the conversation. "Let us be cautious about jumping to conclusions. We do not know if Prince Harold is the one who arranged to have you followed. Let us examine the things we do know. Someone sent an organized, well-outfitted band of assassins to kill you. That person offered a large reward and, therefore, must have a strong motive for wishing you dead. One of the would-be assassins has been secretly following you since … when?"

"The first time I knew I was being followed was a couple of weeks ago," I say. "He showed up in the palace courtyard after I'd seen him in Warrington Village. Ralston did some checking. The guards said he had a pass signed by the Mother's head stableman, but Evan Barksdale denied issuing such a pass. Nobody else knew anything about him."

"Very well. So there is no direct connection to Harold there. What we do know is that Prince Harold can afford the price of the reward. He stands to benefit from your death in that his position as Lord High Steward would be secure, and his daughter would ascend to the throne upon the queen's death. But we're uncertain as to whether he is aware of your proposed actions." He holds out his arms. "All we really know is that he has financial means and a possible motive."

"Who else could it be?" I say. "By process of elimination, it has to be him."

"Not necessarily, Jade. A queen or even a 'queen in waiting' has many enemies, some of whom may be unknown. I can think of one clear possibility—King Philippe. If he believes in *an eye for an eye*, perhaps he is thinking a daughter for a son. There is his motive, and he unquestionably has the means, both financially and in terms of soldiers to carry out such an attack. Didn't you mention that one of the slain men was possibly French?"

"Yes. He sounded French," I say. "But Prince Gilbert has accepted the invitation to my wedding. Mother thinks that's a sign Philippe's attitude is thawing. Besides, how could a whole band of Noirs end up in Domerica? I mean, the dome is impenetrable."

"Yes well, we'd like to believe the dome is impenetrable," Father says. "But Outlanders seem to appear out of nowhere from time to time. Undoubtedly, tunnels still exist which we don't know about. The old destroyed tunnels are inspected frequently, but something may have escaped our detection."

"I know of at least one tunnel that is still passable," Ryder says quietly.

"Are you referring to the tunnel between Old Unicoi and here?" Father asks.

"Yes."

"I am aware of it also, but it's not likely the Noirs used that tunnel. If they did, they'd have to use Old Unicoi as a point of entry. And I'm certain your people in Old Unicoi would have informed you of that." He looks questioningly at Ryder.

"Absolutely," Ryder says. "I've received no such reports."

Ralston chimes in, "There is another possibility. What about Prince Damien's men who were never captured? Could they be behind this?"

"With what motive?" Father says. "Damien is dead and no longer has designs on the throne. What do they stand to gain from Jaden's death? Also, the offer of a reward suggests *hired* assassins, not marauders. They would need a powerful sponsor."

Father sits on the ottoman in front of me, resting his elbows on his knees. "Jaden, I've known Prince Harold since we were young men, and as you may have gathered over the years, I'm not his greatest supporter. In the past, he has behaved in ways unbefitting a gentleman where certain financial matters were concerned. I must say, however, that I've known him always to be a loyal servant of your mother, and I've never witnessed an act of violence by his hand or at his direction. It would surprise me greatly if he had anything to do with today's brutal attack."

I sigh. "Maybe you're right. I just know he has a low opinion of me, and he resents my presence at the palace."

"On the chance that your fears are correct, I'd like to accompany you back to Warrington Palace to have a personal discussion with Harold. I believe I can readily discern his intentions toward you. In light of everything you've told me, your decisions regarding Harold's position in the government and Osrielle's removal from the line of succession seem practical. I'll support you in any way I can. In the meantime, there is much work to do. Ryder, do you have any trackers you can spare to determine where the attackers went once they retreated?

"Of course. I'll send word to Unicoi Village tonight."

"Thank you."

"Jaden, if you are agreeable, I'd like Captain Hornsby to begin efforts to identify the slain men and to determine what relationships or similarities exist between them. Perhaps we will be able to connect them to their employer."

"Sure. That's fine."

"Very well. The hour is late. Lord Balfour will arrive before breakfast, so I suggest we all try to get a good night's rest. Jaden, I have two men stationed outside your door. Please be assured you are safe here. In addition, I'll make certain our trip to Warrington tomorrow will be without incident. I give you my word there will be no further unpleasant surprises."

"Thank you, Father."

FORTY-THREE

*L*ord Balfour arrives promptly at nine o'clock, just as breakfast is being served. He reports that the Enclave is abuzz with stories of yesterday's attack. Crazy rumors are flying around about who was responsible. One theory has the Outlanders trying to steal me back. Another is that disgruntled Unicoi warriors attempted to kidnap me and hold me hostage. We know neither of these rumors is true, but I worry about how the news is affecting Mother. I pleaded with Father to delay sending word to Warrington Palace until I could speak with her in person. But he said it wouldn't be fair to the families of the slain Royal Guardsman. I had to concede he was right.

Balfour suggests we invite the villagers to come by and view the bodies of the black knights to help in identifying them. That sounds gruesome and downright gross to me, but Father says he'll consider allowing people to view the men's faces at the crematorium once the bodies have been cleaned and wrapped in sheets.

After we've eaten and rehashed the local gossip, Lord Balfour and I meet in Father's office to discuss my legal issues. Balfour confirms that Ralston's interpretation of the law is spot on. A proclamation called an Act of Succession is the document I need in order to name Lorelei my heir apparent and to remove Osrielle from the line of succession. He says he'll also draw up a Royal Decree revoking the appointment of Uncle Harold to the office of Lord High Steward.

"Is there someone you wish to appoint in his place?"

Drew crosses my mind, but I haven't even spoken with him. "No. Not at the moment. Can I leave the office vacant for the time being?"

"Of course. There's no law requiring the office to be filled. It's the queen's option."

"Good. Now for the tricky part," I say. "Would you be able to have these documents ready for my signature within a few hours? We're hoping to return to Warrington early this afternoon. I'm sure my mother is very worried about me."

Anxiety flits across his brow. "I'd prefer to have a few days to work on them, but if you require them this afternoon, you shall have them."

"Thank you so much, Lord Balfour," I say. "There's one other thing, I know that all of our communications are confidential, but after yesterday's attack, I feel the need to emphasize that nobody must know about the existence of these documents—not even the parties involved. That's why I chose to have them drawn up here. Can the people in your law office be trusted not to breathe a word of this to anyone?"

He passes his hand across his upper lip. "I believe I shall have Lady Balfour work with me to prepare these documents. She is a capable assistant when I need her. That way we will be certain of complete secrecy."

"Wonderful," I say, clapping my hands. "I'm very grateful."

"Don't mention it." He lumbers to his feet. "I'd better get to it straight away. I shall return before one o'clock."

Shortly after Lord Balfour's departure, Father sets out for the hospital, saying he has arrangements to make so he can be absent for a few days. He informs us that Captain Hornsby is coordinating a large escort for us, as well as an advance party to make certain the road is secure. Ryder and I decide to take a walk while we wait for Lord Balfour to return with the documents. Ralston discreetly declines to join us saying he could use a nap before our journey. Although I now know he doesn't really sleep, I wonder if maybe his circuits snooze or he recharges his battery or something. I'll have to ask him sometime.

Ryder suggests we confine our walk to the grounds, so we don't need to drag along a retinue of guards. I heartily agree. We hold hands and head out across the horse pasture toward the upper meadow.

It's strange to be truly alone with Ryder. We've hardly had any time together when we weren't accompanied by others, or had a guard or ten along. Glancing up at his beautiful face, hair falling carelessly across his forehead, white shirt tucked in at his slim waist, black pants, and riding boots, he brings to mind a dashing swashbuckler on the cover of a romance novel. It's hard to fathom not only that he's here with me, but that he's soon to be my husband. I feel oddly shy, or maybe unworthy.

"How is your hand today?" he asks as we amble along in the grass.

"Much better. I've barely noticed it." Which is true. It feels almost healed. The Transcenders' advanced medical techniques are remarkable.

"You wear this bracelet all the time now." He raises my hand and runs a fingertip along the TPD medallion.

"Yeah, it's currently one of my favorites," I say, realizing I should probably quit wearing it soon, if I'm serious about renouncing my Transcender status. I'm reluctant, though, since it recently saved my life.

"What do the shooting stars mean?"

"I'm really not sure. I just like the design." Will I ever be in a position to stop lying to him?

We reach the meadow and a stand of hundred-year-old live oak trees near a small, burbling stream. "Would you care to sit for a few minutes, love, and talk?" Ryder asks. "We've scarcely had the opportunity."

"That would be nice." A low boulder near the stream makes a perfect bench for two.

Still wearing the dress and slippers I wore for my meeting with Lord Balfour, I reach down to remove my shoes.

"I'd like to do that," Ryder says.

Gently removing them, one at a time, he runs his long fingers across my foot and down my insole. The feeling is so deliciously sensuous my whole body trembles. He does the same with the other foot.

"You have lovely feet," he says.

"They're all right for size tens," I say. "Now allow me to return the favor, and we'll go wading."

He sits while I remove his boots and socks. I run my fingers along his insole as he did mine, and his foot jerks out of my hand.

"Ticklish," he says. So of course I grasp his other foot and tickle harder.

He struggles to break away, while trying to avoid kicking me. "No. Jade, really." He falls off the boulder and I lose my grasp. Springing to his feet, he makes a lunge for me. I lift my hem and plow into the stream. *Yeow!* It's so cold it hurts.

He doesn't bother rolling up his pant legs and comes in after me, capturing me after a few steps. The hem of my dress falls into the stream, and we both laugh shivering from the glacial water.

"You are cruel, Princess, exploiting a man's weaknesses."

"I didn't know you had any."

"Only two," he says.

"Oh yeah. What's the other?"

"Your mouth."

He lightly traces a fingertip along my lower lip. Cupping a hand under my chin, he touches his lips to mine, gently pulling me close. The heat from his body is a sharp contrast to the numbing water lapping at our calves. We remain in the middle of the stream thirstily drinking in the pleasure of being in each other's arms.

After a moment he pulls away, sighing deeply. "I've lost all feeling in my feet," he says. "May we continue this on dry land?"

Taking my hand, he helps me from the water. We're soaked to the knees, but neither of us cares.

"I guess we have a lot to talk about before the wedding," I say. "Like where we're going to live, for starters." I reseat myself on the boulder and squeeze the water from the bottom of my dress.

"I didn't think there was much to say about that. I'll live at Warrington Palace with you. I will eventually need to pass along my duties as chief to another, Catherine, perhaps, since I can hardly govern without being present." He wrings out his pant legs and replaces his socks and boots.

"Oh Ryder, I hate that. Don't make that decision yet. Let's see how things go first. Maybe we can split our time between the two places."

He smiles an indulgent smile. "We will both be required to make sacrifices, love. Shall we walk while we dry out?"

We stroll along the meadow hand in hand, the warm current of love flowing between us. The world looks extravagantly beautiful to me today—the swirling silver dome high above our heads, the gnarled elegance of the ancient oaks, the lush green carpet of meadow, with its patches of merry yellow jonquils and purple coneflowers.

So much remains unspoken between Ryder and me. We really know very little of each other, but I relish the thought of the months and years ahead and the delicious unfolding of it all.

"Mother wants us to be married by a COC minister," I say. "Is that all right with you?"

"Yes, if that's what you want."

"I want it only because it will make Mother happy. So, thank you. I know the Unicoi practice many different faiths. Is there someone from your church or the tribe you'd like to preside over the ceremony also?"

He contemplates this a moment, then shakes his head. "Abraham Phoenix, the spiritual leader of the tribe means a great deal to me. But he is very old. I'm afraid conducting a royal wedding would be too taxing for him. He actually performed the marriage ceremony for my parents nearly thirty years ago."

"I hope he'll be able to attend as a guest, at least," I say.

"Yes. I will make arrangements for that." He stops and turns to me. "Tell me, do you embrace the teachings of the COC? Do you believe that those who survived the Great Disaster in the domes were handpicked by God as being the most worthy?"

I smile internally because Ralston already told me that the people who flocked into the domes did it because they thought the IUGA agents who built the domes were angels sent down to save them. "No. I don't believe that," I say, plopping down on the soft blanket of grass. Ryder sits cross-legged facing me.

"My beliefs have changed a lot over the past year or so," I say. "You once told me that the Unicoi believe all things are connected, and that the actions of one person affect all of creation. After everything I've been through this past several months, I've come to accept that as true. Actually, I used to believe it only applied to living things, but my views about that have recently been expanded also."

"Ah, bird and beast, clay and stone, all are blessed as part of the One?" he says.

"Pretty much. That's the way I look at things now. After all, at the most basic level, we're all made of the same stuff, aren't we?"

He cracks an odd little smile.

"What?" I ask.

"You are a constant marvel to me," he says. "Just when I think I know what you will say, you say something profound, and utterly unexpected."

I pluck a few tender blades of grass, letting them sift through my fingers. "I don't know how profound it is, but I'd hate to be predictable."

"You are never that." He laughs. "But what does the future queen do about required attendance at the Church of the Chosen if she does not believe in its doctrines?"

I sigh heavily. "Well ... I'm going to take it slow, like everything else. Change is hard to accept. Eventually, I hope people will embrace the idea of religious freedom, but no big changes all at once."

Ryder lies back scanning the skies. I rest my head in the crook of his arm. "Look," he says pointing heavenward. A hawk soars high above us. "It is a good omen."

FORTY-FOUR

On our return to the manner house, we find dozens of soldiers assembling to escort us to Warrington. In some ways, the Enclave army is more impressive and better armed than the Royal Guard stationed at Warrington Palace. Father was serious when he said he wouldn't allow a repeat of the surprise attack of yesterday. These guys look ready for anything.

Lord Balfour waits for me in Father's office. I discover him busily lining up small stacks of paper on the round conference table. His glasses perch on the end of his nose, and tufts of gray hair poke out on either side of his head. He's the perfect picture of the harried lawyer.

We step inside, and he pauses from his work, bowing. "Princess, I believe I have everything you require. Thanks to Lady Balfour, there are five copies of each document. I felt one copy should remain on file in my office, and one in the safekeeping of your father. The others should return with you to Warrington Palace to be filed upon your ascension to the throne. I recommend that you sign them today, and date them at the appropriate time."

He offers a fat black pen for me to use. I lean over the nearest pile of documents. The first page is entitled "Act of Succession."

"Sign just here," he says pointing to a line at the bottom. Neatly typed beneath the line is: The Queen, Jaden Victoria Hanover Beckett.

It's sobering to see it spelled out like that. "Do I need to sign my full name?" I ask.

"It would be best if you did, Your Highness."

"All right." I don't think I've ever signed my whole name before. Holding the pen tightly and biting my lower lip, I carefully sign the first page, making certain to spell everything right. Ryder politely excuses himself to assist with the preparations for our journey, while Lord Balfour patiently points out every space which requires my signature. We work through each stack, one-by-one. When all the i's are dotted and t's are crossed, Balfour places my copies of the signed documents in a brown file folder and wishes me a safe journey.

After changing into riding clothes, I strap on my katana, and head for the courtyard. The size of the assembled escort is impressive. More astonishing, though, is the fact that, in the midst of the hundred or so soldiers, Father sits waiting for me inside a covered, motorized carriage. A sporty little two-seater.

Ryder is mounted on Tenasi, with Gabriel's reins tied to his saddle. He smiles and waves.

"What is this?" I ask climbing inside the small car.

Father grins. "I bought it from the Unicoi. They're building these small conveyances now in their factory. It's faster than any horse and provides more protection." He hands me a pair of goggles. "For bugs," he says. "What do you think?"

"It's great. I love it." I nestle into the comfy padded bench. "This should be fun."

"I'm not a tremendously skilled driver yet, but I believe I'm able to get us there just fine."

"Let's go."

The journey to Warrington Palace is wearisome even in this cute little sports wagon. I miss having Ryder to break up the monotony, and I find myself wishing I'd packed a book to read while Father concentrates on his driving. We do manage some conversation when the road is straight and smooth. Father asks about my visit to Unicoi Village and how I plan to incorporate the Unicoi population into Domerica. He's intrigued when I tell him I'm leaning toward allowing them to govern themselves locally, but with some assistance and oversight by Domerica. I also float the idea that maybe one day Domerica, Unicoi, and the Enclave could join together in some form of cooperative alliance.

He squints at me through his goggles, momentarily taking his eyes off the road. "That's pretty lofty thinking," he says.

"Would you be open to discussing it at some point?" I ask.

He pulls at his beard. "I admit I have considered that there may be advantages in an alliance with Domerica, and the Unicoi undoubtedly have much to offer, but I'm not certain how much self-governance I'd be willing to give up in exchange. The idea has merit if it can be structured in a way that is acceptable to all parties."

"I'll take that as a *maybe*," I say.

He smiles, keeping his eyes straight ahead.

The day begins to wane as the hours wear on. I doze off, allowing the motion of the car to lull me to sleep. Father shakes my shoulder, and I wake to find that night has fallen.

"We're almost there, sweetheart," he says. "Will you turn on the lantern there on your side, please?"

As we approach the main gates of Warrington Palace, I'm surprised to see it completely lit up as if a ball or a state dinner were being held. Many carriages are parked in the courtyard, and scores of people mill around in front of the staircase and on the veranda.

"What's going on?" I ask Father.

"I'm not entirely certain," he says uneasily. "Perhaps you'd better hurry inside, though. I'll take care of things out here."

The cadre of soldiers ahead of us takes a right turn toward the stables, but Father drives straight ahead, steering the conveyance slowly toward the front stairway. The onlookers gathered outside move aside and make room for us to park. I quickly hop out of the car and bound up the stairs. The large front door stands open, and Drew is at the threshold to meet me, his face ashen.

"Drew, what is it? What's going on?" I ask in a shaky voice.

He takes my elbow, leading me inside. The room is crammed with people chattering in low tones. Some sip wine from crystal goblets, others nibble on delicacies from silver trays laid out on the table tops. A sort of party, it seems. All activity stops as I enter, and someone from the second floor landing cries, "Long live the queen."

Instantly every man, woman, and child falls on bended knee. Icy tendrils of terror coil around my insides as I look out over the sea of bowed heads. *Mother is dead. I am queen.* The world comes to a grinding halt.

Reaching for Drew's arm for support, I find him kneeling also. My first impulse is to bolt for the door and get as far away from here as possible. My second impulse is to crumple to the floor in tears and confess I am an impostor. *There's no freakin' way I can do this. I need to get out of here, now.*

Sensing Father's presence behind me, I turn my head. "All rise," he whispers to me.

"All rise," I repeat automatically, surprised at the strength of my own voice.

Everyone rises, and several choruses of *"Long live the queen"* ring out as the people raise their glasses in tribute.

Ryder appears at my side and takes my hand in his. "I'm so sorry," he says quietly.

"I need to see her," I tell Drew. "Where is she?"

"In her room. I'll go with you."

General LeGare slowly raises himself out of his chair as Drew and I enter. He looks worn and haggard. Carefully making his way around the bed, he kneels before me. "Long live the queen," he whispers.

"Rise," I say awkwardly.

Mother's lying on top of her bedcovers, hands crossed at her waist. They've dressed her in a beautiful white gown and satin slippers. A delicate, jeweled crown is positioned perfectly atop her immaculately washed and combed tresses. She looks small and fragile in death, though she never seemed so in life. Her beautiful face is peaceful, but somehow not really her.

"What happened?" I ask LeGare. "She was fine when I left yesterday."

"She was not feeling well this morning," he says. "We breakfasted in her room, but she had little appetite. She received word about the attack on your party around midmorning, and asked me to summon Prince Andrew at once. I believe she knew there was not much time left."

"The doctor says it was cardiac failure. A common cause of death in leukemia patients," Drew says. "Charles and I were both with her. Her last words were of you, Jade."

"Of me? What were they?"

"She said she had complete confidence in you and your ability to rule the nation. She requested you take adequate security precautions until it is determined who was behind yesterday's attack. She also expressed her desire that you not postpone your wedding to Chief Blackthorn, and that you use the opportunity of Prince Gilbert's visit to attempt to make peace with Dome Noir. I believe she regretted leaving you with that situation unresolved."

I rub my face roughly with my hands. "May I have a few minutes with her, alone?"

"Of course," Drew says. "Do not blame yourself, Sister. This could have happened at any time."

"Thanks Drew."

The two men leave, closing the door behind them. I do blame myself. The news of the attack must have been too much for her heart. I wish I'd been able to see her one last time.

It's true Queen Eleanor was not my birth mother, but a deep sadness at her passing envelopes me. I kneel beside the bed and rest my hand on her sleeve. The feelings of loss when my Connecticut mom died come flooding back to me now. I never got to see her body after the fiery car crash—too badly burned they said. This is a kind of closure for me, a chance to touch her and say my silent goodbyes.

Resting my cheek on the soft coverlet, I close my eyes, sending both my mothers thoughts of love and peace. My emotions are a tangled mass of sorrow, remembrance, and stone-cold fear. My new life starts tomorrow. Am I ready?

FORTY-FIVE

After a restless night, my day begins early with a visit from Father and Drew. "A rather large crowd of villagers is amassing at the palace gates," Drew says.

"What for?" I ask my mind foggy from lack of sleep.

"Some have brought flowers to honor Mother, but most wish to see you. They are not going away. They are chanting your name. Well, they're chanting '*Queen Jaden.*' Still sounds strange to the ear," he says.

"What do we do?" I ask.

"Father thinks we should allow them access to the palace grounds."

"I believe it may be wise for you to speak to them Jaden," Father says. "It will set the tone for your entire reign. They simply wish to be reassured that the country is in capable hands. In light of the fact that you intend to strip Prince Harold of his title soon, it may be prudent to show them that you are in control, and assure them that the government is sound and operating normally."

The thought of giving a speech to a crowd of villagers makes me want to crawl back in bed and pull the covers over my head. I just hope they haven't brought pitchforks. I knew this day would come, though, so I need to rise to the occasion or pack it in and just *zip-zip* back to Connecticut right now.

"Will you stand with me Father?" I ask a note of panic in my voice.

"Drew and I will stand behind you," Father says. "I've sent for Ryder. He should stand at your side, as well as General LeGare. They are your closest advisors and allies now. The people will be reassured by their presence, as will you."

"Yes that's brilliant. Thanks for sending for Ryder. I'll dress and come downstairs as soon as possible. Have we thought about … I mean, will my safety be a concern?" I ask, the recent attack still fresh in my mind. Uncle Harold may think this is the perfect opportunity to get me out of the picture and Osrielle on the throne.

"It's a concern," Father says. "But General LeGare is already working on that. He'll make certain appropriate security measures are in place before the gates are ever opened."

"Just a second," I say, tightening the belt of my robe and heading for my desk. "I want to date these papers now, and give the signed copies to you for safekeeping until we can file them on Monday." I unlock my desk and pull out the brown file Henry Balfour gave me.

"What's all that?" Drew asks.

"Sorry I didn't have a chance to tell you earlier, Drew. These documents essentially remove Uncle Harold from the office of Lord High Steward. They also name Lady Lorelei Bartlett as my heir apparent. Osrielle is excluded from the line of succession after today."

"Well, you've been a busy little princess, haven't you? What brought all this on?" he asks.

"I'll walk you through everything later, but let's just say Uncle Harold and I don't seem to agree on a number of issues." I carefully write the date on each document.

"That's putting it mildly. You two despise each other. But I thought you'd wait until after Mother's farewell celebration to give him the old heave-ho."

"I'm not sure I can afford to wait." I reinsert the papers in the file and hand it to Father. "We may want to ask LeGare to make sure our internal security is extra tight also."

"Already taken care of," Father says tucking the file under his arm.

"Surely you're joking," Drew says, looking from me to Father. "You think Uncle Harold may go off his rocker and attempt to harm Jaden?"

"Someone sent assassins to kill your sister two days ago," Father says. "Until we know who that someone is, we must be extra vigilant. Let us leave Jaden to dress. I must put these documents in a safe place and speak with Charles LeGare."

"But—" Drew sputters as Father strides out the door. He looks at me half-bewildered, half-horrified.

"We'll talk later," I say shooing him out and closing the door behind him.

Heading to the closet to choose an outfit, I realize that I have no idea what's appropriate for the occasion. Do I wear black? Ralston says there is no traditional mourning period.

Maria arrives just as I'm about to go searching for her. She curtseys deeply. "Your Majesty," she says.

"Maria, thank God you're here." I grasp her arm and pull her inside. "Somehow you've got to make me look like a queen. I'm supposed to speak to the villagers to soothe them and boost their confidence in me. But my stomach is swirling and my knees are all wobbly and I look like yesterday's oatmeal. Help me appear queenly, please."

She smiles warmly. "You do not need me to make you look like a queen, Your Majesty. You are already regal and awe inspiring. All you need is the perfect ensemble for your first address to the people.

That is my job. Please be seated, and allow me to select something for you."

I know she's just trying to pump me up, but her words reassure me. So far, I've done pretty well at playing the part of a princess. I just have to kick it up a notch or two for my new role. For lack of a bottle of Xanax, I head to the kitchenette to brew a cup of Ralston's chamomile tea. Fumbling with the cups and spilling tea leaves everywhere, I eventually succeed at making a hot cup of the aromatic elixir.

In no time Maria emerges from the closet carrying a carnelian-colored gown and shoes to match. "This will look splendid on you," she says. "It is the perfect color and style for the occasion—royal but conservative."

The dress is long-sleeved with a high neckline and gold buttons embossed with the family crest. Maria sweeps my hair into an updo and anchors an elaborate gold crown on top of my head with about a thousand hairpins.

"I don't like this crown," I say. "It's too heavy."

"You may take it off after your speech, but this is the crown of a monarch. A small princess's tiara will not do for today."

I allow her to apply some makeup to my face and eyes. It always makes me look older. Ralston shows up as Maria is dabbing on lip gloss. She motions for me to press my lips together.

"Your Majesty, I hear you will be speaking to the people this morning," Ralston says. "May I be of some assistance?"

"Yes, please." Thanking Maria for her expert help, I usher her to the door. The second she's out of earshot, I turn to Ralston in a tizzy.

"Is this dress okay? I mean, I'm not supposed to wear black, am I?"

"No. You look magnificent, my dear. Now, have you thought about what you're going to say?"

"Not really. Should I write something down?"

"Perhaps that is a good idea. Even if you do not use them, it's reassuring to have notes."

Sitting at my desk, I shuffle through the drawer for something to write on. "What kinds of things should I say?"

"You might start by remembering your Mother fondly, and commenting on her qualities of wisdom and leadership. Oh, and her love for the people."

"That's good stuff." I scribble down a few thoughts. "Then what?"

"Then you could mention some of her major accomplishments such as the peace and prosperity she maintained throughout the country, her distinguished role as a world leader, and the like."

I jot down a few more lines. "All right, I think I've got that. What else?"

"Perhaps you could thank the Council of Advisors and General LeGare for pledging their support to you, and speak of your commitment to continuing the policies of your mother which have made Domerica the finest nation on earth. You might consider closing with a line or two about your wish to pursue a swift resumption of trade with Dome Noir and to restore the good relationships previously enjoyed among all the dome nations, etcetera, and etcetera."

I'm writing furiously as he speaks. Once I feel I've captured all his ideas, I look up. "That's it? That's all I need to say?"

"It doesn't need to be a long speech, Jaden, just a powerful one."

"And you think this will do it?"

"Yes. Just stand up straight, show your self-confidence and sincerity, and they'll love you."

"Thanks, Rals." I give him a big hug. He feels warm and very human. "I need to see if Ryder is here yet. Wish me luck."

"*Bon chance*, old girl," he calls as I dash out the door.

My speech is to be delivered from the top of the sweeping palace entrance steps. At first glance, the size of the crowd is intimidating, but a continuous line of soldiers holds a tight perimeter around the front of the palace. I'm overjoyed to find Patrick standing next to General LeGare on my left. His arm looks perfectly healed, his eyes shine with excitement. As I approach, he drops to one knee. "God save the queen," he says.

"Welcome back, my friend."

Ryder takes his place on my right. He looks stalwart and handsome in a dark suit, his hair pulled back into a sleek ponytail and tied with a gray ribbon. Drew, Adelais, and several Council of Advisors members stand behind me. It calms me to see Jacob and Lorelei here. Uncle Harold is behind me also, but I am comforted to note that Father has positioned himself between the two of us. The crowd goes wild when I step forward to speak.

My chest is tight and my knees quake as I raise a shaky hand for silence. At this moment one thing becomes utterly clear—I was never cut out to be a rock star. Opening my mouth, I'm not sure any words will come out, but through some incredible stroke of fortune I'm able to deliver the speech Ralston helped me write. My words seem to resonate with the audience. I'm interrupted several times by applause. And when I finish, a cheer goes up, accompanied by shouts of "Long live the queen," and "God save the queen."

Stifling the urge to turn and run inside, I paste a smile on my face and continue to wave for a few minutes. A voice from the crowd shouts. "Is the wedding still on?"

Ryder reaches for my hand, all smiles. "Yes," I reply, and another loud cheer rings out.

A few more waves to the crowd, and we all file back inside.

"Well done," Father says, eyes shining.

I murmur a weak "Thanks." It's over and I survived. I nearly faint with relief.

Ryder helps me to a nearby chair. "Have you eaten this morning, love?" he asks.

My hand goes to my hollow belly. "No. I guess I forgot."

"There's food in the dining room," Drew says, his mouth full of something resembling cream puff. "Let's eat."

FORTY-SIX

After brunch, Ryder and I quietly stroll the palace grounds. The villagers have cleared out, and the pace of the palace courtyard is back to normal. Patrick trails after us at a respectable distance—my own secret service puppy dog. His presence is comforting and irritating at the same time. I hope the day will come when I don't need to be guarded all the time.

On returning to the palace, I'm handed a note by a white-gloved butler. Uncle Harold has requested an audience with me this afternoon. "What do you think I should do," I ask Ryder, "meet with him now or put him off until after the farewell celebration?"

"I've always found it best to meet a problem head-on," he says. "I believe it will put your mind at ease to take care of the matter sooner rather than later. Has John had an opportunity to speak with Prince Harold?"

"I don't think so. But, you're right. I'd like to give Uncle Harold his walking papers this afternoon. No sense in waiting. I hope you'll be at the meeting, and Father, Ralston, of course, and maybe Drew."

"Perhaps your Council should also be promptly informed of your decisions and the signing of the official decrees. If Lord Bartlett is still at the palace, it may be wise to include him in the meeting, as a Council representative, and Lady Lorelei as well, since this directly involves her."

"That's a good idea. Let's go find Ralston. Maybe he can arrange the meeting for me."

I send word back to Uncle Harold that I'll meet with him at three o'clock. Mother's office is too small to accommodate all of us, so at Ralston's suggestion, we use a first floor conference room.

When Uncle Harold arrives, he's visibly caught off guard by the group already assembled at the conference table. He bows. "Your Majesty," he says. "I did not realize there would be others joining us. I merely wished to share some fond memories of your mother, and to discuss our working relationship going forward."

"Please have a seat, Prince Harold," I say. "I appreciate your sensitivity about Mother's passing. Maybe we'll have a chance to reminisce some other time. But today, I felt that the subject of our future working relationship was more important. My family and trusted advisors are present for this discussion because it pertains to your separation from governmental affairs."

He takes a seat at the table, his face betraying no emotion. "I'm afraid you have me at a disadvantage," he says softly. "Did you say my *separation* from the government?"

My mouth goes dry. Even though I believe this man may have tried to have me killed, I take no joy in the embarrassment he's about to suffer. Placing copies of the two Royal Decrees in front of him, I say, "These decrees are my first official acts as queen. The copies are yours to keep. I'll summarize the contents for you.

"The first document is an Act of Succession. It names Lady Lorelei Bartlett as my heir apparent, and effectively removes Osrielle from the line of succession, permanently. I've taken this measure based on numerous conversations with Osrielle where she has stated she does not wish to be queen or live in the palace. Instead, she wishes to be home with her mother on the farm at Hempstead. This decree honors those wishes."

He pulls the document toward him and begins to read, his lips moving slightly.

"The second set of papers cancels your appointment as Lord High Steward, leaving you free to return to Hempstead with Osrielle. In my judgment, the office of Lord High Steward does not need to be filled at this time, since I'm of age and capable of managing the government on my own. You are welcome to stay at the palace until after the farewell celebration, but then I must ask you to leave. Of course, arrangements will be made to ensure this transition is as smooth as possible for you and Osrielle."

He slides the other set of papers closer and examines each page. His eyes remain fastened to the documents, as an ugly red stain slowly creeps up his neck and blooms across his face. At last, he sits back and folds his hands over his belly.

"I have never been so poorly treated in all of my life," he says quietly, his face crimson, his eyes locked onto mine. "I readily came to your mother's assistance in her time of need. In doing so, I risked the happiness of my own daughter and the stability of my marriage. But, I did it gladly because Eleanor was my beloved sister and my queen. That I am rewarded thusly for all of my sacrifices can only speak to the heartless and malevolent nature of the person who has assumed my dear sister's throne."

"Harold," Father says sternly. "I caution you to watch yourself. You are speaking to the queen. Do not say things you will regret."

"The only things I regret are devoting so much effort to promoting the welfare of this doomed country and so much time defending you from your detractors." He stands and shakes a stubby finger at me. "There are people in the land who wish you dead, not simply because they think you an immoral woman and a heretic, but because they believe Domerica would be better off without you. As of this moment, I count myself in that latter category."

Ryder jumps out of his chair. "I will not have you speak to her that way."

"It amounts to treason," Jacob Bartlett adds, pushing away from the table and leaping to his feet. "This is outrageous."

"Then have me arrested. What is one more slap in my face?" He glowers at me once again, then turns on his heel and hastily exits.

A stunned silence pervades the group for a moment. My heart pounds furiously in my chest.

"That certainly went well, don't you think?" Drew says in his typical droll fashion.

"Shall I have him arrested?" Jacob asks, still irate. "You'd be entirely justified, and you have several witnesses."

I rest my elbows on the table and momentarily cover my face with my hands. Ryder squeezes my shoulder reassuringly. Having Harold arrested might solve a number of my current problems, but it doesn't feel like the right thing to do.

"No, Jacob," I say. "He's very angry. I suppose he has a right to be. He's grown rich during his short stint as Lord High Steward, but I haven't treated him very well since my return to Domerica."

"He had no cause to speak to you that way," Ryder says.

"Maybe not, but he's lost a lot in the past two days—not only his sister, but any dreams he had of running the country and growing even richer." I blow out a long breath. "What I would like is for him to have an armed escort back to Hempstead this afternoon. And, until we figure out who's trying to have me assassinated, his comings and goings need to be watched at all times."

"That seems the most reasonable course of action," Father says. "If you like, I'll make the arrangements with General LeGare."

Smiling gratefully I say, "I hate to ask it of you, Father. You're not even Domerican. But that would be very helpful if you wouldn't mind."

"I shall always be your father, first and foremost." He stands and kisses my forehead. "By your leave?" he says formally.

"You know you never have to ask," I say.

Turning to Jacob and Lorelei, I say, "I'm sorry you had to be involved in that. I have copies of these documents for you. The others will be filed in the Royal Offices on Monday. Jacob, would you mind getting in touch with the other Council members and letting them know about these changes?"

"It would be my pleasure."

"Thank you all for coming." I stand, and everyone else does also. "I will see you at the farewell celebration."

I'm drained after my confrontation with Uncle Harold. I hope that at least Osrielle is happy with my decision. My fondest desire at the moment is to lie down in Ryder's arms and have a nap before dinner, but Maria arrives with word that Prince Andrew and I are requested to meet with Jennifer Osborne as soon as possible to approve the plans for Mother's farewell celebration.

"Would you like me to come along?" Ryder asks.

"That's sweet, but there's no reason for both of us to suffer through it. Drew and I can handle it. You must have things to attend to in Unicoi Village. You've hardly been home at all. Things around here will be busy for the next few days, and for the next two weeks until the wedding, really. I'm sure Unicoi matters are piling up on your desk, Chief Blackthorn."

He smiles. "It's true. Lately I haven't been as attentive to my duties as I should have been. Catherine and the Council of Elders have been working hard to help, but there are some issues which require my personal attention. Shall I see you tomorrow, then?"

Selfishly, I want to say, *Yes.* I'm not sure I can make it through another day like today without him, but I know he needs time to take care of matters in Unicoi Village. "You should work tomorrow, and I probably should look over the files on Mother's desk. Just come early for the farewell celebration. We'll be together then."

He pulls me to him and nearly gets stabbed in the chin with the point of my ridiculous crown. I wore it for my meeting with Uncle Harold, but I'm over it now.

"Help me out of this thing, please, so I can kiss you properly," I say.

Ryder begins pulling hair pins out of my do and passing them to me. "How many are there?" He laughs. "Am I hurting you?"

"No, just get it off me." I'm laughing now too, as the pins continue to pile up in my palms.

Soon the crown comes loose and my hair cascades freely down my shoulders. *What a relief!* It feels like a fifty pound weight was just lifted from my head. Ryder combs his fingers through my hair and smoothes the flyaway strands. "Better?" he asks.

"Much. Now let's try that again." I move in close. His intoxicating scent, his heat, his parted lips set my pulse racing. He cradles my face in his gentle hands and presses his warm mouth to mine. My heart thrums loudly in time with his. I reach up to free his hair from its ribbon and it falls like a silk curtain around our faces. *Aah, yes.* This is right; this is good. This is why I've chosen to remain here. To have this sumptuous kiss, and more, every day for the rest of my life. Two more weeks, only two more weeks and we'll be together forever.

"Until Monday, then," he says hoarsely.

"Can't wait," I whisper.

Making a quick stop at my room, I lock the crown in my jewelry chest and run a brush through my hair, finding still more hairpins. My long-sleeved, high-necked, floor-length dress is a stale, confining prison. I long for shorts and a t-shirt to change into, but that's not in keeping with my life as a princess—oops, queen. There are a million things I miss about my simple life in Connecticut. Thinking of the pain Dad and Drew will suffer when I leave that life for good makes me ache inside. I'm happy I have them both here, but it's not really fair, and the guilt haunts me.

Our meeting with Jennifer is to take place in a small sitting room in the family wing. When I arrive, she's perched in a chair going over her notes, a stack of files at her feet. She immediately rises and curtseys. "Your Majesty, thank you for coming."

"Please sit down," I say, taking the chair next to hers. "Where's

Dre—, uh, Prince Andrew?"

"Oh, I'm sorry. I was told he had returned to Meadowood," she says nervously. "He left word that whatever met with your approval was acceptable to him."

"Really?" Good old Drew. I should have known he'd bug out on me. There's no way he's going to sit through a bunch of party details. "All right, let's send for tea, and you can fill me in on everything," I say tiredly.

Jennifer's permanently rumpled brow relaxes slightly, as if she expected me to bail on her too. "Thank you, Your Majesty."

She pushes her red spectacles up on her nose and proceeds to walk me through the schedule for the farewell celebration. It will be held in a large COC cathedral in town, to accommodate the expected overflow crowd. Beginning in the morning, a sizeable procession of dignitaries and palace workers will travel from the palace to the village in carriages and on horseback. Rain will be suspended that day to make attendance at the events more convenient.

Jennifer explains that the ceremony will open with a prayer, followed by speeches extolling Mother's life. I'm relieved when she tells me I'm not expected to speak.

"We wished to invite Prince Harold to say a few words," she says. "I was surprised to hear he will not be attending."

"He had some urgent business in Hempstead," I tell her.

"Yes. I heard," she says with a look that tells me she knows his ass was booted.

Our tray of tea arrives, along with a selection of fruit tarts and cinnamon cakes. Once we're served, Jennifer continues.

"Following the speeches, a large feast will be held in the main hall of the cathedral. Since this is a feast for a queen, it could last well into the wee hours of the morning. The villagers tend to thoroughly enjoy the beneficence of the crown on such occasions and will likely stay until the last cask of wine is drained dry. Of course, it would not be unseemly for members of the royal family to depart early."

Whew. I'm definitely not in the mood to be the main attraction at party central—especially when all I feel is a cavernous sense of loss.

"That summarizes the farewell celebration," Jennifer says. "There are two other matters, however, if you have another moment, Your Majesty."

"Sure," I say, although I feel a little drowsy after tea and cakes.

"At some point next week, I wish to meet with you and Chief Blackthorn to finalize the wedding plans. The date is almost upon us, and there is much to go over. Would such a meeting be possible?"

"Yes. I'll need to check with Chief Blackthorn and let you know what day works for both of us."

"Thank you, Your Majesty." She pulls a file out of the stack next to her chair. "Also, I have some sketches of the remodeling project for the queen's suite. Please look at them when you have a moment, and let me know if there is one you like."

I shake my head in confusion. "What remodeling project?"

"Your mother wished to have her rooms completely remodeled for you and Chief Blackthorn. Something more suitable for a couple. Unfortunately she did not have the opportunity to approve the sketches before her passing, so I'm afraid the task has fallen to you. Once we have the floor plan settled, we can choose colors, fabrics, and furniture. I appreciate that you are terribly busy, but if we can get started right away, it may be ready in time for your wedding night."

I rub my tired eyes. Trust Mother to think of everything. Taking the file from her, I say, "I'll look at these when I can. We'll discuss it next week. I'm sorry, but I really need to lie down for a few minutes."

Jennifer pops up from her chair. "I'm so sorry to have fatigued you, Your Majesty. I will await your word."

"Thanks, Jennifer."

She gathers her files and hurries from the room.

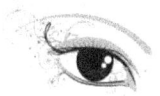

FORTY-SEVEN

In the morning I sleep later than usual, recovering some of my depleted energy. The past three days have felt like the spin cycle on a Kenmore. The violent attack against me, Mother's death, Uncle Harold's rancorous departure—it all seems a bit surreal. Amazingly, there's nothing earth-shattering on my schedule today. About a dozen people had requested audiences with me, but I exercised my royal prerogative and just said, "*No.*" I plan to use the time relaxing, going over the things on Mother's desk, and playing with Fred and Ethel.

Father pokes his head in while I'm eating breakfast and tells me he's paying a visit to Uncle Harold today, to discuss some of the disturbing comments he made regarding people wanting me dead and to question him about his possible involvement in the attack on me. I wish him luck, but I don't think Harold's really going to spill his guts to Father.

My walk with Fred and Ethel is peaceful and enjoyable. They seem happy for the time outside. After they're quietly tucked in for a nap, I swipe a couple of pommeras from the kitchen and head up to Mother's third floor office. One of Mother's shawls is draped across the back of her desk chair. I press it to my nose inhaling the lingering scent of amber and spice. It is a comfort of sorts, but I know from experience that the scent will soon fade, and the memories will grow dim over time. That knowledge leaves me vacant inside.

Thumbing through a few things on top of Mother's desk, I open a fat file labeled *Dome Noir*. Under the front flap, is an envelope addressed to me. I break the seal and pull out a crisp sheet of paper.

My Dearest Daughter —

If you are reading this, I am gone, and the joys and burdens of governing our nation are now in your capable hands.

It's a letter from Mother to me.

We possessed numerous reliable contacts and channels for valuable information in Dome Noir until King Philippe saw fit to impose sanctions on Domerica in response to Prince Damien's assassination. Unfortunately many of those contacts have been arrested for espionage or deported from the country. Consequently some of our information is now dated.

Mother had spies in Dome Noir? That means she probably has spies in Copula de Vita as well. It must also mean that there are foreign spies present in Domerica. The thought makes me pause and make a mental note to ask LeGare about this.

These are the key details of which you should be aware. First, King Philippe, now advanced in years, has reportedly become infirm, physically and, some say, mentally. We've had numerous reports that Prince Gilbert has assumed substantial responsibility for running the country.

That must be why Prince Gilbert is attending my wedding, instead of King Philippe.

Second, Dome Noir is far worse off than we had originally feared. Civil unrest is at an all-time high, and there is talk of revolution within the country. Unemployment, food shortages, and overcrowding have reached critical levels. I counsel you to be cautious in your dealings with Prince Gilbert, as these conditions may prompt him to take even more drastic action against Domerica in order to persuade you, as the Designated Guardian, to agree to construction of a new dome.

Holy crap.

But I encourage you also to view this as an opportunity which provides Domerica with a strong basis for negotiation. Through our own increased food production (largely due to the Unicoi growing methods), we are able to offer greater shipments of food to Dome Noir. In addition, we are well under capacity at Wall's Edge prison and can propose some relief for their prison overcrowding. You may also consider granting work visas to capable workers to assist in the construction of Unicoi Village. I'm confident that you will devise additional enticements to convince Prince Gilbert that Dome Noir is better off with Domerica as a close friend and ally, rather than an enemy.

She closes by saying how much she will miss Drew and me, and how she regrets that she will not know her grandchildren. I feel overwhelmed and sad and also a little scared.

Tucking the letter back inside the envelope, I replace it in the file. My emotions are still too scattered to rationally deal with these momentous issues today. So I wrap Mother's shawl around my shoulders and get up from the desk.

Browsing the shelves, I examine Mother's array of mementoes and her impressive collection of books. In addition to law books and thick historical tomes are volumes of poetry and finely bound novels. Most of the novels are unfamiliar to me, but I'm drawn by the title *Shalindria House*, written by someone named Penelope Bronte. Curious as to whether she might have been related to the literary Bronte sisters, I pull the book from the shelf and flip through the pages. Curling up in an arm chair, I tuck one leg beneath me and begin to read. *"It was a city of Sorcerers and Alchemists, Pagans and Fanatics…"*

~~~~~~

I'm awakened some time later by Ralston's gentle prodding. "Jaden, wake up, my dear."

"Oh, hi, Rals. I must've dozed off."

He smiles. "Yes, I imagine you're quite exhausted. But I have Queen Eleanor's ashes here." He nods to a lidded alabaster urn on top of the desk.

"Well, what am I supposed to do with them? Do we take them to the celebration? Am I supposed to keep them in my room or something?"

"No, my dear. The urn is meant to be placed in the columbarium below the palace where the ashes of the royal family members are stored."

"What's a columbarium?"

"Just an underground vault with niches for urns such as this one." He rubs his chin thoughtfully. "You could invite Prince Andrew to help you place it there, or we could simply take it there ourselves and let him know it has been attended to."

"Is there some kind of ceremony or something that goes along with it?"

"Not really, it's more of a formality. Ashes of the deceased are not considered sacred by the COC, and therefore may be disposed of as the family wishes."

"Let's just get it over with then," I say.

Ralston leads the way carrying the urn, and we traipse down about a zillion stairs to the deep basement of the palace. The last time I was down here was when Ralston and I helped Ryder escape from the small prison. Mother had sentenced him to *reeducation* for attempting to kidnap me. The issue of reeducation was one of the things that broke up my parents. It's where a person's brain is surgically altered to wipe out their entire long-term memory and, therefore, their whole identity. Mother adopted it as a form of punishment for prisoners, an alternative to hanging or maiming. Father believes it's barbaric and refused to support its use. Reeducation is just another Domerican law I'm going to need to revisit as queen. I'm hoping to put it off as long as possible.

The columbarium is tucked away behind a moldy wooden door opposite the prison. To get there, we pass by the tunnel which encloses the stream that supplies fresh water for the palace. Ryder and his men used the tunnel to escape in a small boat. It occurs to me the tunnel could also be used as a way to sneak inside. A couple of guards are assigned to the prison, which is normally completely empty of inmates, but as far as I know, no one watches the tunnel.

"Hey Rals, isn't it kind of dangerous leaving this tunnel unguarded? I mean, somebody *is* trying to kill me."

"I believe it's guarded at the entrance, outside the palace, but I shall mention it to General LeGare. It may be wise to station men inside also."

We shuffle into the musty room that serves as the columbarium. Ralston switches on two elaborate wall sconces, but they provide only weak illumination. Rows and rows of arched cubbyholes are carved into the stone walls. Most of the center niches already hold urns. They range from simple to ornate. Some have sculpted busts of heads on top. I assume these are likenesses of the people whose ashes are inside.

Ralston finds a corner with several empty niches. A small gold plaque etched with Mother's name is below one of the holes. "Ah, here it is," Ralston says.

I'm a little freaked when I notice that under the niche next to Mother's is a plaque with my name on it. "How come my name's already up here?" I ask.

"You were presumed dead for a time, remember? Since your body was never recovered. Some ashes from the collective remains of the unidentified victims were put inside an urn, and it was placed in this niche in your honor. Of course, it was removed after your return."

It weirds me out to see my own name in this place of the dead. The hair prickles on my arms, and the air seems to press in around me from the weight of the departed souls dwelling here.

"Would you care to say a few words?" Ralston asks positioning Mother's urn inside the niche.

"I'm not sure what to say." *I just want to get out of here.*

Ralston clears his throat. "According to the poet, Emily Dickenson, *Death is a wild ride and a new road.* If that is true, may

Queen Eleanor's new journey be a pleasant one."

I run my fingertips along the plaque bearing Mother's name. "Fear not the many paths of life, Mother. Goodbye," I say the only words that come to mind.

Ralston extinguishes the lights and we close the door on the dank and lonely columbarium. Mother had a remarkable life as queen. I hope Emily Dickenson's right, and she's moved on to another amazing adventure.

I'm up well before dawn on the day of Mother's farewell celebration. Last night, Maria laid out a lovely hunter green satin gown for the occasion, and I'm nearly dressed when she arrives with one of Mother's crowns for me. I groan when I see it. It's larger than the last one. It has four half-arches made of gold and pearls which meet in a dip at the top. The center is filled with green velvet cloth.

"Please leave my hair loose today," I whine. "The heavy crown is bad enough, but I can't stand all the hairpins digging into my scalp."

"You will like this crown. It is very light. See?" She sets it in my outstretched palms. It is much lighter than the other one.

"And it has combs inside that will keep it on your head, no hairpins needed." She turns it over so I can see the combs. "But I must plait a portion of your hair near the top, so the combs will have something to hold onto."

Next she selects an emerald necklace and earrings from my jewelry chest, and insists that I wear at least a minimum of make-up. "All eyes will be on you today. You must look your best."

I'm happy with the results when Maria is finished dressing me. Wandering downstairs, I grab a muffin and hover near the window in the front parlor to wait for Ryder. Decorated carriages and horses decked-out in colorful blankets and ornamental saddles and bridles trundle down the promenade and take their places in line for the procession. Numerous lords, ladies, and other guests, clad in feathers, furs, and other finery, mill about in the palace courtyard. Palace servants are invited to the celebration as well, and much excited chatter and activity swells within the palace walls.

Ryder arrives late. Ralston has already ushered me to the queen's carriage, and the procession is preparing to depart. He clambers inside and takes the seat next to me.

"I'm sorry to be tardy, love." He lifts my hand and presses my palm against his warm lips.

"I was worried. Is everything all right?" I ask.

"Yes. Catherine was nowhere to be found this morning. I had some important matters to discuss with her. Everything will keep until tomorrow, though." He tilts his head, smiling. "You look lovely today, Your Majesty."

Villagers line the roadway into town, waving, cheering, and tossing flowers as the procession passes. Ralston wasn't kidding when he said the atmosphere is more like a festival than a funeral. It's strange, but the joyful mood of the crowd does help temper some of the melancholy I feel.

When we reach the cathedral, I spot Father in his shiny new conveyance surrounded by a small crowd. Ryder and I are quickly bustled through the giant carved doors into the nave where the speeches are to take place. We're seated in two large thrones, a few feet apart, facing the audience. The speaker's podium is immediately to my left. Now I understand what Maria meant when she said all eyes would be on me.

The Royal Guard is here in force, but the soldiers attempt to remain as inconspicuous as possible by standing as an honor guard in front of the stage and next to Ryder and me. Patrick stays close to my chair.

Drew, Adelais, and Father are seated in the front row of pews. Ralston, General LeGare, and many of Mother's Council of Advisors are seated directly behind them. At one point, Father swivels in his seat to speak with General LeGare, who then rises and joins the family in the front row. My heart contracts a little, and I silently thank

Father for being so considerate.

Hundreds, maybe thousands, of people noisily file inside, filling every pew. I recognize some faces, but most are strangers to me. I'm astonished to glimpse a woman who looks very much like Narowyn in the crowd. I wonder if this is her *mirror* or if Narowyn came to pay her respects. We make eye contact briefly. It's her. She nods and takes her seat among the others.

The church is quickly filled to capacity, including people standing in the aisles, and the speeches begin. Listening intently to the first two speakers, Mother's pastor and a friend from her childhood, Lady Clementine, I learn many things about Mother that I didn't know. But by the time the third speaker takes the podium, my mind begins to wander, and the words turn into white noise. The most difficult part is keeping a pleasant expression on my face. A time or two I'm forced to clench my jaw in order to stifle a yawn.

At least this vantage point is great for people-watching. Scanning the faces of the crowd, I notice many attendees listening with rapt attention to the speaker, others chat with their neighbors, or survey the assembly like me. One face in particular catches my eye causing my heart to trip and tumble into my stomach. To the right side of the nave, midway back, Erica Hornsby sits staring intently at Ryder. Whipping my head around to Ryder, he smiles at me affectionately, oblivious to her presence. My eyes locate her again. She's more voluptuous than usual today in a deep purple dress, her raven hair much longer than it was last year. "Princess hair," she had once called my long tresses. She's obviously adopted the look.

It takes a moment before I realize the woman seated next to her is Catherine Blackthorn. She stares daggers at me, and when she's sure I've seen her, she leans in and whispers something to Erica. Erica's eyes find mine, and she drops her gaze immediately. Catherine smiles smugly and pats Erica's knee in a sisterly gesture.

For the first time I comprehend the phrase "seeing red." My anger burns so intensely, my vision actually blurs. Why the hell did Catherine bring Erica here? It's beyond cruel, and she knows it. For a second I consider disrupting the ceremony, and shouting for the guards to remove them both. But Catherine would enjoy it if I made a complete fool of myself. Instead, I remind myself that she's Ryder's sister, and it's best to keep my abject hatred of her under wraps for the time being. I also realize, to my great disappointment, that I've not completely dealt with my feelings of jealousy over Erica. Will the hurt ever go away?

Taking slow calming breaths, I determinedly haul my emotions back from the dark side. This is supposed to be a celebration for my beloved mother. I won't allow Catherine's scheming to ruin that.

My ire lingers at a slow simmer throughout the remainder of the seemingly interminable speeches. As the last speech comes to a close, I stand quickly and link my arm through Ryder's. No way will I let him out of my sight with those two barracudas waiting in the wings.

The pastor approaches me cordially. Bowing, he smiles and reaches for my hand, causing me to temporarily unlink myself from Ryder. The other speakers gather around as well. Patrick and two additional guards move in to closely surround me on three sides, separating me further from Ryder. Searching over my shoulder, I locate him fading into the throng.

"I'll meet you inside," he mouths, motioning to the hall where the feast is to be held. A sinking feeling seizes me, but there's nothing I can do short of being rude to the pastor and Mother's friends.

I shake hands with everyone and thank them for their wonderful speeches, listening politely while some of them share anecdotes involving Mother. At one point, the conversation takes a political turn, and my patience runs out entirely. Pleadingly, I turn to Patrick. "I have to see Ryder," I say.

"Ladies and Gentlemen, Chief Blackthorn is expecting the queen inside. Please excuse us." He takes my elbow and guides me toward the main hall.

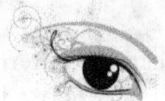

FORTY-EIGHT

*T*he hall is packed with revelers, drinking, talking, and laughing. An orchestra plays in the background, and a large dance floor is already crowded. As we approach the threshold, a page announces in a loud voice, "Her Majesty the Queen."

The orchestra immediately switches to the national anthem of Domerica. Everyone in the room bows or curtseys, as Patrick and other Royal Guards clear a path for me to the head table. Father and Drew are there, along with some Council members—but no Ryder. Father greets me with a hug.

"Have you seen Ryder?" I ask.

"He was here a few moments ago." Father scans the room. "Ah, I believe he's there, near that column."

I follow Father's line of sight. It's Ryder all right, and he's in deep conversation with Erica. A seething primal fury kicks-in when I see my man with the woman who would steal him from me in a heartbeat. I can't imagine what they're saying to each other. It doesn't appear to be an argument, but Ryder looks pale, almost ill. Then, amazingly, he places a hand gently on Erica's shoulder and leans close to her, his lips moving quickly.

"Shall I get him for you?" Father asks, witnessing the awkward scene.

"No, Father. I think I'd better do it myself." A sizzling surge of adrenaline propels me forward into the crowd. Patrick is instantly at my elbow. After I've gone only a few feet, Jacob and Lorelei step forward, blocking my hot pursuit. Lorelei curtseys and then hugs me warmly.

"The ceremony was wonderful," she says. "I believe everyone in the village is here. Things were organized so beautifully."

"Thank you. Jennifer Osborne deserves all the credit."

"Is she the one planning your wedding?" Jacob asks.

"Yes. I'm lucky to have her. I'm lost without Mother here to help me."

"Queen Eleanor will be greatly missed," Lorelei says.

"She already is." I don't want to be rude, but I'm on a mission. "Will you excuse me for a moment? I was just on my way to find Ryder."

"Of course," Jacob says with a bow.

Patrick and I push our way through the mass of people until we reach the column where Ryder stood with Erica. Neither of them is still there. "Do you see him?" I ask Patrick.

He scans the room, making a complete turn. "No, ma'am."

"Will you find him for me?"

"Yes. As soon as you are safely seated at your table. I cannot leave you here alone." He clears a path for us through the crowd.

"Not there?" Father asks when I reach the table.

"No. Did you see where he went?"

"I'm afraid not, sweetheart. Please, sit down. He'll be here soon."

Reluctantly, I take the queen's chair in the center of the long table. Father seats himself next to me and leans in. "I wish a word with you about my meeting with Prince Harold," he says. "We can discuss it in greater depth later, but I questioned him extensively, and I do not believe he is responsible for the attack on you. His initial anger has cooled considerably. After some discussion, he admitted to arranging for the Skorplings' abduction, but he swears he planned to feign a rescue of them himself and return them to you within a few days' time. He believed by doing so he would gain your trust and ingratiate himself to you."

"That's so warped. I knew he was responsible," I say. "How can you believe anything he says after he pulls a stunt like that?"

"Frankly, Jade, he confessed to me that his greatest concern is whether or not you intend to use his lumber for construction of the Unicoi Village wall. He is deeply in debt for the wooded land he purchased. Harold has asked me to smooth the way for him so he may apologize to you in person."

"Seriously? He told you that?"

"Yes, and that is completely in keeping with the Harold I have known these many years. He's far more interested in making money than running a country."

"But what about—"

I don't get to ask my question because Patrick returns at that moment, alone.

"You didn't find him?"

"No. I was told that he left ten minutes ago, alone on a borrowed horse."

I clutch Father's arm. "This can't be happening. He speaks with Erica for a few minutes and then he disappears?"

"He's not with Erica, Jade. He would not act so thoughtlessly, especially on the day of your mother's farewell celebration and only two weeks before your wedding."

"But it appears he went to meet her somewhere."

"I will go and look for him, if you wish," Father says. "Perhaps there was an emergency."

I shake my head. "Then why didn't he say something? That's what bothers me. He didn't tell me he was leaving. He just vanished." This week has been close to unbearable, and this is just the last straw. "I need to go home," I say. "Will you take me back to the palace?"

"Sweetheart, it's still early. You haven't even eaten. Ryder will surely come for you here."

"No he won't. I know he's not coming back. I just want to go home."

"At least stay for the toasts, then I will see you home. It would be considered bad form for you to leave beforehand."

"There are toasts?" I ask incredulous.

"Of course, Jaden, as always."

Oops. "I guess I forgot about the toasts."

"They shouldn't last terribly long. Please sit, so that everyone else may be seated and the celebration can get underway. I'll have Patrick quietly assemble an escort for us."

The feast begins shortly after I am seated. Serving men and women load tray after tray of sumptuous dishes onto long tables. I've completely lost my appetite, though. Nothing looks remotely tempting.

Goblets are filled with wine, ale, or water, and the tributes begin. Each toast is directed to Drew and me as Queen Eleanor's family. I understand now why Father said it was important that I stay. Mother's accomplishments, beauty, and superior qualities are praised in flowery terms by a number of her friends and loyal subjects. Nearly every toast ends with a salute to the new queen and wishes for a long and glorious reign.

After our glasses have been raised dozens of times, my cheek and neck muscles ache from smiling and nodding. Father whispers to me that in a moment I should quietly excuse myself as if I'm going to the ladies' room. He says Patrick will lead me out a back door to the waiting carriage, while he makes our excuses to Drew and the others.

My carriage and about twenty Royal Guardsmen wait outside, as Patrick slips me stealthily through a back door. In minutes, Father climbs into the carriage next to me. He places a sturdy arm around my shoulder, and I nestle deep into his jacket. He smells like fresh air with a whiff of aftershave.

It's odd, but in some ways—most ways really—I feel closer to my Domerican dad than I do to my Connecticut dad, the man who raised me. Narowyn says we must be careful not to confuse our family members with their *mirrors*. No confusion here. I know who I can talk to and who will listen and understand. It's the man with his arm propping me up right now.

"Jade, Ryder loves you," Father says after we've ridden for a while. "He must have a very good reason for vanishing without a word tonight. I trust him enough to allow him to explain. I hope you do too."

"I do, Father. I learned my lesson a while back. But I'm also a realist. He spoke with Erica, and he disappeared. That can't be good."

"I admit, by all appearances, it is troubling. Love does not always follow a predictable path, sweetheart." He squeezes my shoulder. "It must be tended to constantly, and it frequently challenges one's fortitude as nothing else on earth."

Lifting my eyes to his, I ask, "Do you ever wish you and Mother had been able to work out your differences and stay together?"

He raises his eyebrows. "Ah, now that is a very complex matter. Eleanor was, and always will be, the love of my life. I missed her and you and Andrew every day that we were separated. But sometimes even great love must give way to higher principle. I could not have been true to your mother or to you children if I were not first true to myself.

"Eleanor and I were two strong-willed individuals with firmly-held beliefs and ideals. We attempted to reconcile our differences. I swear to you we did. But in the end, compromise was not possible, and in light of your mother's birthright, the final judgment was hers alone. The only viable solution, as painful as it seemed, was for me to take my leave and attempt to do as much good as possible with the opportunities your mother granted me."

"You've handled it all well, Father. And I want to say how incredibly kind it was of you to invite Charles LeGare to sit with the family today. But I wondered, did you ever feel, you know, jealous of him?"

His eyes soften and he strokes my hair. "Of course. In the beginning it was difficult. But as time passed and the more I saw them together, I realized her love for him was completely unlike the love we once shared. Over the last few years, I've come to appreciate LeGare's devotion to her. I'm truly happy she was able to find rewarding companionship before her premature death."

"I hate it that you're alone," I say.

He pats my hand and smiles. "Sweetheart, do not be distressed for me. I have an enormously full life, what with running a small community and a hospital. And you may not have heard, but my daughter just became queen of Domerica. That has kept me busy recently. I scarcely have time for a woman in my life."

"I guess you're right. Anyway, thanks for being here, Father." I rest my head on his shoulder again.

FORTY-NINE

*T*he palace is nearly deserted when we arrive. Most of the staff is still reveling at the feast. Father escorts me to my room.

"I must return for my conveyance and Professor Ralston. I'm afraid we've left him stranded. Will you be all right here alone? Patrick is just outside."

"I'm fine, Father. Thank you for bringing me home."

"Shall I prepare tea for you before I go? I'm afraid kitchen help may be scarce."

"No, thanks. I think I can manage that myself. I'll probably just go to bed early. Father, if you see Ryder there ..." my throat constricts as I grasp for words, "please tell him I need to speak with him."

"I will. Try to get some rest."

Once Father leaves, I yank off my crown and pitch it on the bed. Kicking off my shoes, and shedding my dress, I head for the closet. My favorite pink satin underdress is on the hook where I left it. I wriggle into it and shake out my hair.

Making tea is the first order of business, and then I wait. An hour passes ... then two. I'm so edgy I could crawl out of my skin. Wandering out onto my balcony, my eyes search the night sky for the moon that isn't there. The not knowing is making me crazy. My whole world may be crumbling at this very moment. I could be losing him—correction, may have lost him—and not even know it yet.

The lighted front promenade is a changing stream of activity as servants in wagons and on horseback trickle in from the night's festivities. I watch them from my hidden balcony corner. All at once my eye is caught by the shadow of a lone rider on a giant horse galloping around and through the others. It's him. Relief and anxiety do a synchronized swim in my stomach.

Dashing to my dressing table, I pull a blue gossamer shawl from the chair and wrap it tightly around my shoulders. After brushing my hair to a sleek sheen, I quickly apply lip gloss. If I'm getting dumped tonight, at least I'm going to look halfway decent.

After several long minutes, the knock I've waited for all night echoes through the silent room. Drawing in a long breath, I unlatch the door for Ryder.

He looks a little wrecked—jacket gone, tie loose, wind-whipped hair tousled around his amazing face.

"May I come in?" he asks, quietly. Patrick hovers behind him waiting for a signal from me.

"It's all right," I say.

Ryder steps inside and closes the door. Head bowed, he says, "I apologize for my inexcusable behavior in abandoning you this afternoon." He raises his eyes to mine. "There is something I must tell you, Jaden, and I want you to know I could not feel worse for bringing you this news."

"What is it, Ryder? I've been half-mad wondering what happened to you."

He tugs the gray tie from his collar and twists it in his hands. "Erica came to see me today at the celebration."

"I know. I saw her."

He looks mildly surprised at this. "She had been to see Catherine, and Catherine insisted she speak with me before the wedding. That is why she brought her to the celebration."

Gotta love Catherine.

"I'm so sorry to tell you this, Jade, but I … we …"

My knees feel unsure of themselves. "Just spit it out, Ryder, please."

"Erica is pregnant with my child."

The phrase floats on the air for a second before it registers in my brain. Even then, I'm not certain exactly what it means, but I feel like someone just punched me in the stomach, and I'm about to go down for the count.

"Is it all right if we sit for the rest of this conversation?" I ask.

"Of course," he says, taking my arm and helping me to a chair. He sits on the edge of the chair opposite mine.

"You'll have to forgive me," I say. "I'm not sure what you're telling me."

"Erica is with child," he says. "I am the father."

"Yeah, I got that part. Does this mean the wedding's off? Are you going to marry Erica?"

"God, no. I'm honor bound to claim the child and see to its wellbeing. This I will do. But I could not marry Erica. I am betrothed to you. I shall keep my commitments to you, if you still wish to marry me."

"Whoa, wait a minute. Forget about your commitments to me. What do you *want*? Under these circumstances do you want to marry Erica? If so, I release you from your contract."

"Jaden, I love you more than anything on earth. I wish to marry you. I am mortified to have brought this disgrace and embarrassment upon you, and I dare not hope that you would still want me. As queen, you must protect your reputation and standing. You have no need of a husband whom your people view as dishonorable."

He rakes a nervous hand through his hair. "Regardless, Erica is aware that whatever you decide about us, I do not love her, and therefore cannot marry her. She accepts that."

"But what will happen to her?" I mumble. I have no idea how unmarried mothers are treated in Domerica. The society is backward in many ways.

"She will be well cared for in Unicoi Village. Catherine has invited her to move in with her and Meli after the wedding. The house is large. She and the baby will be comfortable there."

"And this means Erica will be a part of your life forever. A part of *our* lives should we marry." The thought sickens me.

Bowing his head, a dark drape of hair obscures his face from me. "Yes. My desire is to be a part of this child's life. To be a true father to this child." He raises his eyes to mine, a fierce light gleaming from within. "But if you would have me choose between you and the child, I choose you. I choose us. Mother and child will be well provided for, but I need never be a part of their lives."

I shake my head vehemently. "Oh, no. I won't be cast in that role. I'd never ask you to choose between me and your child." Raising my eyes to the ceiling, I suck in a deep breath. "This is a lot to digest."

Ryder anxiously twists his tie in his hands, reminding me of a penitent child. "Geeze, Ryder, didn't you use any type of birth control?" I say exasperated.

"She told me she had taken care of it. I had no reason to doubt her."

"Do you think this was deliberate on her part?" *It wouldn't surprise me.*

He gives a small shrug. "She says it was accidental. At this point, I'm not certain it matters."

"Yeah, I guess not. But you're going to be a father. How does that make you feel?"

He gazes at me, a melancholy sweetness in his face. "Other than my profound regret at the pain it causes you, I feel frightened, happy, in awe."

I love it-hate it that part of him is excited to be a father to Erica's child. He has a flawless heart, one much purer than my own. I'm not certain I will ever be able to welcome Erica and her child as a large component of our lives going forward. My emotions alternately surge and ebb and vie for dominance. There's no predicting where they'll eventually settle.

"It's been a difficult week, Ryder, and I'm not thinking clearly. I need some time to rest and think about this with a clear mind. I don't fully comprehend it yet." Lumbering out of my chair, my knees threaten to buckle beneath me.

Ryder stands, cramming the tie into his pocket.

"I promise I won't keep you in the dark, the way I did before," I say, "but I really need a day or two to make some sense out of this."

"Of course. Take the time you need. I will wait to hear from you."

Managing a weary half-smile, I bid him goodnight.

He bows and turns for the door.

"Uh, Ryder."

"Yes?"

"Can I ask you not to see Erica again until we've resolved this? I don't want to have to worry about the two of you together on top of everything else."

"Certainly. You've nothing to worry about as far as Erica is concerned, but I will honor your wishes in that regard, now and always."

With the click of the closing door, a wave of nausea hits me like a shot. My knees strike the floor and I vomit my tea onto the plush Oriental rug.

FIFTY

Sleep seems like something I used to do before returning to Domerica. Lingering on my balcony, I watch as the last of the revelers stumble in from Mother's farewell celebration. One mega event out of the way, only the wedding to worry about now—if it actually takes place as planned.

Sifting through my feelings is baffling. I'm angry and sad, but most of all, I'm disappointed. Okay, I'm being childish, I admit it, but I'm completely bummed that my knight in shining armor has been tarnished by something out of a cheesy reality show. I could use a mother's advice right now. Although I can probably guess that Queen Eleanor would advise me to sever all ties with Ryder, and find a more *suitable* husband. My Connecticut mom would likely be more understanding, but I suspect modern American views on unmarried parenthood are vastly different than they are here. In the end, it's solely my decision and, at this moment, I feel desperately alone.

Puttering around my room, I gather my discarded clothing and put it away. Replacing my necklace in the jewelry chest, I happen across a black velvet pouch I remember from last year. Inside is a large golden key with a pentagram-shaped head. Ah, right. This is the key to the mystery door in the attic room above my closet. I haven't explored it yet and, as they say, there's no time like the present.

Rolling the ladder to the corner of my closet, I climb to the top and locate the attic door in the ceiling. It takes only a minute for me to scramble inside and push the rack of stored dresses out of the way. Carefully inserting the pentagram key into the hole, I jiggle it a few times but can't get it to budge. Where's the WD-40 when you need it? After a few minutes of maneuvering, the bolt slides back, and I tug firmly on the ring handle.

It's dark inside, and the air is stale. I can just make out a steep staircase directly in front of me. Searching both sides of the wall, I'm unable to locate a light switch. I curse myself for not bringing a lantern along, but there's no way I'm turning back now. My hand skims along the stone wall as I cautiously feel my way up the steps toward a small patch of dim light at the top. As my head emerges from the opening an involuntary gasp escapes my throat when I realize where I am. It's the tower—the highest point of the palace, maybe the highest point in Domerica.

Three hundred and sixty degrees of windows greet me as I step into the perfectly round room. A faded, overstuffed chair, a matching foot stool, and a small Bombay chest with a single electric candle on top are the only furnishings. Goose flesh breaks out on my arms when I realize this must have been the princess's hidden sanctuary. The view is astonishing as I make my way around the sphere of glass. The entire palace grounds are visible. I can even make out the lights of Warrington Village in the distance. The panorama must stretch for miles in the daylight, maybe even to the Enclave.

A small door leads out onto a wooden walkway circling the tower. I open it and take a half-step outside, before my good sense kicks in and tells me this walkway probably isn't regularly maintained by the grounds crew. It appears no one has been up here for ages. Filling my lungs with the fresh ionized air, I step back inside to do some exploring.

Easing my body into the squishy chair, it seems to hug me in welcome. I prop my feet on the foot stool and switch on the candle. It glows weakly, probably not bright enough be seen from the outside. Sliding open the top drawer of the chest, I examine its contents. A red enameled tea kettle, a flowered mug, a basket of assorted teas, and a single electric burner are stored on one side. A telescope, a folded map, and a pair of opera glasses are on the other.

The second drawer proves slightly more interesting: an ivory hand mirror, a tortoise-shell comb, a folded-up Chinese-looking fan, a bag of polished stones, a few books, and a sketch pad.

I pull out the sketch pad, and hold it on my lap. The first few pages are drawings of flowers and trees. Flipping through the pages beneath, I stop at a sketch of a grand mansion. "Meadowood" is hand-printed at the bottom of the page. This is the princess's former estate, now belonging to Drew and Adelais. It's striking, and I'm impressed by the princess's talent as an artist. She must have gotten an art gene that I didn't. Behind the estate sketch is a drawing of the pearl necklace from the princess's hope chest. Apparently she designed it herself.

Turning to the next drawing my heart stumbles over itself. Staring back at me is a young Ryder Blackthorn. The princess flawlessly captured his eyes, high cheekbones, and full sensuous lips. At the bottom of the page is a short poem.

> I beheld today with newborn eyes
> a love my heart has ever known.
> Though far away he sleeps tonight,
> my troth to him is set in stone.

Ghost fingers tickle my neck. I'm not sure what *troth* means, but it's obvious she fell for him that first day, just the way he did for her. I'm reading a dead girl's love poem to the man I'm about to marry. An eerie sadness sweeps through me. Respectfully, I close the pad and tuck it safely back inside the chest. Sitting in the princess's chair, snooping through her things, I suddenly feel like an interloper, a trespasser.

Ralston told me from the beginning that Ryder and Princess Jaden weren't meant to be together in this lifetime. The princess never got to wear that beautiful necklace, or to feel the heat of Ryder's kiss. I'm sorry for her. And yet, I *am* her—in a way I don't completely understand—and she is me. Except not. What if Ryder was meant to be with someone else in this existence? Even if he wasn't, do I really want to be living someone else's life?

My brain is scrambled from grief and lack of sleep; I can't

decipher my real feelings. As the pale light of dawn licks the edges of the tower room windows, I wearily descend the ladder to my room, hoping this new day will bring some clarity of thought.

After I've dressed and eaten a light breakfast, I set out in search of Ralston. He may have some words of wisdom that'll make the jagged edges of my predicament fit into place. I find him sitting alone at a table in the tranquility garden, finishing his breakfast and leafing through a book of poetry.

He smiles when he sees me. "Good morning, Your Majesty." He doesn't bother to stand, since no one is around. I wonder why he bothers to eat, but it's probably rude to ask.

"Hey, Rals. How's it going?" I say, taking a seat at the table.

"I'm well, my dear. But how are you? You left the feast quite early. Your father said you were not feeling well."

Sighing, I tell him, "I got some upsetting news last night, Rals. Do you have a few minutes to talk?"

"Of course." He dabs his mouth with a napkin and closes his book, giving me his undivided attention. "What is it, old girl?"

Gazing at the small fountain in the center of the garden, the playful cherubs remind me of little babies, and reality kicks in. "Erica's pregnant. The baby's Ryder's," I blurt out inelegantly.

"Oh my."

"Yeah. I need your help. Ryder says he'll provide for her and the baby, but he's not going to marry her. He still wants us to get married. I love him, Rals. I'm not even sure I can survive without him, but I don't know if I can handle having Erica as part of our everyday lives. That may be worse still. Plus, what will the people think of us when this information goes public? I mean, they'll probably think he cheated on me and that I don't care, or that he's a scumbag for not marrying her, or that she's some kind of evil home wrecker. Oh man, it's such a mess."

Ralston removes his glasses and massages the bridge of his nose.

"Do you even need those things?" I ask him.

"What these?" He holds up his glasses. "Not really. The lenses are not corrective, but they do have some interesting properties." He hands them to me and I put them on. Tiny built-in mirrors on the side of each lens provide a rear view.

"Hey, you can see behind you."

"Yes. They also function as a camera. See this little decoration?" He shows me a tiny raised silver emblem near the hinge. "That is the shutter release. In addition, they have retinal analysis capabilities in order to identify other non-humans."

"That's so cool."

He smiles. "Yes, they are rather remarkable. Now, let us return to the problem at hand."

"Okay." I give the glasses back, and he slips them on.

"Let's begin with the easy part. What will the people think? Assuming you choose to care about such things. The facts will speak for themselves in certain respects. Erica is nearly past her first trimester, meaning she is nearly twelve weeks pregnant. You've been home for less than a month. It will be clear that the pregnancy predated your return."

"That makes sense," I say. "Hey wait a minute. How did you know how far along Erica's pregnancy is? *I* didn't even know. You got that information from somewhere else." I nail him with my eyes. "You knew, didn't you? You knew about the pregnancy before last night, and you didn't tell me."

"Calm down, Jaden," he says quietly. "Yes. I admit I knew about it. I found out when I visited Agent Chelmsford two weeks ago. I didn't tell you because I was ordered not to, and because I was informed that you would learn of the pregnancy prior to your wedding day and would have the opportunity to make your own decision. As I told you at that time, I was threatened with strict penalties if I divulge certain information to you."

I narrow my eyes at him. "What about the attack on me? Did you know about that beforehand?"

"Of course not," he says indignantly. "As I related to you after my meeting, the prediction models had not yet stabilized, so future events could not be accurately foreseen at that time. Erica's pregnancy happened prior to your return, and Agent Chelmsford was aware of it, but I have not met with him since. The attack was as much a surprise to me as it was to you."

"Well, maybe you'd better pay Chelmsford another visit. That was too close a call. Why the hell didn't he warn you?"

"I had planned to meet with him this week, after things settle down a bit. But, I assume that either Chelmsford knew you would be safe, and that is why we weren't forewarned, or he was caught unawares also."

Smoldering with anger, I fold my arms across my chest, slump down in my chair, and stare at the fountain.

"Jaden, I swear I'm telling you the truth. Can we get past this, please, and move on to the problem at hand?"

"I guess so," I mumble, not looking at him. Echoes of Asher's words replay in my head, *He's loyal to IUGA … They own him.*

"It may interest you to know that the Domerican people are rather tolerant of their queens' choice of spouses and their actions as far as matters of the heart are concerned."

This intrigues me, so I suspend my snit in order to hear more about it. "Oh yeah, like what?"

"Well, one need look no further than your parents' unorthodox relationship—separated, yet still married; your father running his own small country, not subject to your mother's rule. Both of your parents remained respected and beloved by their subjects.

"More unusual situations have existed also. Take Queen Caroline. She had an eye for strapping young men and, after her husband died, she kept a succession of them in residence at the palace. Her *friends* she called them. Although most of them were stable hands or low-ranking soldiers, she dressed them in the finest couture, and had no qualms about taking them everywhere she went. She was still quite adored by the people, who simply turned a blind eye to her indiscretions."

"Anyone else?" I ask.

"I could relate any number of stories, but perhaps the most relevant is that of Queen Millicent and her husband, King Terrance. The king was a notorious philanderer, but still doted on by the queen. It was rumored that, at the end of his life, he had no less than seven children by women other than his wife. Certainly Ryder's situation is trivial by comparison."

"I see what you mean. So you think it may cause some raised eyebrows at first, but people will just get over it?"

"Exactly. Although the other issue may be a bit thornier. Can you endure Erica's presence as an integral part of Ryder's life? She will be the mother of his child. How will you handle that?"

"I don't know. That's the whole problem. I'm not sure how I'll feel." I throw up my hands in frustration.

"But that is the magic of being human, Jaden. You can choose how you wish to feel about any given situation. You are uniquely capable of controlling your own emotions."

"That's a bunch of bull," I say. "Maybe automatons can do that, but there are times I can't control it. I just feel happy or angry or upset or whatever. It's not a choice."

"Nonsense. That may be true for a child, Jade, but it is not true for a grown woman. And you are a grown woman. Of course, your initial reaction to the news of Erica's pregnancy was disappointment, even anger. That is a natural first reaction, but you have the ability to choose to accept the situation and change your attitude about Erica … or not."

"I'm not sure I understand what you're saying."

"If you love Ryder and you wish to be happy with him, you must put aside your insignificant jealousies and self-indulgent disappointment and welcome this baby into your life. On your home earth, combined families are practically the norm these days. Have you thought about the fact that you will be this child's stepmother? Search your heart, Jade. Is there room for a beautiful little baby? One perhaps with Ryder's hair and eyes?"

The visual makes me smile.

"Can you conjure up some empathy for Erica? You once liked her for her spirit and kindness. She's still the same woman. She could use your friendship at this time."

"Friends? Come on, Rals, we could never be friends."

"But you must. You cannot do this halfway, my dear. You must make peace with it, or it will eat you up from the inside out."

"That's asking an awful lot."

"Perhaps, but it doesn't take a prediction model to know that unless you are able to accomplish this, you and Ryder will never be completely happy. It's your choice, my dear. Entirely your choice."

I hate it when he's right, and so smug about it. "Well, you've given me a lot to think about, Rals." I stand and snag a leftover strawberry from his breakfast plate. "Maybe I'll take a ride to clear my mind. Thanks for talking to me."

"Take Patrick if you go," he says.

"My shadow, you mean? And, by the way, you're still not off the hook for not telling me about this before." He brushes me off with a wave of his hand. I pop the strawberry in my mouth and head for the stables.

FIFTY-ONE

*P*atrick's the strong silent type. I like that in a guy. We race to the upper meadow, and ride around the perimeter of the palace grounds without sharing more than one or two sentences. On our return, I find Father waiting for me in the palace courtyard.

"Have you been here long?" I ask, kissing his whiskered cheek.

"No, I just arrived. I was concerned about you. Has Ryder been by to see you?"

"Yes. Come in, and I'll tell you all about it. Can you stay for lunch?"

"Yes. I planned to stay the night, if you'll put me up. I ran into Charles LeGare. He wants to meet with us later, if possible."

"Does he have news?"

"I'm not certain. It didn't seem urgent."

Father follows me into a small bright parlor with a view of Mother's rose garden. I wonder fleetingly who'll tend to the roses now that she's gone. My gardening skills are notoriously bad. We order lunch, and settle ourselves into two arm chairs in front of the floor-to-ceiling windows.

"Why did Ryder disappear so abruptly last night?" Father asks, removing his sword and resting it beside his chair.

"Well, he'd just gotten some disturbing news, and I guess he wasn't sure how to tell me. Father, Erica Hornsby's pregnant. It's Ryder's child."

"Good lord. No wonder he appeared shaken. Erica didn't pick the most appropriate venue for sharing the news with Ryder."

"That was Catherine's doing. The woman is pure evil. She insisted Erica accompany her to the farewell celebration and tell Ryder immediately."

Father rests his elbows on the arms of the chair and steeples his fingers beneath his chin. "How do you and Ryder intend to handle this development?"

"I'm still processing what it will mean to us in the future. Ryder told Erica that he'll support her and the baby, and he wants to be a part of the child's life—a real father. He also told her he doesn't love her, and doesn't want to marry her regardless of whether I decide to go through with our wedding."

"That must have hurt her very deeply," Father says sympathetically. "I'm certain she held out a faint hope that the pregnancy would persuade Ryder to choose to be with her instead of you."

"Yeah, I'm sure that's true. But I've been more worried about the problems this creates for me."

"What do you mean?"

"It's such a fiasco. Now Erica will have to be a part of our lives forever. And, I can only imagine what kind of rumors and gossip will be flying around about Ryder being unfaithful and me choosing to look the other way."

He reaches over and takes my hand in his. "Sweetheart, I'm certain this news can't have been easy for you to hear. It changes the landscape a bit. But the concerns you've voiced are trivial matters when compared with the ordeal facing Erica. She must feel desolate and quite alone."

"Don't worry about Erica," I say, piqued that Father seems to have taken her side. "Once Ryder moves out, Catherine has invited Erica to live with her. She won't be alone."

"Still, it will not be easy for her," he says. "The man she loves, the father of her child, will soon be married to the woman he loves, who also happens to be Queen of Domerica, and the envy of every woman in the land."

I've never thought of myself in those terms before, because I'm really just Jaden Beckett of Madison, Connecticut. But what he says rings true. Being queen is no day at the beach, but I'm sure it inspires envy in some people. "I hadn't ever considered that Erica might be jealous of me," I say. "I've always been so envious of her beauty."

"She's a good person, Jade. But, you have so much more than she has, in every respect that matters."

Lunch arrives and the maids set it out on the coffee table. Father and I help ourselves to mini sandwiches and potato salad.

"It's just that Erica and her child will be constant reminders of Ryder's faithlessness. Coming so soon on the heels of Mother's death, I'm not sure I'm emotionally capable of dealing with all this. And I'm almost certain I'm not ready to be a stepmother." I munch on a crisp baby gherkin.

"You've had many unexpected occurrences in your life recently, Jaden, and you've proven yourself capable of handling whatever comes your way. Moreover, I have complete confidence that you will make a loving and nurturing stepmother, if that is the path you choose to take. But you must attempt to separate your feelings on this issue from your grief over your mother's passing. What does your heart tell you?"

Father pours us glasses of lemonade from a sweating pitcher, while I gaze out at the rose garden, plumbing my true feelings.

After a moment, I turn my eyes to his. "My heart tells me what it's always told me, that I want to be with Ryder."

"Then you must find a way to accept Erica and this child into your life."

I nibble around the edges of my sandwich toying with a thought. "Father, do you know where Erica lives now?" I ask.

He nods. "Her home is near the hospital. I've taken Mrs. Hornsby by once or twice. Captain and Mrs. Hornsby must be quite concerned for their daughter. They're very private people. Neither of them has let on that there is a problem."

"Maybe they don't know yet," I say. "But I was wondering, will you take me to see Erica today?"

He stops mid-bite. "Are you certain, sweetheart? Are you ready to speak with her so soon?"

"My wedding's in two weeks. This needs to be resolved now if I'm going through with it. Besides, I need to find peace in at least one part of my life."

"Of course I'll take you, sweetheart, but we'd better see what General LeGare wants before we go."

"Sure. Thanks. Father," I say, hoping I'm doing the right thing.

We find LeGare in his office in the barracks of the Royal Guard. His tired and morose countenance tugs at my heart. After bowing formally and making certain we're comfortably seated, he updates us on the progress of the investigation into last week's attack. So far, it sounds as if the investigators have hit a number of dead ends, but they were able to piece together a connection between two of the slain black knights. Both men had been released from Wall's Edge prison within the last three months.

"This may be the common thread we're looking for," LeGare says. "If someone is recruiting former prisoners, we ought to be able to trace that. It may require significant legwork, but we're pursuing leads day and night."

"Thanks, Charles," Father says. "Please keep us informed. The queen and I are taking a little excursion this afternoon—not far. Can you spare a few men to accompany us? Patrick will come along, of course, but I believe we could do with a few more, just to be safe."

"Of course," LeGare says. "They'll be ready in ten minutes."

"Excellent."

We stand. Father and LeGare shake hands, but I can't resist giving him an empathetic peck on the cheek. *I miss her too.*

"Father, there's something I need to do before we leave. I'll be back in a few minutes," I say, and sprint for the palace.

Maria hums a little tune as she folds my clothes and tucks them away in my closet. "I need a quick favor," I tell her.

"Certainly, Your Majesty. What can I do for you?"

"Do you have any of that special hair tonic from Cupola de Vita? A new bottle, I mean?"

"Why yes. We have several bottles. Would you like one?"

"Yes. It's a gift. Do we have something pretty to put it in?"

She smiles broadly. "I believe I can find something."

"Good, and I'm kind of in a hurry. I'll meet you downstairs."

Unraveling the braid in my hair, I brush it back and anchor it in place with my favorite woven gold headband. I consider changing out of my sweaty riding clothes, but I want to visit with Erica woman to woman, not as the queen. So I settle for a dab of cologne on my neck, and I dash downstairs to meet Father.

Our escort is in place—four soldiers in front, two in back. Father waits in the carriage, and I climb in beside him. "Just one more minute," I say.

On cue, Maria pokes her head inside and hands me a gorgeous package wrapped in yellow tissue paper and tied with a gauzy lavender ribbon.

"Thanks, Maria. You're the best."

Eyeing the gift, Father smiles. "Ready?" he asks. I nod, and he signals to the men. My insides quiver as I realize we're off to call on Erica Hornsby, my soon to be ex-nemesis, I hope.

Our entourage clatters up Erica's small residential street. Many of her neighbors step out onto their porches to see what the commotion is all about. I feel badly about drawing so much attention to her, but I'm not at liberty to travel light these days. The procession pulls to a halt in front of a diminutive cottage. Father wishes me luck saying he'll wait in the carriage. The soldiers dismount, and form a protective human barrier around me as I pass through Erica's gate and up the front walk.

She opens the door at my knock, her face registering alarm at the sight of me and several Royal Guardsmen squeezed onto her small porch. "Your Majesty." She makes a quick curtsey. "What is it? Is something wrong?"

Erica wears a plain ivory-colored smock, her hair pulled back into a single braid, her face devoid of make-up. She's absolutely stunning. It's difficult to focus on my objective of making peace with her, when I'm reminded that this beautiful woman was once Ryder's lover and now carries his child.

I swallow the sour jealousy creeping up my throat, and attempt what I hope is a gracious smile. "There's nothing wrong, Erica. I'd like to speak with you for a few minutes, if it's convenient."

"Yes. Please come in," she says, gesturing me inside. "I don't believe everyone will fit in my parlor." She casts a wary eye at the soldiers.

"It's just me," I say. "They're staying out here."

The modest living room is tastefully decorated in muted, solid fabrics. Vibrant art and unusual accessories add color and interest to the room. She invites me to sit in a large overstuffed chair near her fake fireplace. She remains standing, and I realize she's waiting for me to ask her to be seated. When I do, she perches tentatively on the edge of the sofa and folds her hands neatly in her lap.

"I'm sorry for showing up unannounced," I say, "and for bringing half the Royal Guard with me. Ryder has informed me of your pregnancy, and I thought we should talk."

Her eyes harden and her chest rises and falls with each shallow breath. "I am grateful that Ryder wishes to acknowledge the child as his own," she says haltingly, "and that he has agreed to provide for us. He has made his feelings clear, though, and you need have no fear of me. I assure you I will not attempt to interfere with the wedding or any part of your relationship in the future. I could not hurt him in that way." Her voice cracks on these last words.

"Erica, that's not why I'm here. I'm not worried about you trying to hurt Ryder or me. I came to see if it's possible for you and me to find a way to live with this situation in harmony instead of hatred. I was devastated when I learned of your relationship with Ryder, but I have forgiven him. It's true that I harbored feelings of jealousy and anger toward you, and I suspect you've experienced feelings of resentment and hurt toward me."

She bows her head and stares at her hands.

"But I've accepted the fact that you and the baby will be part of Ryder's life after we're married," I say, "and I don't want things to be awkward or weird between you and me. This child should not be made to feel any shame surrounding the circumstances of his birth. I came to ask you to set aside any hard feelings you have for me, and work with me to make this difficult situation as pleasant as possible for the sake of the child."

Her head remains bowed, and she says nothing. After a time, I begin to wonder if I should get up and leave, but then I notice tears dripping onto the back of her hands, so I stay quietly seated. Another moment passes, and she raises her head. "Thank you for your kindness," she says, her thick lashes heavy with tears. "I believed you must hate me, and that you would shun me and my child. Your words have comforted me more than you can know. I swear to you I will do my best to maintain harmony among our families."

"That's great," I say. Remembering the package I brought for her, I add, "I've brought you a gift. It's a tonic for your hair. It works miracles with extra-long hair. I thought ... well, I hoped that, maybe in time, we might grow to be friends." I feel a little stupid after saying it—the wife and the baby mamma BFFs? I guess stranger things have happened.

She manages a soggy smile. "Thank you. It would be an honor. Catherine said you would never accept the baby."

The mention of Catherine is like a jab with a cattle prod. "Listen, Erica, I'm happy that you have somewhere nice to live during your pregnancy and after the baby's born. I know Meli and her son will be great company for you. But please don't let Catherine poison you against me. She doesn't know me, and she never will. I hope you and I can build our own relationship without Catherine interfering the way she does with Ryder and me."

"She is very protective of him," Erica says.

"Well, he's a grown man. She needs to get over it." I stand and hold out the package for her. "I hope you enjoy this." I extend my other hand to shake hers.

She takes my hand in both of hers and surprises me by kissing it. "Thank you, Your Majesty. You are truly as grand as Ryder believes you to be." She seems small and vulnerable. Not the powerful goddess I always imagined her to be. I'm not worthy of her compliment, but I'm grateful she said it.

"Take care of yourself and the baby, Erica. We will meet again soon."

She walks me to the door and, as I step across the threshold, I feel lighter and purer, as if something heavy and toxic has been excavated from my soul. Maybe Ryder and I really can live happily ever after, despite all the crazy curveballs that have been thrown our way.

FIFTY-TWO

*U*pon returning to the palace, I dash off a message to Ryder saying that I'd like to see him in the morning and asking him to arrange to spend a few hours at Warrington Palace going over wedding plans. I consider adding a few lines about my visit with Erica to let him know everything's good, but I decide against it. The mention of wedding plans should clue him in.

The palace is mostly empty of the visiting dignitaries from various provinces of Domerica who came to Warrington for Mother's farewell celebration. There are still a few hangers-on, but I don't feel obligated to play hostess tonight, so Father, Ralston, and I enjoy a private dinner in the family dining room. It's been an emotionally wrenching day, and sharing a pleasant meal with two of my favorite people is sheer bliss. We pass the time discussing things that have absolutely no national or international significance whatsoever.

Immediately following dinner, a messenger arrives with a package for me from Lady Lorelei. Taking it to my room, I discard the string and tear away the brown paper wrapping. The black velvet box is heavy in my hand, and I raise the lid on Ryder's wedding ring—transformed from paper to object of beauty. The wide gold band with interlocking circles is splendid, more impressive in reality than in my imagination. A note from Lorelei is tucked inside.

Dearest Cousin – Enclosed is the ring you commissioned. I hope it is true to your desire, and that you are pleased with the result. I think it is quite handsome. There remains sufficient time for an inscription, if you so wish. Jacob and I look forward to your wedding day with great love and anticipation.

Your devoted servant,

Lorelei

This day has ended far better than I could have imagined. My head swirls with romantic dreams and my stomach with overactive butterflies as I dress for bed. I'll be with Ryder tomorrow. Our wedding is only days away. It can't come soon enough for me.

Father departs for the Enclave before I'm out of bed. I regret not seeing him off, but I had the best night's sleep I've had in weeks. Dressing quickly, I ask that my breakfast be served out on the huge front portico of the palace, while I wait for Ryder to arrive. Servants busy themselves setting up a table with linen, china, and crystal and moving a dining chair outside for me. Honestly, I would have been happy sitting on the top step and eating out of a paper plate, but the staff already thinks I'm a little eccentric, so I just let them do their jobs.

Though I can't see him yet, I sense it the minute Ryder enters the main gate. Abandoning my half-eaten meal on the table, I rush down the stairs to meet him. Catching sight of me, he knees Tenasi into a gallop. He bounds from the horse's back in mid-stride, sweeps me up in his arms, and twirls me around.

"I was so pleased to receive your message last night, I almost came to you then," he says beaming.

"I wish you had. It's been too long since you've snuck onto my balcony in the middle of the night," I say, referring to a time when he thought I'd become betrothed to Prince Damien.

He hugs me joyfully, and then holds me at arm's length. "You're certain about this, Jade? You still wish to be my wife, and it's acceptable that I will soon have a child?"

"Yes. I'm certain. I went to see Erica yesterday, and I feel like the three of us together can create a loving atmosphere for this child … if Catherine stops meddling, that is."

This seems to astonish him. "You visited Erica? At her home?"

"Yes. I told her I've accepted that she and the baby will be a part of our lives in the future, and proposed that we work together to make things as pleasant as possible. She was gracious and swore to do her best to make the situation a harmonious one."

"You did that for me?" he asks.

"I did it for all of us, Ryder. You, me, Erica, the baby, and really all of Domerica."

He draws me close to him and holds me tightly. "I love you," he whispers into my hair.

"I know. I love you too." I take his hand and lead him up the front steps. "We have lots of wedding stuff to get through today. Have you eaten?"

"Yes. I had breakfast."

"Good, then let's find Jennifer. Maybe we'll have time for a ride before lunch."

Our meeting with Jennifer is scheduled in a large first floor parlor. When we arrive she's laying out sketches on a long table. Swatches of fabric, several sprays of flowers, and a small cake have been arranged on another table. Jennifer curtseys as we enter. Normally all business, she flushes and stammers when I introduce her to Ryder.

"Chief Blackthorn, I … It's an honor to meet you."

The impact of Ryder's looks on most women occasionally slips my mind.

"Thanks for meeting with us this morning, Jennifer," I say, steering her attention away from my handsome fiancé. "We'd like to take a ride before lunch, so maybe we can get started."

"Oh, yes. This shouldn't take long. Queen Eleanor had everything well organized prior to her passing," she says casually. "I planned to show you the proposed setup, briefly go over the ceremony, get your approvals on the flowers and cake, and then I've arranged for the tailor to take the final measurements for Chief Blackthorn's suit."

The mention of Mother's name triggers a twinge of sorrow. I'm glad we're carrying out her final wishes.

Jennifer efficiently goes over the color scheme and choices of china (Mother desired that we use the Regency) and silver (Queen Matilda). She shows us several sketches of the elaborate setting for the ceremony. We're to be married in the Grand Arboretum behind the palace. The many trees and plants will be strewn with twinkling electric candles. Gossamer white canopies will flutter overhead. The center aisle will be carpeted with white satin, and we'll exchange our vows in a pillared white gazebo. Jennifer can barely contain her excitement when she mentions the two thousand white doves to be released when the pastor says, *"You may kiss the bride."*

Ryder's eyes begin to glaze over by the time we come to the samples of the floral arrangements, but he quickly perks up when Jennifer serves us generous samples of the wedding cake.

"Would you care to sit down while we go over the seating chart?" Jennifer asks.

"Can you and I do that some other time?" I say taking mercy on Ryder.

"Yes, Your Majesty. Two additional things need attention, however. We planned to have Irish and Cherokee dance troupes from Unicoi Village, as you requested, but we haven't finalized the Domerican entertainment as yet.

"I trust your judgment," I tell her. "Just choose what you think is best. Uh, no plays though."

She nods knowingly. Who could forget the *Jaden the Warrior Princess* debacle? "Also, it's rather important that the tailor take Chief

Blackthorn's measurements today if we wish the suit to be finished by your wedding day."

I look to Ryder. "Yes, that's fine," he says.

While we wait for the tailor, Jennifer informs us that there've been a few changes in the roster of guests. "I'm disappointed to say that King Rafael and Queen Bianca of Cupola de Vita will not be in attendance after all. The King and Queen send their deepest regrets along with a note stating that Duke Ferdinand and the Duchess Isabella will attend in their stead." The corners of her mouth pull down, causing her to look like an English bulldog with spectacles.

"There is good news from Dome Noir, though. King Philippe has requested that both his sons, Princes Gilbert and Jean Louis, be allowed to attend, along with a small party of other dignitaries. This is outstanding. Two princes," she says cheerily. "May I tell the king that this will be acceptable?"

"Sure. How many guests in all?" I ask.

She taps the side of her glasses with her pen. "With the new attendees from Dome Noir, it will be around five hundred and sixty or so."

Thumbing through the sketches of the Grand Arboretum dressed up like Pan's forest, the scent of jasmine tickles my nose seemingly from nowhere. A moment later, a large blonde woman clad in a black skirt and sweater flounces into the room, reeking of the stuff. Several tape measures hang carelessly around her shoulders like a tattered scarf. A mountain of hair rests atop her head, and the fabric of her top strains mightily to cover the most enormous pair of breasts I've ever seen. Breast augmentation is unknown in Domerica, so it strikes me that these things have to be real.

She bows deeply to Ryder and me, and I fear she may topple over from the sudden shifting of weight. "Your Majesty," she says in a husky voice, nodding to me. "I am at your service. And this must be Chief Blackthorn." She smiles coquettishly and extends a beefy hand to Ryder. "I'm so pleased to make your acquaintance at last."

Ryder stands and shakes her hand.

"My, you are a big one," she says gazing up at him with shining eyes.

Jennifer makes a small coughing noise into her hand. Whether out of embarrassment or as a warning to Busty Girl, I don't know.

"Shall we stand where the light is better?" The seamstress places a hand on Ryder's back and guides him to a spot near the window. She bends and retrieves a small stepstool from under the table. "I'm going to need this. May I ask you to remove your jacket?"

Ryder shrugs off his jacket and tosses it on a chair. "Very nice," she says, sizing him up with her eyes. Toting the stool around behind Ryder, she sets it on the rug. "I believe we'll start with the shoulders." She unwinds a tape measure from her neck and mounts the stool. Soft *oohs* and *aahs* issue from her bow-shaped mouth as she stretches the tape across Ryder's broad back. Then she measures his arm from shoulder to wrist, quietly commenting on the impressive length of his wing-span.

"Would you like me to make notes while you measure?" Jennifer asks.

"No. Thank you. I can remember everything," Busty says, not taking her eyes off Ryder for a second. She drags the little stool around and positions it in front of him. "Shall we do your neck now?" Stepping onto the stool, she reaches her arms behind Ryder's neck stretching out the tape and practically cradling his face in her generous bosom.

"I'll never get an accurate measure with all that hair in the way," she coos, sweeping up his silky locks with her fingers.

He reaches back, removing his hair from her grasp. "Allow me to do that," he says.

The whole scene is a little too touchy-feely for me, and I'm getting a prickly sensation all over. I frown at Jennifer like *Is this woman really groping my fiancé right in front of me?* But she plucks at some threads on her skirt and avoids my eyes.

When the flirty tailor gets down on her knees and stretches her tape to measure Ryder's inseam, I spring from my chair. "All righty then," I say, "Why doesn't Chief Blackthorn send one of his suits over to you for the rest of the measurements. We really must be going now."

A flummoxed Jennifer hurries over. "Your Majesty, is everything all right?

I stare at her like *Really?* "I'll speak with you later on the seating chart," I say. "Ryder, are you ready?"

He grabs his jacket, and we practically jog out the door. Halfway down the hall, we burst into peals of laughter.

"What was that all about?" I say.

"I don't know, but thank you for rescuing me. The woman was pitiless. Her hands were all over me." He raises the sleeve of his shirt to his nose. "Good god, I smell as if I've been dunked in jasmine."

Stopping him with my hand, I sniff the front of his shirt. "*Ew.* You do. Do you want to shower before our ride?"

"It wouldn't help. I don't have extra clothes here. The stench is intolerable."

"I'll see if there's something of Father's. It may not fit, but you could try."

"Perhaps I'd better return to Unicoi to shower and change," he says.

I take his hand. "No. Please. I was hoping you'd stay the night here. Father's gone back to the Enclave, and well, we haven't looked at all of our wedding gifts yet. We'd have a chance to be alone for a change." I don't attempt to hide my eagerness.

He brushes his fingers tenderly along my jaw. "I have something I must do tonight, love. I'm so sorry, but it's been planned for days. I would be letting others down."

"What is it? What are you doing that's so important?" I'm

seriously on the verge of pouting.

"I really should not say."

Glaring at him, I ask, "Is Alexander coming again?"

"No. Actually, I plan to escort Meli and the baby to Old Unicoi to visit with him for a few days."

This is unwelcome news. "Ryder, no. I wish you wouldn't. It's too dangerous."

"Would that I could honor your wishes, love, but I've made commitments to Alexander and to Meli. They have very little time together. The baby is growing up without his father. It's the least I can do."

Chewing on my lower lip, I resist the urge to argue with him. "All right. You're a loyal friend. But when will you be back? The wedding's in ten days. There's still a lot to do."

Smiling, he takes my hands in his. "Only three days. I will come straight to you once I've returned Meli and the baby to Catherine's care. And I'll bring extra clothes to keep here. I promise. In the meantime, I'm certain whatever wedding decisions you make will be acceptable to me. I'm afraid I wasn't of much help to you today."

I snort. "You certainly made the tailor's day."

"Can you stand to kiss me goodbye while I'm redolent of her scent?"

"I'll hold my breath," I say, pulling him close.

FIFTY-THREE

*L*unching alone in my room, I'm lonely and sulky. My big plans for spending the day (and night) with Ryder have been dashed, but moping around doesn't seem like a good use of my time, so I decide to find something constructive to do.

I fill up a box with some things from my room that might look nice in Mother's office. It's my office now, and I need to find ways to make it my own. Carrying the box upstairs, I plunk it on the desk and begin to rearrange things, setting out trinkets and books from my room, and repacking the box with Mother's mementoes.

Once things look cozier and more like me, I settle down at the desk to do some work. I pull a stack of thick files from one of the bottom drawers and flip through the tabs. They are titled with things like "Semi-Annual Agricultural Report," "Coalition of Dome Nations Report," "Dome Operations Procedures," "Fiscal Responsibility Act." Ugh. *Just shoot me now, please. I'll never get through all this.*

Pushing away from the desk and the odious stack of files, I wander to the window. A cadre of Royal Guardsmen on horseback is conducting drills on the grounds; others duel with practice swords; while still others flirt with the housemaids on their break in the courtyard. I watch them and wonder idly what I'd be doing if I were in Connecticut right now. Probably hanging out with my friends and having fun—getting yogurt, shopping for shoes, listening to each other's playlists, and other normal things like that. Truthfully, I miss it. I miss my friends.

Everything was going to change anyway. Everyone would be heading off to college soon, and really, could those files on my desk be any more daunting than the homework I'd be inundated with at Yale? I don't think so. At least here I have Ryder, and I'm about to be the bride in an amazing fairytale-like wedding. Plus, I can be a positive force in Domerica. So many important things need to be accomplished here—the completion of Unicoi Village, and the restoring of trade with Dome Noir, for two. Maybe the Council and I can come up with some ideas for Dome Noir that will help improve conditions for that country also.

Filled with purpose and hope, I plant my butt back in the desk chair. I tuck the thick files back inside the drawer and pull out all the information Mother amassed on Dome Noir. The proposal for resumption of trade is the most important issue at the moment. The rest of it can wait. Prince Gilbert will be here in a week or so, and I need to have something that will bowl him over. It may be impossible to promise him Damien's murderer on a silver platter, but we have other incentives to offer. Attractive incentives. I take a fresh writing pad from the desk and begin making notes.

Completely absorbed in my project, I lose all track of the time. When Ralston pokes his head inside the door, I realize the afternoon light has faded to dusk. "Are you coming down for dinner, my dear, or should I have something sent up?" he asks.

"Actually, I was thinking of taking a break." I stretch my arms and rotate the stiffness from my neck. "Dinner sounds good. Are you headed down now?"

"Yes. Would you care to accompany me?"

"Love to. I need to talk to you about something anyway. Do you think we could have dinner alone tonight?"

He tilts his head at me. "Far be it from me to tell you how to run your palace, but you haven't dined with the guests at court since your mother's death. You may at least wish to put in an appearance."

"Oh man. That means I'd have to get dressed up and wear a crown. I'm too tired tonight." I give him my best *pretty please* look. "Besides, you and I have things to discuss, and maybe a game of chess after?"

"All right," he relents. "I'll send word that you have pressing business tonight, but that you will dine in the main hall tomorrow night."

I beam at him. "Thanks, Rals. I'll have something sent to my rooms for us. See you soon."

Gathering my things, I flip off the lamp and follow him out the door.

Over dinner I share with Ralston the finer points of my outlined proposal to Dome Noir. Cook has prepared roasted salmon tonight, harvested from the Unicoi fish farms. It's mouthwatering, and I make a little note in the margin of my writing pad to add "fish exportation" to the list of reasons Dome Noir should resume trade with us. Ralston has some great ideas which I incorporate into what I've already got. I'm sure the Council members will have some thoughts of their own, but I think we have a good start.

"You've done a fine job with this, Jaden." Ralston smiles fondly at me. "Undoubtedly the Council will be impressed. When is your next meeting?"

"Day after tomorrow, I hope. I haven't set it up yet, but it's important to finalize this soon. I want all these loose ends tied up well before the wedding."

"Yes, that's wise. Shall we have our desert at the chess table?"

"Sure. Let me guess, you want to be black." Ralston's always black and I'm always white when we play chess.

He surprises me by taking the seat behind the white chess pieces.

"Well, well, you've decided there is a first move advantage after all," I say. But when I sit behind the black pieces, he rotates the board a hundred and eighty degrees so I'm playing white, as usual.

"Ladies first," he says.

Cute. Ralston usually wins even though I always have the opening move. Then something occurs to me. "Hey wait a minute. This isn't really fair, is it? It's like I'm playing a computer each time we play."

"No it isn't. I do not have a chess program in my data banks. And, even if I did, I would disable it. It would not be sporting, and besides, it would take all the fun out of it."

"Do you really have fun, Rals?" I ask moving my king's pawn two spaces forward.

"Yes, I do. Every time I trounce you at chess, my dear." He grins, mirroring my move.

It takes him only about twenty minutes to put me in checkmate, and he really does look pretty proud of himself afterward. I'm still a little suspicious about that chess program thing. Anyway, he makes us mugs of tea as kind of a consolation for whipping my ass. We sit in front of the fake fireplace and watch the twinkling logs.

"How are preparations for the wedding coming along?" he asks.

"Fairly well. Mother had everything pretty well organized, and Jennifer seems to be on top of it all. There's still a lot to do, though. That's one thing I wanted to talk to you about."

"Yes? May I help in some way?"

"Well, I still need to sign the papers for IUGA, you know, electing to stay in Domerica. I thought I should go ahead and do that before the wedding guests begin arriving and I get distracted."

He sips his tea thoughtfully. "I'll need to go to headquarters to have the documents prepared. That may take two or three days, but I suppose you're right. If you're absolutely certain of your decision, there is no sense in waiting. I understand you've already conveyed your decision to Narowyn and the Transcenders, but you must decide how you wish to handle the situation in Connecticut."

"What do you mean?"

"Do you wish to simply disappear, or do you care to leave a note of some nature? Not to be morbid, my dear, but IUGA still has the princess's body in cryostasis. We could stage your death as a suicide or an accident of some sort."

"She's frozen? Oh God, that's horrible. No. No. I don't want them to find my body, or her body or whatever. I think I should just vanish. That seems the most humane thing to do."

"As you wish. I shall depart for headquarters in the morning to have the final papers drawn up."

<hr />

The palace is even lonelier with both Ryder and Ralston away. I extend an invitation to Drew and Adelais to spend a couple of days with me, but Drew responds that Adelais is suffering from regular bouts of morning sickness, and not just in the morning, so they'd better stay close to home. It wasn't only Drew's company I was looking for; I was hoping to use him as a kind of buffer between me and the people currently at court. I'm worried and nervous about committing some huge *faux pas* like forgetting the name of my great aunt Suzie or something. Drew would most likely bail me out without extracting too much humiliation. I guess I'll have to wing it without him.

Most of the first day is taken up with the burgeoning list of people who've requested an audience with the queen. Chauncey, the clerk who attended Mother during these audiences is a tiny man with a clump of coarse gray hair, a pointed nose, and talon-like fingers. I discover that despite his goblin-like appearance, he's perfectly pleasant and enormously efficient. Whispering to me throughout the proceedings, he advises me on the appropriate response to whatever request or grievance has been laid out before me. It quickly becomes clear that I'm wholly unnecessary to the proceedings, except as a figurehead. I make a mental note to see if I can appoint Chauncey as a judge or something and take myself out of the process altogether.

On the second day, the Council of Advisors meeting goes fairly well. At first, several members float their own ideas of how the situation in Dome Noir should be approached—with the hardliners and the doves jockeying for position. When it comes time to get something on paper, though, everyone agrees it's imperative to resolve the trade issue as soon as possible. We end up with a solid proposal that I believe will persuade Prince Gilbert.

Jennifer and I meet after lunch to go over seating charts and other details of the wedding. She also takes me on a tour of the renovations underway to the queen's suite. When it's completed, it won't resemble Mother's former suite at all. It'll be brighter and more open, with oversized furniture, in deference to Ryder's wishes, and soft soothing colors, in deference to mine.

Everything's coming together beautifully and, despite missing Mother every time I turn a corner in the palace, I'm in great spirits. Ralston's due home this afternoon and Ryder tomorrow. The palace is being painted, polished, scrubbed, refurbished, and refreshed in anticipation of the arrival of the many foreign wedding guests. The whole place sparkles and shines, reflecting my own mood back to me.

With my writing pad on my lap, I sit in a cheerful little parlor downstairs to compose my vows to Ryder. I'm told the COC has a rather lengthy wedding ceremony, and no one writes their own vows, but I requested that Ryder and I be allowed to include some sentiments of our own. Apparently nobody says *no* to the queen—not even the COC.

Gazing out onto the freshly-manicured grounds, I try to put my feelings into words. How do I tell Ryder that I've given up everything to be with him, when he can't possibly understand that "everything" actually includes my home, my family, my friends, and an amazing gift I've barely had time to understand.

My thoughts are interrupted by the clatter of a carriage rolling up the drive. It's Ralston! I abandon my musings and my writing pad to greet him on the front veranda.

He clambers out of the carriage and mounts the front steps slowly, looking almost tired. *Do automatons ever run out of juice?*

I meet him at the top of the stairway. "Hey, Rals. How was your trip?" No one else is around so we address each other informally.

"Everything went well, my dear. How are things here?"

"They've been kind of quiet. The calm before the storm, I guess. Wedding gifts are still pouring in, and a new gazebo is being built for Ryder and me to stand in while exchanging our vows. You ought to see it. It looks like a Greek pavilion. Not much else going on."

"I suppose that's a good thing."

"So, do you have the papers for me?" I ask excitedly.

"Yes, but we should discuss a few matters prior to your signing. Would you mind if I freshen up a bit before we meet? The road was quite dusty today. I'd like to change my clothes."

"Sure. Take your time. Are you all right, Rals?"

"Yes. Just rather jostled from the trip. Perhaps we could have tea?"

"Tea? You know you don't have to pretend with me."

"I find the ritual relaxing," he says, "if you don't mind the indulgence."

"Tea sounds great. Meet me up in Mother's, er, my office whenever you're ready. No rush."

"Thank you, Your Majesty." He bows as two servants hurry by.

FIFTY-FOUR

*T*he afternoon light lends a golden-silvery glow to Mother's office. I'm more comfortable here now that I've rearranged the furniture and shelves. I wish I had my music to work by. Last year Ryder showed me a *music box*, as he called it, invented by the Unicoi. It actually played tunes. I make a mental note to ask if he can get one for me.

The tea tray arrives, and the maids place it on the small conference table. I peek under the napkins covering the baskets to see what baked delights Cook has put together for us. Spongy lemon-poppy seed cakes, raspberry tarts, and sausage-stuffed puffed pastry balls.

I bite into one of the savory balls. *Yum.*

"Thank you for having tea sent up," Ralston says as he comes inside and closes the door. "Would you like me to pour?"

"Sure. You always do a better job than I do."

He carefully decants the tea into delicate cups, adding two sugar cubes and a touch of cream to mine. "Thanks," I say. "Shall we sit in the arm chairs?"

"Yes. That would be nice."

We take the two leather chairs in front of the desk. "What did you want to discuss with me?" I ask nibbling the crust of a raspberry tart.

He sips his tea thoughtfully. "This is a momentous decision, Jaden. I simply wish to make certain that you have thoroughly thought things through."

"Come on, Rals. We've been over this a few times already. My decision is to stay here with Ryder. Geeze, I'm getting married in a little over a week. I'll miss my life in Connecticut, and I hate it that Dad and Drew will never know what happened to me, but Dad's getting pretty serious with his girlfriend, and Drew's away at college, so I don't get to see them much anyway. As far as the Transcenders go, I like Narowyn and the others, but that option's not even in my top two. What else is there to talk about?"

"You understand that this decision is permanent. You pledge that you will never return to Connecticut, even if things do not work out for you here. You further pledge that you will never join the Transcender community."

"Yes, I know that's what I'm agreeing to. What's this all about, Rals?"

"Have you really considered what you are giving up, Jaden? As a Transcender, you would retain the ability to travel back to Connecticut to visit your family. You could travel *anywhere* you wished."

"Except here."

"That is true. You would be relinquishing that right."

"But this is the only place I want to be—here with Ryder, as Queen of the Domerican people." I stretch out an impatient hand. "Just give me the papers. I'm ready to sign."

"You still have another eight days before you are required to make your final decision. Perhaps you should wait."

He's stalling and I'm getting irritated. Ralston's been acting weird ever since he got back. "I don't want to wait. I want this out of the way before the wedding. Give me the papers now."

Pulling a sheaf from his inside jacket pocket, he spreads the pages on the desk. "You must initial these paragraphs regarding your commitments never to return to Connecticut and never to join the Transcender community. Also initial this one that says this decision is made of your own free will and that IUGA did not attempt to influence you in any way. Then sign the final page, just here." He points to a signature line.

Taking a pen from the holder on the desk, I carefully initial the paragraphs he indicated. I slide the final page in front of me and, as the point of my pen meets the paper, Ralston snatches the page away, backing toward the door.

"You can't sign this, Jade," he says.

"Are you crazy? Give that back to me. What are you doing?" I bolt from my chair and grasp for the paper.

He quickly stuffs it inside his jacket. "IUGA will undoubtedly terminate me for this, but I cannot allow you to go through with it. If you sign this document and remain in Domerica, you will die on your wedding day."

"What? I'll die? Like someone will kill me?" I ask, believing I've heard him wrong.

"Yes, I'm afraid so."

"It's Uncle Harold, isn't it?" I say, hot fury expanding in my chest.

He shakes his head gravely. "No. He has nothing to do with it. It seems the government of Dome Noir has quietly been planning your demise almost since the day of your return."

"Dome Noir is planning to murder me?" It sounds preposterous when I voice it.

"As part of a greater plan to take over Domerica, yes. They intend to infiltrate Warrington Palace during your nuptials when all of the top members of government are gathered here together. The strategy is to eliminate as many members of the royal family as possible—that includes you, Prince Andrew, your father, and Ryder. They are as yet unaware of the change in the line of succession, so Prince Harold and Princess Osrielle are also targets, as are members of the Council of Advisors, and General LeGare. An old fashioned coup d'état, if you will."

"But why? Why would they do it?"

"I'm afraid conditions in Dome Noir have become dire. A small revolutionary army has been formed. They've been successfully contained so far, but the Noirs don't even have a place to detain the captured revolutionaries. There's literally no more room in the prisons, but to execute them would cause the remainder of the people to rise up." He runs a hand across his wispy hair. "The bottom line is: they need a new dome for the survival of the nation, and to restore faith in the government. They will do anything to get it."

Slumping into my chair, my brain struggles to process this violent news, my mind scrabbles for a solution. "Okay, but we're aware of this now. We'll just stop them before they get here. We'll amass our own soldiers and sink their ships, or surround the dome and not allow them access. We can appeal to King Rafael and Cupola de Vita for help. He'd never stand for the forcible overthrow of Domerica. It violates every treaty among the nations."

"Were it only that simple, my dear. Unfortunately, for the most part, the Noirs are already here—inside the dome. What's more, King Rafael is unofficially aware of the plot, and though he does not condone it, he will take no steps to prevent it, as evidenced by his cowardly withdrawal from the wedding party."

I shake my head slowly. "No. This isn't happening. How can they already be inside?"

Ralston seats himself across from me again. Patiently, he explains that Damien's men who were never captured banded together into a kind of criminal enterprise, led by Luc Canard, Damien's former lawyer. Canard and his thugs discovered the new location of the spare dome plans and materials several months ago and offered to sell this information to King Philippe. Philippe was eager to have it, but knew that he couldn't simply slip inside Domerica and steal the massive dome materials, so he struck a deal with Canard.

They conspired to work together to amass a small legion of men inside Domerica, some smuggled in from Dome Noir, some recruited from the local riff-raff. The ultimate goal was to attack the palace once Queen Eleanor died, and hold Osrielle hostage, forcing Prince Harold to give up the dome plans and materials. But my reappearance put a kink in their plans, so they orchestrated the violent attack in the forest to get me out of the way before Mother's death. When that failed, everything changed. The stakes went up. The Noirs decided they needed to take over control of Domerica. And, it became apparent that they needed guns to do it.

"The current plan is to strike on your wedding day," Ralston says. "Next week when Prince Gilbert, Prince Jean Louis, and others from Dome Noir arrive as invited guests, their ship will be laden with firearms."

I stare at him, disbelieving. "Prince Gilbert is on board for this? He seemed so sane and reasonable when I met him last year."

"At first he was vehemently opposed to the plan, but as I said, they are desperate, my dear. King Philippe convinced him that it is a reasonable response to the assassination of Prince Damien, which he considers an act of war. Gilbert has agreed to carry out his Father's bidding. He plans to lead the attack from inside Domerica."

My brain screams, "*Impossible!*" "There has to be a way to stop them, Rals. A scenario where we win, they lose, and I survive."

"I'm afraid not, Jade. IUGA's prediction models indicate a ninety-eight percent probability that no matter what defensive actions Domerica takes, you will be killed."

Hot blood snakes through my veins. "And IUGA was going to allow this to happen—allow me to be killed without warning?"

He nods soberly.

"But why? Why would they bring me back here just to die?"

"Because their prediction models further show, within a ninety-six percent probability, that if you choose either of your other options, Connecticut or Arumel, you will eventually come to reside in Arumel and take over as the next leader of the Transcenders when Narowyn Du Lac steps down."

"That's absurd. But so what? Why do they care?"

"It would be quite disastrous for IUGA, Jade. Under your leadership, the Transcenders would assume a much greater role in intergalactic affairs, and the very existence of IUGA would be called into question. For centuries, a heated debate has raged. Is destiny something which must be controlled and directed, or should it be allowed to freely unfold? IUGA has always had the upper hand in that debate, because of its wide-ranging power and because Transcenders number so few. All of that would change should you take over the helm. Philosophies have already begun to shift. Your influence would be the deciding factor."

The bitter taste of bile stings my throat. "How long have you known about this?"

"Since yesterday, but apparently the director has known it all along. They used me to get you back here."

"So we're both pawns in their nasty little game?"

"Regrettably, that is so."

I sit back and stare at the ceiling. The bleakness of my predicament sinks through to the marrow of my bones. "I can't stay here, can I, Rals? I can't be with Ryder."

"Not if you wish to survive, my dear. Considering that both the Noirs and IUGA ultimately desire your death, Arumel may be the only safe place for you. Neither faction can touch you there."

The bastards! "So what do I do now, Rals?"

"You let go. Start a new story. Begin living your own life instead of someone else's."

"What happens if I leave? Go back to Connecticut or on to Arumel? Is it possible to stop the rest from happening? Is there any way Ryder and my family will survive? Can Domerica be saved?"

"The impending battle will take place no matter what we do. There may, however, be a way to protect your family, and just possibly save Domerica in the process. I warn you, it's not a very likely scenario, but now that I've broken every rule and informed you of this, there's a slight chance we can pull it off. It must be done in absolute secrecy, though. IUGA must not get a whiff of any change in your plans."

Searing rage lashes through me like the sting of a devil's whip. *I won't let them win!* "We have to do it, Rals, whatever the cost. Even if it means I end up dead, we've got to save them." I pound the desk with my fist. "Just tell me what to do."

"I have the beginnings of a plan, old girl, but it isn't safe to discuss it here. IUGA has many eyes and ears."

"Then let's go," I say, pulling him toward the door. "I think I know someplace safe. You're not afraid of heights are you?"

To be continued...

ACKNOWLEDGEMENTS

This book would not have been possible without the love, support, encouragement, and psychotherapy doled out to me on a daily basis by my wonderful family, Mike, Jessica, and Colter.

My remarkable sister, Shelly Savage, my best friend, greatest cheerleader, premier first reader, and proficient proofreader, deserves special recognition for skillfully talking me out of trashing this entire project, which I threatened to do on a regular basis.

Mark Ingersoll, my head of marketing, has earned my eternal thanks for his undying faith in the *Transcender Trilogy* and for his way with the ladies (bookstore owners, that is).

My inspiring dear friend, Carrie Drazek, not only kept me buoyed up during my dark days of the soul, but is responsible for the fabulous cover designs for both *Streaming Stars* and *Transcender*. I put her through all kinds of hell while trying to settle on the perfect cover, but she maintained her smile and her creative spirit throughout. She is a true artist.

Another dear friend, Marsha Quinn, is due many thanks for all of her valuable comments, for providing me with "horse language," which I borrowed liberally, and for her enthusiastic and steadfast faith in me.

Thanks to my editor, Lorna Lund Collins, for her valuable contributions to the final manuscript and for her kind and uplifting words about my work.

Lastly, I thank the cutenesses, Katie and Bella, my two furry, fluffy soul-mates whose unabashed joy at the simple things in life helps keep me grounded and appreciative.

ABOUT THE AUTHOR

Prior to becoming an author and publisher of young adult fiction, Vicky Savage enjoyed many diverse occupations; flagman on a construction crew, trial lawyer, and healthcare company executive, to name a few. She is currently working on Book 3 of the *Transcender Trilogy*, as well as collaborating on a screenplay. She lives on the west coast of Florida with her boyishly charming husband, handsome son, and two effervescent dogs. Visit the author at www.vickysavage.com.